John Sandford is the pseudonym of a Pulitzer Prize-winning journalist and novelist. Born and educated in Iowa, Sandford has a black belt in Shotokan karate. He enjoys wilderness canoeing and in 1980 paddled solo down the Mississippi River from its source to New Orleans. He is married with two children, and lives in Minnesota.

John Sandford is the author of *Rules of Prey* and *Shadow Prey*, and has recently published in hardback the sequel to *Eyes of Prey – Silent Prey*.

Praise for John Sandford and *Eyes of Prey*:

'A resourceful, high-octane yarn in which super-sleuth Lucas Davenport gets to grips with horror and homicide in Minneapolis.' *Sunday Express*

'Engrossing . . . one of the most horrible villains this side of Hannibal the Cannibal.' *Ricmond-Times Despatch*

'Sandford is a cunning writer, and consistently avoids the routine or expected with intelligent and surprising new wrinkles.' *Washington Post*

'When it comes to portraying twisted minds, Sandford has no peers.' *Associated Press*

'Sandford grabs you by the throat and never lets go.' *Robert B. Parker*

'A web of suspense . . . compelling and skillfully executed.' *Orlando Sentinel*

By the same author

JOHN SANDFORD

Eyes of Prey

Grafton
An Imprint of HarperCollinsPublishers

Grafton
An Imprint of HarperCollins*Publishers,*
77–85 Fulham Palace Road,
Hammersmith, London W6 8JB

Special overseas edition 1991
This edition published by Grafton 1992
9 8 7 6 5 4 3 2 1

First published in Great Britain by
GrafatonBooks 1991

ISBN 0 586 21131 4

Set in Times

Printed in Great Britain by
HarperCollinsManufacturing Glasgow

1

Carlo Druze was a stone killer.

He sauntered down the old, gritty sidewalk with its cracked, uneven paving blocks, under the bare-branched oaks. He was acutely aware of his surroundings. Back around the corner, near his car, the odor of cigar smoke hung in the cold night air; a hundred feet farther along, he'd touched a pool of fragrance, deodorant or cheap perfume. A Mötley Crüe song beat down from a second-story bedroom: plainly audible on the sidewalk, it had to be deafening inside.

Two blocks ahead, to the right, a translucent cream-colored shade came down in a lighted window. He watched the window, but nothing else moved. A vagrant snowflake drifted past, then another.

Druze could kill without feeling, but he wasn't stupid. He took care: he would not spend his life in prison. So he strolled, hands in his pockets, a man at his leisure. Watching. Feeling. The collar of his ski jacket rose to his ears on the sides, to his nose in the front. A watch cap rode low on his forehead. If he met anyone—a dog-walker, a night jogger—they'd get nothing but eyes.

From the mouth of the alley, he could see the target house and the garage behind it. Nobody in the alley, nothing moving. A few garbage cans, like battered plastic toadstools, waited to be taken inside. Four windows were lit on the ground floor of the target house, two more up above. The garage was dark.

Druze didn't look around; he was too good an actor. It wasn't likely that a neighbor was watching, but who could know? An old man, lonely, standing at his window, a linen shawl around his narrow shoulders . . . Druze could see him in his mind's eye, and was wary: the people here had money, and Druze was a stranger in the dark. An out-of-place furtiveness, like a bad line on the stage, would be noticed. The cops were only a minute away.

With a casual step, then, rather than a sudden move, Druze turned into the darker world of the alley and walked down to the garage. It was connected to the house by a glassed-in breezeway. The door at the end of the breezeway would not be locked; it led straight into the kitchen.

"If she's not in the kitchen, she'll be in the recreation room, watching television," Bekker had said. Bekker had been aglow, his face pulsing with the heat of uncontrolled pleasure. He'd drawn the floor plan on a sheet of notebook paper and traced the hallways with the point of his pencil. The pencil had trembled on the paper, leaving a shaky worm trail in graphite. "Christ, I wish I could be there to see it."

Druze took the key out of his pocket, pulled it out by its string. He'd tied the string to a belt loop, so there'd be no chance he'd lose the key in the house. He reached out to the doorknob with his gloved left hand, tried it. Locked. The key opened it easily. He shut the door behind him and stood in the dark, listening. A scurrying? A mouse in the loft? The sound of the wind brushing over the shingles. He waited, listening.

Druze was a troll. He had been burned as a child. Some nights, bad nights, the memories ran uncontrollably through his head, and he'd doze, wretchedly, twisting in the blankets, knowing what was coming, afraid. He'd wake in his childhood bed, the fire on him. On his hands, his face, running like liquid, in his nose, his hair, his mother

6

screaming, throwing water and milk, his father flapping his arms, shouting, ineffectual . . .

They hadn't taken him to the hospital until the next day. His mother had smeared lard on him, hoping not to pay, as Druze howled through the night. But in the morning light, when they'd seen his nose, they took him.

He was four weeks in the county hospital, shrieking with pain as the nurses put him through the baths and the peels, as the doctors did the skin transplants. They'd harvested the skin from his thighs—he remembered the word, all these years later, *harvested*, it stuck in his mind like a tick—and used it to patch his face.

When they'd finished he looked better, but not good. The features of his face seemed fused together, as though an invisible nylon stocking were pulled over his head. His skin was no better, a patchwork of leather, off-color, pebbled, like a quilted football. His nose had been fixed, as best the doctors could, but it was too short, his nostrils flaring straight out, like black headlights. His lips were stiff and thin, and dried easily. He licked them, unconsciously, his tongue flicking out every few seconds with a lizard's touch.

The doctors had given him the new face, but his eyes were his own.

His eyes were flat black and opaque, like weathered paint on the eyes of a cigar-store Indian. New acquaintances sometimes thought he was blind, but he was not. His eyes were the mirror of his soul: Druze hadn't had one since the night of the burning. . . .

The garage was silent. Nobody called out, no telephone rang. Druze tucked the key into his pants pocket and took a black four-inch milled-aluminum penlight out of his jacket. With the light's narrow beam, he skirted the car and picked his way through the litter of the garage.

7

Bekker had warned him of this: the woman was a gardener. The unused half of the garage was littered with shovels, rakes, hoes, garden trowels, red clay pots, both broken and whole, sacks of fertilizer and partial bales of peat moss. A power cultivator sat next to a lawn mower and a snowblower. The place smelled half of earth and half of gasoline, a pungent, yeasty mixture that pulled him back to his childhood. Druze had grown up on a farm, poor, living in a trailer with a propane tank, closer to the chicken coop than the main house. He knew about kitchen gardens, old, oil-leaking machinery and the stink of manure.

The door between the garage and the breezeway was closed but not locked. The breezeway itself was six feet wide and as cluttered as the garage. "She uses it as a spring greenhouse—watch the tomato flats on the south side, they'll be all over the place," Bekker had said. "You'll need the light, but she won't be able to see it from either the kitchen or the recreation room. Check the windows on the left. That's the study, and she could see you from there—but she won't be in the study. She never is. You'll be okay."

Bekker was a meticulous planner, delighted with his own precise work. As he led Druze through the floor plan with his pencil, he'd stopped once to laugh. His laugh was his worst feature, Druze decided. Harsh, scratching, it sounded like the squawk of a crow pursued by owls. . . .

Druze walked easily through the breezeway, stepping precisely toward the lighted window in the door at the end of the passage. He was bulky but not fat. He was, in fact, an athlete: he could juggle, he could dance, he could balance on a rope; he could jump in the air and click his heels and land lightly enough that the audience could hear the *click* alone, like a spoken word. Midway through, he heard a voice and paused.

8

A voice, singing. Sweet, naive, like a high-school chorister's. A woman, the words muffled. He recognized the tune but didn't know its name. Something from the sixties. A Joan Baez song maybe. The focus was getting tighter. He didn't doubt that he could do her. Killing Stephanie Bekker would be no more difficult than chopping off a chicken's head or slitting the throat of a baby pig. Just a shoat, he said to himself. It's all meat. . . .

Druze had done another murder, years earlier. He'd told Bekker about it, over a beer. It wasn't a confession, simply a story. And now, so many years later, the killing seemed more like an accident than a murder. Even less than that: like a scene from a half-forgotten drive-in movie, a movie where you couldn't remember the end. A girl in a New York flophouse. A hooker maybe, a druggie for sure. She gave him some shit. Nobody cared, so he killed her. Almost as an experiment, to see if it would rouse some feeling in him. It hadn't.

He never knew the hooker's name, doubted that he could even find the flophouse, if it still existed. At this date, he probably couldn't figure out what week of the year it had been: the summer, sometime, everything hot and stinking, the smell of spoiled milk and rotting lettuce in sidewalk dumpsters . . .

"Didn't bother me," he had told Bekker, who pressed him. "It wasn't like . . . Shit, it wasn't like anything. Shut the bitch up, that's for sure."

"Did you hit her? In the face?" Bekker had been intent, the eyes of science. It was, Druze thought, the moment they had become friends. He remembered it with perfect clarity: the bar, the scent of cigarette smoke, four college kids on the other side of the aisle, sitting around a pizza, laughing at inanities . . . Bekker had worn an apricot-colored mohair sweater, a favorite, that framed his face.

9

"Bounced her off a wall, swinging her," Druze had said, wanting to impress. Another new feeling. "When she went down, I got on her back, got an arm around her neck, and *jerk* . . . that was it. Neck just went pop. Sounded like when you bite into a piece of gristle. I put my pants on, walked out the door. . . ."

"Scared?"

"No. Not after I was out of the place. Something that simple . . . what're the cops going to do? You walk away. By the time you're down the block, they got no chance. And in that fuckin' place, they probably didn't even find her for two days, and only then 'cause of the heat. I wasn't *scared*, I was more like . . . hurried."

"That's something." Bekker's approval was like the rush Druze got from applause, but better, tighter, more concentrated. Only for him. He had gotten the impression that Bekker had a confession of his own but held it back. Instead the other man had asked, "You never did it again?"

"No. It's not like . . . I enjoy it."

Bekker had sat staring at him for a moment, then had smiled. "Hell of a story, Carlo."

He hadn't felt much when he'd killed the girl. He didn't feel much now, ghosting through the darkened breezeway, closing in. Tension, stage fright, but no distaste for the job.

Another door waited at the end of the passage, wooden, with an inset window at eye level. If the woman was at the table, Bekker said, she would most likely be facing away from him. If she was at the sink, the stove or the refrigerator, she wouldn't be able to see him at all. The door would open quietly enough, but she would feel the cold air if he hesitated.

What was that song? The woman's voice floated around

him, an intriguing whisper in the night air. Moving slowly, Druze peeked through the window. She wasn't at the table: nothing there but two wooden chairs. He gripped the doorknob solidly, picked up a foot, wiped the sole of his shoe on the opposite pantleg, then repeated the move with the other foot. If the gym shoe treads had picked up any small stones, they would give him away, rattling on the tile floor. Bekker had suggested that he wipe, and Druze was a man who valued rehearsal.

His hand still on the knob, he twisted. The knob turned silently under his glove, as slowly as the second hand on a clock. The door was on a spring, and would ease itself shut. . . . And she sang: Something, Angelina, *ta-dum*, *Angelina*. Good-bye, Angelina? She was a true soprano, her voice like bells. . . .

The door was as quiet as Bekker had promised. Warm air pushed into his face like a feather cushion; the sound of a dishwasher, and Druze was inside and moving, the door closed behind him, his shoes silent on the quarry tile. Straight ahead was the breakfast bar, white-speckled Formica with a single short-stemmed rose in a bud vase at the far end, a cup and saucer in the center and, on the near end, a green glass bottle. A souvenir from a trip to Mexico, Bekker had said. Hand-blown, and heavy as stone, with a sturdy neck.

Druze was moving fast now, to the end of the bar, an avalanche in black, the woman suddenly there to his left, standing at the sink, singing, her back to him. Her black hair was brushed out on her shoulders, a sheer silken blue negligee falling gently over her hips. At the last instant she sensed him coming, maybe felt a rush in the air, a coldness, and she turned. *Something's wrong*: Druze was moving on Bekker's wife, too late to change course, and he knew that something was wrong. . . .

*   *   *

11

Man in the house. In the shower. On his way.

Stephanie Bekker felt warm, comfortable, still a little damp from her own shower, a bead of water tickling as it sat on her spine between her shoulder blades. . . . Her nipples were sore, but not unpleasantly. He'd shaven, but not recently enough. . . . She smiled. Silly man, must not have nursed enough as a baby . . .

Stephanie Bekker felt the cool air on her back and turned to smile at her lover. Her lover wasn't there; Death was. She said, "Who?" and it was all there in her mind, like a fistful of crystals: the plans for the business, the good days at the lakes, the cocker spaniel she had had as a girl, her father's face lined with pain after his heart attack, her inability to have children . . .

And her home: the kitchen tile, the antique flour bins, the wrought-iron pot stands, the single rose in the bud vase, red as a drop of blood . . .

Gone.

Something wrong . . .

"Who?" she said, not loud, half turning, her eyes widening, a smile caught on her face. The bottle whipped around, a Louisville Slugger in green glass. Her hand started up. Too late. Too small. Too delicate.

The heavy bottle smashed into her temple with a wet crack, like a rain-soaked newspaper hitting a porch. Her head snapped back and she fell, straight down, as though her bones had vaporized. The back of her head slammed the edge of the counter, pitching her forward, turning her.

Druze was on her, smashing her flat with his weight, his hand on her chest, feeling her nipple in his palm.

Hitting her face and her face and her face . . .

The heavy bottle broke, and he paused, sucking air, his head turned up, his jaws wide, changed his grip and smashed the broken edges down through her eyes. . . .

12

"Do it too much," Bekker had urged. He'd been like a jock, talking about a three-four defense or a halfback option, his arm pumping as though he was about to holler "*Awright!*" . . . "Do it like a junkie would do it. Christ, I wish I could be there. And get the eyes. Be sure you get the eyes."

"I know how to do it," Druze had said.

"But you must get the eyes. . . ." Bekker had had a little white dot of drying spittle at the corner of his mouth. That happened when he got excited. "Get the eyes for me. . . ."

Something wrong.

There'd been another sound here, and it had stopped. Even as he beat her, even as he pounded the razor-edged bottle down through her eyes, Druze registered the negligee. She wouldn't be wearing this on a cold, windy night in April, alone in the house. Women were natural actors, with an instinct for the appropriate that went past simple comfort. She wouldn't be wearing this if she were alone. . . .

He hit her face and heard the thumping on the stairs, and half turned, half stood, startled, hunched like a golem, the bottle in his gloved hand. The man came around the corner at the bottom of the stairs, wrapped in a towel. Taller than average, too heavy but not actually fat. Balding, fair wet hair at his temples, uncombed. Pale skin, rarely touched by sunlight, chest hair gone gray, pink spots on his shoulders from the shower.

There was a frozen instant, then the man blurted "Jesus" and bolted. Druze took a step after him, quickly, off balance. The blood on the kitchen tile was almost invisible, red on red, and he slipped, his feet flying from beneath him. He landed back-down on the woman's head, her pulped features imprinting themselves on his black jacket. The man, Stephanie Bekker's lover, was up the stairs. It

13

was an old house and the doors were oak. If he locked himself in a bedroom, Druze would not get through the door in a hurry. The man might already be dialing 911. . . .

Druze dropped the bottle, as planned, and turned and trotted out the door. He was halfway down the length of the breezeway when it slammed behind him, a report like a gunshot, startling him. *Door*, his mind said, but he was running now, scattering the tomato plants. His hand found the penlight as he cleared the breezeway. With the light, he was through the garage in two more seconds, into the alley, slowing himself. *Walk. WALK.*

In another ten seconds he was on the sidewalk, thick, hunched, his coat collar up. He got to his car without seeing another soul. A minute after he left Stephanie Bekker, the car was moving. . . .

Keep your head out of it.

Druze did not allow himself to think. Everything was rehearsed, it was all very clean. Follow the script. Stay on schedule. Around the lake, out to France Avenue to Highway 12, back toward the loop to I-94, down 94 to St. Paul.

Then he thought:

He saw my face. And who the fuck was he? So round, so pink, so startled. Druze smacked the steering wheel once in frustration. *How could this happen? Bekker so smart* . . .

There was no way for Druze to know who the lover was, but Bekker might know. He should have some ideas, at least. Druze glanced at the car clock: 10:40. Ten minutes before the first scheduled call.

He took the next exit, stopped at a Super America store and picked up the plastic baggie of quarters he'd left on the floor of the car: he hadn't wanted them to clink when he went into Bekker's house. A public phone hung on an exterior wall, and Druze, his index finger in one ear to

14

block the street noise, dialed another public phone, in San Francisco. A recording asked for quarters and Druze dropped them in. A second later, the phone rang on the West Coast. Bekker was there.

"Yes?"

Druzc was supposed to say one of two words, "Yes" or "No," and hang up. Instead he said, "There was a guy there."

"What?" He'd never heard Bekker surprised, before this night.

"She was fuckin' some guy," Druze said. "I came in and did her and the guy came right down the stairs on top of me. He was wearing a towel."

"What?" More than surprised. He was stunned.

"Wake up, for Christ's fuckin' sake. Stop saying 'What?' We got a problem."

"What about . . . the woman?" Recovering now. Mentioning no names.

"She's a big fuckin' Yes. But the guy saw me. Just for a second. I was wearing the ski jacket and the hat, but with my face . . . I don't know how much was showing. . . ."

There was a long moment of silence; then Bekker said, "We can't talk about it. I'll call you tonight or tomorrow, depending on what happens. Are you sure about . . . the woman?"

"Yeah, yeah, she's a *Yes*."

"Then we've done that much," Bekker said, with satisfaction. "Let me go think about the other."

And he was gone.

Driving away from the store, Druze hummed, harshly, the few bars of the song: *Ta-dum, Angelina, good-bye, Angelina* . . . That wasn't right, and the goddamned song would be going through his head forever until he got it. *Ta-dum, Angelina.* Maybe he could call a radio station and they'd play it or something. The melody was driving him nuts.

He put the car on I-94, took it to Highway 280, to I-35W, to I-694, and began driving west, fast, too fast, enjoying the speed, running the loop around the cities. He did it, now and then, to cool out. He liked the wind whistling through a crack in the window, the oldie-goldies on the radio. *Ta-dum* . . .

The blood-mask dried on the back of his jacket, invisible now. He never knew it was there.

Stephanie Bekker's lover heard the strange thumping as he toweled himself after his shower. The sound was unnatural, violent, arhythmic, but it never crossed his mind that Stephanie had been attacked, was dying there on the kitchen floor. She might be moving something, one of her heavy antique chairs maybe, or perhaps she couldn't get a jar open and was rapping the lid on a kitchen counter—he really didn't know what he thought.

He wrapped a towel around his waist and went to look. He walked straight into the nightmare: A man with a beast's face, hovering over Stephanie, the broken bottle in his hand like a dagger, rimed with blood. Stephanie's face . . . What had he told her, there in bed, an hour before? You're a beautiful woman, he'd said, awkward at this, touching her lips with his fingertip, so beautiful. . . .

He'd seen her on the floor and he'd turned and run. *What else could he do?* one part of his mind asked. The lower part, the lizard part that went back to the caves, said: *Coward.*

He'd run up the stairs, flying with fear, reaching to slam the bedroom door behind him, to lock himself away from the horror, when he heard the troll slam out through the breezeway door. He snatched up the phone, punched numbers, a 9, a 1. But even as he punched the 1, his quick mind was turning. He stopped. Listened. No neighbors, no calls in the night. No sirens. Nothing. Looked at the phone, then finally set it back down. Maybe . . .

He pulled on his pants.

He cracked the door, tense, waiting for attack. Nothing. Down the stairs, moving quietly in his bare feet. Nothing. Wary, moving slowly, into the kitchen. Stephanie sprawled there, on her back, beyond help: her face pulped, her whole head misshapen from the beating. Blood pooled on the tile around her; the killer had stepped in it, and he'd left tracks, one edge of a gym shoe and a heel, back toward the door.

Stephanie Bekker's lover reached down to touch her neck, to feel for a pulse, but at the last minute, repelled, he pulled his hand back. She was dead. He stood for a moment, swept by a premonition that the cops were on the sidewalk, were coming up the sidewalk, were reaching toward the front door. . . . They would find him here, standing over the body like the innocent man in a Perry Mason television show, point a finger at him, accuse him of murder.

He turned his head toward the front door. Nothing. Not a sound.

He went back up the stairs, his mind working furiously. Stephanie had sworn she'd told nobody about their affair. Her close friends were with the university, in the art world or in the neighborhood: confiding details of an affair in any of those places would set off a tidal wave of gossip. They both knew that and knew it would be ruinous.

He would lose his position in a scandal. Stephanie, for her part, was deathly afraid of her husband: what he would do, she couldn't begin to predict. The affair had been stupid, but neither had been able to resist it. His marriage was dying, hers was long dead.

He choked, controlled it, choked again. He hadn't

17

wept since childhood, couldn't weep now, but spasms of grief, anger and fear squeezed his chest. Control. He started dressing, was buttoning his shirt when his stomach rebelled, and he dashed to the bathroom and vomited. He knelt in front of the toilet for several minutes, dry heaves tearing at his stomach muscles until tears came to his eyes. Finally, the spasms subsiding, he stood up and finished dressing, except for his shoes. He must be quiet, he thought.

He did a careful inventory: billfold, keys, handkerchief, coins. Necktie, jacket. Coat and gloves. He forced himself to sit on the bed and mentally retrace his steps through the house. What had he touched? The front doorknob. The table in the kitchen, the spoon and bowl he'd used to eat her cherry cobbler. The knobs on the bedroom and bathroom doors, the water faucets, the toilet seat . . .

He got a pair of Stephanie's cotton underpants from her bureau, went down the stairs again, started with the front door and worked methodically through the house. In the kitchen, he didn't look at the body. He couldn't look at it, but he was always aware of it at the edge of his vision, a leg, an arm . . . enough to step carefully around the blood.

In the bedroom again, and the bathroom. As he was wiping the shower, he thought about the drain. Body hair. He listened again. Silence. *Take the time*. The drain was fastened down by a single brass screw. He removed it with a dime, wiped the drain as far as he could reach with toilet paper, then rinsed it with a direct flow of water. The paper he threw into the toilet, and flushed once, twice. Body hair: the bed. He went into the bedroom, another surge of despair shaking his body. He would forget something. . . . He pulled the sheets from the bed, threw them on the floor, found another set and spent five minutes putting them on the bed and rearranging the blankets and the coverlet. He wiped the nightstand and the headboard, stopped, looked around.

Enough.

He rolled the underpants in the dirty sheets, put on his shoes and went downstairs, carrying the bundle of linen. He scanned the living room, the parlor and the kitchen one last time. His eyes skipped over Stephanie. . . .

There was nothing more to do. He put on his coat and stuffed the bundle of sheets in the belly. He was already heavy, but the sheets made him gross: good. If anybody saw him . . .

He walked out the front door, down the four concrete steps to the street and around the long block to his car. They'd been discreet, and their discretion might now save him. The night was cold, spitting snow, and he met nobody.

He drove down off the hill, around the lake, out to Hennepin Avenue, and spotted a pay telephone. He stopped, pinched a quarter in the underpants and dialed 911. Feeling both furtive and foolish, he put the pants over the mouthpiece of the telephone before he spoke:

"A woman's been murdered . . ." he told the operator.

He gave Stephanie's name and address. With the operator pleading with him to stay on the line, he hung up, carefully wiped the receiver and walked back to his car. No. Sneaked back to his car, he thought. Like a rat. They would never believe, he thought. Never. He put his head on the steering wheel. Closed his eyes. Despite himself, his mind was calculating.

The killer had seen him. And the killer hadn't looked like a junkie or a small-time rip-off artist killing on impulse. He'd looked strong, well fed, purposeful. The killer could be coming after him. . . .

He'd have to give more information to the investigators, he decided, or they'd focus on him, her lover. He'd have to

19

point them at the killer. They'd know that Stephanie had had intercourse, the county pathologists would be able to tell that. . . .

God, had she washed? Of course she had, but how well? Would there be enough semen for a DNA-type?

No help for that. But he could give the police information they'd need to track the killer. Print out a statement, Xerox it through several generations, with different darkness settings, to obscure any peculiarities of the printer . . .

Stephanie's face came out of nowhere.

At one moment, he was planning. The next, she was there, her eyes closed, her head turned away, asleep. He was seized with the thought that he could go back, find her standing in the doorway, find that it had all been a nightmare. . . .

He began to choke again, his chest heaving.

And Stephanie's lover thought, as he sat in the car: Bekker? Had he done this? He started the car.

Bekker.

It wasn't quite human, the thing that pulled itself across the kitchen floor. Not quite human—eyes gone, brain damaged, bleeding—but it was alive and it had a purpose: the telephone. There was no attacker, there was no lover, there was no time. There was only pain, the tile and, somewhere, the telephone.

The thing on the floor pulled itself to the wall where the telephone was, reached, reached . . . and failed. The thing was dying when the paramedics came, when the glass in the window broke and the firemen came through the door.

The thing called Stephanie Bekker heard the words "Jesus Christ," and then it was gone forever, leaving a single bloody hand print six inches below the Princess phone.

2

Del was a tall man, knobby, ungainly. He put his legs up on the booth seat and his jeans rode above his high-topped brown leather shoes, showing the leather laces running between the hooks. The shoes were cracked and caked with mud. Shoes you'd see on a sharecropper, Lucas thought.

Lucas drained the last of his Diet Coke and looked over his shoulder toward the door. Nothing.

"Fucker's late," Del said. His face flicked yellow, then red, with the Budweiser sign in the window.

"He's coming." Lucas caught the eye of the bartender, pointed at his Coke can. The barkeep nodded and dug into the cooler. He was a fat man, with a mustard-stained apron wrapped around his ample belly, and he waddled when he brought the Diet Coke.

"Buck," he grunted. Lucas handed him a dollar bill. The bartender looked at them carefully, thought about asking a question, decided against it and went back behind the bar.

They weren't so much out of place as oddly assorted, Lucas decided. Del was wearing jeans, a prison-gray sweatshirt with the neckband torn out, a jean jacket, a paisley headband made out of a necktie, and the sharecropper's shoes. He hadn't shaved in a week and his eyes looked like North Country peat bogs.

Lucas wore a leather bomber jacket over a cashmere sweater, and khaki slacks and cowboy boots. His dark hair was uncombed and fell forward over a square, hard face, pale with the departing winter. The pallor almost hid the white scar that slashed across his eyebrow and cheek; it became visible only when he clenched his jaw. When he did, it puckered, a groove, whiter on white.

Their booth was next to a window. The window had been covered with a silver film, so the people inside could see out but the people outside couldn't see in. Flower boxes sat under the windows, alternating with radiator cabinets. The boxes were filled with plastic petunias thrust into what looked like Kitty Litter. Del was chewing Dentyne, a new stick every few minutes. When he finished a stick, he lobbed the well-chewed wad into a window box. After an hour, a dozen tiny pink wads of gum were scattered like spring buds among the phony flowers.

"He's coming," Lucas said again. But he wasn't sure. "He'll be here."

Thursday night, an off-and-on hard spring rain, and the bar was bigger than its clientele. Three hookers, two black, one white, huddled together on barstools, drinking beer and sharing a copy of *Mirabella*. They'd all been wearing shiny vinyl raincoats in lipstick colors and had folded them down on the barstools to sit on them. Hookers were never far from their coats.

A white woman sat at the end of the bar by herself. She had frizzy blond hair, watery green eyes and a long thin mouth that was always about to tremble. Her shoulders were hunched, ready for a beating. Another hooker: she was pounding down the gin with Teutonic efficiency.

The male customers paid no attention to the hookers. Of the men, two shitkickers in camouflage hats, one with a folding-knife sheath on his belt, played shuffleboard bowling. Two more, both looking as if they might be from the neighborhood, talked to the bartender. A fifth man, older, sat by himself in front of a bowl of peanuts, nursing a lifelong rage and a glass of rye. He'd nip from the glass, eat a peanut and mutter his anger down into his overcoat. A half-dozen more men and a single woman sat in a puddle of rickety chairs, burn-scarred tables and cigarette smoke at the back of the bar, watching the NBA play-offs on satellite TV.

"Haven't seen much crack on TV lately," Lucas said, groping for conversation. Del had been leading up to something all night but hadn't spit it out yet.

"Media used it up," said Del. "They be rootin' for a new drug now. Supposed to be ice, coming in from the West Coast."

Lucas shook his head. "Fuckin' ice," he said.

He caught his own reflection in the window glass. Not too bad, he thought. You couldn't see the gray thatch in the black hair, you couldn't see the dark rings under his eyes, the lines beginning to groove his cheeks at the corners of his mouth. Maybe he ought to get a chunk of this glass and use it to shave in.

"If we wait much longer, she's gonna need a cash transfusion," Del said, eyeing the drunk hooker. Lucas had staked her with a twenty and she was down to a pile of quarters and pennies.

"He'll be here," Lucas insisted. "Motherfucker dreams about his rep."

"Randy ain't bright enough to dream," Del said.

"Gotta be soon," Lucas said. "He won't let her sit there forever."

The hooker was bait. Del had found her working a bar in South St. Paul two days earlier and had dragged her ass back to Minneapolis on an old possession warrant. Lucas had put the word on the street that she was talking about Randy to beat a cocaine charge. Randy had shredded the face of one of Lucas' snitches. The hooker had seen him do it.

"You still writing poems?" Del asked after a while.

"Kind of gave it up," Lucas said.

Del shook his head. "Shouldn't of done that."

Lucas looked at the plastic flowers in the window box and said sadly, "I'm getting too old. You gotta be young or naive to write poetry."

"You're three or four years younger'n I am," Del said, picking up the thought.

"Neither one of us is a fuckin' walk in the park," Lucas said. He tried to make it sound funny, but it didn't.

"Got that right," Del said somberly. The narc had always been gaunt. He liked speed a little too much and sometimes got his nose in the coke. That came with the job: narcs never got out clean. But Del . . . the bags under his eyes were his most prominent feature, his hair was stiff, dirty. Like a mortally ill cat, he couldn't take care of himself anymore. "Too many assholes. I'm gettin' as bad as them."

"How many times we had this conversation?" Lucas asked.

"'Bout a hundred," Del said. He opened his mouth to go on, but they were interrupted by a sudden noisy cheer from the back and a male voice shouting, "You see that nigger fly?" One of the black hookers at the bar looked up, eyes narrowing, but she went back to her magazine without saying anything.

Del lifted a hand to the bartender. "Couple beers," he called. "Couple Leinies?"

The bartender nodded, and Lucas said, "You don't think Randy's coming?"

"Gettin' late," Del said. "And if I drink any more of this Coke, I'll need a bladder transplant."

The beers came, and Del said, "You heard about that killing last night? The woman up on the hill? Beat to death in her kitchen?"

Lucas nodded. This was what Del had been leading up

to. "Yeah. Saw it on the news. And I heard some stuff around the office. . . ."

"She was my cousin," Del said, closing his eyes. He let his head fall back, as though overcome with exhaustion. "We grew up together, fooling around on the river. Hers were the first bare tits I ever saw, in real life."

"Your cousin?" Lucas studied the other man. As a matter of self-defense, cops joked about death. The more grotesque the death, the more likely the jokes; you had to watch your tongue when a friend had a family member die.

"We used to go fishing for carp, man, can you believe that?" Del turned so he could lean against the window box. *Thinking about yesterdays.* His bearded face drawn long and solemn, like an ancient photo of James Longstreet after Gettysburg, Lucas thought. "Down by the Ford dam, just a couple blocks from your place. Tree branches for fishing poles. Braided nylon line, with dough balls for bait. She fell off a rock, slipped on the moss, big splash . . ."

"Gotta be careful . . ."

"She was, like, fifteen, wearing a T-shirt, no bra," Del said. "It was plastered to her. I said, 'Well, I can see it all, you might as well take it off.' I was kidding, but she did. She had nipples the color of wild roses, man, you know? That real light pink. I had a hard-on for two months. Stephanie was her name."

Lucas didn't say anything for a moment, watching the other man's face, then, "You're not working it?"

"Nah. I'm no good at that shit, figuring stuff out," Del said. He flipped his hands palm out, a gesture of helplessness. "I spent the day with my aunt and uncle. They're all fucked up. They don't understand why I can't do something."

"What do they want you to do?" Lucas asked.

"Arrest her husband. He's a doctor over at the U, a pathologist," Del said. He took a hit of his beer. "Michael Bekker."

"Stephanie Bekker?" Lucas asked, his forehead wrinkling. "Sounds familiar."

"Yeah, she used to run around with the political crowd. You might even have met her—she was on the study group for that civilian review board a couple of years ago. But the thing is, when she was killed, her old man was in San Francisco."

"So he's out," Lucas said.

"Unless he hired it done." Del leaned forward now, his eyes open again. "That alibi is a little too convenient. I personally think he's got a loose screw."

"What're you telling me?"

"Bekker feels wrong. I'm not sure he killed her, but I think he might've," Del said. A man in a T-shirt dashed to the bar with a handful of bills, slapped them on the bar, said, "Catch us later," and ran three beers back to the TV set.

"Would he have a motive?" Lucas asked.

Del shrugged. "The usual. Money. He thinks he's better than anyone else and can't figure out why he's poor."

"Poor? He's a doctor. . . ."

"You know what I mean. He's a doctor, he oughta be rich, and here he is working at the U for seventy, eighty grand. He's a pathologist, and there ain't no big demand for pathology in the civilian world. . . ."

"Hmph."

Out on the sidewalk, on the other side of the one-way window, a couple shared an umbrella and, assuming privacy, slowed to light a joint. The woman was wearing a short white skirt and a black leather jacket. Lucas' Porsche was parked next to the curb, and as they walked by it, the man stopped to look, passing the joint to the girl. She took a hit, narrowed her eyes as she choked down the smoke and passed the joint back.

"Gotta get your vitamins," Del said, watching them. He reached forward and quickly traced a smiley face in the condensation on the window.

"I heard in the office . . . there was a guy with her? With your cousin?"

"We don't know what that is," Del admitted, his forehead wrinkling. "Somebody was there with her. They'd had intercourse, we know that from the M.E., and it wasn't rape. And a guy called in the report. . . ."

"Lovers' quarrel?"

"I don't think so. The killer apparently came in through the back, killed her and ran out the same way. She was working at the sink, there were still bubbles on the dishwater when the squad got there, and she had soap on her hands. There wasn't any sign of a fight, there wasn't any sign that she had a chance to resist. She was washing dishes, and *pow*."

"Doesn't sound like a lovers' quarrel . . ."

"No. And one of the crime-scene guys was wondering how the killer got so close to her, assuming it wasn't Loverboy who did it—how he could get so close without her hearing him coming. They checked the door and found out the hinges had just been oiled. Like in the past couple of weeks, probably."

"Ah. Bekker."

"Yeah, but it's not much. . . ."

Lucas thought it over again. A gust of rain brought a quick, furious drumming on the window, which just as quickly stopped. A woman with a red golf umbrella went by.

"Listen," Del said. "I'm not just sitting here bullshitting. . . . I was hoping you'd take a look at it."

27

"Ah, man . . . I hate murders. And I haven't been operating so good. . . ." Lucas gestured helplessly.

"That's another thing. You need an interesting case," Del said, poking an index finger at Lucas' face. "You're more fucked up than I am, and I'm a goddamned train wreck."

"Thanks . . ." Lucas opened his mouth to ask another question, but two pedestrians were drifting along the length of the window. One was a very light-skinned black woman, with a tan trench coat and a wide-brimmed cotton hat that matched the coat. The other was a tall, cadaverous white boy wearing a narrow-brimmed alpine hat with a small feather.

Lucas sat up. "Randy."

Del looked out at the street, then reached across the table and took Lucas' arm and said, "Take it easy, huh?"

"She was my best snitch, man," Lucas said, in a voice like a gravel road. "She was almost a friend."

"Bullfuck. Take it easy."

"Let him get all the way inside. . . . You go first, cover me, he knows my face. . . ."

Randy came in first, his hands in his coat pockets. He posed for a moment, but nobody noticed. With twelve seconds left in the NBA game, the Celtics were one point down with a man at the line, shooting two. Everybody but the drunk hooker and the bitter old man who was talking into his overcoat was facing the tube.

A woman came in behind Randy and pulled the door shut.

Lucas came out of the booth a step behind Del. *She's beautiful*, he thought, looking at the woman past Del's shoulder; then he put his head down. *Why would she hang with a dipshit like Randy?*

Randy Whitcomb was seventeen and a fancy man, with a gun and a knife and sometimes a blackthorn walking stick with a gold knob on the end of it. He had a long freckled face, coarse red hair and two middle teeth that pointed in slightly different directions. He shook himself like a dog, flicking water spray off his tweed coat. He was too young for a tweed coat and too thin and too crazy for the quality of it. He walked down the bar toward the drunk hooker, stopped, posed again, waiting to be seen. The hooker didn't look up until he took a hand out of his coat and slid a church key down the bar, where it knocked a couple of quarters off her stack of change.

"Marie," Randy crooned. The bartender caught the tone and looked at him. Del and Lucas were closing, but Randy paid them no attention. He was focused on Marie like fire: "Marie, baby," he warbled. "I hear you been talking to the cops. . . ."

Marie tried to climb off the stool, looking around wildly for Lucas. The stool tipped backward and she reached out to catch herself on the bar, teetering. Randy slid around the corner of the bar, going for her, but Lucas was there, behind him. He put a hand in the middle of the boy's back and pushed him, hard, into the bar.

The bartender hollered, "Hey," and Del had his badge out as Marie hit the floor, her glass shattering.

"Police. Everybody sit still," Del shouted. He slipped a short black revolver out of a hip holster and held it vertically in front of his face, where everybody in the bar could see it.

"Randy Ernest Whitcomb, dickweed," Lucas began, pushing Randy in the center of his back, looping his foot in front of the boy's ankles. "You are under . . ."

He had Randy leaning forward, his feet back, one arm held tight, the other going into his pocket for cuffs, when Randy screamed, "No," and levered himself belly-down onto the bar.

Lucas grabbed for one of his legs, but Randy kicked,

thrashed. One foot caught Lucas on the side of the face, a glancing impact, but it hurt and knocked him back.

Randy fell over the bar, scrambled along the floor behind it and up over the end of it, grabbed a bottle of Absolut vodka and backhanded it at Del's head. Then he was running for the back of the bar, Lucas four steps behind him, knowing the back door was locked. Randy hit it, hit it again, then spun, his eyes wild, flashing a spike. They were all the fashion among the assholes. Clipped to a shirt pocket, they looked like Cross ballpoint pens. With the cap off, they were six-inch steel scalpels, the tip honed to a wicked point.

"Come on, motherfucker cop," Randy howled, spraying saliva at Lucas. His eyes were the size of half-dollars, his voice high and climbing. "Come on, motherfucker, get cut. . . ."

"Put the fuckin' knife down," Del screamed. His gun pointed at Randy's head. Lucas, glancing at Del, felt the world slowing down. The fat bartender was still behind the bar, his hands on his ears, as though blocking out the noise of the fight would stop it; Marie had gotten to her feet and was staring at a bleeding palm, shrieking; the two shitkickers had taken a step away from the shuffleboard bowling machine, and one of them, his Adam's apple bobbing up and down, was fumbling at the sheath on his belt. . . .

"Fuck you, cop, kill me," Randy shrieked, doing a sidestep shuffle. "I'm a fuckin' juvenile, assholes. . . ."

"Put the fuckin' blade down, Randy. . . ." Del screamed again. He glanced sideways at Lucas. "What d'ya wanna do, man?"

"Let me take him, let me take him," Lucas said, and he pointed. "The shitkicker's got a knife." As Del started to turn, Lucas was facing Randy, his eyes wide and black, and he asked, "You like to fuck, Randy?"

"Fuckin' A, man," Randy brayed. He was panting, his tongue hanging out. Nuts: "Fuck-in-A."

"Then I hope you got a good memory, 'cause I'm gonna stick that point right through your testicles, my man. You fucked up Betty with that church key. She was a friend of mine. I been looking for you. . . ."

"Well, you got me, Davenport, motherfucker, come get cut," Randy shouted. He had one hand down, as he'd been shown in reform school, the knife hand back a bit. Cop rule of thumb: An asshole gets within ten feet of you with a knife, you're gonna get cut, gun or no gun, shoot or no shoot.

"Easy, man, easy," Del shouted, looking at the shit-kicker. . . .

"Where's the woman? Where's the woman?" Lucas called, still facing Randy, his arms wide in a wrestler's stance.

"By the door . . ."

"Get her. . . ."

"Man . . ."

"Get her. I'll take care of this asshole. . . ."

Lucas went straight in, faked with his right, eluded Randy's probing left hand, and when the knife hand came around, Lucas reached in and caught his right coat sleeve, half threw him and hit him in the face with a roundhouse right. Randy banged against the wall, still trying with the knife, Lucas punching him in the face.

"Lucas . . ." Del screamed at him.

But the air was going blue, slowing, slowing . . . the boy's head was bouncing off the wall, Lucas' arms pumping, his knee coming up, his elbow, then both hands pumping, a slow motion, a long, beautiful combination, a whole series of combinations, one-two-three, one-two, one-two-three, like working with a speed bag . . . the knife on the floor, skittering away . . .

31

Suddenly Lucas was staggering backward; he tried to turn, and couldn't. Del's arm was around his throat, dragging him away. . . .

The world sped up again. The people in the bar stared in stunned silence, all of them on their feet now, their faces like postage stamps on a long, unaddressed envelope. The basketball game was going in the background, broadcast cheers echoing tinnily through the bar.

"Jesus," Del said, gasping for breath. He said, too loudly, "I thought he got you with that knife. Everybody stay away from the knife, we need prints. Anybody touches it, goes to jail."

He still had a hand on Lucas' coat collar. Lucas said, "I'm okay, man."

"You okay?" Del looked at him and silently mouthed, *Witnesses*. Lucas nodded and Del said loudly, "You didn't get stabbed?"

"I think I'm okay. . . ."

"Close call," Del said, still too loud. "The kid was nuts. You see him go nuts with that knife? Never saw anything like that . . ."

Steering the witnesses, Lucas thought. He looked around for Randy. The boy was on the floor, face-up, unmoving, his face a mask of blood.

"Where's his girlfriend?" Lucas asked.

"Fuck her," Del said. He stepped over to Randy, keeping one eye on Lucas, then squatted next to the boy and cuffed his hands in front. "I thought you were gonna get stuck, you crazy fuck."

One of the hookers, up and wrapping a red plastic raincoat around her shoulders, ready to leave, looked down at Randy and into the general silence said, in a long, calm Kansas City drawl, "You better call an ambulance. That motherfucker is *hurt*."

32

3

Bekker was of two minds.

There was an Everyday Bekker, the man of science, the man in the white lab coat, doing his separations in the high-speed centrifuge, the man with the scalpel.

And then there was Beauty.

Beauty was up. Beauty was light. Beauty was dance. . . .

Beauty was the dextroamphetamines, the orange heart-shaped tablets and the half-black, half-clear capsules. Beauty was the white tabs of methamphetamine hydrochloride, the shiny jet-black caps of amphetamine, and the green-and-black bumblebees of phendimetrazine tartrate. All legal.

Beauty was especially the *illegals*, the anonymous white tabs of MDMA, called ecstasy, and the perforated squares of blotter, printed with the signs of the Zodiac, each with its drop of sweet acid, and the cocaine.

Beauty was anabolic steroids for the body and synthetic human growth hormone to fight the years. . . .

Everyday Bekker was down and dark.

Bekker was blood-red capsules of codeine, the Dilaudid. The minor benzodiazepines smoothed his anxieties, the Xanax and Librium and Clonopin, Tranxene and Valium, Dalmane and Paxipam, Ativan and Serax. The molindone, for a troubled mind. All legal.

And the illegals.

The white tabs of methaqualone, coming in from Europe.

Most of all, the phencyclidine, the PCP.
The power.

Bekker had once carried an elegant gold pillbox for his medicines, but eventually it no longer sufficed. At a Minneapolis antique store he bought a brass Art Deco cigarette case, which he lined with velvet. It would hold upward of a hundred tablets. Food for them both, Beauty and Bekker . . .

Beauty stared into the cigarette case and relived the morning. As Bekker, he'd gone to the funeral home and demanded to see his wife.

"Mr Bekker, I really think, the condition . . ." The undertaker was nervous, his face flickering from phony warmth to genuine concern, a light patina of sweat on his forehead. Mrs Bekker was not one of their better products. He didn't want her husband sick on the carpet.

"God damn it, I want to see her," Bekker snapped.

"Sir, I have to warn you . . ." The undertaker's hands were fluttering.

Bekker fixed him with a cold stare, a ferret's stare: "I am a pathologist. I know what I will see."

"Well. I suppose . . ." The undertaker's lips made an O of distaste.

She was lying on a frilly orange satin pad, inside the bronze coffin. She was smiling, just slightly, with a rosy blush on her cheeks. The top half of her face, from the bridge of the nose up, looked like an airbrushed photograph. All wax, all moldings and make-up and paint, and none of it quite right. The eyes were definitely gone. They'd put her together the best they could, but considering the way she'd died, there wasn't much they could do. . . .

"My God," Bekker said, reaching out to the coffin.

A wave of exultation rose through his body. He was rid of her.

He'd hated her for so long, watching her with her furniture and her rugs, her old paintings in the heavy carved frames, the inkwells and cruets and compotes and Quimper pots, the lopsided bottles dug from long-gone outhouses. She'd touch it, stroke it, polish it, move it, sell it. Caress it with her little piggy eyes . . . Talk about it, endlessly, with her limp-wristed antiquarian friends, all of them perched on rickety chairs with teacups, rattling on endlessly, *Mahogany with reeded legs, gilt tooled leather, but you almost couldn't tell under the horrible polish she'd absolutely poured on the piece, well, she obviously didn't know what she had, or didn't care. I was there to look at a Georgian tea table that she'd described as gorgeous, but it turned out to be really very tatty, if I do say so. . . .*

And now she was dead.

He frowned. Hard to believe that she had had a lover. One of those soft, heavy pale men who talked of teapoys and wing chairs . . . unbelievable. What did they do in bed? Talk?

"Sir, I really think . . ." The undertaker's hand on his arm, steadying him, not understanding.

"I'm okay," Bekker said, accepting the comforting arm with a delicious sense of deception. He stood there for another minute, the undertaker behind him, ignored. This was not something he'd want to forget. . . .

Michael Bekker was beautiful. His head was large, his blond hair thick and carefully cut, feathering back over small, perfect ears. His forehead was broad and unlined, his eyebrows light, near-white commas over his startlingly blue deep-set eyes. The only wrinkles on his face were barely noticeable crow's-feet: they enhanced his beauty, rather than detracted from it, adding an ineffable touch of masculinity.

Below his eyes, his nose was a narrow wedge, his nostrils small, almost dainty. His chin was square, with a cleft, his complexion pale but healthy. His lips were wide and mobile over even white teeth.

If Bekker's face was nearly perfect, a cinema face, he had been born with a body no better than average. Shoulders a bit too narrow, hips a little too wide. And he was, perhaps, short in the leg.

The faults gave him something to work for. He was so close. . . .

Bekker exercised four nights a week, spending a half-hour on the Nautilus machines, another hour with the free weights. Legs and trunk one night, arms and shoulders the next. Then a rest day, then repeat, then two rest days at the end of the week.

And the pills, of course, the anabolic steroids. Bekker wasn't interested in strength; strength was a bonus. He was interested in shape. The work broadened his apparent shoulder width and deepened his chest. There wasn't anything he could do about the wide hips, but the larger shoulders had the effect of narrowing them.

His legs . . . legs can't be stretched. But in New York, just off Madison Avenue, up in the Seventies, he had found a small shop that made the most beautiful calfskin half-boots. The leather was so soft that he sometimes held the boots against his face before he put them on. . . .

Each boot was individually fitted with the most subtle of lifts, which gave him an inch and made him as near to perfect as God would come with Nordic man.

Bekker sighed and found himself looking into the bathroom mirror, the bathroom down the hall from his bedroom, the cold hexagonal tiles pressing into his feet. Staring at his beautiful face.

He'd been gone again. How long? He looked at his

watch with a touch of panic. Five after one. Fifteen minutes gone. He had to control this. He'd taken a couple of methobarbitals to flatten out the nervous tension, and they'd thrown him outside himself. They shouldn't do that, but they had, and it was happening more and more often. . . .

He forced himself into the shower, turned on the cold water and gasped as it hit his chest. He kept his eyes closed, turned his back, lathered himself, rinsed and stepped out.

Did he have time? Of course: he always had time for this. He rubbed emollients into his face, dabbed after-shave along his jawline, cologne on his chest, behind his ears and under his balls, sprinkled powder across his chest, under his arms, between his buttocks.

When he was done, he looked into the mirror again. His nose seemed raw. He considered just a touch of make-up but decided against it. He really shouldn't look his best. He *was* burying Stephanie, and the police would be there. The police investigators were touchy: Stephanie's goddamned father and her cop cousin were whispering in their ears.

An investigation didn't much worry him. He'd hated Stephanie, and some of her friends would know that. But he'd been in San Francisco.

He smiled at himself in the mirror, was dissatisfied with the smile, wiped it away. Tried a half-dozen new expressions, more appropriate for the funeral. Scowl as he might, none of them detracted from his beauty.

He cocked his head at himself and let the smile return. All done? Not quite. He added a hair dressing with a light odor of spring lilacs and touched his hair with a brush. Satisfied, he went to the closet and looked at his suits. The blue one, he thought.

Quentin Daniel looked like a butcher in good clothes.

A good German butcher at a First Communion. With his lined red face and incipient jowls, the stark white collar pinching into his throat, the folds of flesh on the back of his neck, he would look fine behind a stainless-steel meat scale, one thumb on the tray, the other on your lambchops. . . .

Until you saw his eyes.

He had the eyes of an Irish Jesuit, pale blue, imperious. He was a cop, if he was one at all, with his brain: he'd stopped carrying a gun years before, when he'd bought his first tailored suits. Instead, he had spectacles. He wore simple military-style gold-rimmed bifocals for dealing with the troops, tortoise-shell single-vision glasses for reading his computer screen, and blue-tinted contact lenses for television appearances.

No gun.

Lucas pushed through the heavy oak door and slouched into Daniel's office. He was wearing the leather bomber jacket from the night before but had shaved and changed into a fresh houndstooth shirt, khaki slacks and loafers.

"You called?"

Daniel was wearing his computer glasses. He looked up, squinted as though he didn't recognize his visitor, took the computer glasses off, put on the gold-rimmed glasses and waved Lucas toward a chair. His face, Lucas thought, was redder than usual.

"Do you know Marty McKenzie?" Daniel asked quietly, his hands flat, palms down, on his green baize blotter.

"Yeah." Lucas nodded as he sat down. He crossed his legs. "He's got a practice in the Claymore Building. A sleaze."

"A sleaze," Daniel agreed. He folded his hands over his stomach and peered up at the ceiling. "The very first thing this morning, I sat here smiling for half an hour while the sleaze lectured me. Can you guess why?"

"Randy . . ."

" . . . Because the sleaze had a client over in the locked ward at Hennepin General who had the shit beat out of him last night by one of my cops. After the sleaze left, I called the hospital and talked to a doc." Daniel pulled open a desk drawer and took out a notepad. "Broken ribs. Broken nose. Broken teeth. Possible cracked sternum. Monitored for blunt trauma." He slapped the pad on the desktop with a crack like a .22 short. "Jesus Christ, Davenport . . ."

"Pulled a knife on me," Lucas said. "Tried to cut me. Like this." He turned the front panel of the jacket, showed the deep slice in the leather.

"Don't bullshit me," Daniel said, ignoring the coat. "The Intelligence guys knew a week ago that you were looking for him. You and your pals. You've been looking for him ever since that hooker got cut. You found him last night and you kicked the shit out of him."

"I don't think . . ."

"Shut up," Daniel snapped. "Any explanation would be stupid. You know it, I know it, so why do it?"

Lucas shrugged. "All right . . ."

"The police department is not a fuckin' street gang," Daniel said. "You can't do this shit. We've got trouble and it could be serious. . . ."

"Like what?"

"McKenzie went to Internal Affairs before he came here, so they're in it and there's no way I can get them out. They'll want a statement. And this kid, Randy, might have been an asshole, but technically he's a juvenile—he's already got a social worker assigned and she's all pissed off about him getting beat up. She doesn't want to hear about any assault on a police officer. . . ."

"We could send her some pictures of the woman he worked over. . . ."

"Yeah, yeah, we'll do that. Maybe that'll change her around. And your jacket will help, the cut, and we're getting statements from witnesses. But I don't know. . . . If the jacket wasn't cut, I'd have to suspend your ass," Daniel said. He rubbed his forehead with the heel of his hand, as though wiping away sweat, then swiveled in his chair and looked out the window at the street, his back to Lucas. "I'm worried about you, Davenport. Your friends are worried about you. I had Sloan up here, he was lying like a goddamn sailor to cover your ass, until I told him to can it. Then we had a little talk. . . ."

"Fuckin' Sloan," Lucas said irritably. "I don't want him. . . ."

"Lucas . . ." Daniel turned back to Lucas, his tone mellowing from anger to concern. "He's your friend and you should appreciate that, 'cause you need all the friends you've got. Now. Have you been to a shrink?"

"No."

"They've got pills for what you've got. They don't cure anything, but they make it a little easier. Believe me, because I've been there. Six years ago this winter. I live in fear of the day I go back. . . ."

"I didn't know . . ."

"It's not something you talk about, if you're in politics," Daniel said. "You don't want people to think they've got a crazy man as police chief. Anyway, what you've got is called a unipolar depression."

"I've read the books," Lucas snapped. "And I ain't going to a shrink."

He pushed himself out of the chair and wandered around the office, looking into the faces of the dozens of politicians who peered from photos on Daniel's walls. The photos came mostly from newspapers, special prints made at the

40

chief's request, and all were black-and-white. Mug shots with smiles, Lucas thought. There were only two pieces of color on the government-yellow walls. One piece was a Hmong tapestry, framed, with a brass plate that said: "Quentin Daniel, from His Hmong Friends, 1989." The second was a calendar with a painting of a vase of flowers, bright, slightly fuzzy, sophisticated and childlike at the same time. Lucas parked himself in front of the calendar and studied it.

Daniel watched him for a moment, sighed and said, "I don't necessarily think you should see a shrink—shrinks aren't the answer for everybody. But I'm telling you this as a friend: You're right on the edge. I've seen it before, I'll see it again, and I'm looking at it right now. You're fucked up. Sloan agrees. So does Del. You've got to get your shit together before you hurt yourself or somebody else."

"I could quit," Lucas ventured, turning back to the chief's desk. "Take a leave . . ."

"That wouldn't be so good," Daniel said, shaking his head. "People with a bad head need to be around friends. So let me suggest something. If I'm wrong, tell me."

"All right . . ."

"I want you to take on the Bekker murder. Keep your network alive, but focus on the murder. You need the company, Lucas. You need the teamwork. And I need somebody to bail me out on this goddamn killing. The Bekker woman's family has some clout and the papers are talking it up."

Lucas tipped his head, thinking about it. "Del mentioned it last night. I told him I might look into it. . . ."

"Do it," Daniel said. Lucas stood up, and Daniel put on his computer glasses and turned back to a screen full of amber figures.

"How long has it been since you were on the street?" Lucas asked.

Daniel looked at him, then up at the ceiling. "Twenty-one years," he said after a moment.

"Things have changed," Lucas said. "People don't believe in right and wrong anymore; if they do, we write them off as kooks. Reality is greed. People believe in money and power and feeling good and cocaine. For the bad people out there, we *are* a street gang. They understand that idea. The minute we lose the threat, they'll be on us like rats. . . ."

"Jesus Christ . . ."

"Hey, listen to me," Lucas said. "I'm not stupid. I don't even necessarily think—in theory, anyway—that I should be able to get away with what I did last night. But those things have to be done by somebody. The legal system has smart judges and tough prosecutors and it don't mean shit—it's a game that has nothing to do with justice. What I did was justice. The street understands that. I didn't do too much and I didn't do too little. I did just right."

Daniel looked at him for a long time and then said soberly, "I don't disagree with you. But don't ever repeat that to another living soul."

Sloan was propped against the metal door of Lucas' basement office, flipping through a throw-away newspaper, smoking a Camel. He was a narrow man with a foxy face and nicotine-stained teeth. A brown felt hat was cocked down over his eyes.

"You been shoveling horseshit again," Lucas said as he walked down the hall. His head felt as if it were filled with cotton, each separate thought tangled in a million fuzzy strands.

Sloan pushed himself away from the door so Lucas could unlock it. "Daniel ain't a mushroom. And it ain't horseshit. So you gonna do it? Work Bekker?"

"I'm thinking about it," Lucas said.

"The wife's funeral is this afternoon," Sloan said. "You

42

oughta go. And I'll tell you what: I've been looking this guy up, Bekker. We got us an iceman."

"Is that right?" Lucas pushed the door open and went inside. His office had once been a janitor's closet. There were two chairs, a wooden desk, a two-drawer filing cabinet, a metal waste-basket, an old-fashioned oak coatrack, an IBM computer and a telephone. A printer sat on a metal typing table, poised to print out phone numbers coming through on a pen register. A stain on the wall marked the persistent seepage of a suspicious but unidentifiable liquid. Del had pointed out that a women's rest-room was one floor above and not too much down the hall.

"Yeah, that's right," Sloan said. He dropped into the visitor's chair and put his heels up on the edge of the desk as Lucas hung his jacket on the coatrack. "I've been reading background reports, and it turns out Bekker was assigned to the Criminal Investigation Division in Saigon during the Vietnam War. I thought he was some kind of cop, so I talked to Anderson and he called some of his computer buddies in Washington, and we got his military records. He wasn't a cop, he was a forensic pathologist. He did post-mortems in criminal cases that involved GIs. I found his old commanding officer, a guy named Wilson. He remembered Bekker. I told him who I was, and he said, "What happened, the sonofabitch kill somebody?"

"You didn't prompt him?" Lucas asked, settling behind his desk.

"No. Those were the first words out of his mouth. Wilson said Bekker was called 'Dr Death'—I guess he liked his work a little too much. And he liked the hookers. Wilson said he had a rep for pounding on them."

"How bad?"

Sloan shook his head. "Don't know. That was just his rep. . . . Wilson said a couple of whores got killed while Bekker was there, but nobody ever suggested he did it.

The cops were looking for an Army enlisted man. They never found anybody, but they never looked too hard, either. Wilson said the place was overrun with AWOLs, deserters, guys on leave and pass, guys going in and out. He said it was an impossible case. But he remembers people around the office talking about the killings and that Bekker was . . . he was spooky. Since there were GIs involved, Bekker was in on the autopsies. He either did them himself or with a Vietnamese doc, Wilson couldn't remember. But when he came back, it was like he was satisfied. Fucked out."

"Huh." The printer burped up a number. Lucas glanced at it, then turned back to Sloan. "Did Bekker kill Stephanie? Hire it done?"

Sloan pulled the waste-basket over to his chair and carefully snubbed out his cigarette. "I think it's a major possibility," he said slowly. "If he did, he's cold: we checked on her insurance. . . ."

"Ten million bucks?" Lucas' eyebrows went up.

"No. Just the opposite. Stephanie was starting a business. She was gonna sell architectural artifacts for restoring old homes. Stained-glass windows, antique doorknobs, like that. An accountant told her she could save money by buying all the family insurance through the company. So she and Bekker canceled their old life insurance and bought new insurance through the company. It specifically won't pay off on any violent non-accidental death—murder or suicide—in the first two years of coverage."

"So."

"So she had no insurance at all," Sloan said. "Not that Bekker can collect on. A month ago she had a hundred grand, and she'd had it for a while."

Lucas' eyes narrowed. "If a defense attorney got that into court . . ."

"Yeah," Sloan said. "It'd knock a hell of a hole in a circumstantial case."

"And he's got an alibi."

"Airtight. He was in San Francisco."

"Jesus, I'd find him not guilty myself, knowing all that."

"That's why we need you. If he's behind it, he had to hire a hitter. There are only so many guys in the Cities who'd do it. You probably know most of them. Those you don't, your people would know. There must have been a big payoff. Maybe somebody came into a big hunk of unexplained cash?"

Lucas nodded. "I'll ask around. What about the guy who was in the sack with Bekker's old lady? Loverboy?"

"We're looking for him," Sloan said. "So far, no luck. I talked to Stephanie's best friend and she thought something might be going on. She didn't know who, but she was willing to mong a rumor. . . ."

Lucas grinned at the word: "So mong it to me," he said.

Sloan shrugged. "For what it's worth, she thinks Stephanie might have been screwing a neighborhood shrink. She'd seen them talking at parties, and she thought they . . . She said they quote stood in each other's space unquote."

"All right." Lucas yawned and stretched. "Most of my people won't be around yet, but I'll check."

"I'll Xerox the file for you."

"You could hold off on that. I don't know if I'll be in that deep. . . ." Sloan was standing, ready to leave, and Lucas reached back and punched the message button on his answering machine. The tape rewound, there was an electronic beep and a voice said: "*This is Dave, down at the auto parts. There're a couple of Banditos in town, I just did some work on their bikes. I think you might want to hear about it. . . . You got the number.*"

45

"I'll Xerox it," Sloan said with a grin, "just in case."

Sloan left and Lucas sat with a yellow legal pad in his lap, feet up, listening to the voices on the answering machine, taking numbers. And watched himself.

His head wasn't working right. Hadn't been for months. But now, he thought, something was changing. There'd been just the smallest quieting of the storm. . . .

He'd lost his woman and their daughter. They'd walked: the story was as simple as that, and as complicated. He couldn't accept it and had to accept it. He pitied himself and was sick of pitying himself. He felt his friends' concern and he was tired of it.

Whenever he tried to break out, when he worked two or three days into exhaustion, the thoughts always sneaked back: If I'd done A, she'd have done B, and then we'd have both done C, and then . . . He worked through every possible combination, compulsively, over and over and over, and it all came up ashes. He told himself twenty times that he'd put it behind himself, and he never had. And still he couldn't stop. And he grew sicker and sicker of himself. . . .

And now Bekker. A flicker, here. An interest. He watched the first tickle, couldn't deny it. Bekker. He ran his hand through his hair, watching the interest bud and grow. On the legal pad he wrote:

1. Elle
2. Funeral

How can you lose with a two-item list? Even when—what was it called? a unipolar depression?—even when a unipolar depression's got you by the balls, you can handle two numbers. . . .

Lucas picked up the phone and called a nunnery.

* * *

Sister Mary Joseph was talking to a student when Lucas arrived. Her door was open a few inches, and from a chair in the outer office he could see the left side of her scarred face. Elle Kruger had been the prettiest girl in their grade school. Later, after Lucas had gone, transferred to the public schools, she'd been ravaged by acne. He recalled the shock of seeing her, for the first time in years, at a high school district hockey tournament. She had been sitting in the stands, watching him on the ice, eyes sad, seeing his shock. The beautiful blonde Elle of his prepubescent dreams, gone forever. She'd found a vocation with the Church, she had told him that night, but Lucas was never quite sure. A vocation? She'd said yes. But her face . . . Now she sat in her traditional habit, the beads swinging by her side. Still Elle, somewhere.

The college girl laughed again and stood up, her sweater a fuzzy scarlet blur behind the clouded glass of Elle's office door. Then Elle was on her feet and the girl was walking past him, looking at him with an unhidden curiosity. Lucas waited until she was gone, then went into Elle's office and sat in the visitor's chair and crossed his legs.

Elle looked him over, judging, then said, "How are you?"

"Not bad . . ." He shrugged, then grinned. "I was hoping you could give me a name at the university. A doctor, somebody who'd know a guy in the pathology department. Off the record. A guy who can keep his mouth shut."

"Webster Prentice," Elle said promptly. "He's in psychology, but he works at the hospital and hangs out with the docs. Want his phone number?"

Lucas did. As she flipped through a Rolodex, Elle asked, "How are you really?"

He shrugged. "About the same."

"Are you seeing your daughter?"

47

"Every other Saturday, but it's unpleasant. Jen doesn't want me there and Sarah's old enough to sense it. I may give it up for a while."

"Don't cut yourself off, Lucas," Elle said sharply. "You can't sit there in the dark every night. It'll kill you."

He nodded. "Yeah, yeah . . ."

"Are you dating anybody?"

"Not right now."

"You should start," the nun said. "Re-establish contact. How about coming back to the game?"

"I don't know . . . what're you doing?"

"Stalingrad. We can always use another Nazi."

"Maybe," Lucas said non-committally.

"And what's this about talking to Webster Prentice? Are you working on something?"

"A woman got killed. Beaten to death. I'm taking a look," Lucas said.

"I read about it," Elle said, nodding. "I'm glad you're working it. You need it."

Lucas shrugged again. "I'll see," he said.

She scribbled a phone number on an index card and passed it to him.

"Thanks . . ." He leaned forward, about to stand.

"Sit down," she said. "You're not getting out of here that easy. Are you sleeping?"

"Yeah, some."

"But you've got to exhaust yourself first."

"Yeah."

"Alcohol?"

"Not much. A few times, scotch. When I'd get so tired I couldn't move, but I couldn't sleep. The booze would take me out. . . ."

"Feel better in the morning?"

"My body would."

"The Crows beat you up pretty bad," Elle said. The Crows were Indians, either terrorists or patriots. Lucas had helped kill them. Television had tried to make a hero out of him, but the case had cost him his relationship with his woman friend and their daughter. "You finally found out that there's a price for living the way you do. And you found out that you can die. And so can your kid."

"I always knew that," Lucas said.

"You didn't feel it. And if you don't feel it, you don't believe it," Elle rapped back.

"I don't worry about dying," he said. "But I had something going with Jennifer and Sarah."

"Maybe that'll come back. Jennifer's never said it was over forever."

"Sounds like it."

"You need time, all of you," Elle said. "I won't do therapy on you. I can't be objective. We've got too much history. But you should talk to somebody. I can give you some names, good people."

"You know what I think about shrinks," Lucas said.

"You don't think that about me."

"Like you said—we have a history. But I don't want a shrink, 'cause I can't help what I think about them. Maybe a couple of pills or something . . ."

"You can't cure what you've got with pills, Lucas. Only two things will do that. Time or therapy."

"I'll take the time," he said.

She threw up her hands in surrender, her teeth flashing white in a youthful smile. "If you really get your back against the wall, call me. I have a doctor friend who'll prescribe some medication without threatening your manhood with therapy."

She went with him to the exit and watched as he walked out to his car, down the long greening lawn, the sun flicking through the bare trees. When he stepped from the shelter of the building, the wind hit him in the face, with just a finger of warmth. Spring wind. Summer coming. Behind him, on the other side of the door, Elle Kruger kissed her crucifix and began a rosary.

4

Bekker dressed as carefully as he had cleaned himself: a navy suit, a blue broadcloth shirt, a dark tie with small burgundy comma figures, black loafers with lifts. He slipped a pair of sunglasses into his breast pocket. He would use them to hide his grief, he thought. And his eyes, should there be anyone of unusual perception in the crowd.

The funeral would be a waste of his time. He had to go, but it would be a waste of his time. He sighed, put on the sunglasses, and looked at himself in the mirror. Not bad. He flicked a piece of lint off the shoulder of the suit and smiled at himself.

Not bad at all.

When he was ready, he took one of the Contac capsules from the brass cigarette case, pulled it apart and dumped the powder on the glass top of the bedstand. The Contac people would pee down their pant legs if they'd known, he thought: pure medical cocaine. He snorted it, absorbed the rush, collected himself and walked out to the car.

The drive to the funeral home was short. He liked this one funeral home. He was *familiar* with it. He giggled and just as quickly smothered the giggle. He must not do that. He must not. And then he thought: *Compassionate leave*, and almost giggled again. The University had given him compassionate leave. . . . God, funny as that was, he couldn't let it show.

Phenobarbital? About right for a funeral. It'd give him the right *look*. He took the brass cigarette case from his pocket, keeping one eye on the road, opened it, popped a phenobarbital tab. Thought about it, took a second. Naughty boy. And just a lick of PCP? Of course. The thing about PCP was, it stiffened you, gave you a wooden look. He'd seen it in himself. And that would be right, too, for a grieving husband. But not too much. He popped a PCP tab, bit it in half, spit half back into the cigarette case, swallowed the other half. Ready now.

He parked a block from the funeral home, walked briskly, if a bit woodenly—the PCP already?—down the sidewalk. Minnesota had turned springlike with its usual fickle suddenness. It could revert to winter just as quickly, but for now it was wonderful. A warm slanting sun; red-bellied robins in the yards, bouncing around, looking for worms; fat buds on the trees, the smell of wet grass . . . The warm feeling of the phenobarbital coming on.

He stopped outside the funeral home and took a deep breath. God, it was fine to be alive. Without Stephanie.

The funeral home was built of tan stone, in what some funereal architect must have supposed was a British style. Inside, it was simply cold. A hundred people came to the funeral, people from the decorating world, from the university. The women, he thought, all in their dark dresses, looked at him speculatively as he walked slowly up the aisle. Women were like that. Stephanie not yet cold in the grave . . .

He sat down, blocked out the organ music that seeped from hidden speakers and began toting up the assets. Hard to do with the phenobarbital in his blood, but he persisted. The house was worth better than half a million. The furnishings another two hundred thousand—not even her asshole relatives realized that. Stephanie had bought with an insider's eye, had traded up, had salvaged. Bekker didn't care for the place, but some people considered it a treasure house. For himself, Bekker wanted an apartment, up high, white walls, pale birch woodwork, a few Mayan pieces. He'd get it, and still put a half-million in the mutual funds. He'd drag down seventy-five thousand a year, if he picked his funds carefully. On top of his salary . . .

He almost smiled, thinking about it, caught the impulse and glanced around.

There were a number of people he didn't recognize, but most of them were sitting with people he did, in obvious groups and pairings. People from Stephanie's world of antiques and restoration. Stephanie's family, her father, her brothers and sisters, her cop cousin. He nodded at her father, who had fixed him with a glare, and looked farther back into the crowd.

One man, sitting alone near the back, caught his attention. He was muscular, dark-complected, in a gray European-cut suit. Good-looking, like a boxer might be. And he seemed interested in Bekker. He'd followed his progress up the aisle, into the chair that half faced the coffin, half faced the mourners. Safe behind the sunglasses, Bekker returned the man's gaze. For one goofy minute, Bekker thought he might be Stephanie's lover. But that was crazy. A guy like this wouldn't go for Stephanie, would he? Chunky Stephanie? Stephanie No-Eyes?

Then Swanson, the cop who had interviewed him when he got back from San Francisco, walked into the church, looked around and sat next to the stranger. They leaned their heads closer and spoke a few words, the stranger still watching Bekker. The tough guy was a cop.

All right. Bekker dismissed him, and looked again through the gathering crowd. Philip George came in with his wife, Annette, and sat behind the cop. Bekker's eyes traveled across him without hesitating.

The lover. Who was the lover?

The funeral was mercilessly long. Twelve people spoke. Stephanie was good, Stephanie was kind. Stephanie worked for the community.

Stephanie was a pain in the ass.

Yea, though I walk through the valley of the shadow of death, I will fear no evil: for thou art with me; thy rod and thy staff, they comfort me. . . .

Bekker went away. . . .

When he came back, the mourners were on their feet, looking at him. It was over, what? Yes, he should walk out, one hand on the side rail of the coffin. . . .

Afterward, at the cemetery, Bekker walked alone to his car, aware of the eyes on him. The women, looking. He composed his face: I need a mask, a *grave* mask, he thought. He giggled at the pun. He couldn't help himself.

He turned, struggling to keep his face straight. The crowd was watching, all right. And on the hillside, in the grass, the man in the European suit, watching.

He needed something to enhance his mood. His hand strayed to the cigarette case. He had two more of the special Contacs, a half-dozen methamphetamines. They'd be fine after the barbs.

And a little ecstasy for dessert?

But of course . . .

The funeral was crowded, the coffin closed. Lucas sat next to Swanson, the lead investigator. Del sat with Stephanie Bekker's family.

"Bekker," Swanson mumbled, poking Lucas with an elbow. Lucas turned and watched Bekker go by. Astonishingly good-looking: almost too much, Lucas thought. Like a mythological beast, assembled from the best parts of several animals, Bekker's face seemed to have been assembled from the best features of several movie stars.

"Is he hurt?" Lucas whispered. Bekker was walking awkwardly, his legs like lumber.

"Not that I know of," Swanson whispered back.

Bekker walked to the front of the chapel, stiff-legged, wooden, turned, hesitated and sat down in a chair apart. He never looked at the closed coffin, never spoke, but sat rigid, unbending, his eyes invisible behind dark sunglasses. He remained that way through the funeral, looking neither left nor right. Occasionally his lips moved, as though he were mumbling to himself, or praying. It did not seem an act: the woodenness appeared to be real.

Just before the last prayer, Bekker pursed his lips and, with an odd motion of his hand, wiped the expression away. Odd . . .

He walked from the church as stiffly as he had arrived. Down the steps and out to his car. At the car he turned and looked directly at Lucas. Lucas felt the eyes and stood still, watching, letting their gazes touch. And then Bekker was gone.

Lucas went to the cemetery, curious. What was it with Bekker? Grief? Despair? An act? What?

He watched from a hillside as Stephanie Bekker's coffin was lowered into the ground. Bekker never changed: his beautiful face was as immobile as a lump of clay.

"What do you think?" Swanson asked, when Bekker had gone.

"I think the guy's a fruitcake," Lucas said. "But I don't know what kind."

Lucas spent the rest of the afternoon and early evening putting the word out on his network, a web of hookers, bookstore owners, barbers, mailmen, burglars, gamblers, cops, a couple of genteel marijuana dealers: *Anything on a hit? Any nutso walking around with big cash?*

A few minutes after six, he took a call on his handset and drove back downtown to police headquarters in the scabrous wart of Minneapolis City Hall. Sloan met him in the hall outside the chief's office.

"You hear?" Sloan asked.

"What?"

"We got a letter from a guy who says he was there when Stephanie got killed. Loverboy."

"No ID?"

"No. But there's a lot of stuff in the letter. . . ."

Lucas followed Sloan past the vacant secretary's desk to the inner office. Daniel sat behind his desk, rolling a cigar between his fingers, listening to a Homicide detective who sat in a green leather chair in front of the desk. Daniel looked up when Sloan rapped on the open door.

"C'mon in, Sloan. Davenport, how are you? Swanson's filling me in."

Lucas and Sloan pulled up chairs on either side of the Homicide detective and Lucas asked him, "What's this letter?"

Swanson passed him a Xerox copy. "We were just talking about possibilities. Could be a doper, scared off by Loverboy. Unless Loverboy did it."

"You think it's Loverboy?"

The detective shook his head. "No. Read the letter. It more or less hangs together with the scene. And you saw Bekker."

"Nobody has a good word for the guy," Sloan said.

"Except professionally. The docs at the university say his work is top-notch," Swanson said. "I talked to some people in his department. 'Ground-breaking,' is what they say. . . ."

"You know what bothers me?" Lucas said. "In this letter, Loverboy says she was on her back in a pool of blood, dead. I saw the pictures, and she was face-down next to the wall. He doesn't mention a hand-print. I think he left her there alive. . . ."

"He did," Swanson said, nodding. "She died just about the time the paramedics got there—they even gave her some kind of heart shot, trying to get it going again. Nothing happened, but she hadn't been dead very long, and the blood under her head was fresh. The blood on the floor, though, the blood by the sink, had already started to coagulate. They figure she was alive for fifteen or twenty minutes after the attack. Her brain was all fucked up—who knows what she could have told us? But if Loverboy had called nine-one-one, she might still be around."

"Fucker," Sloan said. "Does that make him an accomplice?"

Swanson shrugged. "You'd have to ask a lawyer about that."

"How about this doctor, the guy she talked with at parties . . ." Lucas asked.

"That's under way," Daniel said.

"You doing it?" Lucas asked Sloan.

"No. Andy Shearson."

"Shit, Shearson? He couldn't find his own asshole with both hands and a pair of searchlights," Lucas said in disbelief.

"He's what we've got and he's not that bad," Daniel said. He stuck the end of the cigar in his mouth, nipped it off, took the butt end from his mouth, examined it and then tossed it into a waste-basket. "We're getting a little more TV on this one—random killer bullshit. I'd hate to see it get any bigger."

"The story'll be gone in a week. Sooner, if we get a decent dope killing," Sloan said.

"Maybe, maybe not," Daniel said. "Stephanie Bekker was white and upper middle class. Reporters identify with that kind of woman. They could keep it going for a while."

"We'll push," Swanson said. "Talk to Bekker some more. We're doing the neighborhood. Checking parking tickets in the area, talking to Stephanie Bekker's friends.

The main thing is, find the boyfriend. Either he did it or he saw it."

"He says the killer looks like a goblin," Lucas said, reading through the letter. "What the hell does that mean?"

"Fuck if I know," said Swanson.

"Ugly," said Daniel. "Barrel-chested . . ."

"Do we know for sure that the goblin's not Bekker? That Bekker was actually in San Francisco?" Lucas asked.

"Yeah, we do," Swanson said. "We wired a photo out, had the San Francisco cops show it to the desk people at Bekker's hotel. He was there, no mistake."

"Hmph," Lucas grunted. He stood up, slipped his hands in his pockets and wandered over to Daniel's wall of trophy photos. Jimmy Carter's smiling face looked back at him. "We're leaning the wrong way with the media. If Bekker hired a killer, the best handle we've got is the boyfriend. The witness . . ."

"Loverboy," said Sloan.

"Loverboy," said Lucas. "He's got some kind of conscience, because he called and he wrote the letter. He could've walked out and we might never have suspected . . ."

"We would have known," Swanson said. "The M.E. found that she'd had intercourse not too long before she was killed. And he did leave her to die."

"Maybe he really thought she was dead," Lucas said. "Anyway, he's got *some* kind of conscience. We ought to make a public appeal to him. TV, the papers. That does two things: it might bring him out of the woodwork, and it might put pressure on the killer, or Bekker, to make a move."

"No other options?" asked Daniel.

"Not if you want to catch the guy," Lucas said. "We could let it go: I'd say right now that the chance of convicting Bekker is about zero. We'll only get him one way—the witness has to identify the killer and the killer has got to give us Bekker on a plea bargain."

"I hate to let it go," Daniel said. "Our fuckin' clearance rate . . ."

"So we get the TV people in here," Lucas said.

"Let's give it another twenty-four hours," Daniel said. "We can talk again tomorrow night."

Lucas shook his head. "No. You need to think about it overnight, 'cause if we're going to do it, we got to do it quick. Tomorrow'd be best, early enough for the early evening news. Before this boyfriend, whoever he is, gets his head set in concrete. You should say flatly that we don't believe the boyfriend did the killing, that we need all the help we can get. That we need him to come in, that we'll get him a lawyer. That if he didn't murder the woman, we'll offer him immunity—maybe you can get the county attorney in on this angle. And that if he still doesn't think he can come in, we need him to communicate with us somehow. Send us letters with more detail. Cut out pictures from magazines, people who most look like the killer. Do drawings, if he can. Maybe we can get the papers to print identikit drawings, have him pick the best ones, change them until they're more like the killer."

"I'll think about it."

"And we watch Bekker. If we make a heavy-duty appeal to the boyfriend and if Bekker really did buy the hit, he'll get nervous. Maybe he'll give us a break," Lucas said.

"All right. I'll think about it. See me tomorrow."

"We gotta move," Lucas urged, but Daniel waved him off.

"We'll talk again tomorrow," he said. Lucas turned back to Jimmy Carter and inspected the former president's tweed jacket. "If it's Bekker who did it, or hired it, if he's the iceman Sloan thinks he is . . ."

"Yeah?" Daniel was fiddling with his cigar, watching him from behind the desk.

"We better find Loverboy before Bekker does," Lucas said.

5

The evening sky shaded from crimson to ultramarine and finally to a flat gray; Lucas lived in the middle of the metro area, and the sky never quite got dark. Across the street, joggers came and went on the river path, stylish in their phosphorescent work-out suits, flashing Day-Glo green and pink. Some wore headsets, running to rock. Beyond them, on the other side of the Mississippi, the orange sodium-vapor streetlights winked on as a grid set, followed by a sprinkling of bluer house lights.

When the lights came on across the river, Lucas pulled the window shade and forced himself back to the game. He worked doggedly, without inspiration, laying out the story for the programmer. A long ribbon of computer paper flowed across the library table, in and out of the puddle of light around his hands. With a flowchart template and a number-two pencil, he blocked out the branches of Druid's Pursuit. He had once thought that he night learn to program, himself. Had, in fact, taken a community college course in Pascal and even dipped into C. But programming bored him, so he hired a kid to do it. He laid down the stories with the myriad jumps and branches, and the kid wrote the code.

The kid programmer had no obvious computer-freak personality flaws. He wore a letter jacket with a letter and told Lucas simply that he'd gotten it in wrestling. He could do chin-ups with his index fingers and sometimes brought a girlfriend along to help him.

Lucas, tongue in cheek, thought to ask him, *Help you do what?*, but he didn't. Both kids came from Catholic colleges in the neighborhood and needed a cheap, private space. Lucas tried to leave them alone.

And maybe she *was* helping him. The work got done.

Lucas wrote games. Historical simulations played on boards, to begin with. Then, for the money, he began writing role-playing quest games of the Dungeons & Dragons genre.

One of his simulations, a Gettysburg, had become so complicated that he'd bought an IBM personal computer to figure times, points and military effects. The flexibility of the computer had impressed him—he could create effects not possible with a board, such as hidden troop movements and faulty military intelligence. With help from the kid, he'd moved the entire game to an IBM 386 clone. A computer database company in Missouri had gotten wind of the game, leased it from him, altered it and put it on line. On any given night, several dozen Civil War enthusiasts would be playing Gettysburg via modem, paying eight dollars an hour for the privilege. Lucas got two of the dollars.

Druid's Pursuit was something else, a role-playing game with a computer serving as game master. The game was becoming complex. . . .

Lucas stopped to change discs in the CD player, switching Tom Waits' *Big Time* for David Fanshawe's *African Sanctus*, then settled back into his chair. After a moment, he put the programming template down and stared at the wall behind the desk. He kept it blank on purpose, for staring at.

Bekker was interesting. Lucas had felt the interest growing, watching it like a gardener watching a new plant, almost afraid to hope. He'd seen depression in other cops, but he'd always been skeptical. No more. The depression—an unfit word for what had happened to him—was so tangible that he imagined it as a dark beast, stalking him, off in the dark.

Lucas sat in the night, staring at his patch of wall, and the sickly smell of Stephanie's funeral flowers came back, the quiet dampness of the private chapel, the drone of the minister, . . . *all who loved this woman Stephanie* . . .

"Dammit." He was supposed to be concentrating on the game, but he couldn't. He stood and took a turn around the room, the *Sanctus* chants banging around in his head. A manila folder caught his eye. The case file, copied by Sloan and left on his desk. He picked it up, flipped through it. Endless detail. Nobody knew what might or might not be useful, so they got it all. He read through it and was about to dump it back on the desk, when a line of the lab narrative caught his eye.

"Drain appeared to have been physically cleaned . . ."

The bedroom and the adjoining bath had been wiped, apparently by Loverboy, to eliminate fingerprints. That demonstrated an unusual coolness. But the drain? That was something else again. Lucas looked for returns on Stephanie Bekker's bed but found nothing in the report. The lab report was signed by Robert Kjellstrom.

Lucas dug in his desk and found the internal police directory, looked up Kjellstrom's phone number and called. Kjellstrom had to get out of bed to take the call.

"There's nothing in the report on hair in the bed. . . ."

"That's 'cause there wasn't any," Kjellstrom said.

"None?"

"Nope. The sheets were clean. They looked like they'd just been washed."

"The report said Stephanie Bekker had just had intercourse. . . ."

"Not on those sheets," Kjellstrom said.

Lucas finished with the file and looked at his watch:

ten o'clock. He walked back to the bedroom, changed from tennis shirt, slacks and loafers to a flannel shirt, jeans and boots, pulled on a shoulder rig with his new Smith & Wesson double-action .45, and covered it with a fleece-lined Patagonia jacket.

The day had been good, but the nights were still nasty, cutting with the last claws of winter. Even the bad people stayed inside. He rolled the Porsche out of the garage, waited in the driveway until the garage door was firmly down, then headed north on Mississippi River Boulevard. At Summit Avenue he considered his options and finally drove out to Cretin Avenue, north to I-94 and then east, past downtown St. Paul to the eastern rim of the city. Three St. Paul cop cars were parked outside a supermarket that had a restaurant in the back. Lucas locked the Porsche and went inside.

"Jesus, look what the fuckin' cat drug in," said the oldest cop. He was in his late forties, burly, with a brush mustache going gray and gold-rimmed glasses. He sat in a booth with three other cops. Two more huddled over coffee cups in the next booth down.

"I thought you guys could use some guidance, so I drove right over," Lucas said. A circular bar sat at the center of the restaurant floor, surrounded by swivel stools, with booths along the wall. Lucas took one of the stools and turned it to face the cops in the booth.

"We appreciate your concern," said the cop with the mustache. Three of the four men in the booth were middle-aged and burly; the fourth was in his twenties, slender, and had tight blue eyes with prominent pink corners. The three older cops were drinking coffee. The younger one was eating French toast with sausage.

"This guy a cop?" the youngest one asked, a fork posed halfway to his mouth with a chunk of sausage. He was staring at Lucas' jacket. "He's carrying. . . ."

"Thank you, Sherlock," an older cop said. He tipped his head at Lucas and said, "Lucas Davenport, he's a detective lieutenant with Minneapolis."

"He drives a Porsche about sixty miles an hour down Cretin Avenue at rush hour," said another of the cops, grinning at Lucas over his coffee cup.

"Bullshit. I observe all St. Paul traffic ordinances," Lucas said.

"Pardon me while I fart in disgust," said the speed-trap cop. "It must've been somebody else's Porsche I got a picture of on my radar about five-thirty Friday."

Lucas grinned. "You must've startled me."

"Right . . . You workin' or what?"

"I'm looking for Poppy White," Lucas said.

"Poppy?" The three older cops looked at each other, and one of them said, "I saw his car outside of Broobeck's last night and a couple of nights last week. Red Olds, last year's. If he's not there, Broobeck might know where he is."

Lucas stayed to talk for a few minutes, then hopped off the stool. "Thanks for the word on Poppy," he said.

"Hey, Davenport, if you're gonna shoot the sonofabitch, could you wait until after the shift change . . . ?"

A red Olds was parked under the neon bowling pin at Broobeck's. Lucas stepped inside, looked down toward the lanes. Only two were being used, by a group of young couples. Three people sat at the bar, but none of them was Poppy. The bartender wore a paper hat and chewed a toothpick. He nodded when Lucas walked up.

"I'm looking for Poppy."

"He's here somewhere, maybe back in the can."

Lucas went to the men's rest-room, stuck his head inside. He could see a pair of Wellington boots under one of the stall doors and called, "Poppy?"

"Yeah?"

"Lucas Davenport. I'll wait at the bar."

"Get a booth."

Lucas got a booth and a beer, and a minute later Poppy appeared, holding wet hands away from his chest.

"You need some towels back there," he complained to the bartender. The man pushed him a stack of napkins. Poppy dried his hands, got a beer and came over to Lucas. He was too heavy, in his middle fifties, wearing jeans and a black T-shirt under a leather jacket. His iron-gray hair was cut in a Korean War flattop. A good man with a saw and a torch, he could chop a stolen Porsche into spare parts in an hour.

"What's going on?" he asked, as he slid into the booth. "You need a starter motor?"

"No. I'm looking for somebody with new money. Somebody who might of hit a woman over in Minneapolis the other day."

Poppy shook his head. "I know what you're talkin' about and I ain't heard even a tinkle. The dopers are sweatin' it, because the papers are saying a doper done it and they figure somebody's got to fall."

"But not a thing?"

"Not a thing, man. If somebody got paid, it wasn't over on this side of town. You sure it was a white guy? I don't know about the coloreds anymore."

He was looking for a white guy. That's the way it went: whites hired whites, blacks hired blacks. Equal-opportunity bigotry, even in murder. There were other reasons, too. In that neighborhood, a black guy would be noticed.

He left Poppy at the bowling alley and headed west to Minneapolis, touched a gay bar on Hennepin Avenue, two more joints on Lake Street and finally, having learned nothing, woke up a fence who lived in the quiet suburban town of Wayzata.

"I don't know, Davenport, maybe just a freak. He wastes the woman, splits for Utah, spends the money buyin' a ranch," the fence said. They sat on a glassed-in porch overlooking a pond with cattails. The lights from another house reflected off the surface of the water, and Lucas could make out the dark shapes of a raft of ducks as they bobbed shoulder to shoulder in the middle of the pond. The fence was uncomfortable on a couch, in his pajamas, smoking an unfiltered cigarette, his wife sitting beside him in a bathrobe. She had pink plastic curlers in her hair and looked worried. She'd offered Lucas a lime mineral water, cold, and he rolled the bottle between his hands as they talked. "If I were you," the fence said, "I'd check with Orville Proud."

"Orville? I thought he was in the joint, down in Arizona or someplace," Lucas said.

"Got out." The fence picked a piece of tobacco off his tongue and flicked it away. "Anyway, he's been around for a week or so."

"Is he setting up again?" He should have known. Proud had been in town for a week—*he should have known*.

"Yeah, I think so. Same old deal. He's hurtin' for cash. And you know the kind of contacts he's got. Fuckin' biker gangs and the muscle guys, the Nazis, everybody. So I says, 'The word's out that it might have been a hit, the husband brought somebody in.' And he says, 'That ain't a good thing to be talking about, Frank.' So I stopped talking about it."

"Huh. You know where he is?"

"I don't want none of this coming back," the fence said. "Orville's a little strange. . . ."

"Won't be coming back," Lucas assured him.

The fence looked at his watch. "Try room two twenty-one at the Loin. There's a game."

"Any guns?"

"You know Orville. . . ."

"Yeah, unfortunately. All right, Frank, I owe you."

" 'Preciate it. You still got that cabin up north?"

"Yeah . . ."

"I got some good deals coming on twenty-five horse Evinrudes."

"Don't push your luck," Lucas said.

"Hey, Lieutenant . . ." Frank grinned, reaching for charm, and his teeth were not quite green.

The Loin was the Richard Coeur de Lion Lounge & Motel on the strip across from Minneapolis-St. Paul International. The place started straight, lost money for a few years, then was picked up by a more creative management out of Miami Beach. After that, it was called either the Dick or the Loin, but Loin won out. As a nickname, it was felt by the people who decided such things, "Loin" had more class. The better gamblers, slicker coke peddlers, prettier whores and less discriminating Viking football players populated the bar and, most nights, the rooms in the attached motel.

The bar was done in red velvet and dark wood with oval mirrors. There were two stuffed red foxes in the foyer, mounted on chunks of driftwood, on either side of a bad reproduction of *The Blue Boy*. Upstairs, the rooms had water beds and pornographic movies on cable, no extra charge.

Lucas walked through the lobby, nodded at the woman behind the desk, who smiled, almost as though she remembered checking him in, and walked up the steps to the single hallway that ran the length of the motel. Room 221 was the last one on the left. He stood outside the door for

67

a moment, listening, then took his .45 out of the shoulder rig and stuck it under his belt in the small of his back. He knocked on the door and stepped back across the hall, where he could be seen through the peephole. The peephole got dark for a moment; then a voice said, "Who is it?"

"Lucas Davenport wants to see Orville."

"No Orville here."

"Tell him. . . ."

The eye left the peephole and a minute passed. Then the peephole got dark again and another voice said, "You alone?"

"Yeah. No problem."

Orville Proud opened the door and looked down the hall.

"No problem?" he asked.

"I need to talk," Lucas said, looking past Orville. Room 221 was a suite without beds. Seven men sat frozen around an octagonal table, their eyes like birds' eyes, picking him up; cards on the table but no chips, ashtrays and bottles of mineral water on the table and the floor by their feet. Behind them, a short man in a hip-length leather coat sat on the heat register. He had a thin pointed beard under delicate gold-rimmed eyeglasses. He looked like Lenin, and he knew it. Ralph Nathan. Lucas put his hand on his hip, six inches from the butt of the .45.

"You're gonna get your fuckin' ass killed someday," Orville said flatly. He stepped into the hall and pulled the door shut behind him. "What do you want?"

"I need to know if there's been any talk about a hit on a woman in Minneapolis. Got herself beat to death, some people think her husband might have hired it. There's a lot of heat coming down."

Orville shook his head, frowning. He didn't need any heat. "A couple of people mentioned it, but I ain't heard a thing. I mean, I think I would've heard. I been scratching around for cash, trying to get back into business, and I been calling everybody I know. There's not a fuckin' thing, man."

"Nobody got rich, nobody bought a car . . . ?"

Proud shook his head. "Not a fuckin' thing. Terry Meller come into a whole load of Panasonic color TVs, fell off the train in St. Paul, but that's about it."

"You're sure?"

"Man, I spent the last three weeks running all over the metro, talking to everybody. That's all I've been doing. There's nothing out there."

"All right," Lucas said, discouraged. "How was Arizona?"

Proud shook his head. "New Mexico. You don't wanna do any time in New Mexico, man. That place is like . . . primitive."

"Sorry to hear it . . ."

"Yeah, sure . . ."

"You check in with me, okay? You got my number?"

Proud nodded, dug in his pocket and came up with a business card printed with a nine-digit number, broken into groups of three, two and four digits, like a Social Security number. He handed the card to Lucas. "Call the last seven numbers, backward. That's my beeper. You want to see me again, phone ahead, huh? Don't come knocking on the fucking door."

"Okay. And I'll give you some free advice, Orville," Lucas said as he stepped away. "Get rid of Ralph. Ralph's a head case and he's looking for somebody to kill. Get yourself a baseball bat or something. If you stay with Ralph, you'll go to Stillwater with him on a murder rap. I guarantee it."

"I hear you," Proud said, but he didn't.

Back in the parking lot, Lucas leaned against the car, thinking it over. They were at a dead end.

Daniel'd have to go for the TV.

6

Beauty danced.

A jig, to music that played only in his brain.

He hopped from one foot to another, his penis bobbing like the head of a blind waxen cave worm, his arms, crooked at the elbow, flapping like chicken wings. He laughed with the pleasure of it, the feel of Persian wool carpet under the bare soles of his feet, the sight of himself in the freestanding mirrors.

He danced and he twirled and he hopped and he laughed. . . .

He felt a wetness on his chest and looked down. A crimson rain was falling on his chest. He touched his nose. His fingers came away sticky, red. Blood. Running across his lips, dripping from his chin, trickling down across his pale, hairless chest to the thatch of hair at his crotch. The music drained from his brain.

"Blood," he moaned. "You're bleeding. . . ."

His heart pounding, Bekker got on his knees, groped under the desk and pulled out his briefcase. Knowing that the police would be in his house, he had thought it prudent to move his medications to his office. He'd not yet returned them to the medicine chest. He fumbled at the tiny combination lock on the case and got it open. Dozens of medical vials were jammed inside, amber plastic with white caps and taped-on labels, mostly prescription, a few over-the-counter dietary supplements. He pawed through them, still dripping blood.

Amobarbital. Dextroamphetamine. Loxapine. Secobarbital. Ethotoin. Chlordiazepoxide. Amiloride. No, no, no, no . . . He should have a color-coding system, he thought; but once he had them back on the shelves, it would be easier. He could put the uppers on top, the downers at the bottom, the smoothers on the second shelf, the vitamins and supplements under that. . . . Haloperidol. Diazepam. Chlorpromazine. No. Where was it? Where? He was sure . . . Ah. Here. Vitamin K. How many? No problem with vitamin K, better safe than sorry. He tossed five caps in his mouth, grimaced and swallowed.

Better. The bleeding was slowing anyway, but the extra K couldn't hurt. He pulled a wad of tissues from a Kleenex box on his desk, pressed it to his nose. He'd bled before. There was no pain, and the bleeding would soon stop. But, he thought, only two this time and I'm bleeding. He'd taken them, why had he taken them, the methamphetamines? There was a reason. . . .

He looked at the corner of his desk, at the brass cigarette case, the lid popped open, an invitation. Three black-coated methamphetamine tablets nestled in one quadrant of the box, sharing space with the phenobarbitals, the butalbitals and the criminals of the crew, all in a single, separate cell: the one remaining pale blue tab of acid, the four white innocuous-looking hits of phencyclidine and the three innocent Contac capsules.

Only three methamphetamines? But he usually kept seven in the box. Could he have taken four by mistake? He couldn't remember, but he felt up, wired, he'd danced for . . . how long? A long time, he thought. Maybe he'd better . . .

He did a phenobarbital to level himself out. And it wouldn't hurt the bleeding, either. Maybe . . . He did one more, then carried the cigarette case, the emergency kit, back to the briefcase, the mother ship, and carefully refilled it.

Still bleeding? Bekker took the Kleenex away from his face. The blood looked black against the blue tissue, but the flow had stopped. He stood and stepped carefully around the clothes he'd strewn on the floor when the amphetamines came on him. Why had he eaten them? *Must think*.

His study was neat, with wooden in boxes and out boxes on the antique desk, an IBM electric on an antique corner table, a wall of shelves filled with books, journals, magazines. On the wall next to the door was a photograph of himself, standing next to an E-type Jaguar. Not his, unfortunately, but a beautiful car. A silver frame around the photograph.

Stephanie smiled from a matching frame, on the other side of the door. She was wearing jodhpurs, why was she . . . ? *Hard to think*. Must. Stephanie? The lover. Who was the lover?

That was the critical question. He'd thought the amphetamines might help him with that. . . . If they had, he couldn't remember.

He sat down in the middle of the floor, his legs spread. Must think . . .

Bekker sighed. His tongue slipped out, tasted salt. He looked down and found himself covered with a dark crust. Crust? He touched his chest with a fingertip. Blood. Drying blood . . .

He got to his feet, stiff, climbed the stairs, hunched over, touching each riser with his hands as he went up, and then went down the hall to the bathroom. He turned the tap handles, started the water running, ducked his head toward the sink, splashed cold water on his face, stood, looked into the mirror.

His face was pink, his chest still liver-red with the blood crust. He looked like the devil, he thought. The thought came naturally. Bekker knew all about the devil. His parents, immersed in the severities of their Christian faith, had hammered the devil into him, hammered in the old, dead words of Jonathan Edwards. . . .

There are in the souls of wicked men those hellish principles reigning, that would presently kindle and flame out into hellfire, were it not for God's restraints.

He'd never seen God's restraints, Bekker had told the preacher one Sunday night. For that he had gotten a beating that at the time he thought would kill him. Had, in fact, not been able to go to school for a week, and had seen not a gram of pity in his parents' eyes.

Bekker, sopping up the blood, looked into the mirror and spoke the old words, still remembered: "*God holds you over the pit of hell, much as one holds a spider or some loathsome insect over the fire, abhors you, and is dreadfully provoked.* Bullshit."

But was it? Did the consciousness go somewhere after death? Was there a pit? The children he'd seen die, that change of gaze at the last instant . . . was that ecstasy? Did they see something beyond?

Bekker had studied the films taken by the Nazis at the death camps, stared into the filmed faces of dying medical experiments, films considered collectible by certain influential Germans. . . . Was there something beyond?

Bekker's rational scientist mind said no: We are no more than animated mud, a conscious piece of dirt, the consciousness no more than a chemical artifact. *Remember thou that thou art dust and to dust thou shalt return.* Isn't that what the Catholics professed? Odd candor, for a Church Political. Whatever his rational mind said, the other parts, the instinctive parts, couldn't imagine a world without Beauty. He couldn't simply *vanish* . . . could he?

He glanced at his watch. He had time. With the proper medication . . . He looked out of the bathroom at the brass box on the bureau.

Michael Bekker, very smooth, a little of the cocaine, just a lick of the phencyclidine, slipped through the halls of University Hospital.

"Dr Bekker . . ." A nurse, passing, calling him "Doctor." The word flushed him with power; or the lick of PCP did. Sometimes it was hard to tell.

The hallway lights were dimmed, for night. Three women in white sat under the brighter lights of the nursing station, thumbing through papers, checking medication requirements. Overhead, a half-dozen monitors, flickering like the components of a rich man's stereo system, tracked the condition of the ICU patients.

Bekker checked his clipboard. Hart, Sybil. Room 565. He headed that way, taking his time, past a private room where a patient was snoring loudly. He looked around quickly: nobody watching. Stepped inside. The patient was sound asleep, her head back, her mouth hanging open. Sounded like a chainsaw, Bekker thought. He went to the bedside table, opened the drawer. Three brown vials of pills. He took them out, half turned to the dim light coming in from the hall. The first was penicillamine, used to prevent kidney stones. No need for that. He put it back. Paramethasone. More kidney stuff. The third vial said "Chlordiazepoxide hydrochloride 25mg." He opened it, looked inside at the green-and-white caps. Ah. Librium. He could always use some Librium. He took half of the tablets, screwed the top back on the vial and put the vial in the drawer. The Librium caps he dropped into his pocket.

At the door, he stopped to listen. You had to be careful in this: nurses wore running shoes, and were silent as ghosts. But if you knew what to listen for, you could

74

pick up the almost imperceptible squawk-squawk-squawk of the shoes on polished tile. . . .

The hall was silent and he stepped out, squinting at his clipboard, ready to look confused if a nurse was in the hall. There were none, and he went on toward Sybil Hart's room.

Sybil Hart had raven hair and dark liquid eyes. She lay silently watching the screen of the television bolted into a corner of her room. An earplug was fitted in one ear, and although the inanities of late-night television sometimes made her want to scream . . . she didn't.

Couldn't.

Sybil Hart lay unmoving, propped semi-erect on her bed. She was not in the ICU proper, but was accessible, where the nurses could check her every half-hour or so. She'd be dead in three weeks, a month, killed by amyotrophic lateral sclerosis—ALS, Lou Gehrig's disease.

The disease had started with a numbness in the legs, a tendency to stumble. She'd fought it, but it had taken her legs, her bowel control, her arms and, finally, her voice. Now, and most cruelly, it had taken her facial muscles, including her eyelids and eyebrows.

As the ALS had progressed and her voice had gone, she'd learned to communicate through an Apple computer equipped with special hardware and a custom word-processing program. When the disease had taken her voice, she'd still had some control of her fingers, and using two fingers and a special switch, she could write notes almost as effortlessly as if she were typing.

When her fingers had gone, the therapist had fitted her with a mouth switch, and still she could talk. When her mouth control had gone, another special switch had been fitted to her eyebrow. Now that was going, was almost gone. Sybil Hart began to sink into the final silence, waiting for the disease to take her diaphragm. When it did, she would smother . . . in another two or three weeks. . . .

In the meantime, there was nothing wrong with her brain and she could still move her eyes. The CNN commentator was babbling about a DEA raid on a drug laboratory at UCLA.

Bekker stepped inside her room and Sybil's eyes shifted to him.

"Sybil," he said, his voice quiet but pleasant. "How are you?"

He had visited her three times before, interested in the disease that incapacitated the body but left the brain alive. With each visit he'd seen further deterioration. The last time she had barely been able to respond with the word processor. A nurse had told him several days before that now even that was gone.

"Can we talk?" Bekker asked in the stillness. "Can you shift to your processor?"

He looked at the television in the corner of the room, but the screen stayed with CNN.

"Can you change it?" Bekker stepped closer to her bed, saw her eyes tracking him. He moved closer, peering into them. "If you can change it, make your eyes go up and down, like you're nodding. If you can't, make them go back and forth, like you're shaking your head."

Her eyes moved slowly back and forth.

"You're telling me you can't change it?" Her eyes moved up and down.

"Excellent. We're communicating. Now . . . just a moment." Bekker stepped away from Sybil's bed and looked down the corridor. He could see just the corner of the nurses' station, a hundred feet away, and the cap on the head of a nurse, bowed over the desk, busy. Nobody else. He went back to the bed, pulled a chair up and sat where Sybil could see him. "I would like to explain my studies to you," he said. "I'm studying death, and you're going to be a wonderful participant."

Sybil's eyes were fixed on him as he began to talk.

And when he left, fifteen minutes later, she looked up at the CNN commentator and began to strain. If only . . . if only. It took twenty minutes, exhausting her, but suddenly there was a click and the word processor was up. Now. She needed a B.

When the nurse came by a half-hour later, Sybil was staring at the word processor. On the screen was a single B.

"Oh, what happened?" the nurse asked.

They all knew Sybil Hart could no longer operate the equipment. They'd left the switch attached because her husband had insisted. For morale. "You must've had a little twitch, there," the nurse said, patting Sybil's unfeeling leg. "Let me get the TV back for you."

Sybil watched in despair as the B disappeared, replaced by the tanned face and stupid shining teeth of the CNN commentator.

Four floors below, Bekker wandered through the pathology lab, whistling tunelessly, lost in not-quite-thought. The lab was cool, familiar. He thought of Sybil, dying. If only he could have a patient just a little early, just five minutes. If he could take a dying patient apart, watch the mechanism . . .

Bekker popped two MDMAs. Beauty broke into his jig.

7

Light.

Lucas moved his head and cracked an eye. Sunlight sliced between the slats in the blinds and cut across the bed. Daylight? He sat up, yawning, and looked at the clock. Two o'clock. Telephone ringing.

"Jesus . . ." He'd been in bed for nine hours: he hadn't slept that long for months. He'd unplugged the bedroom phone, not wanting it to ring if he did manage to sleep. Now he rolled out, yawned and stretched as he walked into the kitchen and picked up the telephone.

"Yeah. Davenport." He'd left the kitchen blinds up the night before and saw, up the block, a woman walking with an Irish setter on a leash.

"Lucas? Daniel . . ."

"Yeah."

"I've been talking to people. We're going with television."

"Terrific. What time's the press conference?" The woman was closer now, and Lucas was suddenly aware that he was standing naked in front of a window that was barely knee-high.

"Tomorrow."

"Tomorrow?" Lucas frowned at the phone. "You gotta do it today."

"Can't. No time. We didn't decide until a half-hour ago—Homicide still doesn't like it."

"They think it makes them look bad. . . ." The woman was one lot away, and Lucas squatted, getting down out of sight.

"Whatever. Anyway, it'll take the rest of the day to get a package together. I've got to meet with the county attorney about the legal angles, figure out if we're gonna try to pull full-time surveillance on Bekker, and all that. We're sorting it out now. I left some messages at your office, but when you didn't get back, I figured you were on the street."

"Uh, yeah," Lucas said. He looked around the kitchen. Unwashed dishes were stacked in the sink and microwave-dinner boxes were crushed into a plastic waste-basket. Bills were piled on the kitchen table with books, magazines, catalogues—two weeks' worth of mail, unopened. He was living like a pig. "Just walked in the door."

"Well, we're gonna do the conference early tomorrow afternoon. Probably two o'clock. We'll want you around. You know, for the PR. Wear the usual undercover rig, you know they like that, the TVs. . . ."

"All right. I'll be down a little early tomorrow, talk it over. But today would be better."

"Can't do it," Daniel said. "Too many details to smooth out. You coming in?"

"Maybe later. I'm trying to get an interview over at University Hospital with a guy who knows Bekker."

When Daniel got off the phone, Lucas peeked over the windowsill and found a redheaded woman staring vacantly at the front of his house while pretending not to see her dog relieve itself in Lucas' bushes.

"God damn it." He crawled back to the bedroom, found his notebook, sat on his bed and called Webster Prentice at the University of Minnesota. He got a secretary and was switched to Prentice's office.

"You think Bekker killed her?" Prentice asked, after Lucas introduced himself.

"Who mentioned Bekker?"

"Why else would a cop be calling me?" the psychologist

said in a jovial fat-man's voice. "Listen, I'd like to help, but you're talking to the wrong guy. Let me suggest that you call Dr Larry Merriam."

Merriam's office was in a building that from the outside looked like a machine, with awkward angles, unlikely joints. Inside, it was a maze, with tunnels and skyways linking it to adjoining buildings, ground-level exits on different floors. Entire floors were missing in some parts of the structure. Lucas wandered for ten minutes, and asked twice for directions, before he found a bank of elevators that would take him to the sixth floor of the right wing.

Merriam's secretary was short, overweight and worried, scurrying like a Disney churchmouse to locate her boss. Larry Merriam, when she brought him back from the lab, was a balding, soft-faced man in a white smock, with large dark eyes and tiny worried hands. He took Lucas into his office, pressed his fingertips to his lips and said, "Oh, dear," when Lucas told him what he wanted. "This is totally off the record?"

"Sure. And nothing'll come back to you. Not unless you confess that you killed Mrs Bekker," Lucas said, smiling, trying to loosen him up.

Merriam's office overlooked a parking garage. The cinder-block walls had been painted a cream color; a small bulletin board was covered with medical cartoons. From behind the desk Merriam mouthed silently, *Shut the door*.

Lucas reached back and eased the door shut. Merriam relaxed, folding his hands over his chest.

"Clarisse is a wonderful secretary, but she does have trouble keeping a secret," Merriam said. He stood, hands in his pockets, and turned to look out the window behind his desk. A man in a red jacket, carrying what looked like a doctor's bag, was walking across the roof of the parking garage. "And Bekker is a troubling subject."

80

"A lot of people seem to be troubled by Mr Bekker," Lucas said. "We're trying to find an angle, a . . ." He groped for the right words.

"An entry wedge," Merriam said, glancing back over his shoulder at Lucas. "You always need one, in any kind of research."

"Exactly right. With Bekker—"

"What's this man doing?" Merriam interrupted, staring down at the roof of the parking garage. The man in the red jacket stopped next to a midnight-blue BMW, glanced around, took a long silver strip of metal from his coat sleeve and slipped it between the window and the weather stripping, down into the door. "I think, uh . . . Is this man stealing that car?"

"What?" Lucas stepped over to the window and looked out. The man below stopped for a moment and looked up at the hospital building, as though he sensed Merriam and Lucas watching. He wouldn't be able to see them through the tinted glass. Lucas felt a pulse of amusement.

"Yeah, he is. Gotta make a call, just take a minute," Lucas mumbled, reaching for Merriam's desk phone.

"Sure," Merriam said, looking at him oddly, then back down at the thief. "Dial nine . . ."

Lucas dialed straight through to the dispatcher. "Shirl', this is Lucas. I'm looking out a window at a guy named E. Thomas Little. He's breaking into a BMW." He gave her the details and hung up.

"Oh, dear," Merriam said, looking out the window, his fingertips pressed to his lips again. E. Thomas Little finally got the door open and climbed into the front seat of the BMW.

"E. Thomas is an old client of mine," Lucas said. The amusement pulsed through him again, felt good, like a spring wind.

"And he *is* stealing the car?"

"Yeah. He's not much good at it, though. Right now he's jerking the lock cylinder out of the steering column."

"How long will it take a police car to get here?"

"Another minute or so," Lucas said. "Or about a thousand bucks in damage." They watched, silently, together, as Little continued to work in the front seat of the car. Sixty seconds after he got inside, he backed the car out of the parking space and started toward the exit. As he was about to enter the circular down ramp, a squad car, driving up the wrong way, jerked to a stop in front of him. Little put the BMW in reverse and backed away, but the squad stayed with him. A minute later he was talking to the cops.

"Very strange," Merriam said, as the cops handcuffed Little and put him in the backseat of the squad. One of the patrolmen looked up at the hospital windows, as Little had, and waved. Merriam lifted a hand, realized that he couldn't be seen, and turned back to Lucas. "You wanted to know about Michael Bekker."

"Yeah." Lucas went back to his chair. "About Dr Bekker . . ."

"He's . . . Do you know what I do?"

"You're a pediatric oncologist," Lucas said. "You treat kids with cancer."

"Yes. Bekker asked if he could observe our work. He has excellent credentials in his own field, which is pathology, and he's also developing something of a reputation among sociologists and anthropologists for work on what he calls the social organization of death. That's what brought him up here. He wanted to do a detailed examination of the chemistry we use, and how we use it, but he also wanted to know how we handle death itself . . . what conventions and structures had grown up around it."

"You agreed?"

Merriam nodded. "Sure. There are dozens of studies going on here all the time—this is a teaching and research hospital. Bekker had the credentials and both the studies had potential value. In fact, his work *did* result in procedural changes."

"Like what?"

Merriam took his glasses off and rubbed his eyes. He looked tired, Lucas thought. Not like he'd missed a night's sleep, but like he'd missed five years' sleep. "Some of it's stuff you just don't notice if you work with it all the time. When you know somebody's about to die—well, there are things that have to be done with the body and the room. You have to clean up the room, you have to prepare to move the body down to Path. Some patients are quite clear-headed when they're dying. So how must it feel when a maid shows up and peeks into the room with a bunch of cleaning stuff, checking to see if you're gone yet? The patient knows we must've told her, 'Well, this guy'll be gone today.'"

"Ouch," Lucas said, wincing.

"Yeah. And Bekker was looking at more subtle problems, too. One of the things about this job is that some medical people can't handle it. We treat kids with advanced and rare types of cancer, and almost all of them eventually die. And if you watch enough kids die, and their parents going through it with them . . . well, the burnout rate with nurses and technicians and even doctors is terrific. And they sometimes develop problems with chronic incapacitating depression. That can go on for years, even after the victim has stopped working with the kids. Anyway, having Bekker look at us, we thought, might give us some ideas about how we might help ourselves."

"That sounds reasonable," Lucas said. "But the way you're talking . . . did Bekker do something wrong? What happened?"

"I don't know if anything happened," Merriam said, turning to look out at the sky. "I just don't know. But after he was here for a week or two, my people started coming in. He was making them nervous. He didn't seem to be studying so much the routines of death . . . the structures, processes, the formalities, whatever you'd call them . . . as watching the deaths themselves. And enjoying them. The staff members were starting to call him 'Dr Death.'"

"Jesus," said Lucas. Sloan had said that Bekker was known as "Dr Death" in Vietnam. "He enjoyed it?"

"Yeah." Merriam turned back and leaned over his desk, his hands clenched on the desktop. "The people who were working with him said he seemed to become . . . excited . . . as a death approached. Agitation is common among the medical people—you take a kid and he's fought it all the way, and you've fought it all the way with him, and now he's going. In circumstances like that, even longtime medical people get cranked up. Bekker was different. He was excited the way people get with an intellectual pleasure."

"Not sexual?"

"I can't say that. There *was* an intensity of feeling on the order of sexual pleasure. In any case, it seemed to people who worked with him that it was definitely pleasure. When a kid died, he registered a certain satisfaction." Merriam stood and took a turn around his chair, stopping to look down at the parking garage. A patrolman had pulled the BMW back into its parking place and was standing beside it, writing out a note to its owner. "I don't know if I should say this, I could expose myself to some criticism. . . ."

"We're off the record. I mean that," Lucas said.

Merriam continued to look out the window and Lucas realized that he was deliberately avoiding eye contact. Lucas kept his mouth shut and let the silence stretch.

"There's a rhythm to death in a cancer ward," Merriam

said eventually, and slowly, as though he were considering each word. "A kid might be an inch from death, but you know he won't die. Sure enough, he improves. Everything backs off. He's sitting up again, talking, watching TV. Six weeks later, he's gone."

"Remissions," Lucas offered.

"Yeah. Bekker was here, off and on, for three months. We had an agreement: He could come in anytime, day or night, to watch. Not much to see at night, of course, but he wanted complete access to the life on the wards. There was some value in that, so we agreed. Remember: He's a university professor with excellent credentials. But we didn't want a guy wandering around the wards on his own, so we asked him to sign in and out. No problem. He understood, he said. Anyway, during his time here, a child died. Anton Bremer. Eleven years old. He was desperately ill, highly medicated . . ."

"Drugged?"

"Yes. He was close to death, but when he died, it came as a surprise. Like I said, there seems to be a rhythm to it. If you work on the ward long enough, you begin to feel it. Anton's death was out of place. But you see, sometimes that *does* happen, that a kid dies when it seems he shouldn't. When Anton died, I never thought much about it. It was simply another day on the ward."

"Bekker had something to do with the death?"

"I can't say that. I shouldn't even suspect it. But his attitude toward the deaths of our patients began to anger our people. Nothing he said, just his attitude. It pissed them off, is what it did. By the end of the three months—that was the trial period of the project—I decided not to extend it. I can do that, without specifying a reason. For the good of the division, that sort of thing. And I did."

"Did that make him angry?"

"Not . . . obviously. He was quite cordial, said he

understood and so on. So two or three weeks after he left, one of the nurses came to me—she doesn't work here anymore, she finally burned out—and said that she hadn't been able to stop thinking about Anton. She said she couldn't get it out of her head that Bekker had killed him somehow. She thought the kid had turned. He was going down, hit bottom and was stabilizing, beginning to rally. She was a second-shift nurse, she worked three to midnight. When she came in the next afternoon, Anton was dead. He died sometime during the night. She didn't think about Bekker until later, and she went back to see what time he had signed out that night. It turned out our log didn't show him signing in or out. But she remembers that he was there and had looked at the kid a couple of times and was still there when she left. . . ."

"So she thinks he wiped the log in case anybody ever went back to try to track unexplained deaths."

"That's what she thought. We talked about it, and I said I'd look into it. I talked to a couple of other people, and thinking back, they weren't sure whether he was here or not, but on the balance, they thought he was. I called Bekker, gave him this phony excuse that we were looking into a pilferage problem, and asked him if he'd ever seen anybody taking stacks of scrub suits out of the supply closet. He said no. I asked him if he'd always signed in and out whenever he visited, and he said he thought so, but maybe, at one time or another, he'd missed."

"You can't catch him in a lie . . ." Lucas said.

"No."

"Were there any other deaths? Like this kid's?"

"One. The second or third week he was on the wards. A little girl with bone cancer. I thought about it later, but I don't know. . . ."

"Were there postmortems on the kids?"

86

"Sure. Extensive ones."

"Did he do them? Do you know?"

"No, no, we have a fellow who specializes in that."

"Did he find anything unusual?"

"No. The fact is, these kids were so weak, they were so near the edge, that if he'd simply reached out and pinched off their oxygen feeds . . . that might have been enough. We'd never find that on a postmortem—not enough to separate it from all the other wild chemical shit we see in cancer cases: massive loads of drugs, radiation reactions, badly disturbed bodily functions. By the time you do a postmortem, these kids are a mess."

"But you think he might have killed them."

"That's too strong," Merriam said, finally turning around and looking at Lucas. "If I really thought that, I'd have called the police. If there had been any medical indication or anybody who actually saw anything or had a reason to believe he'd done it, I'd have called. But there was nothing. Nothing but a feeling. That could simply be a psychological artifact of our own, the insider's resentment of an outsider intruding on what Bekker called our 'rituals of death.'"

"Did he publish?" Lucas asked.

"Yes. I can give you the citations. Actually, I can probably have Clarisse scrounge up some photocopies."

"I'd appreciate it," Lucas said. "Well . . . You know what happened. The other night."

"Bekker's wife was killed."

"We're looking into it. Some people, frankly, think he might have had a hand in it."

"I don't know. I'd kind of doubt it," Merriam said grimly.

"You sounded like you thought he'd be capable. . . ."

"I'd doubt it because if he knew his wife was going to be killed, he'd want to be there to see it," Merriam said. Then, suddenly abashed, he added, "I don't know if I believe that, really."

"Huh," Lucas said, studying the other man. "Is he still in the hospital, working with live patients? Bekker?"

"Yes. Not on this ward, but several others. I've seen him down in the ORs a couple of times and in the medical wards where they deal with the more extreme varieties of disease."

"Did you ever mention to anyone . . . ?"

"Listen, I don't *know* anything," Merriam barked, his soft exterior dropping for a moment. "That's my problem. If I say anything, I'm implying the guy is a killer, for Christ's sakes. I can't do that."

"A private word . . ."

"In this place? It'd stay private for about thirty seconds," Merriam said, running a hand through his thinning hair. "Listen, until you've worked in a university hospital, you've never really experienced character assassination. There are ten people on this staff who are convinced they'll be on next year's Nobel list if only some klutz in the next office doesn't screw them up. If I suggested anything about Bekker, it would be all over the hospital in five minutes. Five minutes later, he'd hear about it and I'd be fingered as the source. I *can't* do anything."

"All right." Lucas nodded. He stood, picked up his coat. "Would you get me copies of those papers?"

"Sure. And if there's anything else I can do for you, call, and I'll do it. But you see the kind of jam I'm in."

"Sure." Lucas reached for the door, but Merriam stopped him with a quick gesture.

"I've been trying to think how to characterize the way Bekker acted around death," he said. "You know how you read about these zealots on crusades against pornography, and you sense there's something wrong with them? A fascination with the subject that goes way beyond any normal

88

interest? Like a guy has a collection of two thousand porno magazines so he can prove how terrible it is? That's how Bekker was. A kind of a pious sadness when a kid died, but underneath, you got the feeling of a real, lip-smacking pleasure."

"You make him sound like a monster," Lucas said.

"I'm an oncologist," Merriam said simply. "I believe in monsters."

Lucas walked out of the hospital, hands in his pockets, thinking. A pretty nurse smiled at him, and he automatically smiled back, but his head wasn't smiling. Bekker killed kids?

The medical examiner's investigator was a fat, gloomy man with cheeks and lips so pink and glossy that he looked as though he might have been playing with an undertaker's make-up. He handed Lucas the file on Stephanie Bekker.

"If you want my opinion, the guy who did her was either a psycho or wanted it to look that way," the investigator said. "Her skull was like a broken egg, all in fragments. The bottle he hit her with was one of those big, thick tourist things from Mexico. You know, kind of blue-green, more like a vase than a bottle. The glass must have been a half-inch thick. When it broke, he used it like a knife, and drove the edges right down through her eyes. Her whole face was mutilated, you'll see in the photographs. The thing is . . ."

"Yeah?"

"The rest of her body was untouched. It wasn't like he was flailing away, hitting her anyplace he could. You take somebody flying on crank or PCP, they're just swinging. They go after a guy, and if the guy gets behind a car, they'll go after the car. If they can't hit you on the face, they'll hit you on the shoulders or chest or back or the soles of your feet, and they'll bite and claw and everything else. This thing was almost . . . technical. The guy who did it is either nuts and it has something to do with the face, with the eyes, or it's supposed to look that way."

"Thanks for the tip," Lucas said. He sat down at an empty desk, opened the file and glanced at the photos.

Freak, he thought.

The file was technical. To judge from body temperature and lack of lividity, the woman had died just before the paramedics arrived. Stephanie Bekker had never had a chance to resist: she had been a strong woman, with long fingernails, and they were clean—no blood or skin beneath them. There were no abrasions on the hands. She'd had intercourse, while alive and probably an hour or so before she'd died. No bruising was evident around the vagina and there were indications that the intercourse had been voluntary. She had washed after the intercourse, and samples taken for DNA analysis might not prove valid. The samples had not yet been returned.

The medical examiner's investigator noted that the house had been undisturbed, with no evidence of a fight or even an argument. The front door had been unlocked, as had a door into the kitchen from the garage. Bloody tracks led into the garage. The outer garage door had also been unlocked, so an intruder could have come through the house from the alley. There was a single bloody hand-print on the wall, and a trail of blood from the point where she'd fallen in the initial attack. She'd lived, the medical examiner thought, for twenty to thirty minutes after the attack.

Lucas closed the file and sat staring at the desktop for a moment.

Loverboy could have done it. If the few solid facts of the case had been given him, Lucas would have bet money on it. But this kind of violence rarely came immediately after a successful sexual encounter; not without some preliminary crockery-tossing, some kind of mutual violence.

90

And then there was Bekker. Everybody had a nervous word for the man.

The fat investigator was washing his hands when Lucas left.

"Figure anything out?" he asked.

"Freak," Lucas said.

"A problem."

"If it's not a freak . . ." Lucas started.

"Then you got a *big* problem," the fat man finished for him, shaking water from his delicate pink fingers.

The days were getting longer. In the pit of winter, dusk arrives shortly after four o'clock. When Lucas arrived at City Hall, there was still light in the sky, although it was well after six.

Sloan had already gone, but Lucas found Del in Narcotics, flipping through a reports file.

"Anything good?" Lucas asked.

"Not from me," Del said. He pushed the file drawer shut. "There were meetings all day. The suits were arguing about who's going to do what. I don't think you'll get your surveillance team."

"Why not?"

Del shrugged. "I don't think they'll do it. The suits keep saying that there's nothing on Bekker, except that some dope cop thinks he did it. Meanin' me—and you know what they think about me."

"Yeah." Lucas grinned despite himself. The suits would like to see Del in a uniform, writing tickets. "Is the press conference still on?"

"Two o'clock tomorrow," Del said. "You been out on your net?"

"Yeah. Nothing there. But I talked to a doc at University Hospital, he thinks Bekker might have killed a kid. Maybe two."

91

"Kids?"

"Yeah. In the cancer ward. I'll use it to jack up Daniel on the surveillance, if I have to."

"Awright," Del said. "Nothing works like blackmail. . . ."

Lucas' answering machine had half a dozen messages, none of them about Bekker. He made two answering calls, checked the phone numbers on the pen register and locked up. City Hall was almost dark and his footfalls echoed through the emptying corridors.

"Davenport . . ."

He turned. Karl Barlow, a sergeant with Internal Affairs, was walking toward him with a sheaf of papers in his hand. Barlow was small, square-shouldered, square-faced and tightly muscular, like a gymnast. He wore his hair in a jock's crew cut and dressed in white short-sleeved shirts and pleated pants. He always had a plastic pocket protector in his breast pocket, filled with an evenly spaced row of ballpoint pens. He was, he professed, an excellent Christian.

An excellent Christian, Lucas thought, but not good on the streets. Barlow had trouble with ambiguities. . . .

"We need a statement on the brawl the other night. I've been trying . . ."

"That wasn't a brawl, that was an arrest of a known pimp and drug dealer on a charge of first-degree assault," Lucas said.

"A juvenile, sure. I've been trying to get you at your office, but you're never in."

"I've been working this Bekker murder. Things are jammed up," Lucas said shortly.

"Can't help that," Barlow said, planting one fist on his waist. Lucas had heard that Barlow was a Youth Football coach and had found himself in trouble with parents for insisting that a kid play hurt. "I've got to make an appointment with a court stenographer, so I've got to know when you can do it."

"Give me a couple of weeks."

"That might be too long," Barlow said.

"I'll come in when I can," Lucas said impatiently, trying to get away. "There's no rush, right? And I might bring an attorney."

"That's your right." Barlow moved in closer, crowding, and poked the sheaf of papers at Lucas. "But I want this settled and I want it settled soon. If you get my drift."

"Yeah. I get your drift," Lucas said. He turned back toward Barlow, so they were chest to chest and no more than four inches apart. Barlow had to move back a half-step and look up to meet Lucas' eyes. "I'll let you know when I can do it."

And I'll throw you out the fuckin' window if you give me any shit, Lucas thought. He turned away and went up the steps. Barlow called, "Soon," and Lucas said, "Yeah, yeah . . ."

He stopped just outside the City Hall doors, on the sidewalk, looked both ways and shook himself like a horse trying to shake off flies. The day had a contrary feel to it. He sensed that he was waiting, but he didn't know for what.

Lucas crossed the street to the parking garage.

8

Pressure. He opened his fist, felt for the tab in his hand, licked it, felt the acidic cut of the drug as well as the salty taste of his own sweat. Too much? He had to be careful. He couldn't bleed today, he'd be in the car. But then the speed was on him and he stopped thinking about it.

He called Druze from a pay phone.

"We have to risk it," he said. "If I do Armistead tonight, the police will go crazy. Meeting could be tough after this."

"Are the cops still hanging around?" Druze sounded not worried—his emotional range might not reach that far—but concerned. "I mean, Armistead's still on, isn't she?"

"Yes. They keep coming back. They want me, but they've got nothing. Armistead will steer them further away."

"They might get something if they find the guy in the towel," Druze said sullenly.

"That's why we've got to meet."

"One o'clock?"

"Yes."

Stephanie's keepsake photos were stuffed in shoe boxes in the sewing closet, stuck in straw baskets in the kitchen, piled on a drawing table in the study, hidden in desk and bureau drawers. Three leather-bound albums were stacked in the library, photos going back to her childhood. Bekker, nude, stopping frequently to examine himself in the house's many mirrors, wandered through the antiques, hunting the photos. In her chest of drawers, he found a plastic bag for a diaphragm—at first he didn't recognize it for what it was— shook his head and put it back. When he was satisfied that he had all the photos, he fixed himself a sandwich, punched up Carl Orff's *Carmina Burana* on the CD player, sat in an easy chair and replayed the funeral in his mind.

He had been fine, he thought. The tough-guy cop. He couldn't read the tough guy, but he had Swanson beat. He could sense it. The tough guy, on the other hand . . . his clothes were too good, Bekker decided.

As he chewed, his eye found a small movement in the far corner of the room. He turned to catch it: another mirror, one of a dozen or so diamond-shaped plates set in the base of a French lamp from the twenties. He moved again, adjusting himself. His eyes were centered in one of the mirrors and, at this distance, looked black, like holes. His genitals were caught in another plate, and he laughed, genuine enjoyment.

"A symbol," Bekker said aloud. "But of what, I don't know." And he laughed again, and did his jig. The MDMA was still on him.

At noon he dressed, pulled on a sweater, loaded the photos into a shopping bag and went out through the breezeway to his car. Could the police be watching him? He doubted it—what else would they expect him to do? Stephanie was already dead; but he'd take no chances.

Out of the garage, he drove carefully through a snake's nest of streets to a small shopping center. No followers. He cruised the center for a few minutes, still watching, bought toilet tissue and paper towels, toothpaste and deodorant and aspirin, and returned to the car. Back through the snake's nest: nothing. He stopped at a convenience store and used the phone on the outside wall.

"I'm on my way."

"Fine. I'm alone."

Druze lived in a medium-rise apartment at the edge of the West Bank theater district. Bekker, still wary, circled the building twice before he left the car on the street, cut through the parking lot and buzzed Druze's apartment.

"It's me," he said. The door opened and he pushed through into the lobby, then took the stairs. Druze was watching a cable-channel show on scuba diving when Bekker arrived. Druze punched the TV out with a remote as Bekker followed him into the apartment.

"Those the pictures?" asked Druze, looking at the bag.

"Yes. I brought everything I could find."

"You want a beer?" Druze said it awkwardly. He didn't entertain; nobody came to his apartment. He had never had a friend before. . . .

"Sure." Bekker didn't care for beer, but enjoyed playing the relationship with Druze.

"Hope he's here," Druze said. He got a bottle of Bud Light from the refrigerator, brought it back and handed it to Bekker, who was kneeling on the front-room carpet, unloading the shopping bag. Bekker turned one of the shoe boxes upside down, and a clump of snapshots fell out on the rug.

"We'll get him," Bekker said.

"Big, flat, blond Scandinavian face. Head like a milk jug, pale, almost fat. Got pretty good love handles on him, a belly," said Druze.

"We knew a half-dozen people like that," Bekker said. He took a hit on the beer and grimaced. "Most likely he's part of the antiques crowd. That could be tough, 'cause I don't know all of them. There's a possibility that he's with the university. I don't know. This affair is the only thing the bitch ever did that surprised me."

"The bad thing is, antiques people are the kind of people who go to plays. Art people. He could see me."

96

"Up on the stage, with the make-up, you look different," Bekker said.

"Yeah, but afterwards, when we go out in the lobby and kiss ass with the crowd, he could see me up close. If he ever sees me . . ."

"We'll figure him out," Bekker said, dumping the last box of photos on the pile. "I'll sort, you look."

There were hundreds of pictures, and the process took longer than Bekker imagined it would. Stephanie with friends, in the woods, shopping, with relatives. No pictures of Bekker . . .

Halfway through the pile, Druze got to his feet, burped and said, "Keep sorting. I gotta pee."

"Mmm," Bekker nodded. As soon as Druze closed the bathroom door, he stood, waited a minute, then quickly padded across the front room to the kitchen and opened the end drawer on the sink counter. Maps, paid bills, a couple of screwdrivers, match-books . . . He stirred through the mess, found the key, slipped it into his pocket, eased the drawer shut and hurried back to the front room as he heard the toilet flush. He'd been here a few times, waiting for the chance at the key. . . . Now he had it.

"Any more candidates?" Druze asked, stepping out of the bathroom. Bekker was back in the center of the photo pile.

"A couple," Bekker said, looking up. "Come on. We're running late."

There were several large blond men, but this was Minnesota. Twice Druze thought he'd found him, but after a closer look under a reading lamp, he shook his head.

"Maybe you should look at them in person. Discreetly," Bekker suggested.

"They're not the guy," Druze said, shaking his head.

"You're positive?"

"Pretty sure. I didn't get the best look at him, I was

on the floor, and he was standing up, but he was heavier than these guys. Fat, almost." He picked up a photo of Stephanie and a blond man, shook his head and spun it sideways back into the pile around Bekker.

"God damn it. I was sure he'd be in here," Bekker said. The photos were scattered around them like piles of autumn leaves; he grabbed a handful and threw them at an empty box, frustrated. "That bitch talked to everybody, took pictures of everybody, never gave anybody a minute's rest. Why wouldn't she have him in here? He's got to be here."

"Maybe he's somebody new. Or maybe she took them out. Have you gone through her stuff?"

"I spent half the morning at it. She had a diaphragm, can you believe it? I found this little plastic pack for it. Cops didn't say anything about that. . . . But there's nothing else. No more pictures."

Druze began scooping the photos together and tossing them into the boxes. "So what do we do? Do we go ahead? With Armistead?"

"There's a risk," Bekker admitted. "If we don't find him, and we do Armistead, he might decide to turn himself in. Especially if he's got an alibi for the time that Armistead gets hit—as far as we know, he's hiding out because he's afraid the cops think he did it."

"If we don't do Armistead pretty soon, she'll dump me," Druze said flatly. "This turkey we're working on now, this *Whiteface*, won't last. And she hates my ass. We're hurting for payroll and I'll be the first to go."

Bekker took a turn around the rug, thinking. "Listen. If this man, Stephanie's friend, turns himself in to the police, they'll tell me, one way or another. I wouldn't be surprised if they have him come look at me, just to make sure I didn't pull something out in San Francisco. Make sure I wasn't the killer and somebody else was out there . . . Anyway, if I can find out who he is, before he has a chance to see you, we can take him. So if we take Armistead, and you stay out of sight, except when you're working . . ."

"And then I'll stay in make-up. . . ."

"Yeah."

"That's what we ought to do," Druze said. "Maybe we can smoke the cocksucker out. If we can't, we can keep working on it. . . ."

"I'll figure him out, sooner or later," Bekker said. "It's only a matter of time."

"How are we going to talk, if the cops stay on you?"

"I've worked that out."

Bekker's neighbor in the pathology department was working in England. Just before he had left, he and Bekker had chatted about their work and Bekker had noticed, idly at the time, that the other man had an answering machine in his bottom desk drawer, an operation manual peeking from beneath it. Late one night, when the office was empty, Bekker had slipped the old-fashioned lock on his neighbor's door, turned the answering machine on and used the instruction manual to work out new access codes for the memo option. He now gave the touch-tone codes to Druze.

"You can call from any touch-tone phone, leave a message. I can do the same to get the message, or leave one for you. You should check every few hours to see if I've left anything."

"Good," Druze said. "But make sure you clean up the tapes. . . ."

"You can erase them remotely, too," Bekker said, and explained.

Druze jotted the code numbers in an address book. "Then we're all set," he said.

"Yes. We should probably stay away from each other for a while."

99

"And we're gonna do Armistead like we planned?"

Bekker looked at the troll, and a smile touched his face. Druze thought it might be simple joy. "Yes," he said. "We'll do Armistead. We'll do her tonight."

The stained-glass windows in Bekker's parlor came from a North Dakota Lutheran church that had lost its congregation to the attractions of warmer climates and better jobs. Stephanie had bought the windows from the church trustees, trucked them back to the Twin Cities and learned how to work in lead. The restored windows hung above him, dark in the night, ignored. Bekker focused instead on the coil that was unwinding in his stomach.

A dark exhilaration: but too soon.

He suppressed it and sat on a warm wine-and-saffron Oriental carpet with a wet clawhammer and the pile of paper towels. He'd bought the hammer months before and never used it. He'd kept it in the basement, hidden in a drawer. Bekker knew just enough about crime laboratories to fear the possibility that a chemical analysis would pick up something unique to the house—Stephanie's refinishing chemicals, glass dust or lead deposits. There was no point in taking chances. He washed it with dishwashing detergent, then sat on the rug and patted it dry with the paper towels. From now on, he would handle it only wearing gloves. He wrapped the hammer in extra towels and left it on the rug.

Plenty of time, he thought. His eyes skittered around the room and found his sport coat hanging on a chair. He got the pill case from its breast pocket and peered inside, calculating. No Beauty tonight. This needed a cold power. He put a tab of PCP on his tongue, tantalized himself with the bite, then swallowed. And a methamphetamine, for the action; usually the amphetamines were Beauty's ride, but not on top of the other. . . .

* * *

100

Elizabeth Armistead was an actress and a member of the board of directors of the Lost River Theater. She'd once played on Broadway.

"Bitch'll never give me a part." Druze had been drunk and raving, the night six months earlier when the deal had occurred to Bekker. "Just like that movie—what was the name? On the train . . . ? She's gonna dump me. She's got the pretty boys lined up. She likes pretty boys. With this face . . ."

"What happened?"

"The company voted to do *Cyrano*. Who gets the lead? Gerrold. The pretty boy. They made him ugly and I'll carry a goddamn pike in the battle scenes. Before this bitch joined up—she supposedly played on Broadway, big deal, but that's why they took her, she can't act—I used to be something. The next thing I know, I'm carrying fuckin' pikes."

"What're you going to do?"

Druze had shaken his head. "I don't know. Finding a job is tough. Up on the stage, with the lights, with make-up, this face is okay. But getting in the door— people look at me, theater people, and they say, Whoa, you're ugly. Theater people don't like ugly. They like pretty."

Bekker had asked, "What if Elizabeth Armistead went away?"

"What do you mean?" But Bekker had caught the quick, feral glint when Druze looked toward him, and he knew the idea was there in the back of Druze's head. If Armistead went away, things would be different. Just like they would be for him, if Stephanie went away. . . .

Bekker had kept the coveralls in a sack at the back of his chest of drawers since he bought them, at a Sears, three months earlier. They were blue, the kind a mechanic might wear. He pulled them over his jeans and sweatshirt,

101

found the matching hat in the closet and put it on. Druze knew about costumes and had put it together for him. This costume said *service*. Nobody would look at him twice.

Bekker glanced at his watch, and the first dislocation occurred, thrilling him: the watch elongated, a Dali watch, draped over his wrist like a sausage. Wonderful. And the power was coming, darkening his vision, shifting everything to the ultraviolet end. He groped in his pocket for the cigarette case, found a tab of the speed and swallowed it.

So good . . . He staggered through the room, feeling it, the power surging along his veins, a nicotine rush times two hundred. He pushed the power back in a corner, held it there, felt the tension.

The time was getting tighter. He hurried down the steps, checked a window to see how dark it was, then carefully picked up the hammer and slid it into his right-hand pocket. The rest of his equipment, the clipboard, the meter and the identification tag, were piled on Stephanie's desk.

The clipboard, with the paper clipped to it, went with the service costume. So did the meter. Druze had found the meter in an electronics junk store and bought it for almost nothing: it was obsolete, with a big analog dial on top, originally made for checking magnetic fields around power lines. The identification tag was Bekker's old hospital ID. He'd laminated it and punched a hole in one end, and hung it from his neck by an elastic string.

He took a breath, did a mental checklist, walked out through the breezeway to the car and used the automatic garage-door opener to lift the door. He drove the long way out of the alley, then continued through the next alley, watching his mirror. Nobody.

Traveling by back streets, he made it to Elizabeth Armistead's house in a little over eight minutes. He would have to remember that. If Druze suspected, he should know the time of his arrival. He just hoped she would be there.

"She does one half-hour of meditation, then drinks an herb tea, then comes down for the warm-ups," Druze said, prepping him. "She's fussy about it. She missed her meditation once and spent the whole show dropping lines."

Druze . . . The original plan had called for Bekker to phone Druze just before he left the house on the way to Armistead's. As soon as Druze got the call, at a remote phone in the theater's control booth, he would call the ticket office with his best California-cool accent. *My name is Donaldson Whitney. Elizabeth Armistead said that she would put me on the guest list for two tickets. I'm in a rush through town, but I have time for her play. Could you call her and confirm?*

They would call and confirm. They always did. Too many bullshitters trying to get in free. Donaldson Whitney, though, was a theater critic from Los Angeles. Armistead would gush . . . and the ticket people would remember. That was the point of the exercise: to create a *last man* to talk to the dead woman, with Druze already in make-up, on stage, warming up . . . alibied. Druze had suggested it and Bekker had found no way to demur.

He could, however, go early; Druze wouldn't have to know. But the cops would figure it out. . . .

And after doing Armistead, he could call as though he were just leaving his house. Then Druze would make his Donaldson Whitney call, and if Armistead didn't answer the phone when the ticket office called her, well, she simply wasn't home yet. That could hardly be Bekker's fault. . . .

Bekker took it slowly the last few minutes down to Armistead's. He'd cruised her house before, and there were no changes. The lots were small, but the houses were busy. One man coming or going would never be noticed. A

103

light burned in Armistead's house, in the back. Her silver Dodge Omni was at the curb, where it usually was. He parked at the side of the house, under a tree heavy with bursting spring buds, got his equipment, leaned back in the seat and closed his eyes.

Like a digital read out: one-two-three-four-five. Easy steps. He let the power out, just a bit; when he looked, the steering wheel was out-of-round. He smiled, thinly, allowed himself to feel the burn in his blood for another moment, then got out of the car, changed the thin smile for a harassed look and walked around the corner to Armistead's house. Rang the doorbell. And again.

Armistead. Larger than he thought, in a robe. Pale oval face; dark hair swept back in a complicated roll, held with a wooden pin. Face slack, as though she'd been sleeping. Door on a chain. She peered out at him, her eyes large and dark. She'd look good on a stage. "Yes?"

"Gas company. Any odor of gas in the house?"

"No . . ."

"We show you have gas appliances, a washer and dryer, a hot-water heater?" All that from Druze's reconnaissance at an Armistead party. Bekker glanced down at the clipboard.

"Yes, down in the basement," she said. His knowledge of her home had confirmed his authority.

"We've had some critical pressure fluctuations up and down the street because of a main valve failure. We have a sniffer here"—Bekker hefted the black box, so she could see the meter—"and we'd like to take some readings in your basement, just in case. There could be a problem with sudden flare-ups. We had a fire over on the next block, you probably heard the fire trucks."

"Uh, I've been meditating. . . ." But she was already pulling the chain. "I'm in a terrible rush, I've got to get to work. . . ."

"Just take a minute or two," Bekker assured her. And he was in. He slipped his hand in his pocket, gripped the hammer, waited until he heard the door close firmly.

"Through the kitchen and down the stairs," Armistead said. Her voice was high and clear, but there was an impatient edge to it. A busy woman, interrupted.

"The kitchen?" Bekker glanced around. The drapes had been closed. The smell of prairie flowers was in the air, and spice, and Bekker realized that it must be her herb tea. The power came out now, out of the corner of his head, and his vision went momentarily blue. . . .

"Here. I'll show you," Armistead said impatiently. She turned her back on him, walking toward the rear of the house. "I haven't smelled a thing."

Bekker took a step behind her, began to draw the hammer, and suddenly blood gushed from his nose. He dropped the meter and caught the blood with his hand, and she saw the motion, turned, saw the blood, opened her mouth . . . to scream?

"No, no," he said, and her mouth closed, halfway . . . everything so slow. So slow, now. "Ah, this is the second time today. . . . Got hit in the nose by my child, just a five-year-old. Can't believe it . . . Do you have any tissue?"

"Yes. . ." Her eyes were wide, horrified, as the stream of blood dripped down his coveralls.

They were on the rug in the front room, and she started to pivot, going for the tissue. The power slowed her motion even more and demanded that he savor this. There could be no fights, no struggles, no chances. She couldn't be allowed to scratch him, or bruise him. . . . This was business, but the power knew what it wanted. She was saying, "Here, in the kitchen . . . ," she was pivoting, and Bekker, one hand clenched to his face, stepped close again, pulled the hammer from his pocket, swung it like

105

a tennis racket, with a good forehand, got his back and shoulder in it.

The hammer hit with a double shock, hard, then soft, like knocking a hole in a plaster wall, and the impact twisted Armistead. She wasn't dead; her eyes were open wide, saliva sprayed from her mouth, her hips were twisting, her feet were coming off the floor. She went down, dying, but not knowing it, trying to fight, her hands up, her mouth open, and Bekker was on her, straddling her. One hand on her throat, her body bucking. Evading the fingernails, hitting with the blunt head of the hammer, her forehead, once, twice . . . and done.

He was breathing like a steam engine, the power on him, running him, his heart running, the blood streaming down his face. *Can't get any on her* . . . He brushed his bloodied face with the sleeve of his coveralls, looked back down, her eyes half open. . . .

Her eyes.

Bekker, suddenly frightened, turned the hammer.

He'd use the claw. . . .

9

The evening dragged; the feeling that he was *waiting* stayed with him.

He thought of calling Jennifer, to ask for an extra visit with their daughter. He reached for the phone once, twice, but never made the call. He wanted to see Sarah, but even more, he wanted to settle with Jennifer. Somehow. End it, or start working toward reconciliation. And that, he thought, was not a process begun with a spur-of-the-moment phone call. Not with Jennifer.

Instead of calling, he sat in front of the television and watched a bad cop movie on Showtime. He switched it off a few minutes before the torturously achieved climax: both the cops and the crooks were cardboard, and he didn't care what happened to any of them. After the late news, he went back to the workroom and began plodding through the game.

Bekker stuck in the back of his head. The investigation was dying. He could sense the waning interest in the other cops. They knew the odds against the case: without eye-witnesses or a clear suspect who had both motive and opportunity, there was almost no chance of an arrest, much less a conviction. Lucas knew of at least two men who had killed their wives and gotten away with it, and a woman who'd killed a lover. There was nothing fancy about any of the murders. No exotic weapons, no tricky alibis, no hired killers. The men had used clubs: a grease gun and an aluminum camera tripod. The woman had used a wooden-handled utility knife from Chicago Cutlery.

I just found her/him like that, they told the answering

cops. When the cops read them their rights, all three asked for lawyers. After that, there wasn't anything to go on. The pure, unvarnished and almost unbreakable two-dude defense: Some other dude did it.

Lucas stared at the wall behind the desk. *I need this fuckin' case.* If the Bekker investigation failed, if the spark of interest diminished and died, he feared, he might slip back into the black hole of the winter's depression. Before the depression, he'd thought of mental illnesses as something suffered by people who were weak, without the will to suppress the problem, or somehow genetically impaired. No more. The depression was as real as a tiger in the jungle, looking for meat. If you let your guard down . . .

Bekker's beautiful face came up in his mind's eye, like a color slide projected on a screen. Bekker.

At twenty minutes after eleven, the phone rang. He looked at it for a moment, with a ripple of tension. Jennifer? He picked it up.

"Lucas?" Daniel's voice, hoarse, unhappy.

"What happened?"

"The sonofabitch did another one," Daniel rasped. "The guy who killed the Bekker woman. Call Dispatch for the address and get your ass over there."

A little spark of elation? A touch of relief? Lucas hammered the Porsche through the night, across the Mississippi, west to the lakes, blowing leftover winter leaves over the sidewalks, turning the heads of midnight walkers. He had no trouble finding the address: every light in the little house was on and the doors were open to the night. Groups of neighbors stood on the sidewalk, looking down toward the death house; occasionally one would cross the street to a new group, a new set of rumors, walking rapidly as though his speed alone would prove to watching cops that he was on a mission of urgency.

Elizabeth Armistead was lying face-up on her living room carpet. A bloodstain marked the carpet under the back of her head, like a black halo. One arm was twisted beneath her, the other was flung out, palm up, the fingers slightly crooked. Her face, from the nose up, had been destroyed. In place of her eyes was a finger-deep pit, filled with blood and mangled flesh. Another wound cut across her upper lip, ripping it, exposing white broken teeth. Her dress was pulled up high enough to show her underpants, which appeared to be undisturbed. The room smelled like a wet penny, the odor of fresh blood.

"Same guy?" Lucas asked, looking down at her.

"Gotta be. I caught the first one, too, and this one's a goddamn carbon copy," said a bright-eyed medical examiner's investigator.

"Anything obvious?" Lucas asked, looking around. The house seemed undisturbed.

"No. No broken fingernails, and they're clean. There doesn't seem to have been a fight, and there's no doubt she was killed right here—there are some blood splatters over there by the table. I didn't look myself, but the other guys say there's no sign of a door or window being forced."

"Doesn't look like rape . . ."

"No. And there aren't any signs of semen outside the body."

A Homicide detective stepped up beside Lucas and said, "C'mere and look at the weapon."

"I saw it when I came in," Lucas said. "The hammer?"

"Yeah, but Jack just noticed something."

They went out in the hallway, where the hammer, wrapped in plastic, was being delicately handled by another cop.

"What?" asked Lucas.

"Look at the head and the claw. Not the blood, the hammer," the second cop said.

Lucas looked, saw nothing. "I don't see anything."

"Just like the fuckin' dog that didn't bark," the cop said with satisfaction. He held the hammer up to a lamp, reflecting light from the shiny hammerhead into Lucas' eyes. "The first time you use a hammer, drive a nail or pull one, you start putting little nicks in it. Look at this. Smooth as a baby's ass. The goddamn thing has never been used. I bet the guy brought it with him, to kill her."

"Are you sure it was his? Not hers?"

The cop shrugged. "The woman's got about six tools— some screwdrivers, a crescent wrench and a hammer. One pack of nails and some picture hangers. They're still in the kitchen drawer. She wasn't a do-it-yourselfer. Why would she have two hammers? And a big heavy one like this? And how'd the guy just happen to get his hands on the second one?"

A bright light swept the front of the house and Lucas half turned.

"TV's here," said the first cop. He stepped away toward the front door.

"Tell everybody to keep their mouths shut. Daniel'll issue a statement in the morning," Lucas said. He turned back to the cop with the hammer.

"So he brought it with him," Lucas said.

"I'd say so."

Lucas thought about it, frowned, then clapped the cop on the shoulder. "I don't know what it means, but it's a good catch," he said. "If it's new, maybe we could check and see where they sell this Estwing brand. . . ."

"We're doing that tomorrow. . . ."

"So what do we know about her?" Lucas asked, pointing a thumb back toward the living room.

110

Armistead was an actress, the hammer-toting cop told Lucas. When she hadn't shown up for a performance, a friend had come to check on her, found the body and called the police. To judge from the body temperature, still higher than the rather cool ambient temperature of the house, she'd been dead perhaps four hours when the medical examiner's investigator had arrived, a few minutes after eleven. There was no sign of a burglary.

"Where's the friend?" Lucas asked.

"Back in the bedroom, with Swanson," the cop said, nodding toward the rear of the house. Lucas wandered back, looking the place over, trying to get a picture of the woman's life-style. The place was decorated with taste, he decided, but without money. The paintings on the walls were originals, but rough, the kind an actress might get from artist friends. The carpets on the floor were worn Orientals. He thought about the rugs at Bekker's house, and stooped to feel the one he was standing on. It felt thin and slippery. Some kind of machine-woven synthetic. Not much of a tie . . .

The bedroom door was open, and when Lucas poked his head in, he found Swanson sitting in a side chair, rubbing the lenses of his wire-rimmed glasses with a Kleenex. A woman was lying face-up on the bed, one foot on the floor. The other foot had made a muddy mark on the yellow bedspread, but she hadn't noticed. Lucas knocked on the jamb and stepped inside as Swanson looked up.

"Davenport," the Homicide cop said. He put his glasses back on and fiddled with them for a second until they were comfortable. Then he sighed and said, "It's a fuckin' bummer."

"Same guy?"

"Yeah. Don't you think?"

"I guess." Lucas looked at the woman. "You found the body?"

She was redheaded, middle thirties, Lucas thought, and

111

pretty, most of the time. Tonight she was haggard, her eyes swollen from crying, her nose red and running. She didn't bother to sit up, but she reached up to her forehead and pushed a lock of hair out of her eyes. They looked dark, almost black. "Yes. I came over after the show."

"Why?"

"We were worried. Everybody was," she said, sniffing. "Elizabeth would go on with a broken leg. When she didn't show up and didn't call, we thought maybe she'd been in an accident or something. If I didn't find her here, I was going to call the hospitals. I rang the doorbell, and then looked through the window in the door and saw her lying there. . . . The door was locked, so I ran over to a neighbor's to call the cops." A wrinkle creased her forehead and she cocked her head forward and said, "You're the cop who killed the Indian."

"Mmmnn."

"Is your daughter okay? I heard on the TV . . ."

"She's fine," Lucas said.

"Jesus, that must have been something." The woman sat up, a quick muscular motion, done without effort. Now her eyes were jade green, and he noticed that one of her front teeth was just slightly crooked. "Are you going after this guy? The killer?"

"I'm helping," Lucas said.

"I hope you get him and I hope you kill the sonofabitch," the woman said, her teeth bared and her eyes opening wide. She had high cheekbones and a slightly bony nose, the craggy variety of Celt.

"I'd like to get him," Lucas said. "When was the last time anybody saw Armistead . . . Elizabeth?"

"This afternoon. There was a rehearsal until about three o'clock," the woman said. She stroked the side of her cheek with her fingertips as she remembered, staring sightlessly at the bedspread. "After that, she went home.

112

One of the ticket ladies tried to call her an hour or so before the play was supposed to start, but there wasn't any answer. That's the last I know."

"Why'd they call? Was she already late?"

"No, somebody wanted in on a free-bee, and she'd have to approve it. But she didn't answer."

"Bucky and Karl are down at the theater, talking to people," Swanson said.

"Did you check Bekker?" Lucas asked.

"No. I will tomorrow, after we've got this nailed down. I'll have him do a minute-by-minute recount of where he was tonight."

"Isn't Bekker the name of that woman who was killed?" asked the woman on the bed, looking between them.

"Her husband," Lucas said shortly. "What's your name, anyway?"

"Lasch . . . Cassie."

"You're an actress?"

She nodded. "Yeah."

"Full-time?"

"I get the smaller parts," she said ruefully, shaking out her red hair. It was kinky and bounced around her shoulders. "But I work full-time."

"Was Armistead dating anyone?" Swanson asked.

"Not really . . . What does Bekker have to do with this? Is he a suspect?" She was focusing on Lucas.

"Sure. You always check the husband when a wife gets murdered," Lucas said.

"So you don't really think he did this?"

"He was in San Francisco when his wife was killed," Lucas said. "This one is so much like it, it almost has to be the same guy."

"Oh." She was disappointed and bit her lower lip. She wanted the killer, Lucas realized, and if she had her way about it, she would have him dead.

113

"If you think of anything, give me a call," Lucas said. Their eyes locked up for a second, a quick two-way assessment. He handed her a business card and she said, "I will." Lucas turned away, glanced back once to see her looking after him and drifted out toward the living room.

The cop with the hammer was talking to a uniform, who had a middle-aged woman in tow. The woman, wearing a pink quilted housecoat and white sneakers, was edging toward the archway that opened into the living room. The cop blocked her with a hip and asked, "So what'd he look like?"

"Like I said, he looked like a plumber. He was carrying a toolbox or something, and I says to Ray, that's my husband, Ray Ellis, Mr and Mrs, 'Uh-oh,' I says, 'it looks like that Armistead woman's got troubles with her plumbing, I hope it's not the main again.' They dug up the main here in this street, the city has, twice since we been here, and we only got here in 'seventy-one, you'd think they'd be able to get that right . . ." She took another crab step toward the arch, trying to get a look.

"You didn't like Ms. Armistead?" Lucas asked, coming up to them.

The woman took a half-step back, losing ground. A flash of irritation crossed her face as she realized it. "Why'd you think that?" she asked. A defensive whine crept into her voice. She'd heard this kind of question asked on *L.A. Law*, usually just before somebody got it in the neck.

"You called her 'that Armistead woman.' . . ."

"Well, she said she was an actress and I said to Ray . . ."

"Your husband . . ."

"Yeah, I said, 'Ray, she don't look like no actress to me.' I mean, I know what an actress looks like, right? And she didn't look like no actress, in fact, I'd say she was plain. I said to Ray, 'She says she's an actress, I wonder what she's really involved in.'" She squinted slyly.

"You think she might be involved with something else?" asked the cop with the hammer.

"If you ask me . . . Say, is that the murder·weapon?" The woman's eyes widened as she realized that the cop was holding a hammer wrapped in a plastic bag.

"Before you get to that," Lucas interrupted impatiently, "the man you saw at the door . . . why'd he look like a plumber?"

"'Cause of the way he was dressed," she said, unable to tear her eyes away from the hammer until the cop dropped it to his side. She looked up at Lucas again. "I couldn't see him real good, but he was wearing one of those coveralls, dark-like, and a hat with a bill on it. Like plumbers wear."

"You didn't see his face?"

"Nope. When I saw him, he was on her porch, with his back to me. I saw his back, saw he had a hat."

"Did you see a truck?"

She frowned. "No, now that you mention it. I don't know where he come from, but there weren't no cars on the street, just Miz Armistead's Omni, which I always notice because Ray had one almost like it, when he was married to his first wife, silver, except it was a Plymouth Horizon."

"Did you see him leave?"

"Nope. I was washing up the dishes."

"All right. Thanks," Lucas said. Nothing. She'd probably seen the killer, but it wouldn't help. Unless . . .

"One more question. Did the guy have plumber's tools or any kind of tools, anything you could see . . . or did he just *feel* like a plumber?"

"Well . . ." She didn't understand the question. "He just *looked* like a plumber. You see him on the sidewalk, you say, 'There goes a plumber.'"

So he might have been a plumber. Or he might have been an actor. . . .

Lucas stepped away, to the arch into the living room. One of the lab cops was videotaping the body and the living room, his lights bleaching out Armistead's already paper-white face. Lucas watched for a moment, then walked outside. The uniform had stretched crime-scene tape around the house and its hedge, and a half-dozen TV cameras were parked just off the curb. He heard his name ripple among the reporters, and the floodlights started flicking on as he walked down the porch steps to the street.

"Davenport . . ." The reporters moved in like sharks, but Lucas shook his head.

"I can't talk about it, guys," he said, waving them away.

"Tell us why you're here," a woman called. She was older for a television reporter, probably in her early forties, about to fall off the edge of the media world. "Gambling, dope? What?"

"Hey, Katie, I really want to leave it to the Homicide people. . . ."

"Anything to do with those guys selling guns . . . ?"

Lucas grinned, shook his head and pushed through to his car. If he stayed to talk, somebody would remember that he was working on the Bekker case and would add it up.

As he drove away, he tried to add it up himself. If the first murder was hired by Bekker, what did the second one mean? There had to be a connection—the techniques were identical—but it was hard to believe that Bekker could be involved. Swanson and the other investigators had been leaning on him: if he had some relationship with this woman, past or present, he'd hardly risk killing her. Not unless he was stupid as well as crazy. And nobody said he was stupid.

116

Lucas stopped for a red light, one foot on the clutch, the other on the gas pedal, idly revving the engine. The first killing had the earmarks of an accidental encounter. A doper goes into a house in a rich neighborhood, looking for anything he can convert to crack. He unexpectedly bumps into the woman, kills her in a frenzy, runs. If it hadn't been for Bekker's reputation with his relatives, if Sloan hadn't made the call to Bekker's former Army commanding officer, the killing might already have been written off as dope-related. . . .

But this second killing looked as though it were planned: The hammer, newly bought and then left behind. Nothing missing from the house. Not like a doper. A doper would have grabbed *something*. Nothing missing from Bekker's house, either . . .

Lucas shook his head, realizing the red light had turned green, then yellow. He was about to pop the clutch to run the yellow, when a black Nissan Maxima, coming up fast from behind, slid a fender in front of him and stopped. Lucas jabbed the Porsche's brake pedal, and the car bucked and died.

"Motherfucker," he said, and pulled the door latch-handle. The other driver was faster. As Lucas pushed open the door, a tall blonde hopped out of the Nissan and walked through Lucas' headlights, a tight smile on her face. TV3. She'd been around for a couple of years and Lucas had seen her on the Crows case.

"God damn it, Carly . . ."

"Stuff it, Lucas," the woman said. "I know how you worked with Jennifer and a couple other people. I want on the list. What happened back there?"

"Hey . . ."

"Look, my fuckin' contract is up in two months, and we're talking, me and the station," she said. "I'm asking sixty and it's like, Maybe yes, maybe no, what've you done

117

for us lately? I need something: you're it." She posed, ankles crossed, fist on her hip.

"What's in it for me?" Lucas asked.

"You want somebody inside Three? You got it."

Lucas looked at her for a moment, then nodded. "I trust you just once," he said, holding up an index finger. "You burn me, you never come back."

"Fine. And it's the same with me. You ever burn me, or even get close, and I'll deny everything and sue your ass," the blonde said. They were both in the street, face to face. A black Trans Am slowed as it passed around them, and the passenger window rolled down. A kid with carefully coiffed hair and a hammered forehead looked out and said, "What's happening?"

"Cop," Lucas said. "Keep moving."

"We're cool," the kid said, then pulled his head inside, and the car accelerated away.

"So what happened?" Carly asked, glancing after the Trans Am, then turning back to Lucas.

"You know about the Bekker killing?"

"Sure."

"This one's identical. A woman named Elizabeth Armistead with the Lost River Theater, she's an actress. . . ."

"Oh shit, I know her. . . . I mean I've seen her. There's no doubt that it was the same guy?" The woman put a long red thumbnail in her mouth and bit it.

"Not much . . ."

"How was she killed?"

"Clawhammer. Hit her on the back of the head, then smashed out her eyes, just like with Stephanie Bekker." The traffic light was running through its sequence again, and the woman's hair glowed green, then gold as the yellow came on.

"Jesus Christ. What are the chances that the other stations'll have it by the morning shows?"

118

"I told the people back there to put a lid on every-thing, pending a release from the chief," Lucas said. "You should have it exclusively, if some uniform hasn't leaked it already. . . ."

"Nobody's talking back there," she said. "Okay, Lucas, I appreciate it. Anything you need from the station, let me know. My ass is in your hands."

"I wish," Lucas said with a grin. The blonde grinned back, and as the stoplight turned red, Lucas added, "There's not much more I can tell you about the murder."

"I don't need more," she said as she turned back toward her car. "I mean, why fuck up a great story with a bunch of facts?"

She left Lucas standing in the street, her car careening around in an illegal U-turn, simultaneously running the red light. Lucas laughed and got back in the Porsche. He had something going, for the first time in months. He was operating again.

And he thought: A copycat? The idea didn't hold up; the murderer's technique with Armistead was too similar to the Bekker killing. There hadn't been enough information in the press to tell a copycat exactly what to do. The killings *had* to be the same guy. The guy in coveralls, the coveralls a way to get inside?

He was edging toward a conclusion: They had another psycho on their hands. But if the guy was a psycho, why had he taken a weapon to Armistead's, but not to Bekker's? He'd killed Stephanie Bekker with a bottle he'd picked up in the kitchen. The Bekker scene made sense as a spur-of-the-moment killing by an intruder, a junkie who killed and got scared and ran. The Armistead scene did not. Yet both by the same guy.

And neither woman was sexually assaulted. Sex, in some way, was usually involved in serial killings. . . .

If Bekker had hired the first killing done, was it possible that he'd set off a maniac?

No. That's not how it worked.

Lucas had worked two serial killers. In both cases, the media had speculated on the effect of publicity on the mind of the killer: Did talking about killers make more killers? Did violent movies or pornography desensitize men and make them able to kill? Lucas didn't think so. A serial killer was a human pressure-cooker, made by abuse, by history, by brain chemistry. You don't get pressure like that from something as peripheral as TV. A serial killer wasn't a firecracker to be lit by somebody else. . . .

Tangled. And interesting. Without realizing it, Lucas began whistling, almost silently, under his breath.

10

The briefing room stank of cigarette smoke, nervous armpits and hot electronics. Twenty reporters crowded the front of the room, Lucas and a dozen more cops hung in the back. Carly Bancroft's early-morning report on the second murder had touched off a panic among the other stations. The press conference had started just after ten o'clock.

"Any questions?" Frank Lester's forehead was beaded with sweat. Lester, the deputy chief for investigations, put down the prepared statement and looked unhappily around the room.

"Lester in the lion's den," Sloan muttered to Lucas. He stuck a Camel in the corner of his mouth. "Got a light?"

Lucas took a book of matches out of his pocket, struck one and held it for Sloan's cigarette. "If you were Loverboy, would you come in?"

Sloan shook his head as he exhaled a lungful of blue smoke. "Fuck no. But then, I'm a cop. I know what treacherous assholes we are. I don't even know if I would've mentioned Loverboy in the thing. . . ."

"About Mrs Bekker's . . . friend, have you done any voice analysis on the nine-one-one tapes?" a reporter asked Lester.

"Well, we've got nothing to match them to. . . ."

"We hear you're calling him 'Loverboy.' . . ."

"Not me, but I've heard that," Lester said grimly.

"Could the killer be going for women in the arts?" a reporter called out. She worked for a radio station and

121

carried a microphone that looked like a Ruger Government Model .22-caliber target pistol. The microphone was aimed at a point between Lester's eyes.

"We don't know," he answered. "Mrs Bekker would only be peripherally in the arts, I'd say. But it could be—there's no way to tell. Like I said, we're not even sure it's the same perpetrator."

"But you said . . ."

"It probably is. . . ."

From the front row, a newspaper reporter in a rumpled tan suit: "How many serial killers have we had now? In the last five years?"

"One a year? I don't know."

"One? There were at least six with the Crows."

"I meant one series each year."

"Is that how you count them?"

"I don't know how you count them," Lester barked.

"By series," a newspaper reporter called.

"Bullshit." Television disagreed. "By the killers."

From the back of the room, a radio reporter with a large tapedeck: "When do you expect him to hit again?"

"How're we gonna know that?" Lester asked, a testy note creeping into his voice. "We told you what we knew."

"You're supposed to be running the investigation," the reporter snapped back.

"I *am* running the investigation, and if you'd ever worked in a market bigger than a phone booth, you'd know we can't always find these guys overnight in the big city. . . ."

There was a thread of laughter, and Sloan said dryly, "He's losing it."

"What the f f f . . . What's that supposed to mean?" the reporter sputtered. The TV cameraman behind him was laughing. TV people ranked radio people, so laughing was all right.

"What's 'fff' supposed to mean?" Lester asked. He turned away and pointed at a woman wearing glasses the size of compact discs. "You."

"What precautions should women in the Twin Cities take?" She had an improbably smooth delivery, with great round O's, as though she were reading for a play.

"Don't let anybody in your house that you're not sure of," Lester said, struggling now. "Keep your windows locked. . . ."

"Who tipped Three, that's what I want to know," another reporter shouted from the back of the room. Carly Bancroft yawned, tried not very hard to suppress a grin, then deliberately scratched her ribs.

When Daniel had scheduled the press conference, he'd expected the police reporters from the dailies and second-stringers from the television stations. With the Armistead killing, everything had changed. He'd passed the press conference to Lester, he said, in an attempt to diminish its importance. It hadn't worked: media trucks were double-parked in the street, providing direct feeds to the various stations. City Hall secretaries were gawking at the media stars, the media stars were checking their hairsprays, and the TV3 anchorman himself, tan, fit, with a touch of gray at the temples and a tie that matched his eyes, showed up to do some reaction shots against the conference. His station had the beat; he had nothing to do with it, but the glory was his, and his appearance gave weight to the proceedings.

The conference started angry and got angrier. Lester hadn't wanted to do it, and every reporter but one had been beaten on it. By the end, the Channel Eight reporter was standing on a chair, shouting at Lester. When she stood on the chair, the cops around her sat down; she wore a very short black leather skirt.

"I guess you gotta get what you can get," Sloan said,

laughing. Lester had fled, and Sloan, Lucas and Harmon Anderson walked together down the hall toward Homicide.

"Department full of fuckin' perverts," Anderson said, adding, "You could see the crack of her ass, if you sat just right."

"Jesus Christ, Harmon, I think that's sexual abuse in the third degree," Lucas said, laughing with Sloan.

"You know why they've got such great voices, the TV people?" Anderson asked, going off in a new direction. "Because they reverberate in the space where most people have brains . . ."

Swanson came slouching down the hall toward them, heavyset, glittering gold-rimmed glasses. "Did I miss it?"

"You missed it," Sloan confirmed. "Anderson got his first look at a woman's ass in twenty years."

"How about Bekker?" Lucas asked.

"Not a thing. We got his ass in here first thing, asked him if he wanted a lawyer, he said no. He said he'd ask if he needed one. So we said, What'd you do? He said he spent the late afternoon working at home, and the evening watching television. We asked what he was watching, and he told us. He was, like, watching CNBC in the afternoon, some kind of stock market shows, and then the news. . . . He went out around nine o'clock to get a bite to eat. We got that confirmed. . . ."

"How about phone calls?"

"He talked to one guy on the phone, a guy from the hospital, but that was late, way after the killing."

"Who called who?" Lucas asked. The four detectives circled around each other as Swanson talked.

"The other guy called in . . ." Swanson said.

"Could have a VCR, tape the shows," Anderson suggested.

"He does have a VCR," Swanson said. "I don't know about taping the shows. Anyway, we got his statement, and

124

shit, there was nothing to say. He didn't know Armistead, doesn't even know if he'd ever seen her on the stage. . . . He was just . . . There wasn't anything there. We sent him home."

"You believe him?" Lucas asked.

Swanson's forehead furrowed. "I don't know. When you're leaning on a guy, like we been leaning on Bekker, scouting around his neighborhood, calling his neighbors, all that . . . and something happened that could clear him, you'd think he'd be peeing all over himself in a rush to prove he didn't do it. He wasn't like that. He was cool. Answered all the questions like he was reading off of file cards."

"Keep up the pressure," Anderson said.

Swanson shook his head. "That ain't gonna work with this guy. I'm starting to think—he's an asshole, but he could be innocent."

They were still talking about it when Jennifer Carey turned the corner.

"Lucas . . ." Her voice was feminine, clear, professional.

Lucas turned in instant recognition. Sloan, Anderson and Swanson turned with him, then moved away down the corridor, furtively watching, as Lucas walked toward her.

"Daniel said you'd be talking afterwards," Jennifer said. She was slender and blonde, with a few thirties wrinkles on a well-kept face. She wore a pink silk blouse with a gray suit, and almost stopped his heart. She and Lucas had a two-year-old daughter but had never married. They'd been estranged ever since their daughter had been wounded.

"Yeah. Didn't see you at the conference."

"I just got here. Where will you be talking? Down at the conference room?" She was all business, brisk, impersonal. There would be more to it than that, Lucas knew.

"Nah. I'll just be around. . . . How are you?"

"I'm working with a new unit," she said, ignoring the question. "Could we get you outside, on the steps?"

"Sure. How've you been?" he persisted.

She shrugged and turned away, heading for the steps. "About the same. Are you coming over Saturday afternoon?"

"I . . . don't think so," he said, tagging along, hands in his pockets.

"Fine."

"When are we going to talk?"

"I don't know," she said over her shoulder.

"Soon?"

"I don't think so," she threw back. "Not soon."

"Hey, wait a minute," he said. He reached forward, hooked her arm and spun her around.

"Let the fuck go of me," she said, jerking her arm away, angry.

Lucas had always worried that women feared him: that he was too rough, even when he didn't mean to be. But her tone cut. He put a hand against her chest and shoved, and she went back against the wall of the corridor, her head snapping back. "Shut up . . ." he snarled.

"You fuck . . ." He thought she was going to swing, and stepped back, then realized that she was frightened and that her hand, coming up, was meant to block a punch. Her wrist looked thin and delicate, and he put up his hands, palms out.

"Just listen," he said, his voice dragging out in a hoarse near-whisper. "I'm tired of this shit. More than tired. I can't stand it anymore. In the past couple of days, I went through to the other side. So I'm telling you: I'm ready to quit. I'm ready to get out. You've been jerking me around for months and I can't deal with it and I won't deal with it. I'm not gone yet, but if you ever want to talk, you better decide soon, because I'll tell you what: You wait much longer and I ain't gonna be there to talk to."

She shook her head, tears starting, but they were tears of anger, and he turned and walked down the corridor. A TV3 producer stepped out into the hallway and looked down toward Jennifer, still flattened against the wall, looked into Lucas' face as he went by, then looked back at Jennifer and said, "Jen, you okay? Jen? What happened?"

As he went out on the steps to meet the cameras, Lucas heard Jennifer answer, "Nothing happened."

All five stations did quick interviews, Lucas standing on the City Hall steps for four of them, suppressing his anger with Jennifer, aware as he talked that it was slowly leaking away, leaving behind a cold hollowness. He did the fifth interview on the street, leaning against his Porsche. When the camera was done, Lucas stepped around the hood of the Porsche to get into the car, looking carefully for Jennifer, half hoping she'd be there, not believing she would be. She wasn't. Instead, a *Star-Tribune* reporter came after him, a dark-haired, overweight man with a beard who always carried a pocketful of sliced carrots wrapped in waxed paper.

"Tell me something," the reporter said. He waggled a carrot slice at Lucas, in a friendly way. "Between you and me—background, not for attribution, whatever. Are you looking forward to hunting this guy?"

Lucas thought for a second, glanced at the last television reporter, who was out of earshot, and nodded. "Yeah. I am. There's not been much going on."

"After busting the Crows, the other stuff must seem small-time. . . ." The reporter gobbled the carrot stick in two quick bites.

"Nah," Lucas said. "But this is . . . interesting. People are dying."

"Will you get him?"

Lucas nodded. "I don't know. But we'd be better off if we could get to Stephanie Bekker's lover. He knows things he doesn't know he knows. . . ."

"Wait a minute," the reporter said, slipping a slender notebook out of the breast pocket of his sport coat. "Can I attribute this last part? Can we go back on the record just for that?"

"Okay. But just that bit: Mrs Bekker's friend—quote me as calling him a friend—has actually seen the guy. He might think he's told us about her, calling nine-one-one, sending the note, but he hasn't. A good interview team would find things in his memory that he has no idea are there. And I'm not talking about giving him the third degree, either. If I could get him ten minutes on the telephone, or if Sloan could . . . I think we'd have a hundred-per-cent-better chance of breaking this thing in a hurry."

The reporter was scribbling notes. "So you want him to come in."

"We want anything we can get from him," Lucas said. He unlocked the Porsche's door and opened it. "Off the record again?"

"Sure."

"Loverboy's our only handle, that's how bad we need him. There's something wrong with this case, and without his help, I don't know how we'll find out what it is."

His anger with Jennifer came back as he drove across town, replaying the scene in the hall. She knew about scenes, knew about drama, knew psychology. She didn't have to be the one who asked him for an interview. She was jerking him around, and it was working. The optimism, the lift of the last few days, was gone. He accelerated out the Sixth Street exit onto I-94. Go home and go to bed, he thought.

Think it over. But his eye caught the sign for the Riverside exit, and without good reason, he took it, then turned left at the top of the ramp and headed down toward the West Bank theater district.

Cassie Lasch was sitting on the floor of the ticket lobby of the Lost River Theater. She was wearing jeans and a pink T-shirt and was digging through a gray plastic garbage bag. Lucas pushed through the revolving door into the lobby, and, as she looked up at him, he stopped short.

"The actress," Lucas said. He paused, his eyes still adjusting to the dim light. "Lasch. Cathy."

"Cassie. How are you, Davenport? Want to help? I'm looking for a clue."

Lucas squatted next to her. The weather was too cold for a T-shirt, but the woman seemed not to notice. Her arms were strong, with long, round muscles that carried up to her neck. And she was tanned, as much as a redhead could tan, too smoothly, by artificial lights. A lifter, Lucas thought. "What clue?"

"The cops were here all morning and I forgot to tell them . . ." She stopped rummaging through the garbage for a moment. A tiny scrap of paper was stuck to the side of her jaw, and her red hair had fallen over her eyes. She brushed it back and said, "Nobody asked about the guy who tried to get on the guest list last night. Remember, I told you that the ticket-office lady tried to call Elizabeth about the free-bee, and couldn't get her?"

"I remember," Lucas said, nodding. He reached over to her cheek, peeled off the scrap of paper, showed it to her and flicked it away.

"Thanks . . . uh . . ." She'd lost her thought, and she smiled up at him, her crooked tooth catching on her lower lip. Her face was just the slightest bit foxy, and mobile. Freckles were scattered lightly over the bridge of her nose.

"The guest list," Lucas prompted.

"Oh, yeah. This guy says he's some big-time reviewer and wants on the list as Elizabeth's friend. I asked the ticket-takers this morning and they said they didn't give out any free-bees last night. Whoever called didn't show up. That could be a clue." She said it seriously, intently, like a Miss Marple with terrific breasts.

"Why is that a clue?"

"Because maybe if he knew Elizabeth, he went over there. . . . I don't know, but he didn't show up."

Lucas thought for a minute, then nodded. "You're right. The list is in here?"

"Somewhere. On a piece of notebook paper from one of those teeny brown spiral notebooks. Probably wadded up."

"So let's dump it out," he said. He picked up the garbage bag by its bottom and shook it onto the lobby rug. Most of the litter was paper, much of it soaked with Coke and 7-Up, and toward the bottom, they found a paper coffee filter full of grounds.

"Ugh. Maybe you shouldn't have done that," Cassie said, wrinkling her nose at the mess.

"The hell with it," Lucas said. "We need the list."

They spent five minutes pawing through the sodden trash, working shoulder to shoulder. She had, Lucas decided, one of the better bodies he'd ever brushed up against. Everything was hard, except what was supposed to be soft, and that looked very soft. Every time she leaned forward, her breasts swelled forward against the thin fabric of the T-shirt. . . . *Jesus Christ, Davenport, you're ready for the peep shows*. . . .

He smiled to himself and picked up a Styrofoam cup. Inside was a paper wad the size of a marble. He unwrapped

130

it, turned it around. At the top somebody had written "Guests" and, under that, "Donaldson Whitney, LA Times."

"This it?"

Cassie took it, looked at it and said, "That's it. Kelly—the ticket-window lady—said the guy was from LA."

Lucas stood, the cartilage in his knees popping. "Got a phone? Someplace quiet?"

"There's one in the office, but there're a couple of people in there. . . . There's another one in the control booth. What do we do about this garbage?" She looked down at the pile of trash on the floor. The coffee grounds were smeared where Lucas had stepped on them.

He frowned, as though seeing it for the first time, and said, "I don't care. Whatever you want."

"Well, fuck that, I didn't put it there," Cassie said. She flipped her hair and turned away. "C'mon, I'll show you the control booth."

She led him down a hall to the theater auditorium. In the light of day, the place was a mess. Black paint was scaling off concrete-block walls, the seatbacks were stained, the overhead light rack was a tangle of electrical wires, ropes, spotlights, outlets and pulleys. At night, none of that would be visible.

The control booth was at the back of the auditorium, up two short flights of stairs. The booth itself was built out of plywood, painted black on the outside, unfinished inside. A barstool and a secretary's swivel chair sat in front of a control panel. Extension and computer cords were fixed to the walls and floors with gaffer tape. A phone was screwed to the wall to the left of the control panel.

Cassie noticed him looking around and said, "No money for luxuries."

131

"First time I've been in a theater control booth," Lucas said.

She shrugged. "They mostly look like this, unless the theater's getting government money."

Lucas used his credit card to call Los Angeles, Cassie leaning against the control panel, arms locked behind her back, listening with interest. Whitney was not at his desk, Lucas was told. He pressed, was switched around, and eventually talked to an arts copy editor who made the mistake of picking up a ringing telephone. He said that Whitney was on vacation.

"In Minneapolis?" Lucas asked.

"Why would he be in fuckin' Minneapolis in April?" the copy editor asked crossly. "He's in Micronesia on a skin-diving trip."

"Well?" Cassie asked, when Lucas had hung up.

"Well, what?"

"Was it him last night?"

"Uh, I appreciate your help, Miss Lasch, but this is police business. . . ."

"You're not going to tell me?" She couldn't believe it. She reached out, took hold of his jacket sleeve and tugged at it. "C'mon."

"No."

"No fair . . ." Her eyes were as large as any he'd ever seen, and dark again, with a spark. She tipped her head, a tiny smile on her face. "I'll show you my tits if you tell me."

"What?" He was surprised and amused. *Amused*, he thought, watching himself.

"Out there in the lobby, you were doing everything but feeling me up, so . . . tell me, and I'll give you a look."

Lucas considered. "This is embarrassing," he said finally.

"I don't embarrass very easily."

"Maybe not, but I do," Lucas said.

Her eyebrows went up. "You're embarrassed? That shows a certain unexpected depth. Do you play the piano?"

She was moving too fast. "Ah, no . . ."

"Quick, Davenport, make up your mind. . . ." She was teasing now.

Lucas put her off: "What do you do besides act? You said you don't get the good parts."

"I'm one of the world's great waitresses. I learned in the theater restaurants in New York. . . ."

"Hmph."

"So how about it?" she pressed.

"You'd have to keep your mouth shut," he said severely.

"Sure. I'm very secretive."

"I'll bet. . . . All right: The *Times* guy is in Micronesia, on a skin-diving trip. Micronesia's in the middle of the Pacific Ocean."

"I know where it is, I've been there," she said. "Then there's no way in hell he could have been here last night."

"No." Lucas glanced around. There was no one else in the theater area, and the booth was even more isolated. "So . . ."

"If you're waiting to see my tits, forget it," she said, crossing her arms over her chest.

"Ha. Rat out on a deal, huh?" he said, grinning.

"Of course. When you want to find out something, first you try treachery—that wouldn't work in this case—and then you make weird sex offers," she said calmly. "Usually, you'll find out what you want to know. I learned that from dealing with agents."

"Fuckin' women," Lucas said. "So casual about the way you break a guy's heart."

"You look thoroughly destroyed," she said.

133

Lucas took a short step toward her, not knowing exactly what he was planning to do. Whatever it was, she didn't back away; but at that moment, a man walked out on the stage below them, and Lucas stopped and looked down. Without a word, and apparently unaware that they were in the booth, the man hit a light switch, stepped to the center of the stage and began juggling. He'd brought a half-dozen baseballs with him, and they spun in a circle, smoothly, without a miss, and then, just as abruptly as he'd begun juggling, he started to tap-dance. Not a simple tap, but a dance almost baroque in its complication, and all the time the balls were in the air.

The man was in blackface. There was something about his head. . . . An effect of the make-up, the wide white-greasepainted lips, the strange flat nose?

Cassie caught Lucas' interest and stepped close behind him and whispered, "Carlo Druze, one of the actors. This is one of his routines."

Druze began to sing, a phony black accent, minstrel-show style, in a shaky baritone, "Way down upon the Swanee River, far, far away . . ."

"We're doing a thing called *Whiteface*, it's like a racial-satire thing. . . ." She was whispering, but Druze apparently heard. He took down the balls in a swift, coordinated sweep.

"I've got an audience?" he called, looking up at the booth.

Lucas applauded and Cassie yelled, "Just us, Cassie and a cop."

"Ah . . ." Was he startled? Lucas wasn't sure. Was there something wrong with his face?

"That was really good, Carlo," Cassie said.

Druze took a bow.

"If only Miz Cassie wuz runnin' d'show," he said, going back to the accent.

"We'll get out of your hair," Cassie said, leading Lucas out of the booth and down the steps toward the exit light.

In the hall on the way back to the lobby, Lucas asked, "Was what's-his-name here last night?"

"Carlo? Yeah. Most of the time, anyway. He was working on the set. He's the best carpenter in the company. And he does great voices. He can sound like anybody."

"Okay."

"He's a tough guy," she added. "Hard. Like his face."

"But he was here?"

"Well, nobody was taking names. But yeah. Around."

"Okay." Lucas followed her down the hall, watching her back and shoulders in the dim light. She looked delicate, like most slender redheads, but there was nothing fragile about her, he realized. "You're a lifter, right?" he said.

"Yeah, some," she said, half turning. "I don't compete or anything. Do you lift?"

"No. I've got some weights in my basement and I've got a routine I do in the morning. Nothing serious."

"Gotta stay in shape," Cassie said, slapping her stomach. They stepped into the lobby, and Cassie stopped suddenly and caught Lucas' arm: "Oh, no," she groaned.

"What?"

"Deep shit," she said.

A man stood over the garbage on the rug. He was dressed all in black, from his knee boots to his beret, and his shoulder-length auburn hair was tied in a stubby ponytail. His hands were planted on his hips, and one foot was tapping in anger. Cassie hurried toward him and he looked up when he heard her coming.

"Cassie," he said. He had a goatee, and his teeth were a brilliant white against the beard. "Did you do this? One of the ticket women said you were looking through the garbage. . . ."

"Uh . . ."

"I did it," Lucas said, his voice curt. Cassie flashed him a grateful look. "Police business. I was looking for information involving the Armistead killing last night."

"Well, are you going to clean it up?" the man asked, nudging a wet ball of paper with the toe of a boot.

"Who are you?" Lucas asked, stepping closer.

"Uh, this is Davis Westfall," Cassie said from behind him. She still sounded nervous. "He is . . . was . . . the co-artistic director with Elizabeth. Davis, this is Lieutenant Davenport of the Minneapolis police. I was showing him around."

"She's been a help," Lucas said to Westfall, nodding at Cassie. "Mr Westfall . . . Miss Armistead's death would put you in sole charge of this theater, would it not? I mean, in one sense, you'd be a . . . beneficiary?"

"Why . . . that would be up to the board," Westfall sputtered. He glanced at Cassie for support, and she nodded. "But we're a non-sexist theater, so I imagine they'll appoint another female to take Elizabeth's place."

"Hmp," Lucas said. He studied Westfall for another moment, skepticism on his face. "No major disagreements on management?" he asked, keeping Westfall pinned.

"No. Not at all," Westfall said. Now he was nervous.

"But you'll be around?"

"Well, yes . . ."

"Good. And don't move this garbage right away. Our crime lab might want to look at it. If they're not here by . . ."—Lucas glanced at his watch—"six o'clock, you can have somebody pick it up."

"Anything we can do . . ." Westfall said, thoroughly deflated.

Lucas nodded and turned to leave. "I'll show him to the door," Cassie said. "I'll make sure it's locked."

"Thank you," Lucas said formally.

At the front door, Cassie whispered, "Thanks. Davis can be an asshole. I'm at the bottom of the heap here."

"No problem," Lucas said, grinning. "And I appreciate the tip on the guest list. It really could turn into something."

"You gonna ask me out?" she asked.

She'd surprised him again. "Mmm. Maybe," he said, smiling. "But why . . ."

"Well, if you're going to, don't wait too goddamned long, okay? I can't stand the suspense."

Lucas laughed. "All right," he said. As he stepped out on the sidewalk, the door clicked shut behind him. He took another step away, toward the car, when he heard a rapping on the door glass. He turned around and Cassie lifted the front of her T-shirt, just for an instant, just a flash.

Long enough: She looked very nice, he thought. Very nice, pink and pale . . . And she was gone.

11

Bekker walked in circles on the Heriz carpet, orbiting the Rococo revival sofa, watching cuts from the press conference on the noon news. He'd heard shorter cuts on his car radio on the way to the hospital, and had gone back home to see it on television. Most of the press conference was nonsense: the police had nothing at all. But the appeal to Stephanie's lover could be dangerous.

"We believe the man who called nine-one-one is telling the truth. We believe that he is innocent of the murder of Mrs Bekker, especially in light of this second murder," the cop, Lester, was saying into the microphones. He was sweating under the lights, patting his forehead with a folded white handkerchief. "After discussions with the county attorney, we have agreed that should Mrs Bekker's friend come forward, Hennepin County would be willing to discuss a guarantee of immunity from prosecution in return for testimony, provided that he was not involved in the crime. . . ."

Lester went on, but Bekker wasn't listening anymore. He paced, gnawing on a thumbnail, spitting the pieces onto the carpet.

The police were all over the neighborhood. They weren't hiding. They were, in fact, deliberately provocative. Stephanie's idiot cop cousin, the doper, had been going door to door around the neighborhood, soliciting information. That angered him, but his anger was for another time. He had other problems now.

"Loverboy," they called him on TV. Who was it? Who

was the lover? It had to be somebody in their circle. Some-body with easy access to Stephanie. He had exhausted himself, tearing at the problem.

Fuckin' Druze, he thought. Couldn't find the face. The face had to be there, somewhere, in the photographs. Stephanie took photographs of everybody, could never leave anybody alone, always had that fuckin' camera in somebody's face, taking snapshots. She had boxes, cartons, baskets full of photos, all those beefy blond Scandinavian males. . . .

Could Druze be wrong? It was possible, but, Bekker admitted to himself uncomfortably, he probably wasn't. He didn't seem unsure of himself. He didn't equivocate. He'd looked at the photos, studied them and said no.

"Bitch," Bekker said aloud to Stephanie's house. "Who were you fucking?"

He looked back at the television, at Lester yammering at the cameras. Anger surged in him: it was unfair, they had twenty men, a hundred, and he had only himself and Druze. And Druze couldn't really look, because if he was seen first . . .

"Bitch," he said again, and gripped by the anger, he pounded out of the parlor, up the stairs, into the bedroom. The cigarette case was with his keys and a pile of change, and he snapped it open, popped two amphetamines and a sliver of windowpane, and closed his eyes, waiting for Beauty.

There. The bed moved for him, melted, the closet opened like a mouth, a cave, a warm place to huddle. His clothes: they gripped him, and he fought the panic. He had felt it before, the shirt tightening around his throat, the sleeves gripping his arms like sandpaper, tightening. . . . He fought the panic and stripped off the constricting shirt, slipped out of his pants and underwear, and threw them out into the room. The closet called, and he dropped to his knees and crawled inside. Warm and safe, with the musty smell of the shoes . . . comfortable.

He sat for a minute, for five minutes, letting the speed run through his veins and the acid through his brain. Fire, he thought. He needed fire. The realization came on him suddenly and he bolted from the cave, still on his hands and knees, suddenly afraid. He crawled to the dresser and reached over it, groping, found the book of matches and scuttled back to the closet, his eyes cranked wide, not handsome now, something else. . . . In the semi-dark of the closet, he struck a match and stared into the flame. . . .

Safe. With the fire. His anger grew and darkened. Bitch. Her face flashed, and melted. Pain flared in his hand, and suddenly he was in darkness. Match gone. He struck another one. Bitch. A bed popped up, not their bed, and strange wallpaper, with fleur-de-lis, where was that? The hotel in New York. With the acid singing through him, Bekker saw himself come out of the bathroom, naked, holding a towel, Stephanie on the phone. . . . Pain in his hand again. Darkness. He dropped the match, struck a third. Bitch. Step into the bathroom to shower; when I come out, she's already on the phone, calling her paint stripper or someone. . . .

His mind stretched and snapped, stretched and snapped, cooled, chilled. Pain. Darkness. Another match. He wiped spittle from his chin, staring at the guttering flame. Pain. Darkness. He crawled out of the closet, the first rush going now, leaving him with the power of ice, of a glacier. . . .

And the answer was there, in the acid flash to New York. He stood up, his mind chilled, precise. Pain in his hand. "Am I stupid?"

Bekker walked out of the bedroom, still nude but unaware of it, down to the study, where he settled behind the big oak desk. He opened a deep drawer and took out a gray plastic box. The tape on the front said "Bills: Paid, Current."

"New York, January . . ." He dumped the box on the desk and combed through the stack of paper, receipts and stubs of paid bills. After a minute he said, "Here . . ."

The phone bill. He hadn't called anyone, but there were six calls on the bill, New York to Minneapolis, four of them to a university extension. He didn't know the number. . . .

Mind like ice. Riding the speed, now. He punched the number into the desk phone. A moment later, a woman answered. "Professor George's office, can I help you?"

Bekker dropped the phone back on the hook, heat flushing the ice from his head. "Philip George," he crowed. "Philip George . . ."

There was work to do, but the drugs had him again and he sat for half an hour, rocking in the chair behind the big desk. Time was nothing in the grip of the acid. . . .

Pain. He looked at his hand. A huge blister bubbled from the tip of his index finger. The ball of his thumb was raw, a patch of burned skin. How had he burned himself? Had there been a fire?

He went to the kitchen, pierced the blister with a needle, smeared both the finger and the thumb with a disinfectant and covered the burns with Band-Aids. A mystery . . . And Philip George.

Bekker pawed through the library, searching for the book. No. No. Where? Must be in the junk, must be in the keepsakes, where could she . . . Ah. Here: *Faculty and Staff, University of Minnesota*.

His own face flashed up at him as he flipped through the pages, then the face of Philip George. Bland. Slightly stupid, somewhat officious, he thought. Large. Blond. Fleshy. How could she? The pain bit into his hand, and confused, he looked at his finger again. How . . . ?

* * *

141

"Carlo?"

"God damn, I thought . . ." Druze was shocked.

"I'm sorry, but this is an absolute emergency . . ."

"Have you seen the television?" Druze asked.

"Yes. And nobody has even begun to look at you. Yet. That's why I'm calling. I found our man."

"Who?" Druze blurted.

"A law professor named Philip George. We've got to move—you've seen the television."

"Yes, yes, where are you?" Druze asked impatiently. "Are you okay?"

"I'm a block down the street, in the VGA supermarket," Bekker said. He was using a convenience phone at the newsrack, and a woman customer was heading toward him with a shopping list in her hand. She'd want the phone. "I've checked and I've checked and there's nobody with me. I guarantee it. But I'm going out the back and down the alley. I'll be at your place sixty seconds after I hang up here. Buzz me in. . . ."

"Man, if anybody sees you . . ."

"I know, but I'm wearing a hat and a jacket and sunglasses, and I'll make sure the lobby's empty before I come in. If you're ready for my buzz . . . I'll come up the stairs. Have the door open."

"All right. If you're sure . . ."

"I'm sure, but I need you to say yes, he's the one."

Bekker hung up and looked around. Was he being watched? He wasn't sure, but he didn't think so. The woman customer was using the phone now, paying no attention to him. An elderly man was going through the check-out with a can of coffee, and the only other people in sight were store employees.

He'd taken a quick trip around the store once before he picked up the phone. There was an exit sign by the dairy case. . . .

142

He got a pushcart and started to the back of the store, checking the other customers. But you couldn't tell, could you? At the dairy case, he waited until he was alone, then left the cart and walked straight out a swinging door under the exit sign. He found himself in a storage area that stank of rotting produce, looking at a pair of swinging metal doors. He pushed through them to a loading dock, walked briskly along the dock and down the stairs at the far end, watching the door behind him.

Nobody came through, nobody looked through. Five seconds later he was in the alley that ran along the back of the store. He hurried down the length of the block, around the corner, another hundred feet and into the outer lobby of Druze's apartment building. He pushed the button on Druze's mailbox, got an instant answering buzz, pulled open the inner door and was inside. Elevator straight ahead, stairs through the door to the right. He took the stairs two at a time, checked the hallway and hustled down to Druze's apartment. The door was open and he pushed through.

"God damn, Mike . . ." Druze's face was normally as unreadable as a pumpkin. Now he looked stressed, uncharacteristic vertical lines creasing the patchwork skin of his forehead. He was wearing a tired cotton sweater the color of oatmeal, and pants with pleats. His hands were in his pockets.

"Is this him?" Bekker thrust the photo of Philip George at Druze.

Druze looked at it, carried it to a light, looked closer, his lower lip thrust out. "Huh."

"It must be him," Bekker said. "He fits: he's blond, he's heavy—he's even heavier in real life than he is in that picture. That photo must be four or five years old. And he wasn't in any of the other photos. And Stephanie was calling him secretly from New York."

143

Druze finally nodded. "It could be. It looks like him. But the guy at the house, I just saw him like that." Druze snapped his fingers.

"It must be him," Bekker said eagerly.

"Yeah. Yeah, I think it is. Give him a couple of more years . . . Yeah."

"God damn, Carlo," Bekker crowed, his beautiful face absolutely radiant. He caught Druze around the neck with the crook of his elbow and squeezed him down, a jock-like hug, and Druze felt the pleasure of approval flush through his stomach. Druze had never had a friend. . . . "God damn, we beat the police."

"So now what?" Druze asked. He felt himself smiling: What an odd feeling, a real smile.

Bekker let him go. "I've got to get out of here and think. I'll figure something out. Tonight, after your show, come up to my office. Even if they're watching me, they won't be inside the building. Call me before you leave and I'll come down and let you in at that side door by the ramp. If you look like you're unlocking the door, they'd never suspect . . ."

Philip George.

Bekker worried the problem all the way back to the hospital. They had to get to George quickly. He stopped at the secretary's desk in the departmental office.

"Lucy, do you have a class schedule?"

"I think . . ." The secretary pulled open a filing cabinet and dug through it, and finally produced a yellow pamphlet. She handed it to him. "Could you bring it back, it's the only one. . . ."

"Sure," he said distractedly, flipping through the schedule. Pain flared in his hand, and he stopped and looked at it more carefully. He should bandage it. . . .

"Lucy?" He went back to the secretary's desk. "Do we

have any big Band-Aids around here? I've burned my thumb. . . ."

"I think . . ." The secretary dug through her desk, found a box of bandages. "Let me see. . . . Oh my God, Dr Bekker, how did you do this . . . ?"

He let her bandage it, then walked down the corridor to his office, unlocked it and settled behind his desk. Law school, George . . . he glanced at his watch. One-thirty. *George: Basic Torts, MWF 1:10-3:00.*

He would be in class. Bekker picked up the phone, called the law school office and twittered at the woman who answered: "Phil George? In class? I see," he said, putting disappointment in his voice. "This is a friend of his over at Hamline, I'm just leaving town, terrible rush, we were supposed to meet one of these nights, and I'm trying to get my schedule together. . . . Do you know if he has classes or night meetings the rest of the week? . . . No, I can't really wait, I've got a seminar starting right now, and it runs late, then I've got a plane. Tried to call Phil's wife, nobody home . . . Yes, I'll hold. . . ."

The law secretary dropped the receiver on her desk and Bekker could hear her walking away. A minute passed, then another, and then she was back: "Yes, tomorrow night, seven to ten, he has preparation for moot court. The other nights are clear here at the school."

"Thank you very much," he said, still twittering. "You've been very kind. What is your name? . . . Thank you very much, Nancy. Oh, by the way, where is the moot-court prep going to be? . . . Okay, thanks again."

He hung up and leaned back in his chair, making a steeple of his fingers. George would be working late. That could be useful. What'd he drive? It was a red four-wheel-drive of some kind, a Jeep. He could cruise by George's house later on. He lived in Prospect Park and probably left the car in the street. . . .

Druze was sure that Bekker was using, but he wasn't sure what it was. An ocean of cocaine flowed through the theater world, but Bekker wasn't a cokehead; or if he was, there was something else involved. At times he was flying, his beautiful face reflecting an inner joy, a freedom; at other times, he was dark, reptilian, calculating.

Whatever it was, it moved through him quickly. He'd been manic when Druze arrived at the hospital. Now he was like ice.

"He'll be out tomorrow night," Bekker said. "I know that's not much time. . . . He drives a red Jeep Cherokee. Fire-engine red. He'll be parked behind Peik Hall."

He explained the rest of it and Druze began shaking his head. "Happy accident? What kind of shit is that?"

"It's the only way," Bekker said calmly. "If we try to pull him out, set him up, we could spook him. If he thinks we might come after him . . . I can't just call him, cold, and ask him to meet me down at the corner. He's got to be a little afraid—that somebody might figure him out, that the killer might come after him. . . ."

"I just wish there was some other way," Druze said. He looked around and realized he was in some kind of examination room. Bekker had met him at a side door, normally locked, and led him down a dimly lit hallway to a red metal door, and had opened it with a key and pulled him inside. The walls were lined with stainless-steel cabinets, a stainless cart sat against one wall, and a battery of overhead lights hung down at the center of the room. Their voices ricocheted around the room like Ping-Pong balls. The room was cold. "It seems pretty . . . uncertain."

"Look, the hardest thing to investigate is a spur-of-the-moment thing, between strangers. Like when you did that

146

woman in New York. How can the cops find a motive, how can they find a connection? If you try to set something up, it leaves traces. If you just go there, where he is, and do it . . ."

"You know he'll be there?" Druze asked.

"Yes. He's got the moot court. He plays the part of the judge, he *has* to be there."

"I guess it's got to be done," Druze said, running his fingers back through his hair. "Jesus, I don't like it. I like things that can be rehearsed. Your wife, that was no problem. This . . ."

"It's the best way, believe me," Bekker said intently. "Look for his car. It should be in the parking lot right behind the building. There's a lot of foliage around the lot—I checked. If he parks there, try to get close to the car, let the air out of one of his tires. That'll give the students time to get away from the building and it'll keep him busy changing the tire while you come up on him. . . ."

"Not bad," Druze admitted. "But God damn, Michael, I've got the feeling that we've kicked the tarbaby. One foot's stuck and now we've got to stick the other one in, trying to get the first one loose. . . ."

"This is the end and we've got to do it, don't you see? For your own safety," Bekker said. "Get him, dump him . . ."

"That bothers me, too. Dumping him. If I just whacked him, and walked away, who's to know? But if I have to take him out to Wisconsin . . . Jesus, I could get stopped by conservation officers looking for fish, or who knows what?"

Bekker shook his head, holding Druze with his eyes. "If we kill him and leave him, they'll know from his eyes that he must be Stephanie's lover—why else would his eyes be cut? But that'll throw the serial-killer pattern right out the window. And how would the killer be able to find the guy? They're already suspicious, and if we killed him and left him in the lot, they'd be all over me."

"We could skip the eyes. . . ."

"No." Bekker was cold as stone. He stepped close to Druze and gripped his arm above the elbow. Druze took a half-step back, chilled by the other man's frigid eyes. "No. We cut the eyes. You understand."

"Jesus, okay," Druze said, pulling back.

Bekker stared at him for a moment, judging his sincerity. Apparently satisfied, he went on. "If we dump him somewhere remote—and I know the perfect place—nobody's going to find him. Nobody. The cops might suspect that he was Stephanie's lover, but they won't know if he ran because he was afraid, or because he was the killer, or if he's dead, or what. They just won't know. . . ."

Druze left the way he'd come, through the side door. Bekker walked back toward his office, rubbing his chin, thinking. Druze was reluctant. Not in rebellion, but unhappy. He'd have to consider that. . . .

In the elevator, he glanced at his watch. He had time. . . .

"Sybil."

Was she asleep? Bekker leaned over the bed and pulled her eyelids up. Her eyes were looking at him, dark and liquid, but when he let go of her eyelids, she closed them again. She was awake, all right, but not cooperating.

He sat beside her bed. "I have to look in your eyes as you go, Sybil," he said. He could feel himself breathing a little harder than usual: his experiments had that effect on him, the excitement. . . .

"Here we are. . . ." He clapped a strip of tape over her lips, rested the heel of his other hand on her forehead and pulled her eyelids up with his index and ring fingers. Her eyes open, he leaned into her line of vision and said, quietly, "I've taped your mouth so you can't breathe, and now I'll pinch your nose, until you smother. . . . Do you understand? It shouldn't hurt, but I would appreciate a signal if you see . . . anything. Move your eyes up and down as you go through to the other side, do you understand? If there is another side?"

He was using his most convincing voice, and quite convincing it was, he thought. "Are you ready? Here we go." He pinched her nose, holding his fingers so she could see it, even if she couldn't feel it. Sybil couldn't move, but there were muscles that could twitch, and they did twitch after the first minute, small tremors running through her neck to his hands.

Her eyes began to roll up and he put his face an inch from hers, looking into them, whispering, urgent. "Can you see it? Sybil, can you see . . . ?"

She was gone, unconscious. He released her nose, placed his hand on her chest, compressed it, lifted, compressed it again. She hadn't been that close, he thought, although she couldn't know that. She'd thought she was dying. *Had* been dying, would have died, if he hadn't released his hand . . .

She owed him this information. . . .

"Sybil, are you in there? Hello, Sybil, I know you're there."

At two, Bekker was home, MDMA burning low in his mind, under control. The episode with Sybil had, ultimately, been unfulfilling. A nurse had come down the hall, gone into a nearby room. He'd left then, thinking it better not to be seen with Sybil. As far as he knew, he hadn't been. He'd gone from her bedside to his office, popped the ecstasy, hoping to balance the disappointment, turned off the lights and left.

He drove past the front of the house on the way to the alley. As he passed, he saw a man, there, at the end of the

149

street. On the sidewalk. Turning his head to watch Bekker go by. Large. Watching. Familiar.

Bekker slowed, stopped, rolled down the window. "Can I help you?" he called.

There was a long moment of silence, then the man sauntered out into the street. He was wearing a leather bomber jacket and boots.

"Mr Bekker, how are you?"

"You're a police officer?"

"Lucas Davenport, Minneapolis police."

Yes. The man at the funeral, the tough-looking one. "Is the police department camped on my porch?" Bekker asked. Safe now—the man wasn't a mugger or revenge-bound relative—the sarcasm knit through his polite tone like a dirty thread in a doily.

"No. Only me," the cop said.

"Surveillance?"

"No, no. I just like to wander by the scene of a crime now and then. Get a feel for it. Helps me think . . ."

Davenport. A bell went off in the back of Bekker's mind. "Aren't you the officer that the FBI agent called a gunman? Killed some ridiculous number of people?"

Even in the weak illumination from the corner street-light, Bekker could see the flash of the cop's white teeth. He was smiling.

"The FBI doesn't like me," the cop said.

"Did you like it? Killing all those people?" The interest was genuine, the words surprising Bekker even as they popped out of his mouth. The cop seemed to think about it for a moment, tipping his head back, as though looking for stars. It was cold enough that their breath was making little puffs of steam.

"Some of them," the cop said after a bit. He rocked from his toes to his heels, looked up again. "Yeah. Some of them I . . . enjoyed quite a bit."

Bekker couldn't quite see the other man's eyes: they were set too deep, under heavy brow ridges, and the curiosity was almost unbearable.

"Listen," Bekker heard himself say, "I have to put my car in the garage. But would you like to come in for a cup of coffee?"

12

Lucas waited at the front door until Bekker got the car in the garage and walked through the house to let him in. Bekker turned on the porch light as he opened the door. In the yellow light, his skin looked like parchment, stretched taut over the bones of his face. Like a skull, Lucas thought. Inside, in the soft glow of the ceiling fixtures, the skull illusion vanished: Bekker was beautiful. Not handsome, but more than pretty.

"Come in. The house is a bit messy."

The house was spectacular. The entry floor was oak parquet. To the left was a coat closet, to the right a wall with an oil painting of a British Isles scene, a cottage with a thatched roof in the foreground, sail-boats on the river beyond. Straight ahead, a burgundy-carpeted staircase curled up to the right. Off the entryway, a room with glass doors, full of books, appeared to the right, under a balcony formed by the stairs. To the left was the parlor, with Oriental carpets, a half-dozen antique mirrors and a stone fireplace. Beautiful and hot. Seventy-five or eighty degrees. Lucas unzipped his jacket and crouched to press his fingers against the parlor carpet.

"Wonderful," he said. The pile was soft as beaten egg whites, an inch or more deep, and as intricately woven as an Arabian fairy tale.

Bekker grunted. He wasn't interested. "Let's go back and sit in the kitchen," he said, and led the way to a country kitchen with quarry-tile floor. Stephanie Bekker had been killed in the kitchen, Lucas recalled. Bekker seemed unaffected by it, pulling earthenware cups from natural oak cabinets, spooning instant coffee into them.

"I hope caffeine is okay," he said. Bekker's voice was flat, uninflected, as though he daily drank coffee with a cop who suspected him of murder. He must know. . . .

"Fine." Lucas looked around the kitchen as Bekker filled the cups with tap water, stuck them in a microwave and punched the control buttons. The kitchen was as carefully crafted as the rest of the house, with folksy, turn-of-the-century wallpaper, dark, perfectly matched wood, and touches of flagstone. While the rest of the house felt decorated, Lucas thought, the kitchen felt lived in.

Bekker turned back to Lucas as the microwave began to hum. "I know nothing at all about cooking," Bekker said. "A little about wine, perhaps."

"You're handling your wife's death pretty well," Lucas said. He stepped up to a small framed photograph. Four women in long dark dresses and white aprons, standing around a butter churn. Old. "Are these, what, ancestors?"

"Stephanie's great-grandmother and some friends. Sit down, Mr Davenport," Bekker said, nodding at a break-fast bar with stools. The microwave beeped, and he took out the cups, the coffee steaming hot, carried them to the bar and sat down opposite Lucas. "You were saying?"

"Your wife's death . . ."

"I'll miss her, but to be honest, I didn't love my wife very much. I'd never hurt her—I know what the police think, Stephanie's idiot cousin—but the fact is, neither of us was much of a factor in the other's life. I suspected she was having an affair: I simply didn't care. I've had female friends of my own. . . ." He looked for reaction in Lucas' face. There was none. The cop accepted the infidelity as routine . . . maybe.

"And that didn't bother her? Your other friends." Lucas sipped at the coffee. Scalding.

"I don't believe so. She knew, of course, *her* friends

would have seen to that. But she never spoke to me about it. And she was the type who would have, if she cared. . . ." Bekker blew on his coffee. He was wearing a tweed jacket and whipcord pants, very English.

"So why not a divorce?" Lucas asked.

"Why should we? We got along reasonably well, and we had this"—he gestured at the house—"which we couldn't maintain if we split up. And there are other advantages for two people living together. You share maintenance chores, run errands for each other, one can take care of business when the other one is gone. . . . There wasn't any passion, but we were quite well adapted to each other's habits. I'm not much interested in marriage, at my age. I have my work. She couldn't have children; her fallopian tubes were hopelessly tangled, and by the time in vitro came around, she was no longer thinking about children. I never wanted any, so there wasn't even that possibility." He stopped and seemed to reflect, took a sip of the scalding coffee. "I suppose other people wouldn't understand the way we were living, but it was convenient and comfortable."

"Hmp." Lucas sipped his own coffee and looked the other man straight in the eyes. Bekker gazed placidly back, not flinching, and Lucas knew then that he was lying, at least about part of it. Nobody looked that guiltless without deliberate effort. "I suppose a prosecutor could argue that since you had no interest in each other, and it made no difference to you whether she lived or died, her death would be very . . . convenient. Instead of having half of this"—his gesture mimicked Bekker's—"you'd have all of it."

"He could . . . if he were particularly stupid or particularly vicious," Bekker said. He flashed a smile at Lucas, a thin rim of white teeth. "I invited you for coffee because of the people you've killed, Mr Davenport. I thought you'd likely know about death and murder. That would give us much in common. I study death as a scientist. I've

154

studied murder, both the victims and the killers. There are several men who consider themselves my friends out at Stillwater prison, serving life sentences. From my research I've drawn two conclusions. First: Murder is stupid. In most cases, it will out, as somebody British once said. If you're going to commit murder, the worst thing you can do is plan it and commit it in league with another person. Conflicts arise, the investigators play one against another. . . . I know how it works. No. Murder is stupid. Murder plotted with someone else is idiotic. Divorce, on the other hand, is merely annoying. A tragedy for some couples, perhaps, but if two people genuinely don't love each other, it's mostly routine legal procedure."

Bekker shrugged and went at the coffee. When he extended his perfect pink lips to the cup, he looked like a leech, Lucas thought.

"What's the second thing you know about murder? You said there were two things," Lucas asked.

"Ah. Yes." Bekker smiled again, pleased that Lucas was paying attention. "To plan and carry out a cold-blooded murder—well, only a madman could do it. Anyone remotely normal could not. Serial killers, hit men, men who plot and kill their wives: all crazy."

Lucas nodded. "I agree."

"I'm glad you do," Bekker said simply. "And I'm not crazy."

"Is that the real reason you invited me in? To tell me you're not nuts?"

Bekker nodded ruefully and said, "Yes, I guess it is. Because I thought you might understand the total-ity of what I'm saying. Even if I had wanted to kill Stephanie—and I didn't—I wouldn't have. I'm simply too smart and too sane." He reached forward and touched Lucas on the arm, and Lucas thought: *The sucker is trying to seduce me. He wants me to like him.* . . . "Your fellow

155

officers have been all over the neighborhood, quite deliberately creating an impression. I can feel it in my neighbors. I'm sure Stephanie's crazy cousin, the dope addict, has told you that I had her killed to get this house, but if you ask her friends, you'll find that I never had much interest in it. The house or the furnishings . . ."

"You could sell it—"

"I was coming to that," Bekker interrupted. He made a brushing motion with his free hand, as though batting away gnats. "I'm not much interested in the house or its furnishings, but I'm not totally unappreciative, either. It is a very comfortable place to live. Success in academia is largely political, you know, and the house is a wonderful backdrop for social gatherings. For impressing those who must be impressed. I would keep it, but . . . I'm afraid Stephanie's crazy cousin may succeed in driving me out. If all my neighbors believe I killed her, remaining here would be intolerable. You might tell that to Del, when you see him. That if I sell, it will be only because he drove me out."

"I will," Lucas nodded. "And if the other officers are creating problems for you . . . I have some pull at headquarters. I'll back them off."

"Really?" Bekker seemed surprised. "Would you?"

"Sure. I don't know whether you were involved in your wife's killing, but there's no reason you should be illegally harassed. I'll look into it."

"That'd be wonderful," Bekker said. Gratitude saturated his voice, but a spark of contempt flared in his eyes. "I'm glad I asked you in: I had an intuition that you'd understand. . . ."

They sat in silence for a moment, then Lucas said, "She was killed here in the kitchen. Your wife."

"Oh, yes . . . . I suppose she was," Bekker said, looking around vaguely.

Wrong reaction, asshole. Bekker had to know where she was killed. He must have thought about it, looked at the spot, carried the image in his head: anyone would, innocent or guilty, crazy or sane. *And that business about a divorce being simply annoying. If you believe that, you're stupider than I think you are.* . . . Lucas waited, expecting more, but Bekker pushed off the barstool and dumped the last of his coffee into the kitchen sink.

"The men you killed, Lucas. Do you think they went anywhere?" His tone was casual.

"What do you mean?" Lucas asked. "You mean, like, to heaven?"

"Or hell." Bekker turned to study him. His voice was no longer casual.

"No. I don't think they went anywhere," Lucas said, shaking his head. "I used to be a Catholic, and when I first started police work, I worried about that. I saw a lot of people dead or dying for no apparent reason . . . not people I killed, just people. Little kids who'd drowned, people dying in auto accidents and with heart attacks and strokes. I saw a lineman burn to death, up on a pole, little bits and pieces, and nobody could help. . . . I watched them go, screaming and crying and sometimes just lying there with their tongue stuck out, heaving, with all the screaming and hollering from friends and relatives . . . and I never saw anyone looking beyond. I think, Michael, I think they just blink out. That's all. I think they go where the words on a computer screen go, when you turn it off. One minute they exist, maybe they're even profound, maybe the result of a great deal of work. The next . . . Whiff. Gone."

"Gone," Bekker repeated. His white eyebrows went up. "Nothing left?"

"Nothing but a shell, and that rots."

"Hah." Bekker turned away, suddenly shaken. "Very sad. Well. I have to get to bed. I have work tomorrow."

Lucas stood, drank the last of his coffee and left the cup on the bar. "I wonder if I could ask something. I'm sure other cops have been all over the house. Could I take a look at the room where Stephanie and her friend were . . . spending time?"

"You mean her bedroom," Bekker said wryly. "I don't see why not. Like you said, the carpets are virtually worn-out from the impact of all the flat feet . . . no offense."

Lucas laughed in spite of himself, then followed Bekker up the long staircase. "I'm down there," Bekker said, when they reached the top. He gestured to the left, but turned to the right. Halfway down the hall, he pushed a door open, reached inside, clicked on a light, stepped back and said, "Here we are."

Stephanie Bekker had slept in an old-fashioned double bed with a rough-cut French frame. The quilt, blankets and sheets were in a heap at the foot of the bed, lying across the frame and partially covering an antique steamer trunk. A dozen magazines on home decorating, antiques and art were piled on the trunk. Near the head of the bed, a Princess phone sat on a bedstand, along with a clock, two more magazines and a Stephen King novel.

A door opened to the left. Lucas stuck his head inside and found a compact but complete bathroom, with a vanity, toilet, tub and shower. A ruby-colored bath towel hung from one of two towel racks. There were traces of fingerprint powder on the vanity, toilet handle, shower handles and towel racks. Lucas turned back into the bedroom, noticed another towel on the red-toned Oriental carpet.

"Just like . . . the night . . ." Bekker said. "The laboratory people said they'd call and tell me when I can clean up. Do you have any idea when that might be?"

"Have they filmed it?"

"I think so. . . ."

"I'll check that, too," Lucas said. He looked at Bekker across the bedroom, measuring him, and asked, "You didn't do it?"

Bekker looked at him now. "No," he said levelly, with the same straightforward, unflinching gaze.

"Well. Nice meeting you," Lucas said.

Outside, the night had turned colder, sliding into frost. The cold air was welcome on his face after the heat of the house. Lucas strolled up the sidewalk, took a right to the alley, looked around and walked down the alley until he was behind Bekker's house. The killer had probably come in this way.

At the side of the house, a light came on, a long narrow shaft gleaming bright at the edge of a curtain. Struck by a sudden impulse, Lucas pushed the gate in the hurricane fence along the backyard. Locked. He glanced around, then vaulted the fence and walked carefully through the dark backyard, feeling with his feet as much as his eyes, wary of loose garbage can lids and invisible clotheslines. . . .

At the side of the house, he moved by inches to the lighted window, put his back to the outside wall, then slowly rotated his head until he could see through the crack.

Bekker was in the study, nude, lurching from one end to the other, chewing convulsively, his face twisted into a mask of pain, terror or religious ecstasy, his eyes turned so far up into his skull that only the whites were visible. He shuddered, twisted, threw out his arms, then collapsed into a leather chair, his mouth half open. For a minute, then two, he didn't move, and Lucas thought he might have had a heart attack or stroke. Then he moved, his arms and legs uncoiling, smoothing themselves into an upright

159

attitude, like that of a king on a throne. Laughing. Bekker was laughing, a mechanical "Ha-ha-ha-ha" choking out of his throat. And still his eyes were looking inward, at God.

Lucas dreamed of Bekker's face. Had to be drugs. Had to be. In the dream he kept arguing that point, that it was drugs; but no drugs were found, and Bekker, lightly restrained by two faceless cops in blue uniforms, would swoop up and screech, *I'm high on Jesus*. . . .

The dream was one of those where Lucas knew he was dreaming but couldn't get out. When the alarm went off, just after one in the afternoon, it was a positive relief. He rolled out, cleaned up and was about to pour a cup of coffee when Del banged on the door.

"You're up," Del said, when Lucas answered.

"Come on in. What's going on?"

"Got some calls on the tip line. Nothing much." He shook a no-nicotine, no-tar cigarette out of a crumpled pack and lit it with a Zippo as they walked through the house to the kitchen. "And Sloan talked to a woman named Beulah Miller this morning—another one of Stephanie Bekker's friends. He asked about the psychologist, and she said, 'Maybe.'"

"But the shrink denies it. . . ."

"So does his wife," Del said. He settled at the kitchen table, and when Lucas held up a pot of coffee, he nodded. "Sloan went back and got her alone. She said he'd had an affair, years ago, and she knew about five minutes after it started. There haven't been any since. And she said that after Sloan went away after the first visit, she went straight back to her husband and asked him. He denied it. Still denies it. And she believes him."

"Has she got a job of her own?" Lucas asked, handing him a cup of hot coffee.

"Sloan thought of that," Del said. "And she does—she's

160

a lobbyist for the Taxpayers' Forum and a couple of other conservative interest groups. She's got a law degree, Sloan says, and she probably makes a pretty good buck."

"So she doesn't need a meal ticket."

"Guess not. Anyway, she suspected that Stephanie was having an affair. They never talked about it, but there were some pretty heavy hints. And she says she thinks they never talked about it because she probably knew the guy, and maybe the guy's wife, and Stephanie didn't know how she'd react. Like she was afraid Miller'd freak out or something."

"So she says it's not her husband, but probably somebody they know. . . ."

"Yeah."

"Did Sloan get a list of possibilities?"

"Naturally. Twenty-two names. But she said some of them were pretty remote possibilities. Sloan's looking at the most likely ones today, the rest of them tomorrow . . . but he got something else you might be interested in."

Lucas raised his eyebrows. "What?"

"Bekker apparently had an affair sometime back, two or three years ago. A nurse. Common talk around the hospital. Sloan got her name and address, went over to see her. She told him to get lost. He pulled the badge, but you know Sloan, he likes people a little too much. . . ."

"Huh. You think . . . ?"

"What I think is, you'd be the perfect guy to talk to her," Del said.

"Why not you?"

"I'd like to come along, but I don't look right to do it by myself," Del said, shaking his long black hair. "I look a little too much like Charlie Manson. People don't let me in the door, even, unless they're assholes. But you—when you put on one of those gray suits, you look like the fuckin' Law."

* * *

Cheryl Clark didn't want to let them in.

"This is about a murder, Miss Clark," Lucas said, cool and official, his ID in her face. "You can talk to us, and the chances are about ninety percent that we'll walk away. Or you can refuse to talk, and we'll take you downtown and let you call a lawyer, and we'll talk to you that way."

"I don't have to talk."

"Yes you do. You don't have the right to refuse to talk. You have the right not to incriminate yourself. If you think you're going to incriminate yourself, then we'll go downtown, you can call a lawyer, we'll get you a grant of immunity from prosecution—and then we'll talk. Or you'll go to jail for contempt of court," Lucas said. His voice warmed up a couple of notches. "Look, we don't want to be jerks—if you haven't done anything criminal, I'm telling you, it'd be a lot easier just to have an informal chat right now."

"I really don't have anything to say," she protested. Her eyes skittered past Lucas to Del, who waited at the foot of the stoop, looking at a motorcycle.

"We'd like to ask anyway," Lucas said.

"Well . . . all right. Come in. But I might not answer," she said.

Her apartment was tidy but impersonal, almost like a motel room. A television was the most prominent piece of furniture, dominating one wall, facing a couch. The couch was covered with a thick green baize that might have been taken off a pool table. A sliding door led to a tiny balcony, with a view toward the Mississippi River valley.

"Is that your boyfriend's Sportster outside?" Del asked, friendly.

"It's mine," Clark said shortly.

"You ride? Far out," Del said. "And you smoke a lot of

162

dope?" He stood in front of the balcony doors, looking out at the river. He was wearing a long-sleeved paisley shirt under a jean jacket, and dirty black jeans with a silver-studded black biker's belt.

"I don't . . ." Clark, dressed in her white nurse's uniform, sat rigidly on her couch. Her eyes, sunk deep in her pale face, were underlined by black smudges. She looked at Lucas. "You said . . ."

"Don't bullshit us," Del said, but in a friendly voice. "Please. I don't give a fuck about the dope, just don't bullshit us. You could get a goddamn contact high off these things." He flicked the curtains with his fingers.

"I don't . . ." she started, then shrugged and said, " . . . smoke a lot."

"Don't worry about it," Lucas said to her. He sat on the couch himself, half turned toward Clark. "You had a relationship with Michael Bekker."

"I told the first officer. It was almost nothing." Her hands fluttered at her chest.

"He's under investigation in the murder of his wife. We're not accusing him, but we're looking at him," Lucas said. "You seem like an intelligent person. What we need from you is . . . an assessment."

"Are you asking me . . . ?"

"Could he kill his wife?"

She looked at him for a moment, then broke her gaze away. "Yes."

"Was he violent with you?"

There was a moment of silence, and then she nodded. "Yes."

"Tell me."

"He . . . used to hit me. With his hands. Open hands, but it hurt. And he choked me once. That time, I thought I might die. But he stopped. . . . He'd go into rages. He seemed unstoppable, but he always . . . stopped."

"What about sexual practices? Anything unusual, bond-age, like that?"

"No, no. The thing is, there almost wasn't any sex." She looked up at Lucas to see if he believed her.

"He's impotent?" Lucas asked.

"He wasn't impotent," she said. She glanced at Del, who nodded, encouraging her. "I mean, sometimes we did, and sometimes we didn't, but he didn't seem driven so much by sex as . . ."

"What?"

Clark's fear of them had slipped into the background and she seemed to be searching for the right phrase, interested despite herself. "He needs to control things. He'd make me do . . . you know, oral sex and so on. Not because it turned him on, I don't think, but because he liked to make me do it. It was the control he liked, not the sex."

"Did he ever use drugs while you were around?"

"No . . . well, he maybe smoked a little marijuana. You know, though, I think he might have used steroids. He has a very good body. . . ." She dropped her eyelashes. "But he had very small testicles."

"Small?"

"Very small . . . almost like marbles," she said. "You know, he lifts weights, and weightlifters sometimes use steroids. Testicles can shrink with prolonged use of ster-oids, so I asked him, and he got angry. . . . That was the time he choked me."

"Did you ever see him dance?" Lucas asked.

"Dance? His dance?" Clark pulled back. "You've been watching him. . . ."

"So you've seen it," Lucas said. Del was frowning at him, confused.

"One time, he beat me up," Clark said in a rush, bounc-ing on the couch. "Not bad, I mean, nothing showed, but

164

I was hurting, and crying, and all of a sudden he started to giggle and jump up and down. I couldn't believe . . . it was like a dance. It *was* a dance, a jig . . ."

"Jesus Christ," Del blurted. "A jig?"

Lucas nodded. "I've seen it. It's gotta be dope. You should talk to your people, see if he's buying on the street."

Del looked at Clark and asked, "Why'd you go along with him?"

She looked up at him and said, "Because he's beautiful."

"Beautiful?"

"He's beautiful. I'd never had a beautiful man." She looked between them, looking for understanding. After a moment, Del nodded.

They left her ten minutes later.

"She knows something else," Lucas said. "She didn't tell us something, and she thinks it might be important."

"Yeah. But there's no way to tell how important it is." Del scratched his head, looking back at the apartment house door. "And if we squeeze, she'll either crack like Humpty-fuckin' Dumpty or call a lawyer. . . ."

"Which is worse . . ."

"Yeah."

They were walking along the sidewalk to the car. "Where's your wife?" Lucas asked suddenly. "I heard she split."

"Yeah. More'n a year ago."

"You gettin' laid?"

"Only by Lady Fingers," Del said, with a dry chuckle. "Look at me, man, I'm a fuckin' wreck. I'm stoned half the time and I'm walkin' around with a gun in my armpit. Who'd go out with me? Other'n maybe a couple of hookers?"

"Yeah." Lucas looked at the other man. "You know

165

what? She kind of liked you. Clark did. Talking about bikes and all. I mean, she's a rider and you're . . . like you are."

Del shook his head. "Man, I can do better'n her."

"You haven't been," Lucas pointed out. "And doing better won't tell us what she knows."

"I'd say twelve or thirteen of them are straight-out nut-cases, and we didn't want to bother you," the dispatcher said, handing Lucas a stack of call slips. "I've marked those. Six of them wouldn't identify themselves at all. You can judge for yourself, but they're a waste of time. . . . There are a half-dozen you ought to get back to. People who knew the Bekkers or Armistead and say they might have a piece of information for you. None of them thought their information was particularly urgent."

"All right. Thanks."

"That last one, she said it was personal."

Lucas looked at it. Cassie Lasch.

He thought about not calling. An easy way out, if you didn't call for long enough. He went home and ate a microwave dinner, aware of the telephone out on the edge of his vision. He lasted an hour before he picked it up.

"You didn't call," Cassie said.

"I'm working. Give me a little time."

"How much time does it take to call? Where do you live?"

"St. Paul."

"Why don't I come over?" she asked.

"Ah . . ." Lucas felt himself freeze for a moment, an impulse to push her away. He was looking at the kitchen table, piled with newspapers and unopened mail, books, some read, some not, a couple of unopened cereal boxes, a stack of unwashed bowls. . . .

He wasn't doing anything. He was barely alive.

"You know where Mississippi River Boulevard is?"

13

Cassie was muscular and intense, and fought him, wrestling across the bed. When they were done, she lay face-down on the extra pillow, while he lay face-up, sweat evaporating from his chest, chilling him.

"Jesus," he said after a while. "That was all right. I was a little worried."

Her head turned. "About what?"

"It's been a while."

She propped herself up on one elbow. "Ah. A little depression?"

"I guess," he said, curiously ready to talk about it. He'd never talked about problems with Jennifer. "I had all the symptoms."

She crawled over him, reaching, switched on the bedside lamp. He winced and turned away from it.

"Look here," she said, showing her wrists to him. There were two whiter lines on the inside of each, parallel, transverse. Scars to be read as clearly as needle tracks.

"What's this shit?" he said. He took her wrists in his hands and stroked the scars with his thumbs.

"What do they look like?"

"Like you cut your wrists," he said.

She nodded. "You win the golden weenie. Fake suicide attempt—that's what the shrinks say. Depression."

"The scars don't look so fake," he said.

"I didn't think so, either," she said, pulling her wrists away. "Are there any cigarettes around here?"

"No. I didn't know you smoked."

"I don't, except after sex," she said.

"Those were pretty heavy cuts. Tell me . . ."

She sat up and pulled her knees under her chin, looking down at him. "This was five years ago. I was never in much danger. A lot of blood, and I had to go to counseling for a few months."

"What's fake about that?" Lucas asked, rolling up on an elbow.

"What the shrinks say is, I was living with this guy and he had a gun, and I knew where it was. And our apartment was on the seventh floor, I could have jumped. And I knew the guy was coming home pretty soon. So they say I really wanted to live and this was just an attempt to draw attention to my condition."

"But the cuts . . ."

"Yeah. The shrinks are full of shit. They can tell you how to talk to someone else, how to deal with personal problems, but they don't know what happens inside your head, unless it's happened to them. I could have jumped out the window. I could have shot myself. But that's not what I thought of. I had this, like . . ."

"Fixation."

"Yeah. Exactly," she said, smiling at him. "See, you *know*. The theater's got a whole oral literature about killing yourself and knives are the way to do it. I fucked it up, did it all wrong—I should have cut myself lengthwise, or at the elbow, but I didn't know that. I could have used little pieces of glass, you get a better cut that way, but I didn't know that, either."

Lucas shuddered. "Glass. I saw that once. You don't want to cut yourself with glass."

"I'll keep that in mind," she said wryly.

"So you cut yourself . . . ?"

"Yep. I just hacked and sat there and bled and cried until my friend came home. They didn't even give me a transfusion at the hospital," Cassie said. "Good thing, too. This was back when there was AIDS in the blood supply. Though who'd ever know, with me fuckin' actors, and all."

"Jesus, that makes me feel good. . . ." He looked down at himself.

"Maybe you oughta run dip it in Lysol . . ." she said.

"Don't have any Lysol—I got some Oven-Off," he said, and laughed. She grinned and patted his leg. "So what were you going to do? Your guns?"

He looked at her for a minute and then nodded. "Yeah. I've got a gun safe down in the basement. It was like they were glowing down there, the guns. Glowing with some kind of gravity, or magnetism, or something. I could feel them wherever I was, pulling me down there. It didn't make any difference if I was on the other side of Minneapolis, I could feel them. I carry a gun, but I never thought about using it. It was the guns in the safe, pulling me down."

"You ever go down? Just to look, or handle them? Stick one in your ear?"

"Nope. I would of felt stupid," Lucas said.

She threw back her head and laughed, but not a happy laugh; an acknowledgment. "I think a lot of suicides are avoided because you'd feel stupid. Or because of the way you'd look afterwards. Like hanging . . ." She gripped herself around the throat and squeezed, crossing her eyes and sticking her tongue out.

"Jesus," he said, laughing again.

She turned serious. "Did you think about it because everything was too painful, or what?"

"No. I just couldn't handle what was going on in my head, this, this *storm*. I couldn't sleep: I'd have these crazy fucking episodes where nine million thoughts would go pounding through my head, and I couldn't stop them. Crazy shit. You know, like the names of people in my senior class, or all the guys on the hockey squad, and all kinds of bizarre shit, and you get crazy because you forget a couple of them."

"That's pretty common," Cassie said, nodding.

"But basically, I thought about the guns because it didn't seem to make any difference whether I lived or died. It was like, Heads I live, tails I die—and if you keep flipping, it'll come up tails, sooner or later."

Cassie nodded. "There was a guy I knew in New York, he used to play Russian roulette with a revolver. About once a year he'd spin that thing, that . . ."

"Cylinder."

"Yeah. Then he'd put the barrel in his mouth and pull the trigger. Right around Christmas time. Said it kept him straight for a whole 'nother year."

"What happened to him?" Lucas asked.

"I don't know. He wasn't that good a friend. He was still alive the last time I was in New York. I could never figure out if he was lucky or unlucky."

"Huh."

She stretched out again, her hands behind her head, and they lay beside each other in comfortable silence for a minute. "Did you have the voice in the back of your head, watching you go through all this shit?" she asked finally.

"Yeah. The watcher. It was like having my own critic back there. My own journalist."

She giggled. "I never thought of it that way, but that's it. Like, the major part of me was hacking away with a bread knife—"

"Ah, fuck, a bread knife?"

"Yeah, the kind with the serrated blade?"

"Ah, Jesus . . ."

"Good brand, too, Solingen . . ."

"God, Cassie . . ."

"Anyway, the big part was hacking away, and this little voice was back there reporting on it, like CNN or something. Kind of skeptical, too."

"Jesus." He reached out and stroked her, from navel to breasts, and back down across her groin to the inside of her knee.

"Pretty gross, huh? Anyway, I'm glad you're getting better."

"I'm not really sure I am. . . ."

"Oh, you are." She patted the bed. "You're here. When you're really depressed, your sex life jumps in a car and leaves for Chicago. I was in this group, as part of the therapy, and every one of the men said so. It wasn't that they couldn't—they just couldn't stand the thought of the complications. Sex is the first thing to go. When it comes back, you're definitely getting better."

The phone rang at eleven o'clock. Lucas woke clear-eyed, rested, already rolling toward the edge of the bed before he was aware of the weight on the other side. He'd slept, and dreamed, and had almost forgotten. . . .

Cassie was lying face-down again, bare as the day she was born, the sheet covering her hips. Her hair had parted on either side of her head, and the light slanting through the venetian blinds played across the sensuous turn of her vertebrae, starting at the nape of her neck, trailing down almost to her just hidden tailbone. He reached down, still aware of the phone, now ringing the fourth time, or fifth, and gently slid the sheet even farther down, onto her legs. . . .

She reached down with one hand and pulled it back up. "Go answer the phone," she grumped, not moving her head.

He grinned and headed for the kitchen, and picked the

171

phone up on the sixth ring. Dispatch. "I've got a call holding from Michael Bekker," the woman said. "Put it through?"

"Yes."

There was a click, a pause, and then Bekker said, "Hello?"

"Yeah, this is Davenport."

"Yes, Lucas. Will you be free tonight, late?" Bekker's voice was low, friendly, carefully modulated. "I've got classes, then a dinner, but I've found something in my wife's papers that I thought was interesting. I'd like to show it to you. . . ."

"Can you tell me on the phone?"

"Mmm, why don't you come over? Somebody'll have to anyway, and I'd prefer it be you. That other police-man . . . he's a bit thick."

Swanson. Not thick at all, although any number of Stillwater inmates had made the mistake of thinking so. . . . "All right. What time?"

"Tennish?"

"I'll see you then."

Lucas hung up and padded back to the bedroom. The bed was empty, and water was running in the bathroom. Cassie was bent over the sink, using his toothbrush. He winced, then reached out and touched her bottom.

"Hi," she said through a mouthful of bubbles, looking into the mirror over the sink. "Done in a minute. Breath like a dinosaur. And I gotta pee."

"I'll run down to the other bathroom," he said. He went down the hall, looked back to make sure she wasn't following, opened a drawer, took out a new toothbrush, peeled the package, removed the brush and hastily stuffed the packaging back in the drawer. He was smiling when he looked at himself in the mirror.

Back in the bedroom, he found the sheets and blankets

172

in a pile on the floor, while she lounged in the middle of the bed.

"Hop in," she said, patting the mattress beside her. "We're right on time for a nooner and we're not even up yet. Ain't it great?"

After Cassie left, in a cab, he spent the rest of the day fooling around, unable to focus much on the case, making call-backs, driving around town, checking the net. He walked past Bekker's house again, and spoke to a neighbor who was raking the winter gunk from his lawn. Stephanie had once had a cocker spaniel, the neighbor said, and when Bekker had had to walk it in the winter, he'd take it up to the corner and then "kick the shit out of it. I saw him out the window, he did it several times." The neighbor's wife, who had been splitting iris bulbs, turned and said, "Be fair, tell him about the shoes."

"Shoes?"

"Well, yeah, the dog had bad kidneys, I guess, and he used to sneak up to Bekker's closet and pee in his shoes."

Lucas and the neighbor started laughing at the same time.

In the evening, an hour before Cassie went on at the Lost River, she and Lucas walked down the block for a cup of coffee. They sat across from each other in a diner booth, and Cassie said, "Ultimately, you're not flaky enough for me. But it'd be nice if we could keep it together for a couple of months."

Lucas nodded. "That'd be nice."

At five after ten, he walked up the steps to Bekker's. Lights blazed from several of the ground-floor windows, and Lucas resisted the temptation to go window-peeking again. Instead he rang the bell, and Bekker came to the door, wrapped in a burgundy dressing gown.

173

"Is that your Porsche?" he asked in surprise, looking past Lucas to the street.

"Yeah. I have a little money of my own," Lucas said.

"I see." Bekker was genuinely impressed. He knew the price of a Porsche. "Well, come along."

Lucas followed him into the study. Bekker seemed skittish, nervous. He would try something, Lucas decided.

"Scotch?"

"Sure."

"I've got a nice one. I used to drink Chivas, but a couple of months ago Stephanie . . ."—he paused on the name, as if calling up her face—"Stephanie bought me a bottle of Glenfiddich, a single malt. . . . I won't be going back to the other."

Lucas couldn't tell one scotch from another. Bekker dropped ice cubes into a glass, poured two fingers of liquor over them and handed the glass to Lucas. He looked at his watch, and Lucas thought it odd that he would be wearing a watch with a dressing gown. "So what'd you find?" Lucas asked.

"A couple of things," Bekker said. He settled behind the desk, leaned back with the scotch and crossed his legs. They flashed from the folds of the dressing gown like a woman's legs from an evening dress. Deliberately, Lucas thought. He thinks I might be gay, and he's trying to seduce me. He took a sip of the scotch. "A couple of things," Bekker repeated. "Like these."

He picked up a stack of colored cardboard slips, bound together with a rubber band, and tossed them across the desk. Lucas picked them up. They were tickets to shows at the Lost River. He thumbed through: eight of them, in three different colors.

"Notice anything peculiar about them, Lucas?" Bekker asked. Using his first name again.

"They're from the Lost River, of course. . . ." Lucas

rolled the rubber band off and looked at the tickets individually. "All for matinees . . . and there are eight tickets for three different shows. All punched, all different shows."

Bekker mimed applause, then held up his glass to Lucas, as if toasting him. "I knew you were intelligent. Don't you find you can always tell? Anyway, the second woman who was killed worked for the Lost River, correct? I went to a couple of evening performances with Stephanie, but I had no idea she was going in the afternoons. So I began to wonder: Could her lover . . . ?"

"I see," Lucas said. A connection. And it seemed to let Bekker out.

"And I also found this," Bekker said. He leaned forward this time, and handed Lucas several letter-sized sheets of paper. American Express account sheets, with various items underlined in blue ballpoint ink. "The underlined charges are for tickets at the Lost River. Six or seven times over the past few months, on her personal card. A couple of them match with the matinee dates and the charge amount is right. And then, on four of the days, there's a dining charge, and none less than thirty dollars. I'd bet she was taking somebody to dinner. That restaurant, the Tricolor Bar, I've been there once or twice, but not in the afternoons . . ."

Lucas looked at the papers, then over the top of them at Bekker. "You should have shown these to Swanson."

"I don't like the man," Bekker said, looking at him levelly. "You, I like."

"Well, good," Lucas said. He drank the last of the scotch. "You seem like a pretty reasonable guy yourself. Pathology, right? Maybe I'll call you on one of my games; you could consult."

"Your games?" Bekker glanced at his watch again, then quickly looked away.

175

What's going on? "Yeah, I invent games. You know, historical strategy games, role-playing games, that sort of thing."

"Hmph. I'd be interested in talking sometime," Bekker said. "Really."

14

Bekker shut the door behind Lucas and dashed upstairs, leaving the lights out. He went to the window over the porch and split the curtains with an index finger. Davenport was just getting into his Porsche. A moment later the car's lights came on, and in another minute it was gone. Bekker let the curtain fall back into place and hurried to his bedroom. He dressed in dark blue slacks, a gray sweatshirt and navy jacket, loafers. He gobbled a methamphetamine and went out the back, through the garage, and got in the car.

A neighborhood restaurant had a pay phone just inside the door. He stopped, dialed, got the answering machine on the second ring—a message was waiting. He punched in the code, 4384. The machine rewound, paused, then Druze's voice blurted a single syllable.

Druze hunched over the wheel, the weight of the night pressing on him.

Like the tarbaby. One foot stuck, then you have to kick with the other one, then you have to punch him, and your fist gets stuck. . . .

This would be the last for him. He'd talk Bekker out of the third killing. There was no need for a third. Not now. He'd seen them on television, and the cops were convinced: one killer, a psycho.

Druze was orbiting a red-brick university building, Peik Hall, watching. Lots of lights, big orange sodium-vapor anti-crime lights, walk lights, globe lights outside the entrances to the university buildings. Lots of trees and shrubbery, too. Good cover. And nobody around.

The night was cold, with heavy broken clouds darting across the sky, a full moon sailing between them; and it smelled of coming rain. A good night for beer and brats and television in the Riverside Avenue taverns with the theater crowd. Druze could never be one of the happy crowd, throwing darts or chattering, but he could sit on his stool at the end of the bar, feeling a little of the reflected warmth. Anything would be better than this—but he had nobody to blame for this but himself. He should have gone after the fat man. . . .

Druze was wearing the ski jacket again, but this time as much for concealment as for protection from the weather. He wouldn't want George to recognize him prematurely.

George's Cherokee was parked in a small public parking lot tucked behind an older building adjacent to Peik Hall. Pillsbury Drive, a cross-campus road, ran past the end of the lot. After ten o'clock there was little traffic—but there was some. Every few minutes or so, a car went past, and the road was smooth enough that you couldn't hear it coming.

One other car was parked in the lot, across from George's. Druze circled the campus complex as long as he dared, then parked his Dodge wagon beside George's Jeep, leaving a full parking space between them. He sat for a moment, watching, then got out, listened a few seconds more. The lot was poorly lit, with most of the light coming from a bowl-shaped fixture on the back of the building.

No people around, unless they were hiding in the bushes. Druze started toward the sidewalk that led past the building, stopped next to a bush of bridal wreath and listened again, ten seconds, twenty. Nothing. He walked back to the Jeep, squatted, took a tire-pressure gauge out of his pocket, reversed it and used the spike to let the air out of the Cherokee's left rear tire. George had to approach from that side; he should see it.

The hissing air sounded like a train whistle in Druze's ears, and it seemed to go on forever. But it didn't. In less than a minute, the tire was flat. Druze stood, looked around again and wandered away.

The parking meters. Jesus Christ.

He walked back and plugged the university's twenty-four-hour parking meters. He'd have to remember to look for the campus cops. They checked the parking lots once or twice a night. A ticket would be a disaster.

Druze didn't feel anything when he killed—revulsion, sorrow, empathy. He didn't fear much, either. But tonight there was an edge of apprehension: it came as he almost walked away from the meters. Suppose he came back, killed George and only then noticed a ticket on his windshield? They'd have him. Or, like Brer Rabbit with the tarbaby, he'd be chasing around the campus, hunting down the cop with the ticket book. He'd have to kill him to get the book. And then . . .

That'd be impossible. That was a nightmare, not a rational possibility. Druze shivered and hunched his shoulders. He hadn't expected to get this tangled.

A woman student, carrying books, walked by on the other side of the street, looking resolutely away from him. He went out to University Avenue, keeping an eye on the lighted windows in Peik. Bekker had scouted the building, told him which ones to watch. . . . A black kid in a red jacket hurried by, on the other side of the street. Another kid, white, wearing a white helmet and a daypack, zipped past on Rollerblades.

Druze sauntered now, moving into actor mode, one hand in his pocket, on the handle of the antique German knife-sharpening steel. The steel was as heavy as a fireplace poker, but shorter, eighteen inches long, tapering like a sword, with a smooth hickory handle. He'd shoved the point of the steel right through the bottom of his pocket. The handle was big enough for the steel to hang there on its own, cold down his leg, out of sight. He'd practiced drawing it. It came out smoothly and swung like a pipe wrench, with better balance. It would do the job. Druze moved off University Avenue and walked across a lawn outside Peik. He was doing a lot for Bekker, he thought, and then: But not only for Bekker. This is for me, I'm the one he'd recognize . . .

At five minutes after ten, three students carrying books came out the front door of Peik Hall. They stopped on the steps for a moment; then one of the men went left, the man and woman right. Another minute passed, and another knot of students came out of the building, talking, and walked away together. A bank of lights went off in the target windows, then another. Druze drifted out toward University Avenue again, then down Pillsbury, toward the parking lot. He walked to the far end of the lot, stepped between two bushes, waited, waited. . . .

Two men walked into the lot, from along the side of the building. He could hear their voices, at first like a faraway typewriter, clacking, then as human speech:

". . . Can't figure out how they won it, given the way the company failed to warn anybody about the gas-tank leaks . . ." The speaker was the shorter of the two men.

"Juries. You have to keep that in mind, always. There's no absolutely good way to predict what they'll do, even with the best screening program. In this particular . . . Oh, shit." The conversation stopped. Druze started back up the sidewalk toward the building. If there were two of them, he'd have to forget it. "Look at the goddamn tire. It's only three months old. . . ."

"You want me . . ." the other man offered. A student, Druze thought.

"No, no, I can change it in two minutes," George said, peering down at the tire in disgust. "But it pisses me off,

180

excuse the expression. I should be able to drive over railroad spikes with those tires. . . . Now, there's a case for you, Mr Brekke. Sue the goddamn tire company for me. . . ."

"Glad to . . ."

There was more talk and a clatter of tools as the slender student stood and watched the heavyset professor dismount the spare from the Jeep. Druze, feeling something almost like relief, thought the student would stay. But after watching for a couple of minutes, the man looked at his watch and said, "Well, my wife will be wondering . . ."

"Go on. This'll just take a minute."

The student was gone, rolling out of the lot, never looking toward Druze's bush. Druze let him go, heard his car accelerate down University. . . . The professor had his jacket off, his shirt sleeves rolled up, and he grunted and cursed in the night. The flat came off, the spare went on. He seemed to know what he was doing, working without wasted motion. With a series of quick twists, the spare was lugged down.

Druze took a deep breath, got a grip on the sharpening steel with his right hand and stepped into the parking lot, jingling his car keys with his left hand, moving slowly.

The professor popped open the back of the Jeep, leaving the keys in the lock—everything was moving slowly for Druze now, everything was in needle-sharp focus—lifted the flat, holding it carefully clear of his trousers, and heaved it inside the Jeep.

Druze was ten feet away, checking, checking. Nobody around. Nothing coming on Pillsbury, no cars: The professor, a big, beefy blond man, slamming the back of the Jeep, now turning at the sound of Druze's keys . . . The keys would be a soothing sound, suggesting that Druze was headed for the last car in the lot. . . .

"Flat tire?" Druze asked.

181

The professor nodded without a flicker of recognition, although Druze was less than a long step away. "Yeah, damn thing was flat as a pancake."

"Got it under control?" Druze asked, slowing. He looked around a last time: Nothing. The handle of the sharpening steel was cool in his hand.

"Oh yeah, no problem," George said, pulling on his jacket. His hands were black with grease from the lug nuts.

"Well . . ." Druze drew the steel behind his leg and stepped on, heading for his car, then pivoted and swung the steel one-handed, half overhead, like a whip, or a machete chopping sugarcane. The steel crashed through the side of George's head, two inches above his right ear. The professor bounced off the Jeep and down. Druze hit him again, but it was unnecessary: the first blow had crushed the side of his head. A sudden stench told Druze that George's bowels had relaxed. Neither he nor Bekker had thought about the stink the body could make in the car.

No reason to be furtive now: if anyone came in the next thirty seconds, it was over. Druze grabbed George under the arms, dragged him to the station wagon. The building lights, which had seemed remote and inadequate a few moments before, now seemed bright as stadium lights. Druze snatched open the wagon's back door and threw the body on the black plastic garbage bags that covered the floor behind the front seat. A short-handled spade was on the floor below the bags. When George's body hit the floor, it landed on the tip of the blade, and the handle popped up, tearing the bags. Druze swore and pushed the handle down, but now the body rolled. . . .

George was heavy, and his legs were still sticking out of the car. Druze struggled, half frantic, trying to bend the legs; then he grappled with the overweight torso, pulling on the sport coat lapels, not seeing the bloody twisted head, trying to lift the torso farther into the car while he pressed the feet in behind. The spade bounded up and down like a teeter-totter, obstructing everything. Druze was sweating heavily by the time he finished.

Never been scared . . . He was scared now. Not badly, but enough to identify the emotion, a feeling that went back to the days of the burning. The hospital baths, where they peeled the dead skin . . . those had scared him. The transplants had scared him. When the doctor had come to check his progress, that had scared him. He hadn't been scared since he'd left the hospital. But he felt it now, a distant tingle, but definitely there. . . .

When George was fully inside the car, on the floor behind the front seat, Druze covered the body with more black plastic garbage bags and then folded the back seats down over it. The seats didn't quite cover it, but to anyone looking casually inside, the wagon would appear empty.

He slammed the door, went back to the Jeep, got the keys out of the back door, shoved them between the curb and the front tire, then checked the meter: ten minutes. Druze took more quarters from his pocket, put in two hours' worth, then went back to the wagon. Nobody around. Nothing but the lights of Minneapolis, over across the river, and the distant sound of an unhappy taxi horn on Hennepin Avenue.

What if the wagon wouldn't start? What if . . . The wagon turned over, and he rolled it out of the lot, took a right. Met no cars. Turned onto University Avenue, let a breath out. Past the frat houses . . . Checked the gas gauge for the hundredth time. Full. He drove down Oak Street, then left, and then onto I-94, and pointed the car east toward Wisconsin.

The drive was eerie. Quiet. He had the feeling that the car was standing still, with the lights zooming by, like a nightmare. A cop crossed the overhead ramp at Snelling.

Druze kept his eyes glued on the rearview mirror, but the cop continued south on Snelling, and out of sight.

He crossed the Fifth Street exit, past Highway 61, and exited at White Bear Avenue. Drove into a Standard station, called the number Bekker had given him, got the answering machine and spoke a single syllable: "*Yes*."

Back on I-94, fifty-five miles per hour all the way, ignoring the signs for sixty-five, through the double bridge across the St. Croix River at Hudson, out of Minnesota and up the Wisconsin side. The interstate mileage signs started on the western ends of each state, so he could count the ascending numbers as he moved deeper into Wisconsin, ten miles, twelve. He took the exit specified by Bekker, heading north.

Four-point-two miles, three red reflectors on a sign at the turn-off. He found it, right where Bekker had said, took the turn-off and bumped down a dirt track. Two-tenths of a mile. The track ended at a simple post-and-beam log cabin, a door in the center, a square window on either side of the door. The cabin was dark. In the headlights, he could see a brass padlock hanging from a hasp on the door.

Beyond the cabin, Druze could see moonlight on the lake. Not much of a lake; almost like a large pond, rimmed with cattails. He turned off the car lights, got out and walked down to the water, his feet groping for the path between the cabin and the water. There was a dark form off to his left, and he stepped next to it, trying to figure out what it was. Boards, on a steel frame, tires . . . a roll-out dock. Okay.

On the opposite side of the lake, he could see a single lighted window but not the house around it. There was no sound but the wind in the trees. He stood for a moment, listening, watching, then hurried back up to the car.

George was easier to handle this time, because Druze

184

didn't have to move so quickly or quietly. He got a flashlight from the glove compartment, then grabbed George by the necktie and the crotch, and hauled him out of the wagon. He threw the body over his shoulder like a sack of oatmeal and carried it down past the end of the track, as Bekker had said, past the tire swing hanging from the cottonwood. He flicked the light off and on, as he needed to spot footing; he was walking diagonally away from the cabin across the lake, so the light wouldn't be visible at the other house.

Blackberry brambles, dead but still armed, plucked at his clothing. Through the brambles, Bekker had said. Just go straight on back, nobody goes out there. Bekker and Stephanie had explored the place three years earlier, when she had been looking for a lake cabin. They'd seen the "For Sale" sign on the way back from another lake, stopped to look, found the cabin vacant, stayed for ten minutes, then moved on. The cabin was primitive: an outhouse, no running water, no insulation. Summer only. Stephanie hadn't been interested, and nobody in the world knew they had been there.

Druze pushed through the brambles until the ground went soft, then dumped the body. He flicked the light on, looked around. He was on the edge of a bleak, rough-looking tamarack swamp. Bekker was right. It could be years before anyone came back here. Or never . . .

Druze walked back to the car, got the spade and went to work. He labored steadily for an hour, feeling his muscles overheat. Nothing fancy, he thought; just a hole. He dug straight down, a pit three feet in diameter, the soil getting heavier and wetter as he dug deeper. He hit a few roots, flailed at them with the spade, cut through, went deeper, covering himself with muck. At the end he had a waist-deep hole, flooded ankle-deep with muddy water. He climbed out of it, beaten, grabbed the body by the necktie and pant-leg, and dumped it headfirst into the hole. There was a splash, and he flicked the light on. George's head was underwater, his feet sticking up. His socks had fallen down around very white ankles, Druze noticed, and one shoe had a hole in the sole. . . .

He stood for a moment, resting, the clouds whipping overhead like black ships, the moon sliding behind one, then peeking out, then going down again. Cold, he thought. Like Halloween. He shivered, and started to fill the hole.

No one saw, no one heard.

He backed the car out, not turning on the headlights until he was down the track. He was in St. Paul before he realized he'd forgotten to cut George's eyes.

Fuck his eyes. And fuck Bekker.

Druze was free of the tarbaby.

Two campus cops cruised past George's Jeep and flashed the meter. More than an hour on the clock.

"*Yes.*"

The single syllable was in his ear, like stone, so hard. George was dead.

Bekker, standing in the hallway outside the restaurant entrance, dropped the phone in its cradle and danced his little jig, bobbing up and down, hopping from foot to foot, chortling. Caught himself. Looked around, guilty. Nobody. And they were clean. There were details to be tidied away, but they were details. After he got rid of the Jeep, there'd be no way to connect him to anything. Well: there'd be one way. But that was a detail.

He glanced at his watch: not quite midnight. Druze should be in Wisconsin by now. Bekker walked out to his car, drove to the hospital, parked. Took the cigarette case from his pocket, opened it in the gloom, popped one of the special Contac capsules, inhaled. The coke hit him immediately, and he rode with it, head back, eyes closed. . . .

Time to go. Nobody was following, but if someone was, he could handle it. He and his friends. He walked through the hospital lobby and took the stairs. Down, this time. Used his key to get into the tunnel and walked through the maintenance tunnel to the next building. Everybody did it, especially in the winter. But the cops wouldn't know.

Careful, he told himself, paranoia . . . there were no cops. The dope was in his blood . . . but what was it, exactly? He couldn't quite remember. There had been some amphetamines, he always did those, and a lick of the PCP; he'd had some aspirin, a lot of aspirin, actually, for an incipient headache, and his regular doses of anabolic steroids for his body and the synthetic growth hormone as part of his anti-aging trip. All balanced, he thought: and for creativity, a taste of acid? He couldn't remember.

He walked out of the next building, pulling his collar up, the brim of his hat down. Peik Hall was three minutes away. He got close, walked behind a building onto Pillsbury, down the street, pulling on his driving gloves. The Jeep was there, right where it should be. He stooped, found the keys, unlocked the door and got inside. This was the risky part. Fifteen minutes' worth. But if he got the car to the airport, the cops might be bluffed into thinking that George had taken off on his own. . . .

The campus cops came back ten minutes later. The Jeep was gone. One of the cops saw something round and flat winking up at her in the headlights, and she said, "Something over there?"

"Where?"

"Right there. Looks like money."

187

She got out, stooped and picked it up. Lug nut. She tossed it in the back of the squad car.

"Nothing," she said.

Bekker took the Jeep out the same way Druze had driven, down to I-94, but westbound, to I-35W, south on I-35W and then on the Crosstown Expressway to the airport. He dropped the Cherokee in the long-term parking garage and left the ticket under the visor. Back on the street, he flagged a cab, keeping his hat down against the wind and against identification.

"Where to?" the cabbie grunted. He wasn't interested in talking.

"The Lost River Theater, on Cedar Avenue . . ."

From the Lost River, it was a twenty-minute walk to the hospital. He went in the way he'd come out, walked up to his office and sat for ten minutes. He remembered to call the answering machine and, using the touch-tone buttons, ordered it to reset. He waited a few more minutes, impatient, then turned off the lights in his office and went back down to his car.

At home, Bekker stripped off his clothes as he walked up the stairs, dropping them wherever they came off. Stephanie would have been outraged; he smiled as he thought about it. He crawled into his closet and took two tabs of phenobarbital, two more of methaqualone, two of methadone, a heavy hit of acid, five hundred mikes. The warmth was incredible. The drugs unwound as they always did—color sequences, clips from life, fantasies, the face of God—then shaded unexpectedly from yellows and reds through pinks into purples; and finally, the fear growing in his throat, Bekker watched the snake uncurl.

The snake was huge, scaleless, more like an eel than a snake, no mouth, just a long cold form unwinding, curling into him.

188

And George was there.

He didn't say anything, George: he simply watched and grew. His eyes were black, but somehow bright as diamonds. He closed on Bekker, the eyes growing larger, the mouth beginning to open, a forked tongue deep inside. . . .

Bekker had killed three whores in Vietnam. He'd done it carefully, confident that he'd never be exposed; he'd worn an enlisted man's uniform, the Class A greens of a spec-5 killed in a Saigon traffic accident, the uniform dumped at Bekker's doorstep in a black satchel that had been with the dead man in his Jeep.

Bekker had strangled the three women. It hadn't been hard. They'd been specialists of a sort, unsurprised when he let them know that he wanted to sit on their chests. More surprised when he pinned their hands. Definitely surprised when he clamped his powerful fingers on their throats, crushing the cartilage with a powerful pinch of his thumb and forefinger . . .

The first one had looked straight into his eyes as she'd died, and it was there Bekker had had his first hint that she'd seen something beyond.

And she was the one who'd come back.

She'd preyed on him, haunted him, followed him with her black eyes. For six weeks he'd doped himself, screaming through the nights, afraid of sleep. He'd seen her in his waking hours, too, in the shiny reflections from his instruments, from mirrors, in panes and fragments of glass . . .

She'd faded, finally, beaten down with drugs. And Bekker had known instinctively that the physical eyes made the difference.

For the next woman, he'd been prepared. He'd pinned her, choked her and, with a stainless-steel scalpel, cut her eyes as she'd died. And slept like a baby.

The third one had died quickly, too quickly, before he could cut her eyes. He had cut them dead, but he still feared that she would follow him into his dreams: that it was necessary to cut the *living eyes*.

But it was not. He'd never seen that one again.

He'd cut the eyes on the old man dying of congestive heart failure, and the old woman with the stroke—they'd delivered those two right to him, in the pathology department, and he still had the taped description of the cutting of the old woman's eyes. And he'd cut the eyes of the boy and the girl from Pediatric Oncology, although he'd had to take a good deal more risk with those. The girl he'd gotten to just before they moved her body out of the hospital. For the boy, he'd had to go to the funeral home and wait his chance.

That had been a bad two days, waiting, the boy out there. . . .

But in the end he'd cut them all.

He hadn't been able to cut George. And George was here now, coming for him.

Deep in his closet, naked, his arms wrapped around his knees, his eyes wide and staring into the beyond, Bekker began to scream.

15

"You're sure?" Lucas asked Swanson. "It's Loverboy?"

Swanson scratched his belly and nodded. "It's gotta be. I went over to Bekker's as soon as I heard. Shook him out of bed. This was about three hours ago, six A.M., and he looked terrible, and I said, 'For the lover, how about Philip George from the law school?' He went like this"—Swanson mimed Bekker's perplexed look—"and he said, quote, If you told me so, I wouldn't be . . . shocked, I guess. I mean, we knew him. Why? Is it him? Unquote. Then I told him about George. He seemed kind of freaked out."

"You got the time George disappeared? It's nailed down? Exactly?"

"Yeah. Within five minutes, I'd bet," Swanson said, nodding. He was unshaven, holding an empty Styrofoam coffee cup, his eyes glassy from fatigue and caffeine. He'd been rousted out of bed at five o'clock, after four hours' sleep. "There was a guy with him, a student, when George started changing the tire. The student was supposed to get right home to his wife, she's pregnant, due anytime, so he was anxious. Anyway, he's got a clock on the dashboard of his car. He said he looked at it going out of the lot, and remembers it was ten-fourteen. He remembers that close. . . ."

"What about this shrink Shearson's been looking at?"

Swanson shrugged. "I always thought that was bullshit, but Daniel wanted him covered."

"Sonofabitch," Lucas said in a black fury. Del was leaning in the doorway, listening, and Lucas bolted past

191

him, out of his office, took a turn down the hallway, then almost trotted back, his face white. "The cocksucker was using me as an alibi. You know that? I'm Bekker's fuckin' alibi. . . ."

"If George is dead," Swanson said. "That's a pretty big if. And if Bekker had something to do with it . . ."

Lucas poked Swanson in the gut with his index finger. "George is dead. And Bekker did it. Believe it." Lucas turned to Del. "Remember when you said the San Francisco alibi was a little too convenient?"

"Yeah?"

"Well, how about this? He invites an investigating *cop* over for a drink, to talk, *he tries to fuckin' seduce me, man*, precisely when the main witness is being taken off. How's that for a motherfucking coincidence?"

Del shrugged. He didn't say "I told you so," but his shoulders did.

Lucas turned back to Swanson, remembering his odd characterization of Bekker. Bekker had looked fine the night before: sleek, even. Beautiful. "You said he looked terrible? What do you mean?"

"He looked fucked up," Swanson said. "He looked like he was a hundred years old. He ain't getting no sleep."

"'Cause he was working a fuckin' murder. That's why. 'Cause he had a murder going down last night," Lucas said. "All right. We're gonna take him down. One way or another"—this time he poked Del—"the motherfucker falls."

Sloan was coming down the hall, rolling an unlit cigarette around between his lips, his hands deep in the pockets of his trench coat.

"Bekker did it?" he asked.

"Fuckin' absolutely," Lucas said grimly.

"Huh," Sloan said. He shifted the unlit cigarette. "You

think he killed George before or after he drove his Jeep out to the airport?"

Lucas looked at him blankly: "Say what?"

"Airport cops listed the bulletin for his Jeep, found it in the long-term ramp. Long-term. Like he ain't planning to come back."

Lucas shook his head. "Bullshit. If George is the one, he ain't running. He's dead."

"We don't know that for sure," Sloan said. "He coulda took off for Brazil. He could of cracked, decided to split."

"Who's talking to his wife?" Lucas asked.

"Neilson, but I'm going over later," Sloan said.

"I tell you, the motherfucker is dead," Lucas said, settling back in his chair. "How's he gonna leave a lug nut in the parking lot? How can you forget to put on a lug nut? You've got the bolt sticking out at you, you can't forget. The flat tire was a set-up."

"How old is the Jeep?" Del asked Sloan.

Sloan shrugged. "New."

"See?" Lucas said with satisfaction. "Flat, my ass."

They were still arguing when Harmon Anderson leaned in the door, a piece of white paper in his hand. "You'll never guess," he said to Lucas. "I'll give you two hundred guesses and betcha a million bucks you don't get it."

"You don't got a million bucks," Swanson said. "What is it?"

Anderson dramatically unfolded the paper, a Xerox copy, and held it up like an auctioneer at an art sale, pivoting, to give everybody a look.

"What is it?" Del asked.

The Xerox showed a painting of a one-eyed giant with a misshapen head, half turned, peering querulously over a hill, a naked sleeping woman in the foreground.

"Ta-da," Anderson said. "The Bekker killer, as seen by Mrs Bekker's lover. A cyclops, is what it is."

"What the fuck?" Sloan said, taking the paper, frowning at it, passing it to Lucas.

"We got it in the mail—actually, this is a copy, they're looking at the original for prints," Anderson said.

"Is the original in black and white?" Lucas asked.

"Yeah, a Xerox. And there's a note from Loverboy. We're sure it's for real, because he goes over some of the stuff he said in the first letter. Calls him a troll, not a giant."

"Jesus," said Lucas, rubbing his forehead, staring at the face of the giant. "I know this guy from somewhere."

"Who? The troll?"

"Yeah. I know him, but I don't know from where."

The other three cops looked at Lucas for a moment; then Sloan said skeptically, "You been talking to any gruff billy goats lately?"

"When was it mailed?" Lucas asked.

Anderson shrugged. "Sometime yesterday, that's all we know."

"Anybody know where this painting comes from?" Lucas asked.

"Not as far as I know . . . We could check it out."

"I mean, if it's from a book, maybe he got it out of the library or something," Lucas suggested.

Sloan and Swanson looked at each other, and then Sloan said, "Right. See, this guy is really freaked out after witnessing this killing, and he's got about a hundred cops on his ass, so he goes down to the library and says, Here's my card, just go ahead and put me in your permanent computer records so Lucas Davenport can come in here. . . ."

"Yeah, yeah, it's weak," Lucas said, waving Sloan off.

"It's not fuckin' weak, it's fuckin' limp."

194

Lucas looked at the photocopy. "Can I keep this?"

"Be my guest," Anderson said. "We only got as many as you can make on a Xerox machine."

Bekker, straight, the morning sun slashing into him, went out to a phone booth and called Druze.

"You didn't do the eyes," he said, when the receiver was picked up.

There was a long silence, and then: "No. I forgot."

"Jesus, Carlo," Bekker groaned. "You're killing me."

Lucas went home at noon, driving through a light, cold drizzle, darker clouds off to the west. He spent five minutes building a turkey sandwich with mustard, put it on a paper plate, got a Leinenkugel from the refrigerator, went and sat in the spare bedroom and stared at the wall.

He hadn't been in the room for months, and dust balls, like mice, half hid under the edge of the guest bed. On the walls were pinned a series of paper charts, laying out possibilities and connections: traces of the Crows case. Most of what he needed to find the men was on the charts, organized, poised, waiting for the final note. He closed his eyes, heard the gunfire again, the screams. . . .

He stood, exhaled and began pulling down the charts, pushing the pins back into the wall. He looked over the names, remembering, then ripped the papers in halves, in quarters, in eighths, and carried them to the study and dumped them into his oversized waste-basket.

The drawing pad was still there, and he sat down, opened it, chose with some care the precisely right felt-tip marker and began to make lists as he ate the turkey sandwich.

Bekker, he wrote at the top of the first sheet. And under that: *Drugs, Times and Places. Friends?* At the top of a second he wrote *Killer*. And below that:

> Looks like troll
> Knows Bekker
> Could be dope dealer?
> Is he paid? Check Bekker accounts
> Theater connection?
> Do I know him?

On the Bekker sheet, he added:

> Cheryl Clark
> Vietnam killings
> Cancer kids

On a third sheet he wrote *Loverboy*, and underneath:

> Cleaned drain
> Changed sheets
> Xeroxed note
> Philip George?

He carried the new charts to the bedroom, pinned them on the wall and stared at them.

Why had the killer gone after George, if indeed he had? If George had known him, why hadn't he said so when he called 911? And if he hadn't known him, why would the killer worry about it? Maybe they worked together, or moved in the same social circles? That didn't fit with the drug thing . . . unless George was a user? Or maybe George was involved with Bekker? What if Bekker, a doctor, was dealing, and a junkie knew that, came into his house . . . but then, why Armistead?

He stood, speculating, trying to come up with something he could hold onto and work with. He found it right away. He thought about it, got his jacket and called Dispatch. As he dialed, he looked out the window: still raining. A cold, miserable slanting spring rain, out of the northwest.

"Could you get in touch with Del and have him meet me

at the office?" he asked when Dispatch came on. "No big rush, this afternoon sometime . . ."

"He's sitting in a bar," the dispatcher said. "He's taking calls there, if you want the number. . . ."

"Sure." Lucas took a piece of paper from his shirt pocket, the Xerox of the painting of the one-eyed giant, and scribbled down the number. When he called, a bartender answered and put Del on. He could meet Lucas at four o'clock. As they talked, Lucas looked at the giant peering at the sleeping woman. The creature had a nearly round head, like a basketball, and thin, wide twisting lips. Where . . . ?

When he finished talking to Del, Lucas pulled out the phone book and called the rare-book room at the university library.

"Carroll? Lucas Davenport."

"Lucas, you haven't been coming to the games. Zhukov is about to go after the Romanians north of Stalingrad. . . ."

"Yeah, Elle told me. She said you needed Nazis."

"No fun for the Nazis from here on out . . ."

"Listen, I need some help. I've got a picture of a one-eyed giant. He's looking over a mountain at a sleeping woman and he's got a club. It's a painting and it's kind of crude. Childlike, but I don't think a kid did it. There's something good about it."

"It's a one-eyed giant, like a cyclops from *The Odyssey*?"

"Yeah, exactly. Somebody said it's a troll, but somebody else said that technically it's a cyclops. I'm trying to figure out what book it came from, if it came from a book."

There was a moment of silence, then the book expert said, "Damned if I'd know. An expert on *The Odyssey* might, but you'd have to get lucky. There are probably about a million different illustrations of cyclopes."

"Shit . . . So what do I do?"

"You say it's crude but good. You mean slick-crude, like a *Playboy* illustration, or . . ."

"No. The more I look at it, the more I think it might be famous. Like I said, there's something about it."

"Huh. Well, you *could* take it over to the art history department. There's a good chance that nobody will be there, and if there is somebody there, he might not talk to you unless you've got a fee statement."

"Hmpf. Okay, well, thanks, Carroll . . ."

"Wait a minute. There's a painter, over there in St. Paul—actually, he's a computer genius of some kind—and he comes in here to look at book illustrations. He's pretty expert on art history. I've got a number, if you want to give him a ring."

"Sure." Lucas heard the receiver being laid on a desk, then a minute of silence, then the receiver being picked up again.

"The guy is a little remote, out in the ozone, like painters get. Use my name, but be polite. Here's the number. . . . And come on back to the games. You can be Paulus."

"Jeez, I don't know what to say. . . ."

When he got the book expert off the line, Lucas dialed the number. The phone rang five or six times and he was about to hang up when it was answered. The painter sounded as though he'd been asleep, his voice gruff, cool. An edge of wariness entered it when Lucas explained he was a cop.

"I got your name from Carroll over at the U. I've got a question that he said you might be able to help on. . . ."

"Computers?" Wary. Lucas wondered why.

"Art. I've got this picture of a giant, a painting, weird-looking. Kind of strong. I need to know where it came from."

The artist didn't ask why. Again, Lucas thought that was odd. "Is the giant biting the head off a dead body?"

198

"No, he's . . ."

"Then it's not Goya. Has the giant got one eye?"

"Yeah," Lucas said. "Big mother, one eye, looking over a mountain . . ."

"At a nude woman in the foreground, lying on the mountainside. Like one of those saints on a Catholic holy card."

"That's it," Lucas said.

"Odilon Redon. The painting's called *The Cyclops*. Redon was French, mostly did pastel. Painted the cyclops around the turn of the century. The nude's got her back to the cyclops, so you're looking right at her . . ."

"Yeah, yeah, that's it. What kind of book would that be in? I mean, obscure, or what?"

"No, no, there are any number of books on Redon. He's in vogue right now. Or was. The library would have something. He's not exactly a household name, but anybody who knows about painting would know about him."

"Hmph. Okay. So probably a book."

"Or a calendar. There are dozens of art calendars around, and art postcards and art appointment books. Depends on what size it is."

"Okay, thanks. That's about what I needed. You say that you'd have to know something about art. . . ."

"Yeah. If you want some kind of index, I'd say maybe one percent of the people walking around on the sidewalk would know about Redon, would know his name. Of those, one in five could tell you a picture he painted."

"Thanks again."

"Always delighted to help the police," the artist said. He sounded like he was smiling.

Del was not smiling. Del was twisting his hands.

"Jesus Christ, it's not hard," Lucas said, squatting beside him. Del sat in the metal folding chair on the visitor's side of Lucas' desk. You just tell her you've been thinking about her. You say, 'I want to apologize for the way I acted, you seem like a really nice woman. You got nice eyes.' Then she'll ask, sooner or later, 'What color are they?' And you say, 'Hazel.'"

"How do I know they're hazel?" Del picked up the phone receiver in one hand, holding down the hang-up button with the index finger of the other.

"'Cause they are," Lucas said. "Really they're brown, but you make it sound nice when you say hazel. She knows she's got brown eyes, but she likes to think they're hazel. She'll think you care more if you say hazel. . . . Christ, Del, when was the last fuckin' time you asked a woman out?"

"'Bout twenty-two years ago," Del said, his head hanging. There was a moment of silence; then they both started to laugh. Del said, "Ah, fuck me," and started punching phone numbers. "Does it have to be tonight?"

"Sooner the better," Lucas said, moving behind the desk. He wanted to be where Del could see his face, in case he needed coaching. The phone rang six times and Del reached out to hang up, when Cheryl Clark answered.

"Ah, is this, ah, Miss Clark?" Del stuttered. Twenty-two years? Lucas shook his head. "Ah . . . this is the cop who was over there with the other cop, I'm the one with the headband. Yeah, Del. Listen, uh, this is got nothing to do with the investigation, you know, but, uh, I been thinking about you, and I finally decided to call. . . . I don't know, you seemed like a pretty nice chick, uh, woman, you know, shit, you had real nice eyes. . . . Uh, huh . . . yeah, kind of, if you'd like to, I was wondering if you'd be interested in a cup of coffee. Un-huh, okay." He turned away from Lucas, hiding his eyes, his voice dropping. "How about Annie's over on the West Bank? Uh, huh. I'll pick you up, is that okay? Uh. Forty-one. Yeah. Yeah. Uh, why,

200

they're hazel, really pretty, you know. . . . Yeah. Okay. Listen, about six-thirty? Get something to eat, a couple burgers? Okay?" By the time he hung up, Del's face was running with sweat.

"Forty-one?" Lucas asked, grinning. "Who the fuck is forty-one?"

"Get off my ass, Davenport," Del said, collapsing in his chair. "I fuckin' did it, okay?"

"All right," Lucas said, turning serious. "Now what'll you talk about?"

"How the fuck do I know? Bekker, of course . . ."

"No. Not about Bekker . . ."

"But why . . . ?"

"This woman has been used all of her life. She's the type, and she'll be very sensitive to it. She lets herself be used because that's the only way she can find relationships. She keeps hoping for something real, but she doesn't believe it's going to happen," Lucas said. He was leaning on the desk, talking rapidly, eyes narrowed, voice urgent, trying to impress his student. "If you come on to her about Bekker, she'll *know*. She'll know we're trying to manipulate her. You'll offend her right down to the soles of her feet. What you do is, you never mention Bekker. You do what all divorced guys do—talk about your ex-wife. Pretty soon she'll start to hint. Wanna know about Bekker? No. You don't want to know about Bekker. You want to talk about you, your ex-wife, her, and how miserable it is to get a relationship going with anyone decent. You say, Fuck Bekker, I don't wanna hear about that shit, that's work. Take her out a couple of times, and she'll start talking about him all on her own. She won't be able to help herself. Just don't push."

"Don't push," Del said. His eyes were like marbles.

"Don't push," Lucas confirmed, nodding.

Del leaned back in his chair, studying Lucas as though

he were a felon, and one he'd just met. "Jesus Christ," he said after a minute, "you are a cruel sonofabitch, you know that?"

Lucas frowned at the tone. "Are you serious?"

"I'm serious," Del said.

Lucas shrugged and looked away. "I do what I've got to do," he said.

He met Anderson on the way out to the car.

"I sent Carpenter down to the library after you called," Anderson said. "He found a book on this Redon dude, and that's the picture all right, but the library's picture was bigger than the one we got. He could only find it in one book, and that hasn't been checked out for two months."

"That's something," Lucas said.

"Yeah? Exactly what?" Anderson asked.

As Lucas drove home, a hard rain began to fall and lightning crackled overhead. A good night for trolls, he thought.

Bekker, God damn it.

16

The rain was steady and cold, driving, slicing through his headlights, the wipers barely able to keep up. Miserable night. A half-dozen black beauties gave him the edge he needed, a couple of purple egg-shaped Xanaxes cooled his nerves.

Not enough, maybe. The flapping of the windshield wipers was beginning to grate on him, and he had to bite his tongue to keep from shouting at them. *Fwip-fwip-fwip*, a torture . . .

Red light. He caught it at the last second, jammed on the brakes and nearly skidded through the intersection. The driver of the car one lane over looked at him, and Bekker had to choke down the impulse to scream at him. Instead of screaming, he went into his pocket, pulled out the cigarette case, tongued a yellow oblong Tranxene and snapped the case shut. He no longer tried to track his drug intake: he was guided by internal signals now, running with his body. . . .

And he was all right; he'd eaten half a handful of downers over the day, and they'd held him together like the skin of a balloon, containing the pressure. But only for a time. The snake was waiting, off in the dark. Then, when it was time to meet Druze, the black beauties pulled him up, out of the downers. He'd be afraid to drive with those downers in his blood. But with the black beauties, driving was a snap. . . . The traffic light changed and Bekker went through, gripping the steering wheel with all his might.

They'd agreed to meet at an all-night supermarket on

University Avenue, a place where the parking lot was usually full. Tonight there were only a few cars in front of the store, and one of them was a baby-blue St. Paul police cruiser. When he saw it, Bekker nearly panicked. Did they have Druze? How did they get him? Had he and Druze been betrayed? Had Druze gone to the police . . . ? No, wait; no, wait; no, wait; wait-wait-wait . . .

There he was, Druze, in the Dodge, waiting, the windows steamed. No cops near the squad car. Must be inside. Bekker parked on the left side of Druze's car, killed the engine and slipped out, watching the lighted entrance of the supermarket. Where were the cops? He opened the back door of his car, got the shovel off the floor, locked the door. He was wearing a rain suit and a canvas hat, and had been out of the car for no more than fifteen seconds, but the water poured off the brim of the hat in a steady stream.

Druze popped the passenger door on the Dodge as Bekker stepped over. He was breathing hard, almost panting. He scanned the rain-blasted lot, then hurled the shovel on the floor of the backseat, on top of Druze's spade, and clambered into the car. With the door shut, he took off the canvas hat and threw it in the back with the shovel. Druze was shocked when Bekker turned toward him. Bekker was beautiful; this man was gaunt, gray-faced. He looked, Druze thought, like a corpse in a B movie. He turned away and cranked the starter.

"Are you all right?" Druze asked, as he put the car in gear.

"No. I'm not," Bekker said shortly.

"This is fuckin' awful, man," Druze said. He stopped at the curb cut, waiting for a stream of traffic to pass. His burned face was flat, emotionless, the scarred lips like cracks in a dried creek bed. "Digging up the dead."

"Fuck it—fuck it," Bekker rasped. A bolt of lightning

zigzagged through the sky to the east, where they were going. "We gotta."

"I can't get the tarbaby out of my head," Druze said. "We can't shake this guy, Philip George." In other people, anger, fear, resentment flowed like gasoline. In Druze, even the violent emotions moved like clay, slowly turning, compressing, darkening. He was angry now, in his muted way, listening to Bekker, his friend. Bekker picked it up, put his hand on Druze's shoulder.

"Carlo, I'm fucked up," Bekker said. He said it quickly, the words snapping off after the last syllable. "I'm fuckin' crazy. I can't apologize for it. I don't want it. But it's there. And honest to God, I'm dying."

Druze took it in, not understanding, took the car onto the entrance ramp for I-94. "I mean, have you tried Valium or whatever?"

"You stupid shit . . ." Bekker's anger burst through like napalm, but he instantly backed off, humbling himself. "I'm sorry. I tried everything. Everything. Everything. There's only one way."

"Dangerous . . ."

"Fuck dangerous," Bekker shouted. Then, quiet again, straining to see through the rain as they accelerated off the ramp and into traffic, his voice formal, that of a man on an emotional seesaw: "A snake. There's a snake in my brain."

Druze glanced sideways at Bekker. The other man seemed to be sliding into a trance, his face rigid. "We were supposed to stay away from each other. If they see us . . ." Druze ventured.

Bekker didn't answer. He sat in the passenger seat, twisting his hands. Six miles later, coming back from wherever he was, he said, "I know. . . . And one of them's no dummy. I had him in for coffee."

"You what?" Druze's head snapped around: Bekker *was* losing it. But no: he sounded almost rational now.

205

"Had him in for coffee. Found him in front of my house. Watching. Lucas Davenport. He's not stupid. He looks mean."

"Tough guy? A little over six feet, looks like a boxer or something? Dark hair, with a scar coming through his eyebrow?" Druze quickly traced the path of Lucas' scar on his own face.

Bekker nodded, his head cocked to one side: "You know him?"

"He was at the theater after you did Armistead," Druze said. "Talking to one of the actresses. They looked pretty friendly."

"Who? Which one?"

"Cassie Lasch. Played the maid in . . . you didn't go to that. She's a second-stringer. Good-looking. I could see this guy coming on to her. She lives in my building."

"You work with her much?"

"No. We're both part of the group, but we've never talked much or anything. Not personally."

"Could she pipe you into what Davenport's thinking?"

"I don't know. She might pick something up. If the guy's smart, I don't need him checking on me."

"You're right," Bekker said, looking at Druze as the Dodge's interior was swept by the lights of an oncoming car. "What was her name again? Cassie?"

"Cassie Lasch," Druze said. "A redhead."

Lightning crashed around them as they crossed the St. Croix River into Wisconsin and headed up the bluff. When they passed the Hudson turn-off, the thunderhead opened. Rain swept across the road, shaking the car, and Druze was forced to slow as they pushed into the dark countryside. By the time they reached the exit to the lake, they were down to forty miles an hour, the last car in an informal convoy.

"What a fuckin' night," Druze said. Lightning answered.

"I couldn't make it another twenty-four hours," Bekker answered. "Is he deep?"

Deep? Ah, he meant George. "More than two feet, anyway," Druze said. "Probably closer to three."

"Should be quick . . . Won't take long," Bekker said.

"You weren't here last night," Druze said sourly. "We're talking about a peat bog. This is gonna take a while."

They missed the turn-off to the cabin. Druze had slowed further on the black-topped county road, driving thirty, then twenty-five, watching for the reflectors that marked the turn . . but they missed them, went a mile too far, had to come back. They saw only one other vehicle, a pick-up, passing in the opposite direction, a man with a hat and a face that was a blurred oval hunched over the steering wheel.

They found the track coming back, turned and picked their way between the high bushes. The rain was tapering off; the thunderhead, still spitting out long chains of lightning, had moved to the north. The cabin popped up in the headlights like a mirage, congealing out of darkness, suddenly, and close. Druze parked in front of it, killed the headlights and said, "Let's do it."

He took a gray plastic raincoat from the backseat and pulled it on. Bekker wore sophisticated foul-weather gear, with a hood like a monk's cowl.

"Take my hat," he said to Druze, snagging it out of the backseat and passing it to the other man.

They got out, the ground firm underfoot, sandy rather than muddy. As the rain slowed, a wind seemed to increase and moaned through the bare birch trees overhead. Past the cabin, perhaps two or three hundred yards across the lake, Bekker could see a blue yard light and, lower, the yellow rectangle of a lighted window.

"This way," Druze grunted. His pantlegs below the rain suit were already wet, and he felt the first tongue of water inside his athletic shoes. He put the spade over his shoulder and, with the flashlight playing on the ground, led the way through the brambles, back to the edge of the tamarack swamp. The ground changed from high and sandy to soft, and finally to muck.

"How much . . ." Bekker started.

"We're here." Druze shined the light on the ground, and Bekker could just pick out an oval pattern of raw earth.

"I kicked some shit over it before I left," Druze said. "In two weeks, you wouldn't be able to find it if you tried."

"We'll do that again before we leave. Maybe get some leaves on it," Bekker said vaguely. Rain ran down his face and collected in his eyebrows, and he sputtered through it. He was disintegrating in the water, falling apart like the wicked witch, Druze thought.

"Sure," Druze grunted. He jammed the flashlight into the branches of a bare bush and scooped up a shovelful of muck. "Dig."

Bekker worked frantically, shoveling, talking to himself, spitting in the rain, digging like a badger. Druze tried to be more methodical but after a few minutes simply tried to stay out of the way. To the north, the thunderhead was still rumbling, and another burst of rain put a half-inch of water in the hole.

"I can't tell . . ." Bekker said, gasping between words, "I can't tell . . . if the water's from the rain . . . or if it's coming up . . . from below."

"Some of both," Druze said. The flashlight caught a lump that looked different, and Druze prodded it with the tip of his shovel. The blade hit something resilient. "I think I got him."

"Got him? Here, let me . . ."

Bekker motioned Druze aside and knelt in the hole, holding the blade of his shovel like a scoop, working like a man in a frenzy, throwing the muck out in all directions.

208

"We got him," he said, breathing hard. A hip, a leg, a shoulder, the sport coat. "Got him got him got him . . ."

Druze stood back, holding the light, while Bekker cleared the mud away from the top of the body. "Shit," he said, looking up at Druze, his pale face the color and consistency of candle wax, "He's face-down."

"I just kind of dumped him . . ." Druze said, half apologetically.

"That's okay, I just have to . . ."

Bekker tried to free the body by pulling on the sport coat, but there was still too much dirt around it and it held George as firmly as if he were frozen in concrete.

"Suction or something," Bekker grunted. His rain suit and his face were covered with mud, but he paid no attention. He straddled what he could see of the body, put his hands around George's neck and tried to pry the head free. "Can't fuckin' get it," he said after a minute.

"We have to clear away."

"Yeah." Bekker went back to the shovel, still using it as a scoop, a pan, and dug around the body, trying to loosen the arms, which were apparently sunk in the mud below. He got the left one first, the hand white as chalk, the fingers rigid and waxy as candles. Then Bekker got part of the left leg and turned his face up to Druze and said, "If you could help just here."

Druze squatted on the rim of the hole, reached in, grabbed George's belt. "Get his head," he said. "Ready? Heave."

George came partway out of the hole like an archaeological artifact on the end of a crane cable. Not stiff, but not particularly loose, either, his legs still anchored in the muck, his head hanging forward . . .

"There," Druze said, and with a heavy pivoting motion

of his shoulders he managed to flip the body onto its side, the legs rolling out of the muck below. Mud caked the nose and mouth, but one eye socket was clear. As the rain washed away the last of the soil, they could see the dead white orb of an eye looking up at them.

"Jesus," Druze said, stepping back.

"I told you!" Bekker screamed. His hand groped in his pocket and came out with a screwdriver. "I told you, I told you, I told you . . ."

He held the corpse's head by the hair and drove the screwdriver first into one eye socket, then the other, over and over, ten times, twenty, thirty, with furious power, screaming, "*I told you*," until Druze grabbed him by the collar and jerked him out of the hole, hollering, "Enough, enough, enough . . ."

They stood looking at each other for a moment, the rain still driving down, Bekker gasping for breath, staggering, Druze afraid he was having a heart attack, and then Bekker said, "Yeah . . . that should be enough."

He took the flashlight from Druze, squatted next to the hole and with an almost gentle hand turned George's head. The eyes were deep bloodless holes, quickly filling with mud.

Bekker looked up, and a long flash of lightning from the distant storm lit him up as clearly as a fly on a television screen. His face was beautiful again, clear, the face of an angel, his white teeth flashing in a brilliant smile.

"That should do it," he said. He let George's head go, and the body flipped face-down into the watery hole with a wet, sucking splash.

Bekker stood up, turning into the rain, letting it wash him. He was bouncing, Druze thought: *Jesus, it's a dance.* And as Bekker danced, the rain slowed, then stopped. Druze was backing away, frightened, fascinated.

"Well," Bekker said a moment later, his labored breath squeezing through the hysterical smile, "I suppose we should fill the hole, should we not?"

The grave filled quickly. The last they saw of Philip George was his right foot, the sock pulled down around the hairless, paper-white ankle, the shoe already rotting with water. Druze beat the surface down with the shovel, then kicked some leaves and brambles over the freshly turned soil. "Let's get the fuck out of here," he said.

They hurried back to the car, and Druze had to jockey it back and forth to turn in the narrow track in front of the cabin. Bekker, his voice clear and easy now, said, "Check the answering machine. Three, four times a day. Call from public phones. When George turns up missing, the cops are probably going to sit on me. If I've got to talk to you . . . the tapes are the only way. And listen, don't forget to press number three, and reset the tape."

"I meant to ask you about that," Druze said, as he wrestled the Dodge onto the black-topped road. "If you reset the tape, isn't the message still there . . . ?"

Across the lake, the yellow rectangle burned in the cabin window. A woman in a pink robe, her hair in curlers, sat under the light reading an old issue of *Country Living*. She was facing an old-fashioned picture window, positioned to look over the lake, when Druze and Bekker got back to the car.

"Richard," she called to her husband, and stood and looked out the window. "There are those headlights again. . . . I'm going to call Ann. I really don't think they were planning to come up tonight."

17

Lucas punched the Porsche down the country highway, hissing along the wet blacktop, past woodlots of unleafed trees and the sodden, dark fall-tilled fields. The day was overcast, the clouds the color of slag iron. A deer, hit by a car, probably the night before, lay folded like an awkward, bone-filled backpack in a roadside ditch. A few hundred yards farther along, a dead badger had been flung like a rag over the yellow line.

He'd been to two hundred murder scenes, all of them dismal. Were murders ever done in cheerful surroundings, just by accident? He'd once gone to a murder scene at an amusement park. The park hadn't yet opened for the season, and although it made a specialty of fun, the silent Ferris wheels, the immobile roller coasters, the awkward Tilt-A-Whirls, the Empty House of Mirrors were as sinister as any rotting British country house on a moor. . . .

He crested a low hill, saw the cop cars parked along the road, with an ambulance facing into a side road. A fat deputy sheriff, one thumb hooked under a gunbelt, gestured for him to keep moving. Lucas swung onto the shoulder, killed the engine and climbed out.

"*Hey, you.*" The fat deputy was bearing down on him. "You think I was doin' aerobics?"

Lucas took his ID out of his coat pocket and said, "Minneapolis police. Is this . . .?"

"Yeah, down there," the deputy said, gesturing at the side road, backing off a step. He tried a few new expressions on his face and finally settled for suspicion. "They told me to keep people moving."

"Good idea," Lucas said mildly. "If the word gets out, you're gonna get about a million TV cameras before too long. . . . How come everybody's parked out here?"

Lucas' collegial attitude loosened the deputy up. "The guy who answered the call thought there might be tracks down there in the mud," the fat man said. "He thought we ought to get some lab people out here."

"Good call," Lucas said, nodding.

"I don't think we'll see any television," the fat man said. Lucas couldn't tell if that made him happy or unhappy. "Old D.T. put a lid on everything. D.T.'s the guy running the show down there."

"Hope we can keep it on," Lucas said, heading toward the side road. "But if they do turn up, don't take any shit from them at all."

"Right on." The deputy grabbed his gunbelt in both hands and gave it a hitch.

The side track was two hundred yards long. At the end of it, Lucas found a nervous gray-haired woman and a pipe-smoking man sitting on the narrow porch of a cabin, both in cable-knit sweaters and slickers. Beyond the cabin, in a tangle of brush and brambles, Swanson was standing in a pod of people, some in uniform, others in civilian clothes.

Lucas walked past the cabin and gingerly into the scrub, staying away from a long strip of yellow police tape that outlined the original track into the raspberry bushes. Halfway back, a uniformed deputy, working on his hands and knees, was pouring casting compound into a footprint. He looked up briefly as Lucas went by, then turned back to his work. He'd already poured some casts farther along the trail.

"Davenport," Swanson said, when Lucas pushed through to the end of the track. Two funeral home attendants in cheap dark suits were waiting to one side, a carry litter with pristine sheets for the uncaring body set carefully by their feet. Two more men, deputies, were working in a muddy foxhole, excavating the body with plastic hand trowels, like archaeologists on a dig. The body was half uncovered, but the face was still down. Swanson stepped away from the group, his face gloomy.

"It's for sure? George?" Lucas asked.

"Yeah. When they went into the hole, they got his foot, and the deputy stopped the digging and called for help. When they started again, they got to his hip, took his billfold out of his pocket. The same guy who found him recognized the name and called for help again. The clothes are right. It's him."

Lucas stepped off to the side to get a better look at the hole. A foot stuck up awkwardly, like a grotesque tree shoot struggling for the sun. A sheriff's deputy in a ball cap and a raincoat came over and said, "You're Davenport?"

"Yeah."

"D.T. Helstrom," the deputy said, sticking out a bony hand. He was a thin man, with a dark, weathered face. Smile lines creased his cheeks at the corners of his mouth. "I've seen you on TV. . . ."

They shook hands and Lucas said, "You were the first guy out here?"

"Yes. The couple back there on the porch . . . ?"

"I saw them," Lucas said. He moved away from the hole with Swanson and Helstrom as they talked.

"They saw some lights over here last night. We have a lot of break-ins in these lake cabins, so I came by and checked it out. There was nothing at the cabin, but I could see somebody had been through the bushes. I went along . . . and there was the grave."

"They didn't try to hide it?" Lucas asked.

Helstrom looked back along the track and cracked a thin

grin. "Yeah, I guess, in a city way. Kicked some shit over the grave. Didn't try too hard, though. They must have figured that with the rain, hell, in a couple of weeks there'd be nothing to find. And they were right. In a week, you couldn't find that hole with three Geiger counters and a Republican water-witcher."

"We're both saying 'they'," Lucas said. "Any sign of how many?"

"Probably two," Helstrom said. "They left tracks, but it was raining off and on all night, so the prints are pretty washed out. We've got one guy in gym shoes, for sure, 'cause we can still see the treads. Then there are prints that don't seem to have treads on them, on top of the treaded prints—but we can't be sure, because the rain might have taken them out. . . ."

"Car?" Swanson asked.

"You can see where the tires were. But I followed it all the way out to the road, and the tread marks were gone."

"But you think there were two," Lucas said.

"Probably two," Helstrom said. "I looked at every track there is, marking the ones to cast; I couldn't swear to it in court, but I'd be willing to bet on it in Vegas."

"You sound like you've done this shit before," Lucas said.

"I had twenty years in Milwaukee," Helstrom said, shaking his head. "Big-city police work can kiss my ass, but I've done it before. We're taking the body over to Minneapolis, by the way. We've got a contract with the medical examiner, if you need the gory details."

Swanson was looking back toward the hole. From where they were standing, all they could see was the foot sticking up and the two men working in the hole, getting ready to move the body. "Maybe we got us a break," he said to Lucas.

"Maybe. I'm not sure how it'll help."

"It's something," Swanson said.

"You know what I thought, when I first dug him up?" Helstrom asked. "I thought, *Ah! The game's afoot.*"

Lucas and Swanson stared at him for a moment, then simultaneously looked back to the hole, where the foot stuck up. "Jesus," Lucas groaned, and the three of them started laughing.

At that instant, one of the deputies, pulling hard, got the body halfway out of its grave. The head swung around to stare at them all with empty holes where the eyes should have been.

"Aw, fuck me," the deputy cried, and let the body slump back. The head didn't turn, but continued looking up, toward the miserable gray Wisconsin sky and the black scarecrow twigs of the unclothed trees.

He thought about it on the way back, weighing the pros and cons, and finally pulled into a convenience store in Hudson and called TV3.

"Carly? Lucas Davenport . . ."

"What's happening?"

"You had a short piece last night about a guy disappearing, a law professor?"

"Yeah. Found his car at the airport. There's a rumor flying around that he was Stephanie Bekker's lover . . ."

"That's right—that's the theory."

"Can I go with . . . ?"

" . . . and they're taking him out of a grave in Wisconsin right this minute. . . ."

"*What?*"

He gave her directions to the gravesite, waited while she talked to the news director about cranking up a mobile unit, then gave her a few more details.

"What's this gonna cost me?" she asked in a low voice.

"Just keep in mind that it'll cost," Lucas said. "I don't know what, yet."

Sloan was working at his desk behind the public counter in Violent Crimes when Lucas stopped by.

"You've been over in Wisconsin?" Sloan asked.

"Yeah. They did a number on the guy's eyes, just like with the women. Did you talk to George's wife yesterday?"

"Yeah. She said it's hard to believe that he was fuckin' Stephanie Bekker. She said he wasn't much interested in sex, spent all his time working."

"Huh," Lucas said. "He could be the type who gets hit hard, if the right woman came around."

"That's what I thought, but she sounded pretty positive."

"Are you going to talk to her again, today?"

"For a few minutes, anyway," Sloan said, nodding. "Checking in, see if she forgot to tell me anything. We got along pretty well. That Wisconsin sheriff called her with the news, she's got some neighbors over there with her. Her brother's going out to identify the body."

"Mind if I tag along when you go?"

"Sure, if you want," Sloan said. He looked at Lucas curiously. "What've you got?"

"I want to look at his books. . . ."

"Well, shit, I'm not doing much," Sloan said. "Let's take the Porsche."

Philip George had lived in St. Paul, in a two-block neighborhood of radically modern homes nestled in a district of upper-middle-class older houses, steel and glass played against brick and stucco, with plague-stricken elms all around. Three neighborhood women were with his wife when Sloan and Lucas arrived. Sloan asked if he could speak to her alone, and Lucas asked if he could look at George's books.

"Yes, of course, they're right down there, in the study," she said, gesturing at a hallway. "Is there anything . . . ?"

"Just wondering about something," Lucas said vaguely.

While Sloan talked to George's wife, the neighbor ladies moved into the living room and Lucas walked through the study, a converted bedroom, looking at books. George had not been an adventuresome reader. He owned a hundred volumes on various aspects of the law, a few histories that appeared to be left over from college, a dozen popular novels that went back almost as many years, and a collection of Time-Life books on home repair. No art books. Lucas didn't know much about art, but he knew that most of the work on the walls was of the professional-decorator variety. Nothing remotely like Odilon Redon.

On the way back to the living room, Lucas scanned the framed photographs hung in the connecting hall. George at bar association meetings, accepting a gavel. George looking uneasy in new hunting clothes, a shotgun in one hand, a dead Canada goose in the other. In two photos, one black-and-white, the other color, he was singing in different bars, arms outstretched, beery faces laughing in the background. Overhead in one, a banner said "St. Pat's Day Bad Irish Tenor Contest"; in the other, a cardboard sign said "Bad Tenors."

Annette George, tired, slack-faced, was sitting at the kitchen table talking to Sloan when Lucas returned from the tour. She looked up, red-eyed, and said, "Anything?"

"Afraid not," Lucas said, shaking his head. "Was your husband interested in art at all? Painting?"

"Well, I mean . . . no. Not really. He thought maybe he'd like to try painting sometime, but he never had the time. And I guess it would have been out of character."

218

"Any interest in a guy named Odilon Redon?"

"Who? No, I never heard of him. Wait, the sculptor, you mean? He did that *Thinker* thing?"

"No, he was a painter, I don't think he did sculptures," Lucas said, now confused himself.

She shook her head. "No . . ."

"There're a couple of photographs in the hall, your husband singing in bad-Irish-tenor contests. . . ."

"Yes, he sang every year," she said.

"Was he good? I mean, was he a natural tenor, or what?" Lucas asked.

"Yes, he was pretty good. We both sang in college. I guess if he had an art form, that was it."

"When he sang in college, what part did he sing?" Lucas asked.

"First tenor. I was an alto and we sang in a mixed choir, we'd stand next to each other. . . . Why?"

"Nothing. I'm just trying to picture him," Lucas said. "Trying to figure out what happened."

"Oh, gosh, the things I could tell you," she said, staring vacantly at the floor. "I can't believe that he and Stephanie . . ."

"If it helps any, I don't believe it, either," Lucas said. "I'd appreciate it if you'd keep that under your hat for the moment."

"You don't believe?" she asked.

"No, I don't . . ."

Later, when Sloan and Lucas were leaving, she asked, "What am I going to do? I'm fifty. . . ."

One of the neighbor ladies, looking at Lucas as if the question were his fault, said, "Come on, Annette, it's all right."

Sloan looked back from the sidewalk: she was still standing there, looking through the glass of the storm door. "What does that mean, about the art? And the Irish-tenor contest?" he asked, turning to Lucas. "And do you really think there's somebody else . . . ?"

"Have you ever heard an Irish-tenor contest?" Lucas asked.

"No . . ."

"I did once, at the St. Pat's Day parade. The guys are *tenors*," Lucas said. "That's a fairly high voice—and especially a first tenor. You must've heard guys singing 'My Wild Irish Rose'? Like that. Our guy on the nine-one-one tape, I don't see how he could sing in a tenor contest. Not unless he had a terrible cold or something."

"Didn't sound like he did," Sloan said, eyes narrowing.

"No. He sounded like a baritone, or even a bass."

"And George wasn't interested in art, or what's-his-name . . ."

"Redon," Lucas said absently. "And this artist I talked to, he said you'd probably have to know a little about art to pull that picture out of your head. It's not one you see every day. As far as I could tell, the Georges don't have an art book in the house."

Sloan looked back at the house. Annette George was gone. "Well, if George wasn't the guy, then the real lover's in the clear. Everybody in the world's assuming that he was the guy."

"Now think about this," Lucas said, moving slowly down toward the car. "If this guy's a serial killer, why'd he go to the trouble of burying George? He didn't care about burying the other two. And dragging a body around the countryside, that's a hell of a risk. What's he hiding about George?"

"And why didn't they bury him the same night he disappeared, instead of waiting? That's even more of a risk," Sloan added.

"It's fucked up. I'm beginning to wonder if we really

know what's going on," Lucas said. They'd reached the car and he leaned on a fender. "We keep looking at Bekker, because we *feel* like he's the guy. But it doesn't make sense from his point of view."

"Tell me," Sloan prompted.

"If Bekker's behind it, why was Armistead murdered? He claims he didn't know her, and we've got no indication that he did. Her friends certainly didn't know Bekker, because they'd remember his face. And if the killer hit George just for the thrill of it, why leave the others but bury George?"

Sloan nodded and sighed. "Like you said, it's fucked up."

"Interesting," Lucas said.

"Gimme the keys," Sloan said. "I wanna drive this piece of shit."

On the way back to City Hall, Lucas told Sloan about the gravesite, and about the deputy's line: "*The game's afoot.*"

"Cracked us up, Swanson and me," Lucas said.

"That ain't bad," Sloan admitted. He had a weakness for wordplay. "*The game's afoot.*"

They were headed west on I-94, and Lucas, in the passenger seat, was looking blankly at a billboard advertisement for South Dakota tourism. Afoot? "Jesus," he said. "When they dusted for prints at Bekker's place, did they do the floor outside her bathroom? The bathroom that opens off her bedroom?"

"Fuck if I know," said Sloan. "Why?"

"Footprints," Lucas said. "The lover, whoever he is, might have wiped all the handles and stuff, but I bet the sonofabitch didn't wipe the floor. And if he didn't, we might still be able to get prints. I mean, since the game is a foot . . ."

*   *   *

221

Cassie came over and cooked Italian, humming in the kitchen, brewing tomato sauce, dancing around and sucking on the wooden spoon as she worked in the spices. She was wearing a fuzzy sweater that clung to her, and Lucas moved around behind her, handling her, stroking her stomach.

"Christ, the muscles are unbelievable," he said.

"I pray to Jane Fonda every morning. . . ."

"Mama's Got a Squeeze Box" came up on the radio and she tried to give him a quick dance lesson. He failed.

"You got the same problem as all large white men: you're afraid to shake your ass," she complained. "You can't dance if you don't move your ass."

"I feel ridiculous when I try to move my ass," Lucas said. He gave it a tentative shake.

"Yeah," she said, nodding, "you do look kinda weird. We could work on it. . . ."

"Maybe I could take banjo lessons or something. . . ."

The phone rang while they ate, and Lucas stepped into the kitchen to pick it up.

"This is Mikkelson," said a deputy medical examiner. "Things are getting strange outside."

"What'd you find?" Lucas asked.

"All kinds of shit. There was fresh blood and fresh fecal matter in George's clothing when he went into that grave. It mixed with the mud before it started to congeal, so it hadn't congealed yet when he went into the hole."

"Which means he wasn't killed until last night . . ."

"That's what you'd think, but that'd be wrong," the medical examiner said. "The holes in his eyes were filled with mud, too, but the holes were made after all the blood had pooled into his chest and arms, a long time after he was killed."

"That doesn't compute," Lucas said, confused.

222

"Only one way," the deputy M.E. said with evident relish. "They had to bury him and then dig him up to do the eyes. We've got some more tests going, but from the tissue evidence, I'd say that's what they did."

"Why?"

"Shit, Lucas, I'm a goddamned doctor, not a fuckin' psychic. But that's what happened. And there's something else, too—some people from your lab brought me over a bunch of footprints from the Bekker house?"

"Yeah?"

"Not a match in the bunch. Not even close."

18

"I need help," Daniel said. "Political help. You know how the city council gets. They think the voters are stupid, they think the voters are gonna run them out of office if we don't catch the guy today. They're getting pissy."

"You got a couple of bad columns, too," Lucas said. They were sitting in Daniel's office, under the watchful eyes of Daniel's political mug shots.

"Yeah, well, what do you expect?" Daniel said. He looked in his cigar humidor, then slammed the lid. "Column-writing is the only job I know where sarcasm passes for intelligence. . . . God damn it, Davenport. I need something, and I don't care what it is."

"Stick full-time surveillance on Bekker," Lucas suggested.

"All right," Daniel said, grasping. "Why?"

"To settle him, one way or another. Tag everybody he talks to, track everywhere he goes. If he's involved, he hired a really strange-looking dude for the killing. We need somebody on the team with enough brains to break off Bekker, if he has to, and go after a likely-looking killer. And we ought to get a court order, tap his phones both at home and at work. We either clear him or we hang him."

"What do you think? Is he the guy?" Daniel asked with genuine curiosity.

"I don't know." Lucas shrugged. "He's the only thing we've got, but everything points somewhere else."

"All right, I'll get the surveillance going," Daniel said. "I can give that out to a couple of people, that we've got a guy

224

being watched. That'll cool some of the council fever. But it'd be nice if we got a little decent PR for a change."

"I was talking to a snitch a few nights ago, and he said a mutual acquaintance came into a bunch of TV sets—maybe a couple hundred of them, a boxcar-load from over in St. Paul. Then I talked to another guy and he says Terry—this is Terry Meller, you remember him? No? He's a longtime semi-bad dude—he says Terry is working out of a rental warehouse off Two-eighty. He says the TVs are stuffed in there, and probably a bunch of other shit. We could get the ERU and a warrant, call up the TV and the papers. . . ."

"I could tell the ERU guys to armor up some of the reporters—we got some extra vests . . ." Daniel said, brightening. The Emergency Response Unit always got air-time. "Give them some good film."

"We won't lose the Bekker story, but we'll look good on this other thing," Lucas said. "And there'll be film. . . ."

"Get a warrant," Daniel said enthusiastically, poking a finger at him. "I'll get the ERU started and some Intelligence guys over to look at the warehouse. Stop down at Intelligence when you leave and give them the location."

"I've got a new friend at TV3, by the way," Lucas said. "She kind of owes me. . . ."

"You feed her that break on George's body?" Daniel asked, looking sideways at Lucas.

Lucas grinned and shrugged. "Maybe something slipped out. But since we're not going to kill the Bekker story, anyway, I want to tell her that I'm going off the reservation. I want to tell her I don't think George is the lover, and I want to make it seem like there's a little controversy between me and the department. Good guy, bad guy, the department being the bad guy. That'll get us better play, and the other stations will come after it, and the papers . . ."

They'd talked about the possibility that Loverboy was still alive, but Daniel was skeptical. "You really think he's still out there?"

Lucas' forehead wrinkled. "Yeah. I know there are some problems with that—like, why was George killed and dumped if he wasn't the lover? I can't figure that out. I mean, he should have been her lover. They knew each other, they were the right age for each other. . . . I don't know. . . . By the way, has Shearson got anything on this shrink he was looking at? Stephanie's other friend?"

"He thinks there's something."

"He ain't exactly the sharpest knife in the dishwasher. . . ."

"Hey, he's okay," Daniel said mildly. "You don't like him because he wears better suits than you do."

"Yeah, but with golf shirts . . ."

"Look," Daniel said. "We know that Bekker didn't kill either George or his wife, not in person. . . ."

"Yeah. And I was sure that he set me up as an alibi on George, but now . . . God damn it, this thing is getting on top of me. And Loverboy's the key. If he's still out there, I want to get to him. Maybe I can make some kind of appeal. Or drop a hint that I'm closing in on him, and that he'd be better off talking to me now—that if he doesn't come in, we'll find him anyway and pack him off to Stillwater on a charge of accessory to first-degree murder."

"I don't know," Daniel said. He rubbed his developing five o'clock-shadow fuzz with the back of his fingers. "My inclination is not to do that."

"Your inclination?"

"Yeah. That's my inclination. But you're an adult. Your ass is in your own hands," Daniel said. Lucas nodded. Daniel was in politics. If Lucas went public and was wrong, Daniel had planted a little ambiguity around the decision process.

"Okay," Lucas said. "And you can tell the mayor we're watching a guy and hustling after Loverboy. . . ."

"He's no dummy, the mayor," Daniel said.

"Yeah, I know, but all he wants is something to feed to the sharks, and that's something."

"Good enough. I'll get Anderson to pull some guys for a surveillance team and we'll get on Bekker by tonight."

Lucas stopped at Intelligence, gave the duty officer the address of Terry Meller's TV warehouse, went to his office and called Carly Bancroft, then talked to the department artist and got a quick sketch done. A half-hour later, he met Bancroft at a Dairy Queen in the Skyway.

"I've got another piece of story for you," he said, nibbling around the edge of his chocolate-dipped cone. "Some of it's points for me—you'd owe me more—but some of it's part of your paycheck. Call it a wash. But I want to get it on the air."

"Let's hear it," she said.

"Everybody's assuming that Philip George was Mrs Bekker's lover and the killer took him out to protect himself."

"Yeah, that's what we're saying," she said.

"I don't think that's right. In fact, I'm pretty sure it's wrong," Lucas said. "I think the guy's still out there. The Loverboy."

She took a lick of her vanilla softie and nodded. "That's an okay story if we can put your name on it. What else?"

"You've got to hint that I'm closing in on the guy—that I'm talking to people and that I've got an identikit picture I'm showing around. I'll show it to somebody you can interview, and they'll know they're supposed to talk to you. They'll describe the guy for you, but I'll refuse to show you the picture."

"That's all fine. What's the pay-off part?"

"I want you to report it as though you got it from a third source. You must use my name, but you can't quote me directly and you can't say I'm the source of the story. You have to say that I've refused comment. . . ."

"That's lying," she said.

"Right. Lying," Lucas agreed. "You have to indicate that you got the story from a secret source in the department, but definitely not me. Suggest that there's an inter-departmental difference of opinion and I've been ordered to keep my mouth shut. And then you've got to do a little background on me, say that Davenport has secret sources that not even other cops know about."

"I don't understand what all this means," she said, a tiny wrinkle appearing between her eyes. "I'd like to know where I'm going, in case I'm going off a cliff."

Lucas finished the chocolate part of the cone, took two licks of the vanilla ice cream, reached back and dumped the cone in a waste-basket. "I do think the guy's out there. I want him to feel threatened, but I don't want to be the threatening guy. I want him to come to me," Lucas said.

She nodded. "All right. We can play it like you said."

"And not a bad story," Lucas said.

"Speaking of which"—she glanced at her watch—"I've got to run."

"What's happening?"

"Some big bust going down somewhere—I don't know exactly what it is, but I'm going in with the ERU."

"Sounds good," Lucas said.

"Sounds like bullshit, but I get to be in the movies," she said. "Film at ten."

Elle Kruger's lips moved silently as she walked slowly along the sidewalk, down the hill past the college duck pond, head bowed. Her hands counted through the large black beads of the rosary hanging down her side. Lucas, who'd missed her at her office, followed fifty feet behind, idly checking out the coeds—most were sweet and blonde and large, as though punched from a German Catholic cookie cutter—waiting until Elle had worked her way through the last decade.

When she'd finished, she released the beads, straightened up and lengthened her step, continuing her stroll around the pond. Lucas hurried after her, and she turned and spotted him coming when he was still fifty feet away.

"How long have you been back there?" she asked, smiling.

"Five minutes. The secretary said you'd be down here. . . ."

"Has something happened?"

"No, not really. I'm puzzled, trying to hack my way through what's happening with this Bekker case."

"A strange case, and getting stranger, if the papers can be trusted," she said, but with an upward inflection, making the statement into a question.

"Yeah. Maybe." He was reluctant to commit himself. "Tell me this: We've got this guy who kills two women, completely destroys their eyes. Then he kills another guy, takes him out and buries him in Wisconsin, and he's spotted purely by chance—some neighbors see his car lights and think he might be a burglar. Turns out he probably buried the body the night before, and he came back for the sole purpose of hacking out the eyes. . . ."

". . . Doesn't want to be watched by the dead," Elle said crisply.

"I was wondering if it might be something like that," Lucas said. "But I was also wondering—would it necessarily have to be sincere? If there was some kind of manipulation going on, could he be doing it for some other reason?"

"Like what?"

"Publicity? Or a deliberate effort to tie the murders together?"

She shrugged. "I suppose he could, but then why go back and hack the eyes out of a man whose body you're trying to hide, and don't expect to be found?"

"Yeah, there's that," Lucas said, discouraged. He thrust his hands into his jacket pockets.

"So it's probably real, and it has implications," she said, looking up at him.

"Like what?"

"He hacked the eyes out of all three people he's killed—at least, all three that we know about. And he did it instantly: he killed the first one, Bekker, and did her eyes at the same time. How did he know that the first one would watch him after she was dead? It would suggest . . ."

"That he's killed before and was watched." Lucas slapped his forehead with the heel of his hand. "Damn it. I missed that."

"He's a very dangerous man, Lucas," Elle said. "In the psychological literature, we'd refer to him as a *fruitcake*."

Restless, Lucas drove to the Lost River. The door was locked, but he could see a woman inside, painting. He rapped on the glass door, and when she saw him, he held up his badge case.

"Cassie around?" he asked when she opened the door.

"There's a rehearsal going on," the woman said. "They're all out on the stage."

Lucas walked through the hall to the theater. The lights were up and people were walking or standing around the stage or the low pit in front of it. Two or three more were sitting in the seats, watching and talking. Half of the whites were in blackface, with wide white-greasepainted lips, while two blacks were in white-face. Cassie saw him and raised a tentative hand, said something to the artistic director, and they both walked over.

"Just looking around, if that's okay," Lucas said. "Would it bother you if I watch?"

"Not much to see," the artistic director said, his grease-painted lips turning down. "You're welcome to stay, but it's mostly people talking."

"We'll be another hour or so . . ." Cassie said. Her green eyes were like lamps peering through the dark paint.

"How about some French food? I mean, later, if you're not doing anything."

"Sounds great." She stepped away and said, "About an hour."

Lucas walked halfway up the rising bank of seats and settled in to watch. *Whiteface* was a brutal but cheerful attack on latter-day segregation. A dozen set pieces were combined with rewritten nineteenth-century show tunes. There were frequent halts to argue, to change lines, to choreograph body positions. Twisting through the set pieces, the troupe kept up a running vaudeville: juggling, tap and rap dancing, joking, banjo-playing.

One manic set involved the two black actors as professional golfers, trying to sneak through a segregated southern country club. Cassie, in a play within a play, took the part of a white southern college belle in blackface, trying to sort out her relationship with a black radical in whiteface.

In a darker piece, a burly man in a wide snap-brimmed felt hat robbed white passersby in a park. Although he was obviously in blackface, none of the victims, when they were talking to the cops, could ever get beyond the blackness, even though they *knew* . . .

When that segment was over, there was a brief, sharp argument about whether it violated the pace and feel of the rest of the show. The two black actors, who were used as arbiters of taste, split on the question. One, who seemed more involved in the technical aspects of playmaking, thought it should go; the other, more interested in the social impact, insisted that it stay.

The artistic director turned and looked up into the seats.

"What do the police think?" he called.

"I think it's pretty strong," Lucas said. "It's not like the rest of the stuff, but it adds something."

"Good. Let's leave it, at least for now," the director said.

When they were done, Lucas sat with Cassie and a half-dozen other actors while they cleaned the paint off their faces. The man who played the mugger was not among them. On the way out, Lucas saw him on the stage, working on a dance he did late in the show.

"Carlo," Cassie said. "He works at it."

They ate and went to Lucas' house. Cassie flopped on the living room couch.

"You know what the worst part of being poor is? You have to work all the time. You're rich, you can take six weeks to veg out. That's what I need: about six weeks of daytime TV."

"Better'n watching the news, anyway," Lucas said. He lifted her legs, sat down on the couch and dropped them in his lap. "At least with the soaps, you *know* you're getting bullshit."

"Hmph. Well, we could get really philosophical about the media and have an intelligent conversation, or we could go fool around," Cassie said. "What'd you want to do?"

"Guess," Lucas said.

Later in the evening, Del called. "Sorry about the other day . . ."

" 'S okay," Lucas said. "What's happening?"

"I've been out with Cheryl twice and she's starting to talk," he said. "I keep telling her I don't want to hear it, and she keeps talking."

"Told you," Lucas said.

"Asshole," said Del. "I actually kind of like her. . . . Anyway, she thinks Bekker might be on some kind of drug. Speed or coke or something. She said he'd sometimes act nuts, he'd be fuckin' her and he'd go a little crazy, start raving, spitting. . . ."

"Sex freak?"

"Well, not exactly. The sex, I guess, was pretty conventional, it's just that he'd kind of lose control. He'd come after her with this really ferocious rush, and then afterwards, it was almost like she was a piece of furniture. Didn't want to hear her talk, didn't want to cuddle up. Usually he'd bring something to read, until he got it up again, and then he'd start freaking out all over."

"Hmph. That's not exactly the worst thing I've ever heard. . . ."

"Well, I'm gonna see her again tomorrow."

"Is there any way we can let Bekker know you're seeing her?"

Del sounded surprised. "What for?"

"Maybe push him a little? We got the surveillance running, so there shouldn't be any problem for her."

"Well . . . yeah, I guess we could work something out. Maybe I could get her to call him, let it slip somehow. . . ."

"Try," Lucas said.

19

The phone rang at three in the morning.

Cassie lay on her back, barely visible in the light from a streetlamp filtering through the blinds, the sheet pulled up around her throat, clutched there with two fists, as though she were dreaming sad dreams.

Lucas tiptoed into the kitchen and picked it up.

The dispatcher, with an overlay of personal concern: "Lucas, this is Kathy, at Dispatch. Sorry to wake you up, but there's a guy on the phone, says he's a doctor, says it's about your daughter. . . ."

His heart stopped. "Jesus. Patch him through."

"I'll push the button. . . ."

There was a moment of electronic vacancy, then the sound of somebody breathing, waiting.

"This is Davenport," Lucas snapped.

There was no immediate response, but the feeling of a presence, a background sound that might have been a distant highway.

"Hello, God damn it, this is Davenport."

A man's voice came back, low, gravelly, atonal, artificially clipped, the words evenly spaced, as though a robot were reading from a script: "There is nothing wrong with your daughter. Do you know who this is?"

Lucas had listened to the tapes. Loverboy. "I . . . yes, I think so."

"Give me your phone number." The voice was from *Star Wars*, from Darth Vader. No contractions. No sloppy constructions. Scripted and pared to the bone. "Do not make a call. I will call you back within five

234

seconds. If your line is busy, I will be gone. I have a pencil."

Lucas gave him the phone number. "You're gonna call . . ."

"Five seconds." There was a click and Lucas said, "Kathy, Kathy? Are you still on the line? God damn it." The dispatcher was gone, and Lucas hung up. A second or two later, the phone rang once.

Lucas snatched it up. "Yeah."

"I want to help, but I can not help directly," the voice grated, still on the script. "I will not come out. How can I help?"

"Did you send us a picture? I gotta know, just for identification."

"Yes. The cyclops. The killer does not look like the cyclops. The killer feels like the cyclops. His head looks like a pumpkin. There's something wrong with it."

"Not to say you're lying, but that sounds like the one-armed man, in that TV show a long time ago," Lucas said, letting a tint of skepticism color his voice. Reaching for control. Cassie came into the kitchen, sleepy, rubbing her eyes, drawn by the tone of his voice.

"Yes, *The Fugitive*," Loverboy said. "I thought of that. Where did you get an artist's drawing of me?"

Loverboy had seen Carly Bancroft on TV3. "Let me ask the questions for a minute, okay? If you get spooked, I don't want you ditching me before I get them out. Do you know of any connection between either of the Bekkers and Philip George?"

"No." There was a moment of hesitation, and then, off the script, voiced a notch higher, inflection: "I've speculated . . ." He changed his mind, and his voice, in mid-sentence: "No." The robot control again.

"Look," Lucas said. "You've got a conscience. We've got a fuckin' monster out there killing people and he

235

might not be done yet. We need every scrap we can get on the case."

"Get Michael Bekker."

"We don't know he's involved."

Back on script, all inflection gone: "He is a monster. But he did not kill Stephanie personally. I did not make that mistake."

"Look, give me the connection between you and George, if you think there is one," Lucas said, going soft. "If you want to stay out there, and you get caught later, I'll testify that you were feeding me information, that you helped, okay? Maybe help you out."

Another pause. Then: "No. I can not. You have thirty more seconds."

"Hold on . . . why?"

"Because you may trace the call. I budgeted two minutes. You have twenty-five seconds left. . . ."

"Wait, wait, we've got to set up some way for me to reach you. . . . If I need you, bad . . ."

"Put an advertisement in the *Tribune* personals. . . . Say you are no longer responsible for the debts of your wife. Sign it 'Lucas Smith.' I will call about this time. Two minutes. Look at Bekker. Stephanie was scared of him. Look at Bekker."

"Gimme one more question, one more," Lucas pleaded. "Why's Bekker a monster? What'd he do to Stephanie . . . ?"

Click.

"God damn it," Lucas said, looking at the phone.

"Who was it?" Cassie asked, moving up beside him. Her soft fingers trickled down his spine, warm, reassuring.

"Stephanie Bekker's lover," Lucas said. He poked a seven-digit number and the other end was picked up instantly: Dispatch.

"This is Davenport. Let me talk to Kathy."

236

"How's your daughter?" the woman asked a second later.

"That was all bullshit," Lucas said. "But it's okay, the guy had to get through to me. I'll need the tapes on your part of the call, so you might want to mark them."

"Well . . . there aren't tapes," the dispatcher said. "He came in on the non-emergency line, the thirty-eight."

"God damn it," Lucas said. He scratched his head. "Listen, write down what you remember he said and give it to Anderson in the morning. Write down everything you remember, what his voice sounded like, the whole nine yards."

"Heavy-duty?" she asked.

"Yeah. Very heavy."

When Lucas hung up, Cassie said, "I think . . . ," but he waved her away and said, "Shhh . . . I've got to remember . . ." She followed him into the bedroom and he flopped onto the bed, lay back and closed his eyes. Remember. Not the words. The feel of the other man. The voice was deep, the words well paced, the sentences clear. When he was off script for a moment, he'd used the word "speculated." He watched TV3.

And, Lucas thought, he looked like George. That's what he had *speculated*, Lucas was sure of it. Lucas had done the same thing: the phony identikit photo he was circulating was a simplified sketch of Philip George.

What else? Loverboy had not gone to the funeral, because he wasn't sure whether George was there. He had done research on Lucas. He knew that Lucas had a daughter and did not live with her. After the Crows case, there'd been quite a bit of press attention to Lucas, to Jennifer and their daughter, so the research wouldn't have been difficult—he might, in fact, simply be operating on memory. But just in case, a check of the libraries again, the newspaper files? He'd talk to Anderson about it.

Lucas opened his eyes. "Sorry, I just had to try to get it down. . . ."

"That's okay—that's how I remember lines," Cassie said.

"He's a smart sonofabitch," Lucas said. He stood up, found his underpants on a chair and pulled them on. "I've got to make a few notes."

She followed him down to the spare bedroom, looked at the charts hanging from the wall. "Wow. Mr Brainstorm."

"Pieces of the puzzle," he said. A sheet of paper, folded in quarters, was lying on the bed. As Cassie looked at the charts on the wall, he unfolded it. The photocopy of the cyclops painting. "The thing is, we know Bekker is goofy, but everything points in some other direction. . . ."

Cassie was still looking up at his charts, but somber now.

"Do you do this for all your cases?" she asked.

"The big complicated ones, yes."

"Have you ever had all the clues up there, posted, but not been able to figure them out until too late?"

"I don't know—I've never thought about it. You hardly get all the information you need to make a case, unless it's simple open-and-shut: you catch a guy red-handed, or five witnesses see a guy kill his wife," Lucas said. "If it's more complicated than that . . . I don't know. I've sent people to prison who claimed to be innocent and still claim they're innocent. I'm ninety-nine percent sure they're not innocent, but . . . you can't always know for sure."

"Wouldn't it freak you out if there was a key piece of information up there, you just didn't see it, and somebody got killed?"

"Mmm. I don't know. You can't blame yourself because a psycho kills people. I'm not Albert fuckin' Einstein."

"So what're you going to do next?" Cassie asked, still wide-eyed.

Lucas tossed the folded Xerox of the cyclops back on the bed. "What any good cop would do at three in the morning. Go back to bed."

Lucas set the alarm for seven. When it went off, he silenced it, slipped out of bed, leaving Cassie asleep, and went to the kitchen to phone Daniel. He caught the chief at breakfast and told him about the call from Stephanie's lover.

"Sonofabitch," Daniel sputtered. "So you're right. But why'd they kill George?"

"He said he didn't know. Actually, he said he'd speculated about it, but didn't want to talk about it. But I know what he was thinking: that he looks like George. And when you sort through all the implications of that, it points at Bekker," Lucas said, and explained.

Daniel listened and agreed. "Now what? How do we get to the guy?"

"We could maybe invent a crisis, put an ad in the paper, stake people out all over town, wire up my line, and when he calls—bam, we're tracing. We might get him."

"Hmph. Maybe. I'll talk to some of the techs about it. But what happens if he calls from Minnetonka?"

"I don't know. The thing is, he's smart," Lucas said. "If we fuck with him, he might just go back into the woodwork. I don't want to risk chasing him away. He can put the finger on a suspect, if we ever come up with one."

"Okay. So let's keep this tight between us," Daniel said. "I'll order a tap on your line and we'll monitor calls. I'll talk with Sloan and Anderson and Shearson and see if we can come up with some kind of pressure that'll get to him to call back."

"I could do that. I figure . . ."

"No. I don't want you chasing Loverboy. I want you focused on the killer or the killers—Bekker and whoever he's working with."

"There's not much there."

"You just keep pushing. Keep moving around. I got all kinds of guys who can do the pony work. I want you on the killer before he does it again."

20

Not knowing the nature of neighborhood friendships around Bekker, and afraid to ask, the surveillance team decided not to seek a listening post among Bekker's neighbors.

Instead the team keyed on the intersections around the front and back of his house. From two parked cars, they could watch the front door directly, and both ends of the alley that ran behind his house. The cars were shuffled every hour or so, both to relieve the tedium and to lessen the possibility that Bekker might grow suspicious of one particular car.

Even so, a jogger, a woman lawyer, spotted one of the surveillance cars within an hour of the beginning of the watch on Bekker and reported it to police. She was told that the car belonged to an undercover detective on a narcotics study, and was asked to keep it confidential. Later that same day she saw a second car and realized that Bekker was being watched. She thought about mentioning it to a neighbor but did not.

The surveillance began in the evening. The next morning, four tired cops took Bekker to work. Four more monitored him in the hospital, but quickly understood that a perfect net would be impossible: the hospital was a warren of passageways, stairs, elevators and tunnels. They settled for containing him within the complex, with occasional eyeball checks of his location. While he was pinned, a narc stuck a transmitter under the rear bumper of his car.

*   *   *

The discovery of George's body was a sensation and a shock. Bekker watched, aghast, a TV3 tape of khaki-clad deputies marching through the brambles near the lakeside cabin, horsing out a litter. The body was covered with a pristine white sheet, wrapped like a chrysalis. A blonde newscaster, with a face as stylistically and cosmetically appropriate for the scene as a Japanese player's is for Noh, intoned a dirgelike report, with the gray skies hanging theatrically in the background.

Bekker, not a watcher of television, found a newspaper TV guide and marked the newscasts. The other stations were on the story, although none had TV3's film.

The next evening, fearing more bad news, he was non-plussed to find himself watching a seemingly interminable story about the recovery of a boxcar full of television sets from a warehouse someplace in Minneapolis. Television sets? He began to relax, switching channels, found television sets everywhere, and television reporters in flak jackets. . . .

If anything important had happened, surely he wouldn't be seeing television sets. . . .

He nearly missed it. He was switching through the channels when he found the blonde again, back in the studio and out of her flak jacket. She delivered another body blow: Davenport, she said, did not believe that Philip George was Stephanie's lover, believed that the lover was still at large, and was circulating an identikit picture of the man. Davenport, she said, was a genius.

"What?" Bekker blurted, staring at the television, as though it could answer him. Could Davenport be right? Had they missed with George? He needed to think. Nothing ephemeral. Needed something to reach him, something to focus. He opened the brass case, studied it. Yes. He lifted it to his face and his tongue flicked out, picking up the capsule the way a frog picks up a fly. Focus.

*   *   *

The flight was not a good one. Not terrifying, like the snake, but not good. He could manage it, though, steering between the shadows where Davenport hid. God-damned Davenport, this case should be done, he should be free. . . .

Bekker came back, the taste of blood on his lips. Blood. He looked down, found blood on his chest again, stirred himself. He'd been away again. . . . What had happened? What? Ah . . . yes. The lover. What to do? To settle, of course.

He staggered to his feet and wandered toward the stairs. To the bathroom, to wash. He went away, came back a few minutes later, his hand on the banister leading up the stairs, his eyes dry from staring. He blinked once. Druze had been uncharacteristically moody on the trip to Wisconsin, the trip to cut George's eyes. Hadn't really understood the necessity of it. Was he pulling away? No. But Druze had changed . . . didn't have moods.

Need to involve him again. Bekker's eyes strayed to the phone. Just one call? No. Not from here. He must not.

He went away once more while he groomed himself and dressed, but he could not remember the content of the trip—if there was any content—when he returned. He finished dressing, took the car out, drove to the hospital. Inside the building, he took the stairs down, hurrying, not thinking.

The quickness of Bekker's move confused the surveillance team. One of the narcs was behind him by ten seconds, walked straight down the hall past the elevators and the staircase door, which were in an alcove. And Bekker was gone. Perhaps the elevator had been waiting, ready to go? The narc hurried back outside and told the team leader, who had a cellular telephone and punched Bekker's office number into it.

"Can I speak to Dr Bekker?" The team leader looked like a mail clerk, short hair, harried, gone to a little weight.

"I'm sorry, Dr Bekker hasn't come in yet."

"I'm downstairs and I thought I saw him just a minute ago."

"I sit right here by the door, and he's not in."

"We've lost him," the narc told the rest of the team. "He's got to be in the building. Spread out. Find him."

Bekker hurried down the steps to the tunnel that led to the next building. He stopped at a candy machine, got a Nut Goodie, then hurried on through the tunnel to a pay telephone.

Druze was not at his apartment. Bekker hesitated, then called information and got the number for the Lost River Theater. A woman answered and, after Bekker asked for Druze, dropped the telephone and went away. Not knowing whether she was looking for Druze or simply had been exasperated by the request, Bekker stood waiting, for two minutes, then three, and finally, Druze: "*Hello?*"

"You heard?" Bekker asked.

"Are you at a safe phone?" Druze's voice was low, almost a whisper.

"Yes. I've been very careful." Bekker looked down the empty hallway.

"I heard that they found the body and that this cop, Davenport, doesn't think George was the lover. . . . And it's not a game they're playing. He's got some good reason to think so."

"How do you know that?"

"Because he's been seeing one of the actresses here, Cassie Lasch. She was the one who found Armistead,

244

and she and Davenport struck up some kind of relationship."

"You mentioned her. She lives in your building. . . ."

"Yeah, that's the one," Druze said. His words were tumbling over each other. "Cassie was telling us this morning that the lover's still out there. I think Davenport's talking to him, but doesn't know exactly who he is. And something else. The cops have supposedly got some kind of picture of me. Not a police drawing, it's something else."

"Jesus, can that be right?" Bekker rubbed his forehead furiously. This was getting complicated.

"Somebody asked Cassie why we wouldn't have seen it on television, if that's true," Druze said. "She said she hadn't seen the picture, but she knew about it and that there was something weird about it. And she was positive about the lover, by the way. She was being mysterious, but I think she knows. I think they're sleeping together, she's getting pillow talk. . . ."

"Damn." Bekker gnawed on a fingernail. "You know what we've got to do? We talked about doing a number three before George came along? I think we've got to do it. We've got to do somebody that doesn't make any sense for either one of us. Somebody completely off the wall."

"Who?"

"I don't know. That's the whole point. Somebody at random. The goddamned shopping-mall parking lots are full of women. Go get one."

There was a moment of silence and then Druze said, "I'm really hanging out there, man."

"And so am I," Bekker snapped. "If there is some kind of drawing of you—if Stephanie's friend sent them something—and if this actress person sees it, then we've got serious trouble."

"Yeah, you're right about that. She sees me every goddamned day and night of my life. . . ."

"What's her name again?" Bekker asked.

"Cassie Lasch. But if we do her . . ."

"I know. We couldn't do it now, but later, next week. . . . If we can get the cops to go hounding off somewhere, maybe she could have an accident. Something unrelated. What floor is she on? High up?"

"Six, I guess. And she did once try to commit suicide. . . ."

"So maybe if she went out a window . . . I don't know, Carlo. We'll work something. But we've got to get the cops going somewhere else. Something not related to the theater or to the university or antiques . . ."

"So . . . are you serious? A mall?" Druze sounded confused, uncertain.

"Yeah. I am. Pick one out on the edge of town. Burnsville would be good. Maplewood. Roseville. You're bright, figure out some way. . . . Pick somebody who looks like she's on a big shopping trip. Get her at her car. Then dump the car with all the packages. Be sure you do the eyes. The thing is, we'll want it to look like it's totally random. . . . You know what? Maybe you could cruise the lots. See if you could get somebody with Iowa plates or something."

"I don't know. . . . I gotta have time to think about it."

"If the lover's out there, we don't have time," Bekker urged. "We've got to lead them away from us, at least until we can pinpoint the guy."

"Jesus, I wish . . ."

"Hey. We had to get rid of them. We deserved to be rid of them. Now we just have to clean up a little bit. Okay?"

Silence.

"Okay?" Bekker demanded.

"Okay, I guess. I gotta go. . . ."

*　　*　　*

Druze was getting sticky: Bekker would have to move on him.

On the way back to his office, Bekker stopped at a men's room and urinated. He went to a sink and was washing his hands when a student came in, looked at him, then casually moved to a urinal. A heavy canvas bookbag hung from his shoulder.

The student looked a little odd, Bekker thought. The jeans and cardigan were okay, the oxford-cloth shirt was all right. . . . He glanced at the student again as he went out.

It was the shoes, he thought, pleased that he'd picked it out. The kid must have just gotten out of the army or something. You didn't see students wearing that kind of black, shiny-toed, oxford anymore. Not since Vietnam, anyway.

In the rest-room, the student listened to Bekker's heels hitting the concrete floor, moving away, then took the radio out of his bag. "I got him," he said. "He was in the can. He's on the basement level, on his way up the west stairs."

At the elevators, another student was waiting to go up, reading one of the free entertainment newspapers. He had shoes like the kid in the rest-room. A new trend? A signal to buy oxford stock? On the other hand, neither of the kids looked exactly like fashion trend-setters. . . .

Back to the office, or up to see the patient? Bekker glanced at his watch. He had time, and nobody coming to see him. A small thrill pulsed through him. Might as well do some serious work.

Bekker rode up to Surgery, nodded to a nurse, and went into the men's locker room, peeled his clothes off and dressed himself in a lavender scrub suit. Technically, he didn't need a scrub suit; he wouldn't be going into Surgery or Burns, where they were most useful. But he liked them. They were comfortable. And he liked them like surgeons liked them, for the aura. . . . When he was wearing a scrub suit, people always called him "Dr Bekker," which they sometimes forgot when he was in the Path area.

With his face, and with the aura of the suit, sometimes he simply went down and relaxed in the cafeteria, let the public look at him. . . .

Not today. When he was dressed, he pulled paper shoe-covers over his loafers, got his clipboard from the locker and headed up another flight of stairs, his heart pounding a bit. It had been a few days since he'd talked to Sybil. He really had to find more time.

At the top of the stairs, he pushed through the fire door and walked down the hall to the nurses' station.

"Dr Bekker," a nurse said, looking up. "You're earlier than usual."

"Had a little extra time." He put on a smile. "Any changes?"

"No, not since you were last here," the nurse said, not managing a smile. "Changes" was Bekker's euphemism for "death." It had taken her a few of his visits to catch on.

"Well, I think I'll wander down," Bekker said. "Anywhere I shouldn't go?"

"Room seven-twelve, we have a radiation treatment there—we're keeping that clean."

"I'll stay away," Bekker promised. He left her at the desk, plowing through the endless paperwork that seemed to afflict nurses. He stopped at two rooms, for show, before heading to Sybil's.

"Sybil? Are you awake?" Her eyes were closed as he stepped into the room, and they didn't open, but he could see that a drip tube leading to her arm was working. "Sybil?"

Still her eyes didn't open. He glanced down the hallway, then stepped up to her bed, leaned forward, placed his fingertips on her forehead, pulled up an eyelid with his thumb and murmured, "Come out, come out, wherever you are . . . ."

The television behind him was tuned to TV3, a game show that apparently involved some kind of leapfrog. He didn't notice; Sybil had opened her eyes and was looking frantically around the room.

"No, no. There isn't any help, dear," Bekker crooned. "No help anywhere."

Bekker spent an hour at the hospital. He was picked up by the surveillance team as he left through the lobby.

"He's got a funny look on his face," the narc said into her purse. "He's coming right at me." She watched Bekker go down the sidewalk, past the bench where she was reading a car issue of *Consumer Reports*.

"What's funny?" the crew chief asked, as the net closed around Bekker again.

"I don't know," the narc said. "He looked like he just got laid or something."

"A look you know well," said a cop named Louis, normally in uniform, but pulled for this job.

"Shut up," the crew chief said. "Stay on his ass and don't spook him. We're doing good."

Halfway across the campus, Bekker did a little jig. He did it quickly, almost unconsciously, but not quite—he caught himself and looked around guiltily before moving on.

"What the fuck was that all about?" the narc asked.

"Potty-mouth," said Louis.

"Shut up," said the crew chief. "And I don't know. We oughta get some video on this guy, you know? I woulda liked to have some video on that." The crew took him home, where another crew picked up the watch. Louis, who liked wisecracks, went back to police headquarters, where he bumped into the police reporter for Channel Eight.

"What's happening, Louis?" the reporter asked. "Workin' on anything good?"

Louis chewed a lot of gum and tipped his head, a wiseguy. "Got a thing going here and there," he said. "Hell of a story, if I could only tell ya."

"You look like you been on surveillance," the reporter suggested. "All dressed up like a human being."

"Did I say surveillance?" Louis grinned. He liked reporters. He'd been quoted several times at crime scenes.

The reporter frowned. "Hey, are you working that Bekker thing?"

Louis' smile faded. "I got no comment. Like, really."

"I won't fuck you, Louis," the reporter said. "But there's a hell of a leak around here somewhere, and TV3 is kicking ass."

Louis liked reporters. . . .

21

Anderson tossed two manila file folders on Lucas' desk.

"Surveillance report, and summary interviews from the theater people and Armistead's friends," he said.

"Anything in them?" Lucas asked. He was leaning back in his chair, his feet on a desk drawer. A boom box on the floor was playing "Radar Love."

"Not much," Anderson said, with a flash of his yellow teeth. He was the department's computer junkie. He dressed like a hillbilly and had once been a ferocious street cop. "Bekker mostly hung around the university, his office, the hospital. . . ."

"All right, I'll take a look," Lucas said, yawning. "If we don't break something soon . . ."

"I'm hearing about it from Daniel," Anderson said, nodding. "That goddamned warehouse raid saved our asses, but there's nothing going on today."

"How many TV sets did we get?"

"One hundred and forty-four: twelve dozen. Hell of a haul. Also thirty Hitachi VCRs, six Sunbeam bathroom scales, about thirty cases of Kleenex man-size bathroom tissues, some water-soaked, and one box of Life-styles Stimula vibra-ribbed rubbers, which Terry said were for personal use only. Wonder if they work?"

"What?"

"Vibra-ribbed rubbers . . ."

"I don't know. I use Good-year Eagle all-weathers myself."

Anderson left, and Lucas picked up the surveillance folder and flipped through it. Bekker had done a jig:

Lucas spotted it immediately and thought back to the night he'd met Bekker and the frenzied dance he'd seen through the window. What was he doing in the hospital? Might be worthwhile checking again . . .

The folders yielded nothing else. Lucas tossed them aside, yawned again, feeling pleasantly sleepy. Cassie was a little rough, a little muscular in her lovemaking. Interesting.

And different. He watched her, comparing her with Jennifer, finding the differences. Jennifer had a tough veneer, developed over years as a reporter. Lucas had the same shell. So did most social workers.

"When you see too much shit in one lifetime, you've got to find a way to deal with it," Jennifer had said once. "Reporters and cops develop the shell as a defense. If you can laugh at a crazy rapist, you know, 'the B. O. Fucker' and all those cute names you cops develop, well, then you don't have to take it so seriously."

"Yeah, right, pass the joint," Lucas had said.

"See? That's exactly what I'm talking about. . . ."

Cassie had no shell. Everything that happened to her, she felt. Psychiatry, she thought, was normal. Most people were screwed up, but it helped to talk about it, even if you had to pay somebody to listen.

Occasionally, when he'd been with Jennifer, Lucas had had a feeling that they both yearned to talk, to let it out, but couldn't. Talking would have made them too vulnerable and, each of them knowing the other, the vulnerability would have been used. . . .

"Hey, you get beat up. People use you, you get played for a sucker," Cassie had said, when he told her about that. "Big fuckin' deal. Everybody gets beat up."

And Lucas had once again found himself trying to dissect his episode of depression: "I've fooled around with a lot of women, ever since I was a teenager. I slowed down a lot after I started dating Jen—slipped up a couple of times, bad, but we were making it until . . you know. But the thing is, when she walked . . . I just stopped. Fell off the cliff. The real pit was last fall, around Thanksgiving, I'd just gotten back from seeing this woman in New York and she'd pretty much called off our relationship. I thought I was crazy. Not crazy crazy, like in the movies. Crazy where you don't get out of bed for two days. You don't pay the mortgage, because you can't get yourself to write a check."

"I once didn't pay my taxes for that reason. I had the money, but I couldn't deal with the government," Cassie had said, not laughing.

"I was down there for three or four months, and when I started feeling like I was moving again, I was afraid of looking at a woman. Any woman. I was afraid that things wouldn't work out, and I'd go back in the pit. I'd rather be celibate than go back in the pit. I'd rather do anything than go back in there. . . ."

"You had it bad," Cassie had said simply. "That's when you need somebody with really big boobs so you can curl up and put your head between them and suck on your thumb."

Lucas had started laughing, trying to get his head between Cassie's breasts. One thing led to another. . . .

Daniel walked into Lucas' office and shut the door. "We got a problem."

"What?"

Daniel ran a hand through his thinning hair, his face caught between anger and confusion. "Tell me the truth: Have you been feeding stuff to Channel Eight?"

"No. I've been working a woman from TV3. . . ."

"Yeah, yeah, I know about that. Nothing going to Eight?"

"No. Honest to God," Lucas said. "What happened?"

Daniel dropped into the visitor's chair. "I got a call from Jon Ayres over at Channel Eight. He says he has a source who tells them that we've got a suspect under surveillance and we're about to make a bust. I denied it. They said they had it pretty solid. I still denied it and told them that false stories could damage our investigation. The guy got huffy, we passed some more bullshit, and he said he'd think about it. . . ."

"That means they're going to use it," Lucas said urgently. "You've got to call the station manager."

"Too late," Daniel said. He pointed at the wall clock. Twelve-fifteen. "It was the lead story on the noon news."

"Sonofabitch," Lucas groaned.

"I know, I know. . . ."

Del stopped by late in the day. "We hit it off and now I can't shut her up about Bekker. She's *insisting* that I investigate him. The problem is, she doesn't know much."

"Like nothing?"

"She thinks he might be on some kind of speed. He gets weird. And here's something: He does have a thing about eyes."

"He does?" Lucas leaned forward. This *was* something. "What?"

"Remember how she told us that he liked to humiliate her? Force her to do blow jobs and so on? When she was doing them, he'd always make her hold her head so he could look in her eyes. Used to say something about the eyes being the hallway to the soul, or something like that . . ."

"These lovely lamps, these windows of the soul . . ." Lucas quoted.

"Who said that?"

"Can't remember. I once took a poetry course at Metro State, I remember it from that."

"Well, he's apparently got a thing for them. He still scares her, when she sees him around the hospital."

"Does she have any idea what he's doing now?"

"No. Want me to ask?"

"Yeah. You'll be seeing her again, huh?"

"Sure, if you want me to pump her some more," Del said.

"I wasn't thinking about that," Lucas said. "I was thinking . . . you look pretty good."

Bekker learned about the police surveillance from Druze. He half expected a call, to warn of a third killing, and every few hours he checked the answering machine.

"TV report on Channel Eight says the cops are doing surveillance on a suspect," Druze said without identifying himself. "I've been watching and I don't think it's me." And he was gone.

What? Bekker couldn't focus, and played it again.

"TV report on Channel Eight . . ."

Surveillance? Bekker reset the tape, his mind working furiously. If they *were* watching Druze and had seen him make this call, would they be able to trace it? He thought not, yet he wasn't sure. But it was unlikely that they would be watching Druze—how would they get to him? The alleged picture? Perhaps.

It was more likely that *he* was the one being watched, if it wasn't just some kind of TV fantasy. The image of the student in the men's room came to him, and the second one at the library. . . .

Not military shoes, he said to himself. Cop shoes . . .

22

The weather patterns were seesawing across the state, Canadian cold and Gulf heat. Druze felt as if he was breathing water. Thunderstorms prowled western Minnesota; TV weathermen said they'd be into the metro area before nine o'clock. From the interstate, Druze could see lightning to the north and west. The storm was too far away for the thunder to be heard.

Maplewood Mall was the northeastern shopping anchor for St. Paul, out in the suburbs. Low crime, high affluence. Boys in letter jackets, teenage girls trying out their new slinks.

Druze cruised the parking lot, watching the shoppers. He wanted a woman leaving the mall. Forties, so she'd fit the profile. If he could get her at the right place, he wouldn't have to move her. Do it right in the parking lot, leave her there. The quicker she was found, the quicker the cops would be turned.

He stopped at a cross-drive and a woman walked in front of his headlights; she wore a cardigan, slacks and high heels, held a purse with both hands, a determined look on her face. A little too old, Druze thought, and not in the right place.

He parked, got out and sauntered toward the mall. A bronze rent-a-cop car rolled slowly through the lot, and Druze headed inside. He'd worked on his face with Cover Mark cosmetics and wore a felt hat with a snap brim, so he wouldn't be particularly noticeable from a range of more than a few feet. Not unless they saw the nose. He pulled the hat farther down on his forehead.

*   *   *

Druze was worried. In the beginning, when he and Bekker had worked through the plan, it had seemed simple. Bekker would take Armistead, and Druze would take Stephanie Bekker. Both he and Bekker would get what they wanted—Bekker his freedom, Druze his security. Both would have solid alibis. If the pressure on Bekker got too great, Druze could take a third. No problem. But then the lover came along. . . .

Was George the right one? He looked like the man in the hall, but the man in the hall had been wearing only a towel, his thinning hair had been wet, his face contorted. Druze had seen him only for an instant. Had he been heavier than George? Now, at this distance, Druze just wasn't sure. He'd looked at too many pictures of people who were almost right. Contaminated with information, he thought.

Bekker . . . He was no longer sure of Bekker. They'd met after a show, in a theater café, Bekker there with Stephanie and some kind of doctors' group from the university. Bekker had been out on the edge of the group, left alone. Druze had come in, also alone, looking for a drink. He'd seen the beautiful man immediately, couldn't take his eyes away: Bekker had so much. . . .

Bekker had been equally fascinated. He'd made the first approach: *Hello there, I think I saw you on the stage a few minutes ago.* . . .

And later, much later, after they were . . . friends? was that right? . . . Bekker had said, "We're the opposite sides of the same coin, my friend, trapped by our looks."

But it hadn't been their appearances that held them together. It had been something else: the taste for violence? what?

He stood next to the atrium rail in the mall, looking down to the lower floor. Shoppers strolled down the length of the mall, some still in careful winter dress, dark, somber, protective, gloves sticking out from coat pockets. Others, the younger ones, had shifted with the Gulf winds, going into summer, T-shirts under light nylon windbreakers, a few of them in shorts, surfers for the boys, tennis shorts for the girls.

He started picking out women. Forties. Somebody attractive. Somebody who might catch the eye of a psycho. There were dozens of them, singles, twos and threes, tall, small, heavy, slender, scowling, laughing, intent, window-shopping, strolling, paying cash, checking receipts, holding up blouses. . . . Druze unconsciously flipped his car keys in the air with one hand, picked them out of the air with the other, tossed them back to the first, and did it again.

And he chose: Eenie meenie minie moe . . .

Nancy Dunen couldn't believe the price of jeans. She never believed. Every time she came in, she thought the last time must have been an aberration, a nightmare. The twins always managed to wear out the back-to-school jeans, bought in September, at the same time in the spring. Two twelve-year-olds, four pairs of jeans, thirty-two dollars a pair . . . she stared blankly into the middle distance, her lips moving, as she calculated. A hundred twenty-eight dollars. My God, where would it come from? Maybe Visa would have a sense of humor about the whole thing.

She held the pants up, checking for flaws in the fabric. Noticed the feminine cut. Twelve years old, and they were getting curves in their pants already. Must be hormones in the breakfast cereal.

A man meandered past the open front of the store. Something wrong with his face, though it was hard to tell exactly what it was. He was wearing an old-fashioned brown felt hat, with the brim snapped down. She was looking past the pants when she saw him; she felt the light *clink* of eye contact, turned away as the man turned away, and she scraped at a knot in the denim with a fingernail. Good eye, Dunen, she thought. She put that pair of jeans back, got another.

Nancy sometimes thought she might be pretty, and sometimes she was sure she wasn't. She kept her dark hair cut short, skimped on the make-up, stayed in shape with a three-time-a-week jog around the neighborhood. She didn't spend a lot of time worrying about whether she was pretty or not, although she claimed she had the best forty-three-year-old butt in the neighborhood. She was settled in her body, in her life. Her husband seemed to like her, and she liked him, and they both liked the kids. . . .

She took the jeans to the cashier's counter, groaned when she saw the Visa charge slip, folded it, dropped it in her purse.

"If my husband finds it, he'll wring my neck," she said to the girl behind the counter.

"Yeah, but . . ." The blonde salesgirl tossed her hair with a smile and made a piano-playing gesture with her hand as she put the jeans in a bag. Husbands can be handled, she was saying. "They're nice pants."

Nancy left the store and, bag in hand, window-shopped at a women's store, but she kept moving. The man with the hat was behind her on the escalator, heading toward the same exit. She noticed but didn't think about it. Let's see, I was out the exit by the cookie stand. . . .

A burly high school kid with a letter jacket and a white-sidewall haircut held the door for her. He was wearing an earring and looked at her butt, and she smiled to herself. When she was growing up, in the fifties, there were older boys with sidewalls, but they'd have cut their own wrists before wearing an earring. . . .

Nancy stepped over a curb and stopped at her car, and fished in her purse for her keys. The man with the hat went by. She almost nodded—they'd sort of looked at each other a few times in the mall—but she didn't. Instead, she popped open the car door, dumped the jeans in the backseat, climbed in and started the engine. She should make it home by eight. What was on TV tonight?

Druze had been ready, the knife-sharpening steel in his pocket, the same one he'd used on George. He had cleaned it meticulously, kept it in his kitchen drawer. And it was ready when he needed it. He followed the woman out of the mall, into the parking lot, ready to close on her, watching for other walkers, for cars turning down the rows, checking the lights. He was ready. . . .

The woman stopped at the first car in the lot, a white Chevy Spectrum. Propped the bag between her hip and the car, began digging in her purse. They were absolutely exposed to the mall. If he moved on her, he would be seen. He glanced back: people on the sidewalk, at the doors, coming, going . . . Shit.

He felt stupid. If he picked a woman inside, there was an excellent chance that she'd be parked somewhere in the open, where he couldn't get to her. Or even that she'd be picked up at the curb by a husband or son. He'd have to wait outside. He went by Nancy Dunen, unconsciously flipped his keys in the air with one hand, picked them out with the other. The woman glanced vaguely at him, then went back to her purse. He never looked back, he heard the door slam and the engine start. . . .

Druze went back to his car, moved it to the edge of the lot, tried a parking space, found he couldn't see out of it, tried another. Good. He parked, turned off the lights and waited. He was parked at an acute angle to a side entry.

People wouldn't naturally look at this area, but he could watch them coming through.

He waited five minutes. Nothing. Then a couple crossed the lot, walking toward the cluster where Druze was parked. A single woman followed them by twenty yards. The couple reached their car; the man walked around to the passenger side to open the door, then opened the trunk to put their packages inside. The single woman reached the cluster as the man closed the trunk and popped open the driver's-side door. By that time, the single woman, unaware that she was being watched, and not more than thirty feet from Druze, was already getting into her car. She backed out at the same time as the couple, and they were gone.

Damn. She would have been a good one, Druze thought. A little young, but that was okay. He slouched in the seat, the hat brim pulled down. People walked in and out of the lighted doors. Eenie meenie minie moe . . .

Kelsey Romm was wearing a scarlet blouse and jeans, with white gym shoes, her hair long, her lipstick dark. She worked part-time at Maplewood and part-time at a convenience store in Roseville, and on weekends at a Target. Sometimes the workload made her sick to her stomach; sometimes her legs ached so bad that she couldn't bend them to sit down. But full-time jobs were hard to find. Economics, her Maplewood boss told her. You could patch together a bunch of part-time employees and avoid all benefits, he said. And it made scheduling easier. It wasn't his fault, he said: he didn't own the store. He was only following orders.

She got the same story at the other places. If she didn't like it, there were plenty of high school kids looking for jobs. It wasn't as if she needed a lot of skill. Scan a code, and a number came up on the cash register. Scan another, and the machine told you the change. Kelsey Romm needed the work. Two kids, both in junior high. Two mistakes, running wild, the girl already into alcohol and who knew what else. She didn't even like them much, but they were hers, no doubt about that.

Kelsey Romm walked with her head down. She always walked with her head down. You didn't see things that way. She didn't see Druze, either. She walked to the car, an '83 Chevy Cavalier, brown, a beater, air didn't work, radio didn't work, tires were going bald, the brakes sounded like they had air in them, the front-seat latch was broken. . . .

She stuck her key in the door lock. She saw the man at the last minute and started to turn her head. The steel caught her behind the ear, and the last thing Kelsey Romm saw in her life was the entrance to the Maplewood Mall, and a kid leaning on a trashcan.

If you'd told her this was the way it would end, she would have nodded. She would have said, "I believe it."

Druze saw her hurry through the entrance and knew instinctively that she'd be coming all the way out. He cracked the car door, so it would open silently. She had her head down and came straight across the lot, heading for the row behind Druze's car. That was fine. That was good. He got out and sauntered down the row, flipped his keys in the air with one hand, picked them out with the other, did it again. There were still a few people on the sidewalks outside the mall, a kid standing by the entrance, looking the other way. This could work. . . .

She came on, paying no attention to him, turned in at an old Chevy. He'd seen where she was going, and made his own move, cutting between the cars. If she had her keys in her hand, he thought, he might be too late. He put

262

his own keys into his pocket, got a grip on the sharpening steel and stepped a little more quickly. She started digging in her purse as she turned in at her car, her head still down. Like a mole, Druze thought. Digging. He was close now, could see the shiny fabric of her shirt, glanced around, nobody . . .

And he was there, swinging, the steel whipping around, the woman cocking her head at the last minute.

The steel hit and bit and she went down, bouncing off the car as the professor had; but the woman made a noise, loud, like the caw of a crow, air from her lungs squeezing out. Druze looked around: he was okay, he thought. The kid by the garbage can might be looking at them . . . but he wasn't moving.

Druze stooped, pulled open the woman's purse, found her keys, unlocked the door, picked her up and shoved her into the Chevy. The car had bucket seats with an automatic-transmission console between them, and she lay humped over the seats, in an awkward, broken position. Druze stood straight, checked the lot again, then got in with her, touched her neck. She wasn't breathing. She was gone.

He used a screwdriver on her eyes.

Bekker was Beauty tonight, a little sting of amphetamine, just a taste of acid. His mind was moving, a facile, glittering thing, a mink of an intellect, and it worked through the problems in what seemed like no time at all . . . although time must have passed . . . it was light outside when he came home, and now, it was dark . . . How long . . . ? He went away again.

Cheryl Clark had called him at his office.

She wanted to come back, he thought. Knew his wife was gone now. Was trying to ingratiate herself. Had news: A cop had been coming around to see her. They wanted to

263

know about his love life, his personal habits. She thought he should know, she said.

Maybe he would see her again. She'd grown tiresome after a while, but there'd been a few nights. . . .

His mind was like liquid fire, the taste of the MDMA in his mouth, under his tongue. What? More? He really should be more temperate. . . . When he came back—came back long enough to know that he would be okay—he'd found the solution to the surveillance. So simple; it had been there the whole time. He had a friend with the authorities, did he not?

The surveillance net picked up Bekker as he left the alley, headed down to Hennepin Avenue and took Hennepin to the interstate. He went to the library, parked and went inside. The net was with him. Looked at a book in the reference section. Headed back to the car. One of the cops in the net looked at the book, a cross-reference directory for St. Paul. He noted the pages: if he'd had time to scan the names, he'd have found Lucas Davenport listed about halfway down the second column. . . .

Across the Mississippi and then south. Nice neighborhood . . . Damn St. Paul addresses, the numbers had nothing to do with the streets. Started at 1 and went however high they needed to go . . .

Davenport's house was not particularly impressive, he thought when he found it, except for the location. One-story rambler, stone and white siding, big front yard. Nice house, but not terrific. Stephanie wouldn't have given it a second look. Lights in the windows.

He rang the doorbell, and a moment later Davenport was there.

"Officer Davenport," Bekker said, nodding, pleased to see Lucas. He had his hands in the pockets of his hip-length leather coat. "You said you would see that I'm not harassed. Why am I followed everywhere?"

Davenport, perplexed, stepped out on the porch. His face was like a chunk of wood, and Bekker stepped back. "What?"

"Why am I being followed? I know they're out there," Bekker said, flipping a hand at the street. "This is not paranoia. I've seen your officers watching me. Young men in college clothes and police shoes . . ."

Davenport's face suddenly tightened, seized by some sort of rictus, Bekker thought. He stepped close and gripped Bekker's coat at the lapels. He lifted and Bekker went up on his toes.

"Put me down . . ." Bekker said. He was strong, but Davenport held him awkwardly close and his arms were bent. He tried to push Davenport away, but the cop held him, shaking, apparently gripped by rage.

"You never come to my house," Davenport rasped, his eyes wide and crazy. "You hear that, motherfucker? The last guy that came to my house, I killed. You come to my house, I'll kill your ass just like I did him."

"I'm, I'm sorry," Bekker stuttered. Davenport was not the cool, rational cop who had walked through Stephanie's bedroom. His eyes were straining open, his head cocked forward on a tense neck, his hands hard as stones.

Davenport shoved Bekker back, releasing him. "Go. Get the fuck out of here."

Bekker staggered. Down the sidewalk, ten feet from the porch, he said, "I just wanted the surveillance pulled, I don't want to be hectored. . . ."

"Call the chief," Lucas said. His voice was cold, brutal. "Just stay the fuck away from my house."

Davenport stepped back inside and shut the door. Bekker stood on the walk for a moment, looking at the

265

door, not quite believing. Davenport had been friendly, he'd understood some things. . . .

Bekker was in his car when his own anger caught him.

Treated like a Russian peasant. Kicked down the stairs. Thrown off. He pounded his palms on the steering wheel. Saw himself striking out, the edge of his hand smashing under Davenport's nose, blood rolling down his dark, bleak face; saw himself kicking, going for the balls . . .

"Fuckin' treat me like that, fuckin' treat me like a . . . a . . . Fuckin' treat me, you can't, you better think about it . . . Fuckin' treat me . . ."

As Bekker drove away from Davenport's house, the net still in place, a teenage boy strolled up to Kelsey Romm's car and peeked inside. Was she fuckin' somebody? What was she . . .

He'd been leaning on a trashcan outside the mall entrance, waiting for something to happen, somebody to show up, when he saw something happen. He didn't know what. There was this guy. . . . He had gotten a videocassette for his birthday, a movie, *Darkman*, his favorite flick. And this guy looked like Darkman, no bandages, but the hat was right. . . . And something happened.

He saw the guy duck inside the car. He was in it for a moment or two; then he got out, went to another car and drove away. It never occurred to the kid to look at the license plate. And he was not the kind of kid who knew his cars. He was just a kid who hung out and watched *Darkman* in the afternoons, after school. . . .

The car with the woman didn't move. When the other car, the Darkman car, was out of sight, the kid considered for a moment, then ambled across the sidewalk, down the long rows of cars. What was she? Was she, like, a hooker, giving blow jobs in the backseat? That'd be something.

He got close, he peeked. . . .

"Aw, Jesus . . . Aw, Jesus . . ." The kid ran toward the mall, his arms milling. Halfway there, he began screaming, "Help . . ."

Lucas, still hot from Bekker's visit, was working on Druid's Pursuit when the watch commander called.

23

A thunderstorm was rolling across Minneapolis when Lucas left his house, lightning crackling through the clouds, storm-front winds lashing the elm branches overhead. He went north, up Highway 280, the lights of downtown Minneapolis to the west, barely visible through the advancing rain. The storm caught him just before he turned east, a few drops splatting off the windshield, and then a torrent, a waterfall, hailstones pecking on the roof, small white beads of ice bouncing off the road in his headlights. He turned east on I-694 and the rain slackened, then quit altogether as he outran the storm front.

From the highway, the mall was screened by an intervening block of buildings, but he could see red emergency lights flashing off window glass. The White Bear Avenue exit was jammed. He put the Porsche on the shoulder and worked his way to the front. A Minnesota highway patrolman ran toward him, and Lucas hung his badge case out the window.

"Davenport," the patrolman said, leaning in the window. "Stay behind me and I'll make a hole in this line."

The patrolman jogged along the shoulder, leading the Porsche to a roadblock. The street was a nightmare tangle of shoppers trying to get out of the mall, gawkers trying to drive past the murder scene, and the normal traffic on and off the interstate. The patrolmen had given up trying to control the crush and had settled for getting as many people out of the mall as possible. At the roadblock, the patrolman leading Lucas said something to the others, and they stopped traffic, directed a car out of the way and let Lucas slip through to the parking lot.

"Thanks," Lucas yelled as he went through. "I came through that storm—it's a bad one, with hail. If you got rain gear . . ."

The patrolman nodded and waved him on.

Television vans and reporters' cars were lined up on the perimeter of the lot, a hundred yards from a battered brown Chevy. All four doors on the car were open and emergency lights bathed it in a brilliant showroom illumination. Lucas left his Porsche in a pod of squad cars and walked toward the Chevy.

"Davenport, over here." A cop in a short blue jacket, who'd been talking to another cop in a sweater, called to him, and Lucas walked over.

"John Barber, Maplewood," said the cop in the jacket. He had pale blue eyes and a long lantern jaw. "And this is Howie Berkson. . . . Howie, go on over and tell that TV bunch it'll be another twenty minutes, okay?"

As Berkson walked away, Barber said, "C'mon."

"Any question whether it's the same guy?" Lucas asked.

Barber shrugged. "I guess not. One of your people is running around out here . . . Shearson? He says the technique is the same. Wait'll you see her face."

Lucas went and looked, and turned away, and they started a circle around the car. "Looks like him," he said sourly. "A copycat couldn't get up that much enthusiasm for it. . . ."

"That's what Shearson said. . . ."

"Where is he, by the way?" Lucas asked, looking around the lot.

Barber grinned. "He said it looked like we had it under control. I heard he's looking at shirts over in the mall."

"Asshole," Lucas said.

"That's the feeling we got. By the way, we found a kid who saw the guy."

"What?" Lucas stopped short. "Saw him?"

"Don't get your hopes up," Barber said. "He was a hundred yards away and wasn't paying too much attention. Saw the guy's car, too, but doesn't have any idea about make or model or even color . . . Didn't get anything. Says the killer looked like a guy from some comic-book movie."

"Then how do you know he saw . . ."

"Because he saw the woman walking out toward her car. He wasn't paying any attention to her, just hanging out, but a minute later, he saw a man by her car, it looked like he was helping her inside. Then, a couple of minutes later, he really doesn't know how long it was, he sees the guy walking away. And the woman never backs the car out. So the kid thinks—he told us before his mother got here—he thinks this woman is a hooker maybe, doing blow jobs in her car, or maybe she's dealing dope. That's the way his head works. And he kind of casually strolls by to take a look. . . ."

"So he saw the guy for sure."

"Seems like it," Barber said.

"Let me talk to him."

The kid was a slender, ragged teenager with skateboard pads on his knees, fingerless gloves, dirty blond shoulder-length hair and a complexion that was going bad. He wore a long-billed hat with the bill turned down and to the side, covering one ear. His mother hovered over him, throwing severe looks alternately at the kid and the police.

"You got a minute?" Lucas asked the kid, when Barber walked him up.

"I guess so, they won't let me go nowhere," the kid answered. He brushed his hair out of his eyes, the same gesture Cassie used, half defense, half necessity.

"We would like to go home sometime," his mother said,

spotting Lucas as an authority. "It's not like . . ."

"This is pretty important," Lucas said mildly. To the kid, he said, "Why don't we take a walk down the mall. . . ."

"Can I come?" asked the kid's mother.

"Sure," Lucas said reluctantly. "But let your boy tell the story, okay? Any help you give him . . . isn't help."

"Okay." Her head bobbed: she understood that.

"So what does this guy feel like?" Lucas asked, as they started down the length of the mall.

The kid's forehead wrinkled. "Feel like?"

"What kind of vibrations did he give off? The Maplewood cop, Barber, says you couldn't see him too clearly, but you must've gotten some vibrations. Barber said you thought he looked like some comic-book guy. . . ."

"Not a comic-book guy, a comic-book *movie* guy," the kid said. "Did you ever see the movie *Darkman*?"

"No, I haven't."

"You oughta. It's a great movie. . . ."

"His favorite," his mother clucked. "These kids . . ."

Lucas put his index finger on his lips and she shut up, her face reddening.

"See, there's this guy Darkman, who gets his face all fuck . . . uh, messed up by these hoods," the kid said, glancing at his mother. "He tries to put his face back together with this skin that he makes—"

"Whoa, whoa," Lucas said. "There was something wrong with his face? The guy in the parking lot?"

"I couldn't see that much, he had this hat. But he moved like Darkman. . . . You gotta see the movie," the kid said with wide-eyed seriousness. "Darkman moves like . . . I don't know. You gotta see it. This guy moved like that. Like, I couldn't see if there was anything wrong with his face, but he *moved* like there was. With his face kind of always turned away."

"Did you see him jump the woman?"

271

"No. I saw her walking out, then I was looking at something else, then I saw him. Then he got in her car, and then he got out, and then he moved away like Darkman. Kind of glided. With that hat."

"Glided?"

"Yeah. You know, like, most guys just walk. This guy kind of glided. Like Darkman. You gotta see the movie."

"All right. Anything else? Anything? Did you see him talk to anybody, did he do a little dance, did he do anything . . . ?"

"No, not that I saw. I just saw him walking. . . . Oh yeah, he was juggling his keys, that's all."

"Juggling his keys?"

"Yeah. Toss them up, then go like this . . ." The kid mimed a man throwing his keys up, made a quick little double step, snagged them with his off hand.

"Jesus," Lucas said. "Just once?"

"Naw, he did it a couple, three times."

They'd stopped walking outside a cutlery store. In the window, a two-foot-long model of a Swiss Army knife continuously and silently folded and unfolded. "What do you do for a living, kid?" Lucas asked. "Still in school?"

"Yeah."

"You got a good eye," Lucas said. "You might make a cop someday."

The kid looked away. "Naw, I couldn't do that," he said. His mother prodded him, but he went on. "Cops gotta fuck with people. I couldn't do that for a living."

Lucas left the kid and his anxious mother with a Maplewood cop and used a pay phone to call Cassie. She was supposed to be off, but there was no answer at her apartment. He tried the theater, but no one answered the phone.

"God damn it." He needed her. He went back outside

and found Shearson and Barber standing at the mall entrance. Shearson had a sack under his arm that might have contained a necktie. Rain swept across the lot beyond them, and the floodlights around the death car had been turned off.

"Find everything you needed?" Lucas asked Shearson, tapping the sack with a finger.

"Hey, I'm out here on my own time," Shearson said. He was wearing a dark cashmere knee-length coat over a pearl-gray suit, with a white shirt, a blue tie with tiny crowns on it, and black loafers. His breath smelled of Juicy Fruit.

"You talk to the kid?" Barber asked.

"Yeah. I'd like to get a stenographer over to his place tomorrow, take a statement," Lucas said. "He told me the guy was juggling his keys, and doing a little dance step when he caught them. I'd like to get him on record for that."

"Give us a call with questions . . ." said Barber.

"You get something?" Shearson asked, eyebrows up.

"I don't know," Lucas said. He trusted Shearson about as far as he could spit a rat. "What's happening with this shrink you've been looking at?"

"He's the Loverboy, all right," Shearson said. "He's hiding something. There aren't a lot of loose ends to pull on. I think we oughta just sit back for a couple days. Until something new comes up. But Daniel's got me covering him like whip on cream."

"Okay . . . Well, I gotta get one last look at this car," Lucas said.

Barber went with him, the two of them hurrying through the rain with a kind of broken-field lope, shoulders hunched, as though they could dodge the raindrops.

"Your buddy's got a great wardrobe," Barber said, tongue in cheek.

"And he'd lose an IQ contest to a fuckin' stump," Lucas said.

The body was being moved out of the car, wrapped in sheets. Another Maplewood cop came over and said, "Nothing in the car that looks like a weapon. Nothing but paper—ice cream bar wrappers, candy wrappers, Ding Dong wrappers. The woman lived on junk."

"All right," said Lucas. To Barber, he said, "Can you keep me up-to-date?"

"I'll fax you everything we got in the morning, first thing. We don't need this clown killing people out here."

Lucas hadn't expected much from the scene itself. If a killer had no relationship with the victim, no apparent motive, no rational method of operation, the only things left to find were witnesses or traceable physical evidence. Because a serial killer could pick the time and place, he could pick a situation that minimized his exposure to witnesses. And evidence left behind—semen, in sex-related cases, or blood or skin samples—didn't help until after the killer was caught.

This attack had been almost perfect. Almost . . .

The storm was dying as Lucas headed west. There was another thunderstorm cell far down to the south, but from I-35W he could see distant jetliner landing lights, going into Minneapolis-St. Paul International from the south, so he knew the storm must be well out downstate.

By the time he got to Cassie's apartment, the rain had diminished to a barely perceptible drizzle. He went into the entry and rang the bell for her apartment, but there was no answer. He continued up the street to the theater, but the windows there were dark. Damn. He needed her.

And he found her. She was sitting on his porch steps, a gym bag between her feet.

"How long have you been here?" he asked from the

car, as she strolled out to the driveway. "How'd you get here?"

"About twenty minutes—I came on the bus. I would have broken in, but the woman next door keeps watching me out her window," Cassie said, grinning. She tipped her head toward a lighted window in the next house. An elderly woman peeked out a lighted window in a side door, and Lucas waved at her. She waved back and disappeared.

"She keeps an eye out," Lucas said. "Besides, you'd need a sledge to get through the doors. . . . Let me get the car inside."

Cassie waited behind the car as he put it in the garage next to his battered Ford four-by-four.

"Sweatsuit and shoes," she said, holding up the gym bag as he dropped the garage door. "I thought we could run along the river."

"In the rain?"

"You could see it going over on the TV radar," she said.

"Okay," he said. He took her elbow in his hand and kissed her on the mouth. "Did you hear?"

"Hear what?" she asked, puzzled by his somber tone.

"We had another killing. Out in Maplewood."

"Oh, no," she said, pressing her fingertips to her lips. "Is it a theater person?"

Lucas shook his head. "Not as far as we know. It's a woman who worked at the mall. They're checking, but she doesn't seem like she'd be a playgoing type. Certainly didn't look like an actress."

"Jesus . . . Like he just picked her out at random?"

"Eenie meenie minie moe," Lucas said. "And I've got something to ask you . . . later."

"What's the mystery?"

"I can't tell you. I want your brain to be fresh. Let's run."

Cassie set the pace along the river until Lucas, puffing,

275

slowed her down. "Take it easy," he said. "Remember, I'm *old*."

"Six years older than me," she said. "At your age, you ought to be able to run a marathon under four, just to be in fair shape."

"Bullshit," he grunted. "If you can run a marathon under six, you're in great shape, for a normal human being, anyway."

"See, you're not hurtin'," she said. "You can still talk." But she slowed the pace and they stopped at a scenic overlook, walked in circles for a minute, then took off again, this time running away from the river.

"I have to stop at a video store," Lucas said. "I want to pick up a movie."

"A movie?"

"A kid at the mall saw the killer. Said he looked like Darkman, in the movie. You see it?"

"No. Heard about it. Supposed to be pretty bad."

"So we watch it for a few minutes."

When they got back to the house, Lucas leaned against the garage door, gasping for breath, dangling the plastic bag with the videocassette in one hand.

"I gotta do this more often," he said. "How far do you think we ran?"

"Three miles, maybe. Enough to crack a sweat."

"I hate to tell you, but I cracked a sweat about two hundred yards out," he said.

"Better take a shower," she said in a low voice. She was standing next to him, and she slipped a hand under his sweatshirt and lightly drew her nails from his nipples to his navel. Lucas shivered and moved against her.

"We've got serious business here," he said, patting her on the butt with the plastic bag.

"Hey—what difference does it make if we look at it now or an hour from now?"

276

He seemed to think about it, stroking his chin. "Hmm. An argument with a certain persuasive force . . ."

"So let's take the shower. . . ."

Lucas, still damp from a second shower, wearing jeans and a T-shirt, popped the cassette into his VCR and turned on the television.

"What are we looking for?" she asked.

"I want to see if this Darkman character brings anybody to mind. Don't study him—just let it percolate."

The movie unwound, Cassie sitting on the floor in front of the TV. "I see why the kid called it a comic-book movie," she said a few minutes into it, when Darkman was blown through his laboratory window by an enormous explosion. "It's all bullshit."

"Doesn't bring anybody to mind?"

"Not yet." She stood up. "Is that peach ice cream still in the freezer?"

"Sure."

She sat with the ice cream, sucking on the spoon, watching intently. During a scene in which Darkman did a macabre dance, an oil funnel on his head, she frowned and shook her head.

"What?" Lucas asked.

"Run that again."

He stopped the movie and reran the dance scene.

"Don't tell me yet," he said.

"Okay. Keep going."

He watched her as the movie continued and she got more and more into it. At the end, she said, "Junk, but some parts were strong."

"So what'd you see?"

She studied him for a moment and then said, "You know, I'm your basic 'Off the Pigs' sort of person."

"Yeah, yeah . . ."

"Me and the people I hang out with."

"Uh-huh."

"And I really hate the idea of police creeping around and monitoring people and all that . . ."

"Come on, come on . . ."

She looked at the blank TV screen, wrinkled her forehead and said, "Darkman reminds me of a guy at the theater. I mean, he's completely different. He's built different, he looks different, but he sort of has . . . the aura of Darkman. He moves like Darkman, sometimes."

"Okay. Don't move."

He hurried back to the spare bedroom, looked around and spotted the Xerox of Redon's *Cyclops* still lying on the bed.

"Close your eyes," he told her, when he got back. "I'm going to hold a paper in front of your face. I want you to look at it for a second, no more, then close your eyes again. You're trying for a momentary impression. . . . Open your eyes when I say 'Open.'"

"Okay . . ."

He held the Xerox in front of her face and said, "Open."

Her eyes opened but didn't close again, and after a little more than a second, he whipped the paper behind his back.

"Jesus," she whispered. "I feel like a fuckin' Judas."

"Who is it?"

"It could be Carlo Druze. You saw him the first day you were at the theater. He was the guy practicing onstage."

"I *knew* it," Lucas said. The thrill of it ran down his spine, and he shuddered. "He's the goddamned juggler, right? The guy you never see without make-up. I knew I'd seen him."

"I feel like . . ."

"Fuck that," he barked. "You saw your friend Elizabeth.

278

You want to look at this woman up in Maplewood? We think he used a screwdriver on her. . . ."

"No, no . . ."

"Are there any good photos of him at the theater? Publicity stuff, anything?"

Cassie nodded, but tentatively. "He's a very scarred man. He doesn't like photo sessions. Sometimes he uses cosmetics to cover up . . . but he's most comfortable in stage make-up. That's how you usually see him in the publicity shots. Full make-up. I don't know if there'd be any raw photos. . . ."

"Can we get in?"

She hesitated. "I could get us inside the building, but the office is locked. And letting you go through the files . . . I don't know."

"C'mon, Cassie," Lucas said, a little less harshly. He reached out and touched her. "You can keep the plans for the fuckin' revolution. I just need a photo of the guy. . . ."

"All right," she said. Then, following him back to the bedroom, she added, "I feel like a shit for saying this, but I keep thinking of more things. . . . Carlo didn't like Elizabeth and she didn't like him."

Lucas, pulling on a shirt, said, "Was she planning to fire him?"

Cassie shrugged. "Who knows? The feeling was, she didn't like him because of his looks. As an actor, he's not bad."

Lucas stopped and looked at her: "Could Druze do this? Is he capable of it? Killing people?"

She shivered. "Of all the people I know . . . yeah, I'd say he's the most likely. But not with passion. I don't understand the eyes. If he wanted to kill somebody, he'd just do it, and walk away."

"Huh. Interesting," said Lucas. He put on a sport

279

jacket, then dug through the bottom drawer of his bureau, found a leather wallet and stuck it in his jacket pocket. "Let's go look."

On the way across town, Lucas said, "When I saw him that time at the theater, I asked you where he was when Armistead was killed. You told me he'd been around all afternoon."

"Yeah..." Her forehead wrinkled. "He was around. But people come and go all the time. Run across the street for a cinnamon roll, down Cedar for a cheeseburger. Nobody notices. The theater's only ten minutes from Elizabeth's house."

"But your impression was that he'd been around. . . ."

"Yeah. I really can't remember, though. . . . A cop interviewed him the day after, maybe he'd know."

"But if he killed Armistead, how does the phony phone call fit?" Lucas asked. "We figured the killer was calling to find out if she was at work. . . ."

"Maybe . . . this sounds stupid, but maybe somebody was just trying to get a free ticket?"

"That's usually what fucks up an investigation, trying to find a reason for everything," Lucas admitted. "But the call was odd. I still think . . . I don't know." They parked in front of a rock bar and looked across the street at the theater's dark windows.

"I don't like this," Cassie said nervously, looking up and down the street. "People come in and out of here all the time. And if anybody found out, I'd lose my job. For sure."

"I doubt it," Lucas said, smiling at her. She didn't like his smile. There was an edge of cruelty to it. "Things can be arranged."

"Like what?"

He looked past her at the front of the theater. "You'd be

surprised how many building, zoning and health violations you can find in a place like that. I doubt an old theater could survive, if somebody really wanted to tote them all up."

"Blackmail," she said.

"Law enforcement."

"Sure," she said, with distaste. "I don't think I could live with that."

She got out of the car and led the way across the street. The theater was dark, but as she opened the door with her key, she called, "Hello? Anybody here?"

No answer. "This way," she said in a hushed voice. They crossed the lobby in the weak light from the street and started down a hallway. Cassie patted the left wall, found a light switch and turned on a single hall light. Lucas followed her to a red wooden door. She tried the doorknob and found it locked. "Damn it. I was hoping it'd be open," she said.

"Let me look," Lucas said. He took a small metal flashlight from his jacket pocket, knelt at the lock, shined the light into the crack between the door and the jamb, turned the knob as far as he could, then turned it back.

"Can you open it?"

"Yeah." He took the wallet, a trifold, from his pocket. He opened it, laid it flat on the floor and slipped out a thin metal blade.

"What're you doing?"

"Magic," he said. He put the blade in the crack between the door and the jamb, and rotated the blade downward; the bolt slipped back. "Shazam."

The office was small, untidy, with lime-green walls, a metal desk with a phone, four chairs, a bulletin board and file cabinets. A faint smell of mildew and old cigarette smoke hung in the air. As Lucas put his lock set back into his pocket, Cassie stepped to one of the file cabinets and

281

pulled open a drawer. Hundreds of eight-by-ten photos were jammed into manila folders. She took out two, a bulging pair, and laid them on the desk.

"He'll be in these," she said. She started going through them, tapping Druze's face wherever she found it. "Here . . . here . . . here he is again."

"He's good at avoiding the camera," Lucas said. He took several of the photos and held them under the light. Druze was always in stage paint or make-up. Sometimes his face was obscured by a hat; at other times by a hand gesture.

"Here's the best one so far," Cassie said, flipping a photo out to Lucas.

Troll, he thought. Druze had a round head, too large for his body. And although he was wearing make-up, there were obvious changes in his skin texture, as if his face had been quilted together. His nose was shortened, ruined.

"That's the best," Cassie said, finishing with the pictures. "But, ah . . ." She glanced at another file cabinet.

"What?"

"If we can get this other cabinet open, we could look through the personnel files. There may be a straight headshot. . . . The cabinet's always locked."

"Let's look," Lucas said. He glanced at the lock on the cabinet, took a pick out of the wallet and had the lock open in less than a second.

"That's fast," Cassie said, impressed.

"For office file cabinets, you get more of a master key than a pick," Lucas said. "I'm not that good with the picks."

"Where do you get them?" she asked.

"I know a guy," Lucas said. He pulled open the top drawer and found a file labeled "Druze." Inside was a block of what once had been eight wallet-sized photos, headshots, straight on, no make-up. Two of them had been cut away with scissors. "Passport shots. And he *does* look like the cyclops, kind of," Lucas said. He went to the office desk, found a pair of scissors in the top drawer, cut out one of the photos and showed it to Cassie.

"Uh-huh." She glanced at it, then went back to the file she was holding.

"What's that?"

She looked up, a piece of notebook paper in her hand, a sad smile on her face. "It's *my* file. There's a note from Elizabeth. It says my work has to be evaluated in case financial circumstances worsen."

"What does that . . . ?"

"She was going to fire me," Cassie said. A tear trickled down her cheek. "Fuckin' theater people, man . . ."

Lucas used the pick to lock the cabinet. The office door locked from the inside, then simply pulled shut. On the way out, they turned off the lights.

Cassie had taken Armistead's note, and when they were back in the car again, she reread it under the dome light. "I can't believe it," she said. "I can't believe she'd do this."

"Well, she's gone—things have changed," Lucas said. "I've seen you act, and you're good. . . ."

"But she was supposed to be my friend," Cassie said, wadding up the note. "We talked together. We were always talking about what we wanted to do."

"Your friends . . . are sometimes different people than you think they are. Most of your friends are halfway made-up. They're what you'd like them to be."

"Do you mind if I sit here and cry for a couple of minutes?"

"C'mon," said Lucas, "that'd really bum me out." He put an arm around her shoulder and kissed her on the forehead, and she grabbed his jacket lapel and buried her face on his shoulder. "C'mon, Cassie . . ."

He stroked her hair and she cried.

24

Daniel, looking from the photograph to Lucas, was stunned. "We got him? Like that?"

"Maybe," Lucas said. "He fits what we know about the killer. He looks right, he acts right, and my friend says he's something of a sociopath. He had reason to kill Armistead. And Bekker gave me those tickets, which suggested that his wife had something going at the theater. . . ."

"We've had two guys full-time on that and as far as they can tell, nobody ever saw her there—or remembers it, anyway," Daniel said. He looked at the photo again. "But this guy *looks* like the cyclops."

"And we've got those American Express charge slips. . . ."

"Yeah, yeah." Daniel scratched his head, still looking at the photo of Druze.

"I think we need to put a team on him. . . ."

"We'll do that, definitely. Since we pulled the team on Bekker . . ."

"The problem is, if Druze saw that story, he might have thought we were watching *him*."

A thin smile creased Daniel's ruddy face. "So for the past two days he's been slinking around with his back to the wall, seeing spies."

"I was thinking . . ."

"Yeah?"

"You could accuse Channel Eight of damaging the investigation, saying they tipped an unnamed suspect to the surveillance and the police have been forced to pull the surveillance after the suspect confronted a departmental officer . . . that being me."

"Yeah. Hmm. It'd back off the TVs a little, too," Daniel said. The grin flicked across his face again. "I'll have Lester do it. He'll enjoy it."

"And if there's a political kickback, you can always blame it on him," Lucas said, grinning himself.

"Did I say that?" Daniel asked innocently, his hand over his heart. "About this guy, Druze . . . maybe we could get some video on him, walking at a distance, show it to this kid out in Maplewood."

"Yeah, good," Lucas said.

"We oughta do that today," Daniel said. He walked around his desk, staring at the photo as if it were a talisman.

"I still think Bekker's in here somewhere," Lucas said. "If Druze and Bekker are talking, maybe we can come up with some phone records."

Daniel nodded. "We can do that, too. All right. Make a list for Anderson, tell him to do it," Daniel directed. "Now, how're you planning to get this picture to Stephanie Bekker's lover?"

Lucas shrugged. "I haven't got that figured. . . ."

"Try this," Daniel said. He sat behind his desk, opened his humidor, stared into it and snapped it shut. "I've been thinking about it. Channel Two still goes off the air sometime after midnight. We ask them to go back on at, say, three o'clock, with the photo. Just for a minute. Nobody'd see it, unless they were accidentally clicking around channels. And the lover would be safe. He could get it on any TV in the metro area, cable or no. And if he's got a VCR, he could record it."

"Great. Have you got any clout with Two?" Lucas asked. Channel Two was the educational station.

"Yeah. Shouldn't be a problem."

Lucas nodded. "Sounds perfect. I'll have an ad in the *Star Tribune* tomorrow morning. When he calls me, I'll try to talk him in. If he won't come, I'll tell him when to watch."

"Until then, we treat Druze as though he was the one. And let's get with the other people on this, so everybody knows what we're doing. . . ." He leaned over his desk and pressed the intercom button. "Linda, get Sloan in here, and Anderson, and the point guys on the Bekker case, everybody who's around. Half an hour . . ."

"We've really got nothing on him yet, it's all speculation," Lucas reminded him.

"We stay with him," Daniel said sharply. "I want to know every step he fuckin' takes. I got a feeling about this guy, Lucas. I get strong vibrations."

"I'm thinking—" Lucas said. He was thinking of cracking Druze's apartment: an informal survey without a warrant.

Daniel stopped him in mid-sentence. "Don't say it. But, uh, it would be nice to know some things . . ."

Lucas nodded, bent over Daniel's desk, opened the humidor and peered inside. Three cigars. He snapped it shut.

"What?" Daniel asked.

"I always wondered what you really had in there. . . ."

The investigation file on Druze was thin. Nothing on NCIC—Anderson had run him against the federal computers as soon as Daniel called the meeting. Druze had been interviewed by Detective Shawn Draper after the Armistead murder, and the interview had been summarized in a half-dozen tight paragraphs. Subject said he was in theater at the time of the murder. Cited several incidents that placed him there. Brief cross-checks with other actors confirmed those incidents. . . .

Daniel, Anderson, Lester, Sloan, Del, Draper, Shearson and three or four other detectives sat in Daniel's office, plotting out the surveillance, while Lucas sat in a corner reading the file. Draper, a large, sleepy man in a knit suit, slumped on a folding chair behind Anderson.

"You interviewed him, Shawn," Lucas said during a break in the discussion. "Did you think, in person, that he looked at all like the cyclops picture? Was there anything . . . ?"

Draper scratched an ear. "Naw . . . I wouldn't say so. I mean . . . he looked fucked up, but he wasn't. . . . Naw."

"Was he solid for an alibi on Armistead?"

"When the chief called about the meeting, I went back and looked at my notes. He really had the evening nailed down, after about seven or seven-thirty. Earlier than that, it was sketchy."

"We think she was killed, what, about seven?" Lucas asked.

"Give or take," Sloan said.

"So he could have done her, then come back and tried to make himself obvious around the place. . . ."

Anderson jumped into the exchange. "Yeah, but he didn't try to cover himself that much for the actual time of the murder. If I'd been doing it, I would have done something to establish myself *before* I went over. Then I would have gone over, done it and come back as fast as I could, maybe with a bunch of doughnuts or something, and established myself again," he said.

"Well, he didn't," Draper said shortly. "He was solid later, but not earlier."

"Hmph," Lucas grunted.

"What?" asked Daniel.

"I'm still trying to fit that phone call in. . . ."

The *Star Tribune* classified-advertising manager said he would see to the ad himself. *Not responsible for the debts of Lucille K. Smith, signed Lucas Smith.* It would appear the next morning.

"This is critical," Lucas said. "Keep your mouth shut, but this is the most important ad you'll run all year."

"It'll be there. . . ."

Lucas called Cassie from the lobby.

"What're you doing here? Oh Gawd, the apartment is a wreck. . . ." Cassie buzzed him through the door. She met him, flushed, at her apartment door.

"Looks nice," Lucas said as he stepped inside. The apartment was small, a kitchen nook opening directly off the living room, a short hall with three doors leading off it, a bathroom, a closet and the single bedroom.

"That's because I just stuffed four days' clothes in a closet, two days' dishes in the dishwasher, and did about a month's worth of cleaning." She laughed, stood on her tiptoes and kissed him, took in the briefcase he was carrying. "What're you doing? You look like Mr Businessman. I was about to leave for the theater."

"I was over at the U and thought I'd stop by," he said. "You have to leave right away?"

She nodded and produced a sleepy-eyed pout. "Pretty soon. Since I read Elizabeth's note, I thought I'd be on time for work."

"Ah . . . well."

"We could take a quick shower . . ." she offered.

"Nah. If we started a shower . . . And I've got to get back to work, anyway. See you after?"

"Sure. We'll be done before eleven."

"I'll take you someplace expensive."

"Shameless sweet-talker, you." She caught his ear and pulled his head down and kissed him again.

"See you. . . ."

* * *

288

He was in.

Druze's apartment was three floors below, and Lucas hadn't wanted to risk raking the lobby locks. That Cassie lived in the same building was not quite pure luck: several other Lost River players lived there, drawn by its proximity to the theater and the low rent. Lucas took the stairs down, emerging a few doors away from Druze's apartment. The hall was empty. Lucas stepped back into the stairwell, took a handset from the briefcase and called the surveillance team leader. At his last check, Druze was at the theater.

"Where is he?"

"Still inside." The team leader didn't know where Lucas was.

"The instant he moves . . ."

"Right."

The theater was less than a block from the apartment. If Druze had to run home for something, Lucas wanted adequate warning. He called Dispatch and gave the dispatcher Druze's telephone number.

"Patch me through . . . let it ring as long as necessary. The guy may be outside mowing the lawn," he said.

"Sure . . ." Jesus, he thought. He had just made the whole dispatch department an accessory to a felony. He put the handset under his arm, so he could hear it if the dispatcher called back, and stepped into the hall. Sixteen doors, spaced alternately down the hall. Plasterboard walls, aging rug. The power rake would clatter, but there was no help for it. He walked down to Druze's apartment and heard the phone ringing. Five times, ten. Nobody. He tried the door, just in case—it was locked—and took the rake from the briefcase. The rake looked like an electric drill, but was smaller, thinner. A prong stuck out of the tip; Lucas slipped it into the lock and pulled the trigger.

The rake began to clatter, a sound like a ball bearing

dropped into a garbage disposal. The clatter seemed to go on forever, but a second or two after it started, Lucas turned the lock and the door popped open.

"Hello? Anybody home?" The phone was still ringing when he stepped inside. "Hello?"

The apartment was neat, but only because there was almost nothing in it. A stack of scripts and a few books on acting were piled into a small built-in bookcase, along with a tape player and a few cassettes. A couch was centered on a television, the remote left carelessly on the floor next to the couch. In his years in the police department, Lucas had been in dozens of cheap boarding-houses and transient apartments, places where single men lived alone. The rooms often had an air of meticulous neatness about them, as though the inhabitants had nothing better to do than arrange their ashtrays, their radios, their hot plates, their cans of Carnation evaporated milk. Druze's apartment had that air, a lack of idiosyncrasy so startling it became an idiosyncrasy of its own. . . .

The telephone was still ringing. Lucas got on the handset and said, "Betty? About that call—forget it."

"Okay, Lucas." A few seconds later, the ringing stopped.

The bedroom first. Lucas didn't know exactly what he was looking for, but if he saw it . . .

He went rapidly through the closets, patting the pockets of the sport coats and pants, checked the detritus on the dresser top, pulled the dresser drawers. Nothing. The kitchen went even quicker. Druze had little of the usual kitchen equipment, no bowls, no canisters, none of the usual hiding places. He checked the refrigerator: nothing but a head of lettuce, a bottle of A.1. sauce, a chunk of hamburger wrapped in plastic, an open box of Arm & Hammer baking soda and a red-and-white can of Carnation. Always a can of Carnation. Nothing in the ice cube trays. Nothing in the bottom drawer of the stove . . .

Druze did have a nice blunt weapon, a sharpening steel. Lucas took it out of the kitchen drawer, swung it, inspected it. No sign of hair or blood—but the steel was exceptionally clean, as though it had been washed recently. He took a piece of modeling clay from the briefcase, held it flat in his hand, and hit it once, sharply, with the steel. The steel stuck to the clay when he pulled it out, but the impression was good enough. He put the steel back into the kitchen drawer, and the clay, wrapped in wax paper, into his briefcase.

The living room was next. Nothing under the couch but dust. Nothing but pages in the books. In a cupboard under the built-in bookcase, he found a file cabinet, unlocked. Bills, employment records, car insurance receipts, tax forms for six years. Check the front closet. . . .

"Damn." A black ski jacket with teal insets. Just like ten thousand other jackets, but still: the lover had seen a jacket like this. Lucas took it out of the closet, slipped it on, got a Polaroid camera from his briefcase, put it on the bookcase shelf, aimed it, set the self-timer and shot himself wearing the jacket—two views, front and back.

When he'd checked the photos, he rehung the jacket. He'd been in the apartment for fifteen minutes. Long enough. He went to the door, looked around one last time. Down the stairs. Out.

"Lucas?" Daniel calling back.

"Yeah." He was sitting in the Porsche, looking at the Polaroids. "Did you get in touch with Channel Two?"

"We're all set," Daniel said. "If he calls you to-morrow night, we can go on the air an hour later. Four o'clock . . ."

"Can I get another picture on?"

"Of what?"

"Of a guy in a ski jacket . . ."

* * *

291

Later:

Daniel paced around his office, excited, cranked. Lucas and Del sat in visitors' chairs, Sloan leaned against the wall, Anderson stood with his hands in his pockets.

"I've got a real feeling," Daniel insisted. Lucas had cut his own face out of the ski jacket photos before he gave them to Daniel. Daniel and Anderson had looked at them, and agreed that it could be the jacket Stephanie Bekker's lover had described. "Almost certainly is, with what we know," Anderson said. "It's too much of a coincidence. Maybe we ought to pick him up and sweat him."

"We've still got to get him with Bekker," Lucas protested.

"What we've got to do is *turn* him against Bekker, if they're really working together," Daniel said. "If we sweat him a little, we could do that."

"We don't have much to deal with," Sloan said. "With the politics of it, with four people dead, the goddamn media would have our heads if we dealt him down to get Bekker."

"Let me deal with the politics," Daniel said. He picked up one of the Polaroids and looked at it again, then up at Sloan. "We could do this: We charge him with first-degree murder, but deal down to second degree with concurrent sentences if he gives us Bekker. Then we tell the press that even though he's getting a second, we're asking the judge to depart upward on the sentence, so it's almost as good as a first. . . ."

Sloan shrugged: "If you think you can sell it."

"I'd make us look like fuckin' geniuses," Daniel said.

"It'd still be nice if we could get something solid," Lucas pressed. "Can we cover his phones, at least? Maybe watch him for a few days before we move? See if we can get him talking to Bekker, or meeting him?"

292

"We couldn't get a warrant for the phones, not yet, there's just not enough," Daniel said. "If Stephanie Bekker's friend comes through, if he confirms this . . . then we get the warrant. And we'll want to put a microphone in his apartment."

"So everything depends on Loverboy," Lucas said. "He's got to call back tomorrow night."

"Right. Until then, we stay on Druze like holy on the pope," Daniel said, running his hands through his thinning hair. "Jesus, what a break. What a fuckin' break . . ."

"If it's true," Anderson said after a moment.

Bekker stood in the bay window, looking past the cut-glass diamonds in the center, out at the dark street, and decided: he had to move. Tomorrow. The cigarette case rode low in his pocket and he opened it, and chose. Nothing much, just a touch of the power. He put a tab of PCP between his teeth and sucked on it for a moment, then put it back in the case. The acrid chemicals bit into his tongue, but he hardly noticed anymore.

The drug helped him concentrate, took him out of his body, left his mind alone to work. Clarified the necessary moves. First the woman, then Druze. Get Druze to come with a last-minute call. The best time would be around five o'clock: Druze always ate at his apartment before walking over to the theater, and the woman would most likely be around at the same time.

No luxuries here, Doctor. No studies. Just do it and get out.

He paced, his legs seemingly in another country, working it out in his mind. If everything went right, it'd be so simple. . . . But he ought to check the gun. Go to Wisconsin, fire a couple of shots. He hadn't fired it in years, not since a trip to New Mexico. He'd bought it originally in Texas, a casual purchase from a cowboy in

El Paso, a drunk who needed money. Not much of a gun, a .38 special, but good enough.

As for the shot . . . he'd have to risk it. If she had a radio . . . Maybe four o'clock would be better. They should be at home then, and the people in the apartments adjoining the woman's would be less likely to be there.

He paced, working it out, working himself up, generating a heat, the light dose of PCP flipping him in and out of otherwhen.

At midnight, pressed by the needs of Beauty, he threw down two tabs of MDMA. The drug roared through him, hammered down the PCP, and he began to dance, to flap around the living room, on the deep carpets, and he went away. . . .

When he returned, breathing hard, he found himself half stripped. What now? He was confused. What? The idea came. Of course. If something went wrong tomorrow—unlikely, but possible; he was confident without being stupid about it—he would have missed an opportunity. Excited now, his hands trembling, he pulled his clothes back on, got his jacket and hurried out to the car. The hospital was only ten minutes away. . . .

He was stuck in the stairwell for five minutes.

He'd gone to his office first, done another MDMA for the creative sparkle and insight it brought, and a methamphetamine to sharpen the edge of his perceptions. Then he went to the locker room and changed into a scrub suit. The clean cotton felt cool and crisp against his skin, touching but not clinging to his chest, the insides of his arms, his thighs, like freshly starched sheets, the pleasure of its touch magnified by the ecstasy. . . .

He left then, alternately hurrying and restraining himself. He couldn't wait. He crept up the stairs, not quite chortling, but feeling himself bursting with the joy of it.

He was careful. If he was seen, it wouldn't be a disaster. But if he was not, it would be better.

At the top of the stairs, he opened the door just a crack, enough so that he could see the nurses' station fifty feet down the hall. He held onto the door handle: if anyone came through unexpectedly, he could react as though he were about to pull the door open. . . .

The nurse spent five minutes on the telephone, standing up, laughing, while he watched her through the crack and cursed her: the drugs were working in his blood, were demanding that he go to Sybil. He held back but wasn't sure how long he could last. . . .

There. The nurse, still smiling to herself, hung up the phone, sat down and pivoted in her chair, facing away from Bekker. He opened the door and quickly stepped through, across the hall, to where her line of vision was cut off. He moved away silently, the surgical moccasins muffling his footsteps, down the hall to Sybil's room.

Her television peered down from the ceiling; it was tuned to the word processor. He frowned. She wasn't supposed to be able to use it. He stepped next to the bed and bent over in the dim light. The processor console sat on a table to the left side of her bed. He reached out, rolled her head: she was wearing the switch. Looking up at the screen, he used the keyboard's arrow keys to move a cursor to the *Select* option, then pressed *Enter*. A series of options came up, including a dozen files. Nine of the files were named. Three were not: they had only numbers.

He was moving the cursor to select the first of the files when he realized that she was awake. Her eyes were dark and terrified.

"It's time," he whispered. The drugs roared and he moved closer to her bedside, peering down into her eyes. She closed them.

"Open your eyes," he said. She would not.

"Open your eyes. . . ." Her eyes remained closed.

"Open your . . . Sybil, I really need to know what you see, there at the end; I need to see your reactions. I need your eyes open, Sybil. . . ." He rattled a key on the keyboard. "I'm looking at your files, Sybil. . . ."

Her eyes opened, quickly, almost involuntarily. "Ah," he said, "so there is a reason I should look. . . ."

Her eyes were flashing frantically from Bekker to the screen. He moved the cursor to the first numbered file and pushed *Enter*. There were two letters on the screen: *MB*.

"Ah. That wouldn't stand for 'Michael Bekker,' would it?" he asked. He erased the letters, moved to the next file. *KLD*. He erased them. "A little message here? Do you really think they would've understood? Of course, with a few more days, you might have been able to squeeze out some more. . . ."

Bekker went to the final file. *ME*. "Got the 'me' done, anyway," he said. He backspaced over the letters, and they were gone.

"Well," he said, turning back to her. "Can I convince you to keep your eyes open?"

She closed them.

"Time," he said. "And this time, we're going all the way. Really, truly, Sybil. All the way . . ."

He stepped to the doorway and glanced down the hall. Nobody. Sybil's eyes followed him across the room and back, dark, wet. Bekker, his eyebrows arched, placed his palm over Sybil's mouth and gently pinched her nose with the thumb and index finger of the same hand. She closed her eyes. With the index and middle fingers of the other hand, he lifted her eyelids. She stared blankly, unmoving, for fifteen seconds. Then her eyes skewed wildly, from side to side, looking for help. Her chest began to tremble and then her eyes stopped their wild careen, fixed beyond him, and began to shine.

"What is it?" Bekker whispered. "Do you see? Are you seeing? What? What?"

She couldn't tell; and at the end, her eyes, the shine still on them, rolled up, the pupils gone. . . .

"*Hello?*"

Panicked, he let go of her nose, backed away from the bed, the hair rising on the back of his neck. He was trembling violently, unable to control himself. She was so close. So close.

"*Hello-o-o?*"

He staggered to the door, barely able to breathe, peeked out. He could see a corner of the nurses' station, but nobody there. Then a woman's voice, two rooms down the hall toward the nurses' station. The nurse: "Did you call me, Mrs Lamey?"

Bekker chanced it, crossed the hall in three long strides and went out through the internal door. He let the door close of its own weight, let it slide shut with a barely audible hiss, then started down the stairs two at a time. Just as the door shut, he heard the nurse's voice again.

"*Hello?*"

She must have seen or heard something, or sensed it. Bekker fled down the stairs, the moccasins muffling his footfalls. He opened the door on his floor, stepped through and from far above heard another, more distant "*Hello?*"

Ten seconds later he was in his office, the door locked, the lights out. Breathing hard, heart beating wildly. Safe. A Xanax would help. He popped one, two, sat down in the dark. He would wait awhile, get his clothes. The MDMA bit him again, and he went away. . . .

Lucas went to pick Cassie up at the theater, and waited while she scrubbed her face, watching again for Druze. And again, Druze was somewhere else.

"How's the play going?" Lucas asked.

"Pretty good. We're actually making some money, which is the important thing. It's kind of funny, has its message. That's a good combination in Minneapolis."

"Sugar pill," Lucas said.

"Something like that."

They ate a midnight snack at a French café in downtown Minneapolis, then went for a walk, looking in the windows of art galleries and trendoid restaurants. Two of them featured raised floors, and the younger burghers of Minneapolis peered down at them through the windows, their fat legs tucked under tablecloths almost at eye level.

"I kept looking at Carlo, I couldn't help it," Cassie said. "I'm afraid he's going to catch me and think I'm coming on to him or something."

"Be careful around him," Lucas said. "If he comes to your apartment, tell him you're in the shower, still wet, or something. Or that you've got me in there. . . . Keep him out. Keep the door shut. Don't be alone with him."

She shivered. "No way. Though . . . there's a funny thing about this. Before I saw those pictures, I might have said, 'Yeah, Carlo could kill somebody.' Now, it's hard to believe that somebody you know could be doing this. Especially the business about the eyes. Carlo doesn't seem out of control; I mean, he could be crazy, but you feel like it would be a real cold crazy. Not a hot crazy. I could see Carlo strangling somebody and never showing any expression: I just can't see him in some kind of frenzy. . . ."

"Could he fake it? Could he be cold enough to do the eyes without feeling it?"

She thought for a moment, then said, "I don't know. Maybe." She shivered again. "But I'd hate to think *anybody* could be that cold. And why would he, anyway?"

298

"I don't know," Lucas said. "We don't know what's going on, yet."

At Lucas' house, in the bedroom, Cassie lay on top of him, a compact mass of muscle. She reached down and grabbed an inch of skin at his waist. "No love handles. Pretty impressive for a guy as ancient as yourself."

Lucas grunted. "I'm in awful shape. I sat on my ass all winter."

"Need a workout?"

"Like what?"

"No sex until you pin me for a three-count?"

"Aw, c'mon . . ."

"You c'mon, wimpy . . ."

They wrestled, and after a time, but not too long, she was pinned.

Beauty arrived home at about the same time. The night's work had been both frightening and exhilarating. A disappointment in some ways, true, but then again: he could go back. He still had Sybil to do. As Lucas and Cassie made love, Bekker ate two more MDMAs and danced to *Carmina Burana*, bouncing around the Oriental carpet until he began to bleed. . . .

25

Lucas heard the first newspaper hit the front porch. That'd be the *Pioneer Press*. The *Star Tribune* should be ten minutes later. He dozed, half listening, drifting from dream to linear thought and back to dream, dream editing reality, Jennifer and the baby, Cassie, other faces, other times. He inserted the *thwap* of the *Star Tribune*; but the dream logic wouldn't buy it, and he woke up, yawned and stumbled out to get the paper. At five-thirty it was still dark, but he could see the heavy gray clouds groaning overhead and smell the rain heavy in the air.

Not responsible . . . Lucas Smith.

He glanced at the comics and went back to bed, falling face-down across the sheets. Cassie's perfume lingered on them, although she'd insisted on going back to her apartment.

"We're getting close on the play. I shouldn't fool around late and get up late. I have to work," she'd said as she dressed.

The perfume was comforting, a sign of society. He slept on her side, dreaming again, until the telephone rang. Startled, he thought, *Loverboy*, and rose through his dreams and snatched at the telephone, almost knocking the lamp off the bed-stand.

"Davenport."

"Lucas, this is Del . . ."

"Yeah, what's happening?" He sat up, put his feet on the floor. Cold.

"I'm, uh, over at Cheryl's. We were talking last night,

and she told me that Bekker has been creeping around her ward. He's been seeing a woman patient almost every day—and the thing is, this woman can't communicate."

"Not at all?"

"Not a thing. Her mind's still okay, but she's got Lou Gehrig's disease and she's, like, totally paralyzed. Cheryl says she's got maybe a week or two to live, no more. Cheryl can't figure Bekker—he's not exactly the social type. Anyway, I thought it might be something."

"Hmph. I got a guy over there. I'll give him a call," Lucas said. "Are you on Druze today?"

"Yeah, I'm about to go over."

"I may see you."

Lucas hung up, yawned, glanced at the clock. After ten, already: he'd slept more than four hours after looking at the paper. He dropped back on the pillow, but his mind was working.

He got up, called Merriam, was told the doctor wasn't in yet, left a message and went off to shave. Merriam called back just as he was about to leave the house.

"There's a woman there, I'd like you to check," he said. "Her name is Sybil. . . ."

Lucas stopped at Anderson's office first.

"Where's Druze?"

"Still bagged out at his apartment."

At his own office, the answering machine showed two messages. *Loverboy?* He punched the message button as he took off his jacket.

"*Lucas, this is Sergeant Barlow. Stop and see me when you come in, please.*" God damn it, he had no time for this. If he could slip out without encountering Barlow . . . The machine clicked and started again.

"*Lieutenant Davenport, this is Larry Merriam. You better come over here right away. I'll leave a note at*

301

*the desk to send you up Pediatric Oncology. I'll be out
in the ward. Talk to the duty nurse and she'll chase me
down.*"

Merriam sounded worried, Lucas decided. He put his
jacket back on and was locking the office door when
Barlow came down the steps at the end of the hall and
saw him.

"Hey, Lieutenant Davenport, I need to talk to you,"
he called.

"Could I stop up later? I'm kind of on the run. . . ."

Barlow kept coming. "Look, we gotta get this done," he
said, his mustache bristling.

Lucas shook him off: "I'm up to my ass. I'll get back to
you as soon as I can."

"God damn it, Davenport, this is serious shit." Barlow
moved so that he was between Lucas and the door.

"I'll talk to you," Lucas said, irritated, letting it show.
They stared at each other for a second; then Lucas stepped
around him. "But I can't now. Talk to Daniel if you don't
believe me."

Barlow hadn't been good on the street. He was a control
freak and didn't deal well with ambiguities—and the street
was one large ambiguity. He'd done fine with Internal
Affairs, though.

IA usually went to work on a cop only if there was a
blatantly public foul-up, and that was okay with most of
the cops in the department, outside of a few hothead
brother-cop freaks. Better IA, the feeling went, than
some outside board full of blacks and Indians and who
knows what, which seemed to be the alternative.

The department had barely managed to fight off a city
council proposal that would have formed a review board
with real teeth. The study commission on that—the
commission Stephanie Bekker had served on—had gone a
bit too far, though, had given the impression that it wanted

302

to get on the cops a little too much. That hadn't gone down well with voters scared by crime. . . .

So a gross screw-up in public would get you an IA investigation. A cop could find himself a target also if he got too deep into drugs, or started stealing too much. Screwing off and getting your partner hurt, that would do it too.

But IA didn't worry much if a pimp got slapped around in a fist-fight. Especially not if he'd pulled a knife. Half of the cops on the force would've shot him and let it go at that, and they would have been cleared by the board. And if the fight had taken place during an arrest on a warrant charging a violent crime, and if the victim of that crime was scarred for life and still around to testify, to be looked at . . .

Where was Barlow coming from? Lucas shook his head. It didn't compute. Anderson was going in the door and Lucas was going out, when Lucas hooked him by the arm.

"You think . . . the guys in the department would like to see me fall? Get taken off by IA?" Lucas asked.

"Are you nuts?" Anderson asked. "What's happening with IA?"

"They're on me for the fight with that kid, the pimp. I can't figure out where it's coming from."

"I'll ask around," Anderson said. "But when the guys decide somebody ought to fall, it's no big secret. You know that. And nobody's talking about you."

"So where's it coming from?" Lucas asked.

Barlow stayed in the back of Lucas' mind all the way to the university campus. He dumped the car in a no-parking zone outside the hospital, stuck a police ID card in the window and went inside. Pediatric Oncology was on the sixth floor. A nurse took him down through a warren of small rooms, past a larger room with kids in terry-cloth robes, sitting in wheelchairs and watching television, into another set of hospital rooms. They found Merriam sitting on a bed, talking to a young girl.

"Ah, Lieutenant Davenport," he said. He looked at the girl in the bed. "Lisa, this is Lieutenant Davenport. He's a police officer with the Minneapolis Police Department."

"What's he doing here?" she asked, cutting straight to the heart of the matter. The girl was completely bald and had a very pale face and unnaturally rosy lips. The chemotherapy aside, Lucas thought, touched with a cold finger of fear, she looked a lot like his daughter would in ten years.

"He's a friend of mine, stopping to chat," Merriam said. "I've got to go for a while, but I'll be back before they start setting up the procedure."

"Okay," she said.

Outside, in the hall, Lucas said, "I couldn't do this." And, "Do you have kids?"

"Four," Merriam said. "I don't think about it."

"So what happened?" Lucas asked. "You sounded a little tense."

"The woman you called about. I went down to see her. She has amyotrophic lateral sclerosis . . ."

"Lou Gehrig's disease . . ."

"Right. She's almost completely incommunicado. Her brain works fine, but she can't move anything but her eyes. She'll be dead in a week or two. And Bekker is trying to kill her."

"What?" Lucas grabbed Merriam by the arm.

"This absolutely defeats me: a goddamn doctor," Merriam said, pulling away. "But you have to see for yourself. Come along."

Lucas trailed behind him as they went down a flight of stairs.

"I went down to find her this morning and stopped to ask

at the nursing station," Merriam said over his shoulder. He pushed through a door at the bottom of the stairs. "The duty nurse had worked overnight, and was working an extra half-shift because somebody was sick. Anyway, I mentioned that I was there to see Sybil and asked if Dr Bekker had been around. The nurse said— you'll have to take this with a grain of salt—she said she didn't see him but she'd *felt* him. Late last night. She said it occurred to her that dirty old Dr Death was around, because she shivered, and she always shivers when she sees him."

"She calls him 'Dr Death'?"

"Dirty old Dr Death," Merriam said. "Not very flattering, is it? So then I went down to talk to Sybil. She's going by inches, but the nurses say she's got an inch or two left. . . ."

Merriam led him past the nurses' station and down the hall, past an exit door and three or four more rooms, then glanced inside a room and turned. Sybil lay flat on her back, unmoving except for her eyes. They went to Merriam, then to Lucas, and stayed with him. They were dark liquid pools, pleading.

"Sybil can't talk, but she can communicate," Merriam said simply. "Sybil, this is Lieutenant Davenport of the Minneapolis Police Department. If you understand, say yes."

Her eyes moved up and down, a nod, and stayed with Merriam.

"And a no," Merriam prompted. They moved from side to side.

"Has Dr Bekker been coming here?" Merriam asked.
Yes.

"Are you afraid of him?"
Yes.

"Are you afraid for your life?"

305

Yes.

"Have you tried to communicate with your eye switch?"

Yes.

"Did Dr Bekker interfere?"

Yes.

"Is Dr Bekker trying to kill you?" Lucas asked.

Her eyes shifted to him and said, *Yes.* Stopped, and then again, *Yes*, frantically.

"Jesus Christ," said Lucas. He glanced at Merriam. "Has he been interested in your eyes? Said anything about . . ."

Her eyes were flashing up and down again. *Yes.*

"Jesus," he said again. He leaned across the bed toward the woman. "You hang on. We'll bring in a camera and an expert interrogator, and we're going to get you on videotape. We're going to slam this asshole in prison for so long he'll forget what the sun looks like. Okay?"

Yes.

"And excuse the 'asshole,'" Lucas said. "My language sometimes gets away from me."

No, her eyes said, sliding from side to side.

"No?"

"I think she means, Don't apologize, 'cause he is an asshole," Merriam said from beside the bed. "That right, Sybil?"

She was like a piece of modeling clay, unmoving, still, except for the liquid eyes:

Yes, she said. *Yes.*

"I'll have somebody here in a half-hour," Lucas said, when they were outside her door.

"You'll have to talk to her husband, just to make sure the legalities are right," Merriam said. "I'll see the director about this."

"Tell him the chief is going to call. And I'll have one

of our lawyers talk to her husband. Can they get all the information from here at your desk?"

"Sure. Anything you need."

Lucas started away, then stopped and turned.

"The kids you think he killed. Did he go after their eyes? I mean, was there anything unusual about their eyes?"

"No, no. I was there for the postmortems, their eyes weren't involved."

"Hmph." Lucas started away again, stopped again.

"Don't let anyone close to her."

"Don't worry. Nobody gets in there," Merriam said.

Lucas called Daniel from a pay phone and explained.

"Sonofabitch," Daniel crowed. "Then we got him."

"I don't know," Lucas said. "But we got something. The lawyers will have to figure out if it'll hold up in court. And it doesn't tie him to these other things."

"But we're moving," Daniel insisted. "I'll send a tape unit over there right now, and Sloan to talk to her."

"Can we put a guy on her door?"

"No problem. Around the clock. You think we should stick a surveillance team on him again?"

Lucas considered, then said, "No. He'll be hyperaware of anything like that. We've got Druze going. . . . Let's see what happens."

"All right. What are you doing?"

"I got a couple more ideas. . . ."

A male duck cruised a female across the college pond, as Elle Kruger and Lucas climbed the sidewalk toward the main buildings. Spring, but a cold wind was blowing. Well off to the west, over Minneapolis, they could see darker clouds, and the blurring underedges that said it was raining.

"The eye fixation could have been created by some kind

307

of traumatic incident, but that seems somewhat unlikely," Elle said. "It's more likely that he's always had a feeling of being watched, and this is his reaction. . . ."

"Then why weren't the kids cut up?"

"Lucas, you're missing the obvious," the nun said. "No good for a gamer."

"All right, tell me the obvious, Sister Mary Joseph, ma'am," he said.

"Maybe he didn't kill the children."

Lucas shook his head. "Thought of that. But Merriam gets these vibrations, and it fits with what he's doing with this Sybil, and the interest in the eyes fits with these other killings. Could be a coincidence, but I doubt it."

"As I said, it is *possible* that he developed the fixation between killings."

"But not likely."

"No."

They walked with their heads down, climbing the hill, and Lucas said, "Would it make any difference when he did the eyes? I mean, could he do them later?"

Elle stopped and looked up at him. "Well. I don't know. This woman who died at the mall—her eyes weren't done until after death."

"Neither were George's, the guy they dug up in Wisconsin. He probably wasn't done for twenty-four hours. . . ."

"That's your answer, then. He does it after death, but apparently it doesn't have to be right away. What are you thinking?"

"Just that if a kid dies and there's going to be a postmortem, you might not want to do the eyes right away. Especially if you had another shot, later."

"Like at the funeral home?"

"Sure. Anytime after the postmortem. He's a pathologist, he's right there with the bodies. He could do the eyes

308

there, right in the hospital, or at the funeral home during a visitation. Who watches a dead body?"

"Do they do anything with the eyes at funeral homes? Would anybody notice?" Elle was doubtful.

"I don't know," Lucas said. "But I can find out."

"What time is it?" she asked suddenly. "I've got a four-o'clock class."

Lucas looked at his watch. "It's just four now."

26

Bekker checked the time as he got out of the car: just four o'clock, right on schedule.

The apartment building was a block away. He had the clipboard under his arm, and the flower box. The gun weighed heavily in one pocket; the tape was much lighter in the other. He walked with his head down against the drizzle.

The rain had arrived just in time, and was a blessing, Bekker thought. The rain suit made perfect sense, and the hood would cover his entire head, with the exception of a narrow band from his eyebrows to his lips. He walked heavily: the PCP always did that, stiffened him up. But it made him strong, too. Focused him. He thought about it, then took the brass cigarette case from his pocket and popped another pill, just to be sure.

He had taken elaborate measures to make sure he hadn't been followed, driving through the looping streets of the lake district, waiting, doubling back, taking alleys. If he was being watched, they were doing it by satellite.

Walt's Appliance faced Druze's apartment building from across the street. The sales level was a rectangular space, four times as deep as it was wide, with wooden floors that creaked when a customer walked among the ranks of white kitchen appliances. The washers, dryers, refrigerators and stoves carried brand names that sounded familiar at first, less familiar after some thought. Walt kept the lights off, unless a customer was on the floor; the interior was usually illuminated only by the weak light from the street, which filtered through the dusty windows with the fading advertising signs.

Like his merchandise, Walt was nondescript. Too heavy. Not so much soft-spoken as noncommittal. A few strands of fading brown hair were combed sideways over a balding head, and plastic-framed glasses perched on the end of a button nose slowly withering with age, like an overripe raspberry. Walt had been a beatnik in the fifties, kept a copy of *Howl* in his desk drawer. Read it more now, rather than less.

He was happy to cooperate with the police, Walt was: genuinely happy. He'd never used the loft anyway, except to store leftover samples of carpet and rolls of cracking vinyl, the remnants of a brief fling with the flooring business. He provided an inflatable mattress, an office chair, a collapsible TV tray and a stack of old *Playboy*s. The watchers brought binoculars, a Kowa spotting scope, a video camera with a long lens, and a cellular telephone. They were happy, warm, out of the rain. Pizza could be delivered, and there was a bakery just down the street.

Another team, not so lucky, watched the back entrance of the apartment building from a car.

The watcher at Walt's sat in the chair, facing the street. The TV tray was at his side, on it a Coke in a paper cup. The spotting scope was on a tripod in front of him. The other cop lay on the mattress, reading a *Playboy*. The watcher saw Bekker lurching through the rain, looked at him through the scope, dismissed him, never even mentioned him to the cop on the mattress. He couldn't see Bekker's face because of the hat, but he could see the oblong lavender box under his arm, the kind used to deliver roses all over the metro area. You recognized them even if you'd never gotten flowers, or given them.

Bekker checked the mailboxes, found her apartment

311

number, used Druze's key to open the lobby door and took the elevator to the sixth floor. Her apartment was the last one on the hall. On impulse, thinking of the gun in his pocket, he stopped one door down the hall and knocked quietly. No response. He tried again. Nobody home.

Good. He slipped a hand in his breast pocket, found the tab of PCP, popped it under his tongue. The taste bit into him. He was ready. He'd primed himself. His mind stood aside, ferocious, and waited for his body to work.

His hand—nothing to do with his mind anymore, his mind was on its own pedestal—knocked on the door and lifted the box so it could be seen from the peephole. There *were* flowers in the box. If there was somebody with her, he could leave them, walk away. Druze? He'd still have to do Druze, but the package wouldn't be nearly as nice.

Bekker stood outside Cassie's door, waiting for an answer.

Four o'clock. Lucas left St. Anne's, heading west toward the rain. Maybe meet Cassie, he thought. Maybe time to catch her before the play. But yesterday she'd almost kicked him out. And then there were the questions about the handling of dead bodies. . . . He knew a funeral director, down on the south side of town. He could ask about the eyes of the children, although the idea disturbed him.

Old Catholic background, he thought. Killing people wasn't so bad, but you didn't want to mess with the dead. He grinned to himself, stopped at a traffic signal. Left, he could take the Ford bridge into south Minneapolis, go to the funeral home. Right, he could cut 1-94 and be at Cassie's in ten minutes.

The lights at right angles turned yellow, and Lucas took his foot off the brake, ready to let out the clutch. Still undecided. Left or right?

"Flowers?" She was smiling, her face completely unaware as she took the box, showing no hint of apprehension. Bekker's body glanced up and down the hall, then drew the pistol and pointed it at her forehead.

"Inside," he snapped, as her eyes widened. "Keep your mouth shut, or I swear to Christ I'll blow your fuckin' brains out," Bekker's body said, his mind applauding. Bekker's body shoved her back with the left hand, holding the pistol with the right. She clutched the box in both hands, her mouth opening, and as she stepped back, he thought for an instant that she was about to scream. "Shut up," he snarled. Saliva bubbled at his lips. "Shut the fuck up."

He was inside then, pulling the door closed behind himself, the gun no more than a foot from her forehead. "Back up, sit on the couch."

She dropped the box and he noticed the muscles in her arms. He wouldn't want to fight her. She backed up until her legs touched the couch, and she half stumbled and sat down. "Don't hurt me," she stuttered. Her face was pale as paper.

"I won't, if you pay attention," Bekker's body said. His mind still floated, directing traffic. "I just need a place to hide for an hour or so."

"You're not with Carlo?" Cassie asked, shrinking back into the couch.

The question caught him, but the drug covered for him. His body was disassociated now, worked by his mind like a puppet on strings, his hands numb. "Who?"

"You're not with Carlo?"

"I'm not with anybody, I'm just trying to hide until the

313

cops get off the street," Bekker said. His body was stiff as marble, betraying nothing, but his mind was working feverishly: *They knew about Carlo.* Christ, were they watching him? They must be. Bekker gestured with the tip of the barrel. "Lie down on the floor. On your stomach. Put your hands behind you."

"Don't hurt me," she said again. She slipped off the couch onto her knees, her eyes large. She was getting old, Bekker's mind thought: she had tiny wrinkles around her eyes and on her forehead.

"I'm not going to hurt you," his body said woodenly. He'd thought about this, what to say. He wanted her reassured, he wanted her to go along. "I'm going to tape your hands behind you. If I were going to hurt you, if I were going to rape you, I wouldn't do that. . . . I wouldn't put your hands under you. . . ."

She wanted to trust him. She turned, looking over her shoulder, and lay down. "Please . . ."

"The gun will be pointing at your head," he said. "I tried your neighbor first, but she wasn't home—so I know I could get away with a shot, if I had to. . . . I don't want to risk it, but I will if you try to fight. Do you understand what I'm saying?"

"Yes."

"Then put your face down on the floor, straight down, and cross your hands. I'll be taping with one hand. The gun's still pointing at you."

She did it: the marvelous power of the gun. She rolled, her hands behind her, and he awkwardly turned a wrap of the two-inch plastic packaging tape around her wrists, then another, then a third.

"Don't move," he said. He didn't say it viciously, but his tongue was thick, slurring the words. That was more frightening than if he'd been screaming at her. . . . He did her ankles, more quickly now that her hands weren't a

314

threat, but still staying clear of a possible kick. When they were tight, he slipped the gun in his coat pocket and went back to her hands, added more tape, tighter now.

"You're hurting me," she said.

He grunted. No point in talking anymore. He had her. He walked around the couch, put one knee across her back to hold her flat, and slapped a palm-sized strip of tape across her mouth. She fought it, but he held her by the hair and wrapped more tape, tangling her hair across her face, plastering it to the sides of her head.

"That should do it," his body said, more to his mind than to her. The bottom part of her face had been encapsulated, leaving her nose and eyes uncovered. He put the tape in his pocket, grabbed her under the arms and dragged her to the bedroom. When she started struggling, he backhanded her across the nose, hard. "Don't do that."

In the bedroom he laid her facedown on the bed and taped her feet to the endboard. He wrapped another length around her neck, once, twice, and led it to the headboard.

"I'm going in the front room to watch television, see if the cops have figured me out," he said. "I want you quiet as a mouse; you're not hurt yet, but you will be if you cause me any trouble."

He closed the bedroom door and turned on the television. Now the tricky part.

Cassie tried to fold her body against the tape. If she could get enough pressure, she might pull free. . . . If she could get up on her feet, even hobble, there were scissors in the bureau, and she might be able to cut the tape. And if her hands were free, she could push the bureau in front of the door and hold him off—throw

315

something through the window, if necessary, scream for help. . . .

But when she tried to fold herself, the tape around her neck threatened to strangle her. She pulled as long as she dared, then released the tension. The tape on her mouth kept her from gasping for the needed air and she strained to get it through her nose, her vision going red for a moment. No good.

She lay still for a moment, calculating. Nobody coming over? No. If Davenport dropped in, like he had the day before . . . Fat chance. She'd have to do it on her own. She tried rolling, rocking back and forth. She was at it for a minute, two minutes, got over on her back, then another half-turn. Was the tape ripping? She couldn't see. She pulled her arm in close to her body and tried to roll again. . . .

Bekker left Cassie's apartment door unlocked and padded down the hall to the stairs. On the way, he wrapped his right hand in a handkerchief. Druze was three floors down and the cops knew something. Bekker didn't know how they knew, but they did, and they'd be watching.

A camera in the corridor? Unlikely. If the cops were secretly watching Druze, they wouldn't do anything that might call attention to themselves. His mind equivocated: the woman had seen him, so he'd have to do her. But he hadn't exposed himself to any watching cops yet, and he might be about to do that. His mind worked at it, and finally told his body to go ahead. To risk it. There was no other way, if the cops were this close to Druze. He opened the door and peeked out: the third-floor corridor was empty. He pulled up his rain hood, hurried to Druze's door and, about to knock, reconsidered. If the apartment was bugged . . .

He scratched on the door. Heard movement inside.

Scratched again. A moment later, the door opened a crack and Druze peered out. Bekker put a finger over his lips for silence and gestured for Druze to step into the hallway. Druze, frowning, followed, looking up and down the hall. Bekker, finger back on his lips, pointed to the door of the stairwell.

"I can't explain it all right now, but we got a problem," he whispered when they were on the stairs. "I talked to Davenport and he said they had a suspect but no evidence. I asked how they were going to catch him, and he said, 'We've got to catch him in the act.' And the way he said it, it sounded like a pun he was making to himself. . . ."

"Aw, shit," Druze said, worried. "What happened to your hand?"

"She bit me. Anyway, I thought I'd come over here, early enough to catch the girl, like we'd talked about. . . ."

"We hadn't talked about it for sure . . ." Druze said.

"Something had to be done and I couldn't risk calling you on the phone," Bekker said. "You may be bugged."

"We don't even know it's me."

"We do now. I went up to her apartment, stuck a gun in her face and taped her up. I was planning to wait until you were at the theater, whack her on the head—you know, do it so they couldn't separate that injury from the injuries in a fall—and then pitch her right out the window. You'd have an alibi, and nobody knows about me."

"What happened?"

"The first thing she said was, 'You're not with Carlo?'" The honesty was there in his voice.

"Aw, God damn it," Druze said, running his fingers through his hair. "And you think the apartment may be bugged?"

"I don't know. But if this woman goes out the window

while you're at the theater, that's one more piece of evidence on your side. . . . They'll know you're not involved, anyway. . . ."

There was something wrong with the reasoning, but Druze, shocked, couldn't figure it. And Bekker said, "Come on up to her apartment. You scare her. We need to find out what the cops know. . . ."

"God, I kind of like her," Druze said.

"She doesn't like you," Bekker answered harshly. "She thinks you're the killer."

Bekker led the way quickly up the stairs, feeling the gun bang against his legs. All clear. In the apartment, he gestured at the bedroom and Druze walked back. Cassie was still facedown on the bed, but she had been struggling against the tape, which had been twisted between her legs and the bed.

"Turn her over, so she can see you," Bekker said, moving to Druze's right side. Druze stooped and grabbed Cassie's near shoulder and hip, to roll her over.

His mind was clear as ice, his body moving with the precision of an industrial robot. Bekker pulled the pistol from his pocket—his mind watched it in slow motion, guiding each small movement of the drawing gesture—with the handkerchief-wrapped hand.

In a single move, Bekker's body put the muzzle an inch from Druze's temple.

Druze sensed the movement, started to turn his head, his mouth opening.

Bekker pulled the trigger.

Dropped the gun.

Recoiled from the blast . . .

The blast, confined in the small bedroom, was terrific, stunning. Bekker jerked back as Cassie arched up, twisting frantically at the tape.

318

Druze simply collapsed, the gun disappearing beneath him.

Cassie's sweater was speckled with Druze's blood and small amorphous shreds of bone and brain tissue.

Bekker's robot-controlled body touched Druze's. Dead. No question of it. The drugs sang in his blood and he went away. He sighed, and came back: Jesus. He'd been gone. How long? He glanced at his watch. Four-twenty. Cassie was staring at him from the bed, her hands working frantically behind her back. He hadn't been gone long, a few minutes at most. He listened. Anybody coming? Not so far. No knocks, no sound of running feet . . .

He looked at Druze on the floor. He'd have to leave him like that, there might be some kind of blood pattern from the shot or something. He couldn't do the eyes, of course. He worried about that, but there was nothing to be done. If Druze was going to take the blame . . .

Cassie.

She'd stopped fighting the tape, but her back was arched, her head turning, trying to see him. He had to hurry: he still had to stop at Druze's apartment, to leave the photos. He started into the kitchen, when a door slammed down the hall, and he stopped. Listened.

Was that a movement? Out in the hall. He strained, listening. The hall was carpeted, would muffle steps. He waited a minute, then a few more seconds.

He couldn't wait longer. He still had to visit Druze's apartment. He patted his chest, confirming that the pictures were there. He'd cut the eyes out. . . .

He'd have to be careful. If the cops had bugged Druze's apartment and realized he was gone, but hadn't left the building, they might be on the way. Maybe he shouldn't try it. If he were caught in the apartment . . . that didn't bear thinking about

Bekker, the PCP pounding in his blood, went into the

kitchen and got a bread knife, the sharpest he could find.

And there again . . . Movement? Somebody in the hall. He froze, listened. . . . No. He had to move.

He didn't do it well, and he didn't do it quickly, but he did it: he cut Cassie's throat from ear to ear, and sat with her, holding her green eyes open with his fingers, as she died.

27

Lucas spent ten minutes at the funeral home with a cheerful, round-faced mortician who wanted to talk golf.

"Damn, Lucas, I already been out twice," he said. He had a putter and was tapping orange balls across a plush carpet toward a coffee cup lying on its side. "It was a little muddy, but what the hell. In another two weeks, it'll be every morning. . . ."

"I need to know about the eyes. . . ."

"So don't talk to me about golf," the mortician complained. He putted the last ball, and it bounced off the rim of the cup. "Nobody wants to talk golf. You know how hard it is to talk golf when you're in the funeral business?"

"I can guess," Lucas said dryly.

"So what exactly do you want to know?" the mortician asked, propping the putter against an easy chair.

They were in a small apartment above the funeral home, where the night man stayed. A lot of people die at night, the mortician said, and if you're not there, they might call somebody else. To the average, unknowledgeable member of the general public, one funeral home was as good as another.

"What about the eyes? Do you leave them in or take them out, or what?"

"Why'd we take them out?" the cheerful mortician asked, relishing the conversation. Lucas was uncomfortable, and he could see it.

"I don't know, I just . . . I don't know. So you leave them in?"

"Sure."

"Do you sew the eyelids shut or glue them shut or anything?"

"No, no, once they're shut, they stay that way."

"How about the viewings? Is there always somebody around?"

"Well, there's always somebody *around*, but not necessarily *right there*. We go by judgment. If we see a street person going into the viewing room, we'd go with him, of course—we don't want to get any rings stolen, or whatever. But if the guy looks straight, if he's a member of the family, then we pretty much let him go. We might check every couple of minutes, but a lot of people, when they're saying good-bye, don't like funeral-home people standing around staring at them. They feel like they're being rushed, you know, like when a salesman stands right next to you in a department store. But it's judgment. One time this whole family warned us about a particular guy, one of the grandfathers. The deceased had this gold plate, probably worth a couple hundred, and this old guy was a thief. So we hung on him. He was kneeling there praying, and he kept looking at us and then praying some more. . . . He must've prayed for half an hour. The family members said that was the longest prayer of his life, by about twenty-nine minutes."

"But theoretically, if somebody wanted to get in and touch a body, or look at its eyes . . . he could do it. If you didn't have some warning."

The funeral home man shrugged. "No theory about it—sure he could. No problem. But what can you do to a dead man in two minutes?"

Lucas kept a handset stashed under the seat, and Del caught him halfway back into the loop.

"Something's happened with Druze," Del said. "He's

gone. The surveillance guys swear there was no way he got out of the building, but he doesn't answer his phone and he's late for rehearsal."

"What do you think? Check his apartment?"

"I don't know. I thought we'd wait a while longer. . . . We've been calling every two or three minutes, so it's not like he's on the can."

"Keep watching. I'll come on up."

He didn't think of her, not right away. The traffic was heavy on Minnehaha Avenue headed north and he was stuck for three blocks behind a dump truck that resisted all of his attempts to pass. Cursing, he finally got around it, and got the finger from a scowling, long-haired truck driver. He hit three red lights in a row, and then she popped up in his mind. Same building. A chill ran through him, and he picked up the handset and called through to Del.

"I have a friend in that building. She's an actress with the same theater Druze is at," he said. "Would you call her?"

"Sure . . ."

Lucas could see the apartments along I-94, six blocks from the theater, when Del called back. "No answer."

"Shit." Lucas glanced at his watch. She should be at the theater. "Could you call the theater, ask for her?"

He was on Riverside, hurrying now, weaving through traffic. He jumped a light, scared a drunk and a student, saw the apartment building ahead.

"Lucas, we called, and she hasn't shown up."

"Ah, Jesus, listen, I gotta check on her. We've been talking about the case. . . ."

"I'll meet you out in front. I've talked to the manager a couple of times."

Del was walking across Riverside when Lucas arrived. Lucas dumped the car and met him on the sidewalk.

"Anything?"

"No. I called the manager, she should be . . . There she is."

The manager was holding the lobby door, and Del introduced Lucas. "This is not official," Lucas said. "She's a personal friend of mine, she's had some serious problems, and she hasn't shown up at work. We're worried."

"Okay. Since you're the police."

They rode up to the sixth floor in silence, listening to the elevator rattle against the sides of the shaft, watching the numbers click on the counter. There was nobody in the corridor outside Cassie's apartment. Lucas knocked on her door. Nothing. Knocked again.

"Open it," he said to the manager, stepping back. She fitted her key to the lock and pushed the door open. Del shoved past Lucas. An odor filled the small front room. . . .

"You stay right fuckin' here, Lucas," Del shouted. He grabbed him by the collar and pulled him out of the doorway, and held the woman back with the other hand. "You stay right fuckin' here. . . ."

Del headed for the bedroom. Lucas pushed past the bewildered woman, right behind him.

Cassie.

Her face was turned away. He *knew*, but he thought *Maybe she's* . . . But the blood was all over the bed, and when he stumbled up to it, and saw her eyes . . . and the huge red gash under her chin, cutting through layers of tape . . . and Druze on the floor beside her, blood everywhere . . .

Somebody moaned, a long, horrible, low-pitched sound, and he realized that it was coming from his own throat, and he reached out and touched her. . . .

"Cassie . . ." He screamed it, and Del pivoted, grabbed him by the jacket and pushed him away like a linebacker

324

working a blocking sled. Del himself screamed, "No, no, no . . ."

The manager, hands clenched in front of her, looked through the bedroom door and then staggered backward, still looking, her mouth hanging open. She ran to the doorway and began retching, and screaming, and retching again, and the stink of vomit overlay the smell of the butchery inside the bedroom. . . .

Lucas strained against his friend, and Del said, "Stay the fuck out, Lucas, stay the fuck out, we need to process, Lucas she's dead, Lucas she's dead. . . ." He pushed Lucas into a chair and picked up the phone.

"We got another one. We need everything you got, apartment six-forty-two. We got two of them, yeah, it's Druze. . . ."

He looked at Lucas, who was back on his feet, ready to go after him. But Lucas walked away from the bedroom and did something that frightened Del more than any effort to look at Cassie: he stood staring at a wall from a distance of no more than a foot, expressionless, unmoving, his eyes open.

"Lucas?" No answer. "Davenport, for Christ's sakes . . ."

"You want to go to the hospital?" Sloan asked.

"What for?" Del had pulled him off the wall, stuffed him into the elevator, guided him to the lobby and held him there.

"Get some dope."

"No."

"You're totally fucked, man. You can't be like this," Sloan said. He was driving the Porsche, while Lucas slumped beside him in the passenger seat.

"Just get me home," Lucas said. The storm was back in his head, the storm he'd feared. Cassie's face. The things he could have done, might have done, that she might have done. Going around, thousands of options, millions

of intricate possibilities, all leading to life or to death . . .
Sybil's face popped into his head.

"We saved the life of a woman who's gonna die in a
week . . ." he moaned.

"But we maybe got Bekker, the lawyers are looking at
the tapes right now."

"Fuck me," Lucas said, dropping his chin on his chest.
He had to cry, but he couldn't.

And then he said, "I went to a funeral home. If I'd come
here . . ."

And then he said, "Every fuckin' woman I see gets hurt.
I'm a goddamned curse on their heads. . . ."

And then he said, "I could've saved her. . . ."

"I gotta make a call," Sloan said suddenly, taking the car
into a convenience-store parking lot. "Just take a minute."

Sloan called Elle Kruger, looking back over his shoulder
at Lucas in the passenger seat of the Porsche. All he could
see was the top of Lucas' head. The nun's phone was
answered by a woman at a switchboard; Sloan explained
that he was calling on a police emergency. The woman said
she'd try to find Elle, and began switching. A moment
later, she came back on to say that the nun was at dinner,
and a friend would get her. She told Sloan to hold on.

"Lucas?" Elle asked when she picked up the phone.

"No, this is his friend Sloan. Lucas has a problem. . . ."

When Sloan returned to the car, Lucas' eyes were
closed, and he was breathing slowly, as though he were
sleeping. "You okay?" Sloan asked.

"That fuckin' Loverboy. If he'd come in, he could've
looked at the picture of Druze the minute I found it, and
we could've busted him. But we had to go through this
newspaper-ad bullshit. . . ."

"Let it go," Sloan said. "Nothing we can do about
it now."

*   *   *

Elle was waiting at Lucas' house with another nun and a small black car.

"How are you?" she asked.

He shook his head, looking down at the driveway. Meeting her eyes would be impossible, too complicated.

"I'll call my friend, get a sedative for you."

"I've got this stuff going around in my head . . ." he said. And the guns: he could feel the guns in the basement. Not heavy, not like last winter, but they were back.

"Let me call my friend." Elle took his arm, then his hand, and led him toward the door like a child, while Sloan and the other nun followed behind.

Lucas woke the next morning exhausted.

The sedatives had beaten him into a dreamless sleep. The storm in his head had dissipated, but he could feel it just over the horizon of consciousness. He slid tentatively out of bed, stood up, swayed, opened the bedroom door and almost fell over the couch. Sloan had pushed it up against the door and was struggling to get up.

"Lucas . . ." Sloan, in a T-shirt and suit pants, with a blanket wrapped around his shoulders, looked tired and scared.

"What the fuck are you doing, Sloan?"

Sloan shrugged. "We thought it might be a good idea, in case you sleepwalked. . . ."

"In case I started looking for my guns?"

"Something like that," Sloan admitted, looking up at him. "You look like shit. How do you feel?"

"Like shit," Lucas said. "I gotta get some dead kids dug up." The blood seemed to drain from Sloan's face, and Lucas smiled despite himself, smiled as a widow might smile the day before her husband is buried. "Don't worry about it. I'm not nuts. Let me tell you about Bekker. . . ."

28

Daniel prowled around his office with his hands in his pockets. He'd pulled the shades but hadn't turned on the lights, and the office was almost dark.

"Homicide is satisfied," he said. "You know I don't clear murder cases on the basis of politics—and there's every indication that we got him. You got him. Bekker is something else."

Lucas was also standing, propped against a windowsill, arms crossed. "If Bekker kills another one and carves her eyes out, then what'll you do? The goddamned press'll be down here with pitchforks and torches."

Daniel threw up his hands in exasperation. "Look, I know this actress woman and you . . ."

"Doesn't have anything to do with it," Lucas said. His head still felt like a chunk of wood. Cassie did have something to do with it, of course. Revenge wouldn't be enough, but it would be something. "Druze may have killed her, but Bekker was behind it."

"Have you talked to the lab people since you came in?"

"No . . ."

"They looked at that jacket in Druze's closet. There was blood on the back of it. You can't see it, because the fabric was black and the blood was soaked in. But it was there, and they've done some preliminary tests. The blood is the same type as Stephanie Bekker's. . . ."

Lucas nodded. "I think Druze killed Stephanie, all right. . . ."

"And George. We got a taxi routing from the airport to the Lost River Theater the night George was done."

"What about Elizabeth Armistead? I'm not so sure about that one. I asked that night, or the next day, and everybody agreed Druze was at the theater most of the afternoon."

Daniel jabbed a forefinger at Lucas: "But maybe not every minute. He could've been gone half an hour and that would have been enough. And the woman who saw the guy at Armistead's said he was in some kind of utility-man get-up. That sounds like an actor to me—we've got Homicide guys over at the theater right now, going through their wardrobe."

"What about the phone call?"

"Come on, Lucas. That so-called phone call doesn't make sense no matter how you cut it. And the kid out in Maplewood is pretty sure that Druze is the guy who did the Romm woman." Daniel took a manila folder from his desk and handed it to Lucas. "They found these in Druze's apartment."

Lucas opened the folder: inside were photographs of Stephanie Bekker and Elizabeth Armistead. The eyes had been cut out. "Where'd they get these?"

"Druze's file cabinet. Stuffed in the back."

"Bullshit," said Lucas, shaking his head. "I went through the file cabinet. These weren't there."

"Maybe he carried them with him."

"And puts them in the file cabinet before he goes upstairs to blow his brains out?" Lucas said. "Look, take this any way you want: as a continuing homicide investigation or just covering your political ass. We've got to stay with Bekker. We can tell the press that the case is cleared, but we've got to stay on him. We can start by exhuming these kids."

"What do we say about that?" Daniel asked. "How do we explain . . ."

"We don't say anything. Why should we say anything

329

to anybody? If we can convince the parents to keep quiet . . ."

Daniel walked around the quiet office, head down, rubbing his hands. Finally he nodded. "Damn, I'd hoped we'd finished with it."

"We're not finished until Bekker falls. You saw the tapes with Sybil, for Christ's sake. . . ."

"And you heard what the lawyers said. A dying woman, maybe paranoid, loaded with drugs? C'mon. I believe her, Merriam believes her, Sloan does, so do you—but there's no way a judge is going to put that in front of a jury."

"Dying declaration . . ."

"Oh, bullshit, Lucas—she didn't make it while she was dying, for Christ's sake. . . ."

"You know what Cassie couldn't understand about the killings? The eyes. She said Druze would never do the eyes. You know what my friend Elle says about them? The shrink. She says he *has* to do the eyes. So if Bekker is nuts, and he kills somebody else . . . Jesus, can't you see it? He'll do the eyes again, and your balls will be hanging from a pole outside the City Hall door."

Daniel pulled on his lip, sighed and nodded. "Go ahead. Talk to the kids' parents. If they say okay on an exhumation, do it. If they say no, come back here and we'll talk. I don't want to go for a court order."

Lucas met Anderson in the hallway.

"You've heard?" Anderson asked.

"What?"

"The lab guys say that Druze didn't have much in the way of nitrites on his hands. He may have had a handkerchief on the gun, but still . . ."

"So what are they saying?"

"Maybe he didn't kill himself. The M.E. says the whole scene is a little weird, the way he did it, the way he must

330

have been standing when he pulled the trigger. Can't figure out how the gun got underneath him, either. The muzzle was three or four inches from his temple when he pulled the trigger, and with the shock of the bullet and the recoil, he should have gone one way and the gun another. Instead, it beat him to the floor."

"The M. E. still working on him?"

"Oh, yeah. They've got samples of everything. I don't know, it's getting curiouser."

Lucas sat in his office, thinking it over, feeling the rats of depression galloping just below the surface of his mind. If he stopped concentrating, they'd be out. He forced his mind into it: Did Druze kill Cassie? Despite the questions, it seemed likely. In most murders, the most obvious answer is correct—and in any crime investigation, there are always anomalies. The gun shouldn't have beaten Druze's body to the floor, but maybe it did.

One of the rats slipped out: If only Cassie had identified him a day earlier and Loverboy had called with a definite identification . . .

Fuckin' Loverboy . . .

Lucas frowned, picked up the phone and called Violent Crimes. Sloan was at home, they said, trying to get some sleep. Lucas called, got him out of bed.

"Last night, when I was doped up. Did anybody call?"

"No."

"Hmph. What time did we identify Druze for television and release the news that it was part of the series . . . ?"

"This morning—I mean, they had Druze's name last night, midnight or so, but just the name. We didn't release the serial-killing business until this morning."

"Huh. Okay, thanks." He let Sloan go, dialed TV3 and got Carly Bancroft. "This is Lucas. Did you make Druze's name on the news last night?"

"No, we had it for the wake-up report," she said. "I could have used a little help. . . ."

"I was . . . out of shape," Lucas said. "What about the other channels? Did they have it?"

"Not as far as I know. We picked up the news release on morning cop checks. Nobody was bitching about getting beat, and they would have, on something like this. When can you talk to us? You found them, right? What—"

"I really can't talk," Lucas said. "I'll call you later."

He hung up and sat in his chair, rubbing his temples. Loverboy hadn't called.

Jennifer's car was in the driveway when he got home. He rolled past it slowly as the garage door went up, and parked and walked out of the garage as she got out of her car.

"How are you?" she asked. She was wearing a black turtleneck under a cardigan, with gold loop earrings visible under her short-cropped blond hair.

"What do you want?" His voice was so cold that she stepped back.

"I wanted to see how you were. . . ."

"Did Elle put you up to this?" Jennifer had her back to the car door and he loomed over her. His hands were in fists, inside his jacket pockets.

"She said you were in trouble."

"I don't need your help. The last time I needed your help, I got my head pushed under," he said. He turned away, walked back into the garage.

"Lucas . . ."

His mind was moving like a freight train, all the facts and suppositions and memories and plans and possibilities flying like boxcars just behind his eyes, unsuppressible. Jennifer. Green eyes. Full lips. Sarah, a bundle, squealing when he tossed her in the air. Jennifer and Sarah together in the delivery room, up at the lake cabin,

Jennifer skinny-dipping in the moonlight, Sarah starting to crawl . . .

He was at a branch, he felt, when ten thousand things were possible, but he couldn't deal with that, with all the branches. . . .

"Just . . . go away," he said.

He tried, but couldn't sleep. Too many suppositions. Finally, glancing at the clock, he called the Minneapolis Institute of Arts and asked how late the gift shop was open. He had just enough time.

He hurried, trying not to think. Just keep moving. Don't worry about the guns. They sit there in the basement and they glow, and fuck 'em, let 'em glow.

The gift shop was empty, except for a bored saleswoman who was dressed so well that Lucas guessed she was a volunteer.

"Can I help you?" she asked.

"Yeah. I'm interested in a dude named Odilon Redon. What've you got? Got any calendars?"

Five minutes later he was back in the car, looking for a scrap of paper. He finally found a receipt from a tire store. He turned it over, flattened it against the Porsche owner's manual on his leg and started a new list.

And later, afraid of the bed, he sat in the spare bedroom with a bottle of Canadian Club and stared at his charts.

The Killer One chart was complete: Druze. A troll, powerful, squat, odd head, murdering Stephanie. No question about that anymore. If he was working with Bekker, must have killed George, because Bekker was with Lucas. Could have killed Cassie. Could have killed Armistead. Could have killed woman at the shopping center—but why? She was entirely out of the pattern. Not at home;

333

not with the academic/art crowd . . . And where did the photos come from, with the missing eyes?

Killer Two: Did he exist? Was it Bekker? Some tracks at the site of the George killing suggested a second man. How would Druze have found George if Bekker hadn't fingered him? (Possibility: He'd watched Stephanie's funeral?) Why would he have driven George's Jeep to the airport? How could he have killed Armistead? Why the phone call—a coincidence, somebody trying to get in free?

The answers were in the pattern, somewhere. Lucas could feel it but couldn't see it.

He took the tire store receipt from his pocket. At the top he'd written "Loverboy."

He looked at it, closed his eyes and let the circumstances flow through his mind.

At six in the morning, he phoned Del. "I gotta come over and talk to you," he said. Del had an affinity for speed.

"Jesus Christ, man, what're you doing up at six o'clock? You're worse'n me. . . ."

Lucas drove across town with the breaking dawn, another cool, overcast day. The drive-time radio programs had started, and he dialed past the jock talk to 'CCO, half listening as he put the car on I-94 toward Minneapolis.

Del met him at the door in a pair of slightly yellowed jockey shorts and a sleeveless T-shirt that Clark Gable would have approved of. When Lucas told him what he wanted, Del shook his head and said, "Lucas, you'll kill yourself."

"No. I just need to stay awake for a while," Lucas said. "I know what I'm doing."

Del looked at him, nodded, went to the bedroom and came back with an orange plastic vial. "Ten hits. Heavy-duty. But don't try to stretch it too far."

"Thanks, man . . ." Lucas said.

334

A woman's voice came from the back. "Del . . . ?"

"In a minute," Del said. He smiled thinly at Lucas. "Cheryl. What can I tell you?"

The speed brightened him up. He turned south, looking at the clock. Almost seven. Sloan would be up.

"How're you feeling?" Sloan's wife asked as she opened the door.

"Everybody wants to know," Lucas said, grinning at her. She was a short woman, slightly plump, motherly and sexy at the same time. Lucas liked her. "Is Sloan out of bed?"

She turned her head. "Sloan? Lucas is here."

"Out on the porch," Sloan called back.

"Does Sloan have a first name?" Lucas asked as he went past the woman.

"I don't know. I never asked," she said.

Sloan was sitting on the sun porch, smoking a cigarette and eating a cherry Moon Pie. A Coke sat on a side table by his hand.

"A real lumberjack breakfast," Lucas said.

"Don't talk loud," Sloan said. "I'm not awake yet."

"I need you to sweet-talk some people for me," Lucas said. Sloan was the best interrogator on the force. People told him things. "I've got the names and addresses. . . ."

"What for?" Sloan asked, taking the slip of paper.

"Their kids died," Lucas said. "We want to dig them up. We want to do it today."

29

Beauty danced and bled and danced and bled and danced until he fell down on his back, his arms thrown wide, his legs spread, a kind of crucifixion on the huge Oriental rug in the dining room. There were no dreams of eyes. There were no dreams of anything. There was nothing at all.

The pain woke him.

Daylight filtered past the blinds and his body trembled with cold, his muscles tight and shaking. He sat up and looked down, thought that somehow he'd gotten muddy, then realized that his chest was caked with dried blood. When he tried to stand, flakes of the blood broke away and fell on the carpet.

Something had changed. He felt it. Something was different, but he didn't know what. Couldn't remember. He tried to find it, but his mind seemed confused and he could not. Could not find it. He went to the bathroom, turned on the water for the tub, watched it pour, the water swirling, and he began to sing just like Mrs Wilson had taught them in the fifth grade:

"*Frère Jacques, Frère Jacques, dormez-vous, dormez-vous?* . . ."

In the tub, the blood dissolved, pink in the water, and Beauty bathed in it, patted it on his astonishing face, and sang every song that a fifth-grader knew. . . .

The mirror was steamed over when he got out of the tub. He was annoyed when this happened, because he could not look into his face, he had to open the bathroom door, had to wait until the cool air cleared it. He always tried to rub the steam away with a towel, but he could never quite clear the mirror. . . .

He opened the door and the cold air flooded around him, and the stimulation almost brought the memory back. Almost . . . The first streak of condensation ran down the mirror. Bekker picked up a towel and wiped. Ah. There he was. . . .

The face was far away, he thought, puzzled. He wasn't that far away. He was right here. . . . He reached out and touched the glass, and the face came closer, and the horror began to grow.

This wasn't Beauty. This was . . .

Bekker screamed, stumbled back, unable to tear his eyes from the mirror.

A troll looked back. A troll with a patchwork face, the wide eyes staring, measuring him. And it all came back, the apartment, the gun, and Druze going down like a burst balloon.

"No!" Bekker screamed at the mirror. He grabbed the hair on both sides of his head, pulled at it, welcoming the pain, trying to rip the troll from his consciousness.

But the eyes, cool, cruel, floated in the mirror, watching. . . . Bekker ran into the hallway: another of her mirrors, mirrors everywhere, all with eyes. He stumbled, fell, crawled down the hall, scampering, naked, his knees burning from the carpet, down to his bedroom like a weasel, groping in panic for the brass cigarette case.

The eyes were everywhere, in the shiny surfaces of the antique bedstand, in the window glass, on the surface of the water in a whiskey tumbler. . . . Waiting. No place for Beauty. He gobbled three blood-red caps of Nembutal 100 mg pentobarbital and the green eggs, the Luminal 30 mg phenobarbital, three of them, four, six. And then the purple eggs, the Xanax 1 mg alprazolam. Too much? He didn't know, couldn't remember. Maybe not enough. He took an assortment of eggs with him, squinting through half-closed eyes, avoiding the shiny surfaces, and whimpering, he crawled into his closet, behind the shirttails and the pantlegs, with the shoes and the odors of darkness. The Nembutal would be on him first; there was a mild rush as they came on, a Beauty rush. Bekker didn't want that. He wanted the calming effect, the sedation; even as he thought it, the rush dwindled and the sedation came on. The Luminal would be next, in an hour or so, smoothing him out for the day, until he could make plans to get at Druze. The Xanax would calm him. . . .

Another voice spoke in his mind, far away, barely rational: Druze. Find Druze.

Bekker looked into his hand, half cupped around the pills. He would find Druze if the medicine held out.

Lucas waited.

The second house was on a slight rise above the street, a greening lawn, neat, flower beds still raw with the spring. A Ford Taurus station wagon was parked in the driveway, the husband's car. He'd arrived just a minute after Sloan and Lucas. Lucas waited in the car while Sloan went inside.

The speed was beginning to bite. Lucas felt sharp and hard, like the edge of a pane of glass; and also brittle. He sat listening to Chris Rea on the tape player, singing about Daytona, his hand beating out the rhythm. . . .

Sloan came straight out the door and across the lawn, the paper in his hand.

"We're clear," he said. "The woman was okay, but I thought her husband was going to freak out."

"As long as we got it," Lucas said.

The machinery of exhumation was fussily efficient. A small

front-loader took off the top five feet of dirt and piled it on a sheet of canvas. Two of the cemetery's gravediggers took off the last foot with shovels, dropped hooks onto the coffin and pulled it out, a corroding bronze tooth.

Lucas and Sloan followed the M.E.'s van back downtown and, as the coffin was unloaded, walked inside to talk to the medical examiner.

When they found Louis Nett, he was pulling a gown over his street clothes. "Have you heard about the other one?" Lucas asked. The second child had been buried in the suburban town of Coon Rapids.

"It's on the way," Nett said. "If you guys want to hang around, I can give you a read in the next couple of minutes . . . depending on the condition of the body, of course."

"What do you think?" Sloan asked.

"Well, she was done by the Saloman Brothers. They're pretty careful, and she hasn't been down that long. I think there's a good chance, as long as the coffin is still tight. If it leaked, you know . . ." He shrugged. "All bets are off."

"We'll wait," Lucas said.

"You can come watch . . ." Nett offered.

"No, no," Lucas said.

"Well, if you don't mind . . . I think I might," Sloan said. "I've never seen one of these."

The medical examiner's office looked like the city clerk's office, or the county auditor's, or any place except one that dealt with the scientific dismemberment of the dead. Secretaries sat in front of smudged computer screens, each desk marked with idiosyncratic keepsakes: china frogs, pink-butted babies, tiny angels with their hands held in prayer, Xeroxed directives from the higher-ups, Xeroxed cartoons from the lower-downs.

In the back room, they were taking apart a long-dead teenage girl.

Lucas looked at one of the cartoons, cut from *The New Yorker*. It showed two identical portly, vaguely Scandinavian businessmen with brush mustaches, conservatively dressed with hats and briefcases, stopped at a receptionist's desk, apparently in Manhattan. The receptionist was talking into an intercom, saying, "Minneapolis and St. Paul to see you, sir . . ."

He turned away from the cartoon, dropped on a couch and closed his eyes, but his eyes didn't want to be closed. He opened them again and stared at the wall, fidgeted, picked up a nine-month-old magazine on bow-hunting, read a few words, dropped it back on the table.

The clock over a secretary's empty desk said four-fifteen. Nett said it shouldn't take more than a couple of minutes. At four-thirty, Lucas got up and wandered around the office, hands in his pockets.

Sloan came back first. Lucas stood up, facing him.

"You called it," Sloan said.

Something unwound in Lucas' stomach. They had him. "The eyes?"

"Cut. Nett says with an X-acto knife or something like it—I figure it was a scalpel. Something that really dug in."

"Can they take photos or something . . . ?"

"Well . . . they're taking the eyes out," Sloan said, as though Lucas should have known. "They put them in little bottles of formaldehyde. . . ."

"Aw, Christ . . ."

30

The day started with an argument.

"I didn't become a psychologist so I could advise you on ways to destroy a mind," Elle Kruger snapped.

"I don't need any ethical qualms dumped on me. I had enough of that in school," Lucas answered. "I need to know what'll happen, what you think'll happen. If it won't work, say so. If it will . . . we told you what he's doing. You want this *monster* creeping around hospitals, snuffing kids? Because you've got a Catholic qualm?"

"That is an extremely offensive phrase," the nun said angrily. "I won't have it."

"Just tell me," Lucas said.

They argued for another fifteen minutes. In the end, she relented.

"If he's the man you think, it could be effective. But if he's as intelligent as you say and if he's thinking clearly, he may see right through it. Then you're ruined."

"We have to push," Lucas said. "We need some control."

"I've told you what I think: It could work. You'd want to just give him a flash, so later he wouldn't be sure if he actually saw it or just imagined it. You can't let him experience the . . . materiality . . . of the image. You wouldn't want to send him a photograph, or anything like that. If he has something solid in his hand, if he can sit and contemplate it, he'll say to himself, *Wait. This is real. How did this go from my mind to reality?* And then he'll be onto you. So you have to deal in images, the more ethereal the better. You need a will-o'-the-wisp."

"A will-o'-the-wisp," Lucas said. "That will do it?"

"There are no guarantees with the human mind, Lucas. You should know that, after last winter."

They stared at each other across her desk until he stood up and started away.

"What're you going to do?" she called after him.

"I'm going to push him," he said.

"God, I need video, I can't stand this." Carly Bancroft sat in the passenger seat of Druze's Dodge, working out of a professional makeup kit. The car was muggy inside, with the two of them working so close. The smell of sweat was pushing through her perfume; Lucas was sure he didn't smell any better.

"You'll be able to talk about it," Lucas said. "That'll be a hell of a story."

"I don't work for a fuckin' newspaper. I don't need words, I need pictures," she said. Lucas had refused to let her bring in a cameraman. She had a thirty-five-millimeter Nikon in a shoulder bag but insisted she felt naked.

"This isn't even supposed to be a story. . . ."

"Stop talking while I work around your mouth."

He felt silly, sitting with his head cranked back, while the reporter worked on him. Lucas tipped the visor mirror down and looked at himself as she painted the side of his face. "It's pretty crude," he said tentatively, trying not to move his lips.

"It's just fine," Bancroft said. "This isn't cosmetic makeup, it's stage makeup. You're lucky I took theater crafts. Hold still, dammit, I've got to shorten your nose."

She'd started by scouring his face with a cleansing cream, then wiped most of it off with tissue. When she finished, his skin still felt oily.

"Supposed to," she said. "That's your base."

His hair was already as dark as Druze's had been, but

she added a blue-gray tone to his beard area, and under his nose, to give him a heavier shadow. Using a powder puff, she put on a transparent powder to set the makeup.

Most of the time was spent blending a series of blue and reddish tones, to give his face the patchwork effect. Additional cosmetics made his face rounder; not quite Druze's pumpkin, but it was the best they could do. A bath towel wrapped around his chest gave him Druze's bulk. The whole process took twenty minutes.

Then they waited.

"On his way," Sloan said with a voice like static.

"Give me the hat . . ." Lucas said. Bancroft passed him a felt snap-brim and he put it on his head. He picked up the handset, pressed the transmit button and asked, "Where is he?"

"He's coming. Two minutes. You ready?"

"Ready," Lucas said. To Bancroft, he said, "Get in the back, in case something weird happens. You try to peek over the door and I'll pull your goddamned head off. And don't stick that fuckin' camera up, either."

"Tell me what happens," she said, as she climbed agilely over the seat. Lucas got a flash of long legs and then her blue eyes.

"You just stay out of sight. . . ."

"Can't I just peek?"

"Two blocks," said Sloan. "We can see the light. It's red. . . ."

"Changing now," said another voice. "Tell me when. . . ."

"It'll be a goddamned short green light," Lucas said to Bancroft. "Get the fuck down."

"Last corner, Lucas. Roll now," said Sloan. Lucas pulled away from the curve, topped a low rise and headed downhill to the light. He could see Bekker's car rolling toward the traffic light, signaling a left turn. The light

343

went yellow, then red, on command from the surveillance car.

Lucas pulled up to the light, stopped, stared through the tinted windshield at Bekker. They didn't think he'd be able to see Lucas' face from this distance, but they weren't sure. Lucas could see Bekker. The traffic light for the cross street went yellow. "Here we go," Lucas said. "Stay down."

Bekker, still signaling a left turn, pulled into the intersection, the surveillance car right on his tail to block any possible pursuit. Lucas moved slowly through the intersection, and as he passed Bekker's car, he looked left, out the window. The coat collar was up, the hat was pulled down, his face was shaded. . . .

His eyes caught Bekker's, and Bekker's head snapped around as though jerked by a wire. Lucas accelerated through the intersection and up the hill.

"He's killed the fuckin' car, I think, he's rolling through the intersection, he can't get the car started," Sloan called.

"He saw me," Lucas called back. To Bancroft, he said, "You can sit up."

"I need some fuckin' video," she moaned. "Davenport, you're killing me. . . ."

Bekker, shocked, sat in his car and cried, tried to start it, sent it bucking in first gear, killed it again, started again. . . .

Bekker didn't think of pursuit. He knew who it was he'd seen.

He'd sat in the closet for a day and a night, alternating between sleep and a half-waking state. He had no idea how many pills he'd taken, or the dosages, but finally, seeing daylight again and the cigarette case empty, and hungry, he crawled out of the closet. The eyes waited in the glass. He stood up, stumbled toward the bathroom, his body racked with pain. He'd gotten cramped in the closet, he hurt everywhere. In the shower, he stood in scalding water, the pain driving the pictures out of his mind. . . .

Out of the shower, he dressed, took a careful black cap, amphetamine, just enough to keep him going, went to the car, saw the eyes in the rearview mirror, tilted the mirror away, started down the street. There was a deli less than a mile away. He was caught by a red light. A station wagon across the street . . .

"Is he going on?" Lucas asked.

"Yeah, he's still going," Sloan said. "He's moving slow, though. I think there's something wrong."

"He's freaked out," Lucas said. "I told you he knew Druze."

"Something definitely wrong," Sloan said. "He's turning around. He's going back out to Twelve. . . ." The net stayed with Bekker as he drove toward downtown.

"Could be heading for the hospital," Sloan called.

Lucas stuck a borrowed police light in the window of the Dodge and raced for the university campus. Bancroft, who'd crawled back into the front seat, pulled a safety belt over her lap and snapped it. "You drive as bad as a cameraman," she said, buckling herself in.

"Don't have a lot of time," Lucas said. "You know where to take the car?"

"Yes." She sounded taut and he grinned. "You'll be paid off after this."

"I'll be paid off and a half," she said. "If the station knew I was doing this . . ."

"What?"

"Now that I think about it, I don't know what they'd do. If I had video, they'd probably be lined up outside the station with their lips puckered. . . ."

*   *   *

345

Lucas hopped out of the car on Washington Avenue, at the base of a footbridge. If Bekker followed his usual route to work, he'd drive beneath the footbridge; but from the roadway, there was no quick way up to it. If he stopped his car and climbed up as quickly as he could, Lucas would still have time to duck into a chemistry building at the end of the footbridge.

"Where is he?" Lucas asked on the handset. He hurried along the sidewalk toward the entry to the footbridge.

"He's coming up to the exit, so you got time," Sloan said. "There he goes, he's off."

Lucas climbed the footbridge, looked west across the Mississippi.

"Davenport . . ." He heard Bancroft on the other side, and turned to look over the rail. She was standing on a wall by the student union, the Nikon to her face. He waved her off and went back to the other side of the footbridge.

"On Washington," Sloan said on the handset. A passing student, a slender, long-haired kid in an ankle-length coat with an ankh on a chain around his neck, looked at him curiously and said, "Can't be Cyrano, with that nose."

"Fuck off, kid," Lucas said. He shaded his eyes as he looked down Washington Avenue toward the river.

"On the bridge," Sloan called on the handset.

"Okay," said Lucas, on his own set.

"Cop?" asked the kid.

"Go away," Lucas said. "You could fuck up something important and I'd have to throw your ass in jail."

"That's a good argument," the kid said, walking hastily away.

Bekker's car was on the bridge, pacing the traffic. Lucas squatted on the far side of the footbridge, out of sight, until Bekker was less than a hundred feet away. He should get just a flash. . . . Now.

Lucas stood up and peered over the bridge. Bekker saw him, swerved. Lucas was gone, hurrying toward the chemistry building.

"He saw you, he's on the side, he's on the side," Sloan called.

"Is he coming?"

"Naw, he's still in his car. . . ."

Bekker sat at the side of the road, his head on the steering wheel. He was afraid to sleep, waiting to move. And now here was Druze, coming back. . . .

He made a U-turn and drove back across the Mississippi, left his car in a dormitory parking lot and walked to the library. A loose net stayed with him, watching. Inside, Bekker scanned an index for the *Star Tribune*, looked up the appropriate issue and wrote down the details about the death of a tramp.

From a phone booth, he called the medical examiner.

"I'm trying to locate my father, who . . . had some mental problems," he said. "We weren't close, I was adopted by another family, but I've heard now from an old friend of his that he died and was buried by Hennepin County last year. . . . I was wondering if you could tell me which funeral homes you use, so I could find out where he's buried."

The county used four funeral homes, selected on an annual bid basis. Walker & Son, Halliburton's, Martin's and Hall Bros. He called them in order. Martin's took his last quarter.

"Martin's . . ." The voice low and already consoling.

"I'm calling about the funeral for a Carlo Druze. . . ."

"That's Friday."

"Will there be a viewing?"

"Uh, well, there usually is, but I'd have to check. Can you hold?"

347

"Yes . . ."

The woman was gone for three or four minutes. When she returned, she asked, "Are you a member of Mr Druze's family?"

"No . . . I'm from the theater. . . ."

"Well, Mr Druze's mother made some tentative arrangements which did not include a viewing, but now we understand that several theater people *will* be coming, so we're planning a viewing from seven to nine o'clock tomorrow night in the Rose Chapel, with burial at Shakopee. We will have to contact his mother again for approval."

"Tomorrow night, from seven to nine . . ." Bekker closed his eyes. The burial was sooner than he'd expected, or dared to hope. Druze had died two days before, and he would be buried in another two days. Bekker had been afraid that it would be a week, or even more, before the body was released. He could hold out for a week, he thought, with the right medication. Longer than that, and he'd have to let go, he'd have to go down and face Druze in the territory of dreams. But now that would not happen. Tomorrow night and it would be over.

31

Bekker saw Druze twice more, or thought he did: he couldn't decide, finally, whether he was seeing Druze or an image within his own eye.

He saw him two blocks from his house, a dark thing drifting around a corner. Bekker stood, his mouth open, the newspaper in his hand, and the figure disappeared like a wisp of black fog. He saw him again at mid-afternoon, passing in a car half a block away. Bekker's eye was caught first by the car, then by the obscured dark form behind the driver's-side glass. He could feel the eyes peering out at him. . . .

He was eating Equanil like popcorn, with an occasional taste of amphetamine; he was afraid to sleep, was living out of his study, from which he'd removed all the glass. If he could spend the day staring at the carpet . . .

He had trouble thinking. He would be all right after Druze was done. He could clear himself out for a while, go off the medications. . . . What? He couldn't remember. Harder to think. The units of thought, the concepts, seemed bound in threads of possibility, the threads tangled beyond his ability to follow them. . . .

He struggled with it: and time passed.

The funeral home was a gloomier place than it had to be, dark red-brown brick and natural stone, with a snaky growth of still leafless ivy clinging to the stone.

Bekker, shaky, anxious but anticipating, black beauties nestled in his pocket, drove past once, twice. There were few cars on the street but several in the funeral home driveway. As he was making his second pass, the front door opened and a half-dozen people came out and stood clustered on the steps, talking.

Older, most of them, they were dressed in long winter coats and dark hats, like wealthy Russians. Bekker slowed, eased the car to the curb, watched the people on the steps. Their talk was animated: an argument? He couldn't tell. After five minutes, the cluster began to break up. In ones and twos, they drifted out to their cars and, finally, were gone.

Bekker tried to wait but couldn't. The pressure to move . . . and there was nobody in sight. He didn't much credit the funeral home receptionist's comment that theater people were expected, but you never knew with theater people. He climbed out of the car, looked around, walked slowly up the driveway to the funeral home. A car cruised past and he turned his head. A man watching him? Druze again? He wasn't sure. He didn't care. In five minutes, he'd be done. . . .

The net was with him:

"He's out of the car, looking at the door," the close man said, driving on by. He didn't look at Bekker, who was walking slowly up the driveway.

There was no place to hide in the Rose Chapel, but the other rooms were worse. Lucas finally decided he could drive a nail through the top panel of one of the double doors, then pull the nail and have a hole large enough to peep through. The manager wouldn't let him use a nail, but did loan him a power drill with a sixteenth-inch bit. When Lucas, standing in the dark behind the doors, pressed his eye to the hole, he could see the entire coffin area.

"Go up there, bend over him," he told Sloan. Del was leaning against the wall, faintly amused. Sloan stood over the coffin and looked back at the doors. The hole was invisible.

"Put your hand on his head, or over it, or something," Lucas called from behind the doors. Sloan put his hand over Druze's head. A moment later, the doors opened.

"Can't see your hand," Lucas said. He looked around the room. "But I think any other arrangement would look wrong."

"Yeah, with the alcove like that," Sloan said, nodding toward the coffin.

Del grinned. "We could, like, put, you know, a spring with a clown under his eyelids, and when Bekker pulls it open, see, it pops up. . . ."

"I like it," Sloan said. "Motherfucker'd have a heart attack. . . ."

"Jesus," Lucas said, glancing toward the body. "I think we'll settle for the hole in the door."

"He's moving," said the voice on the handset.

Sloan looked at Lucas. "You cool?"

"I'm cool," Lucas said.

"So'm I," Del said. He unconsciously dropped his hand back to his hip, where he kept a small piece clipped to his belt. "I'm cool, too."

The receptionist came from Intelligence and spent his nights working undercover. "No problem," he said. "I could win a fuckin' Oscar, the work I do." There were two squads immediately available, and the surveillance team coming in with Bekker.

"He's here," the radio burped ten minutes later. "He's going past."

Bekker rambled through the neighborhood, looking it over, and made another pass at the front of the funeral home before he stopped.

"He's out of the car, looking at the door," the radio said.

"Everybody . . ." Lucas said.

A finger of joy touched his soul. In five minutes . . .

Bekker wore a trench coat and a crushable hat, with leather driving gloves. The scalpel, a plastic tube protecting the point, was clipped in his shirt pocket. The funeral home door, he thought, looked like the door on a bad ski chalet. . . .

The funeral home was overly warm. An antique mirror, like those collected by Stephanie, surprised him just inside the door. He flinched, jerked his eyes away, but found them drawn back. . . .

Druze was gone. Beauty looked back at him. Beauty looked fine, he thought, but tired. Unusual lines crossed his wide brow, gathered at the corners of his eyes. A different look, he thought, but not unattractive. French, perhaps, a world-weariness . . . like the actor with the home-rolled cigarette. What was his name? He couldn't concentrate, his own image floating in front of him like a dream. And then a gathering darkness behind his image, and . . .

He pulled his eyes away. Druze was there, still waiting.

"Buchanan?"

"What?" Bekker jumped. He'd been so engrossed in the mirror that he hadn't heard the funeral home receptionist until the man was virtually on top of him.

"Are you here for Mr Buchanan?" The receptionist seemed ordinary, a thin man in a conservative coat and flannel slacks, a man with no particular relationship to death, although he worked in the middle of it. No imagination . . .

"No . . ." Bekker said, "ah, Mr Druze?"

"Oh, yes. That would be the Rose Chapel. Down to your

352

right . . ." The receptionist pointed like a real estate man giving directions to the third bedroom, the one that was a little too small.

"Thank you."

The funeral home was quiet, all sounds smothered by plush drapes and heavy carpets. To quiet the weeping, Bekker guessed. As he stepped into the Rose Chapel, he glanced back at the receptionist. The man had turned away and seemed about to go down to the next room, when a phone rang in the entry. The receptionist stopped, picked up the receiver and launched into a conversation. Good. Bekker stepped into the chapel.

Lucas stood out of sight, heard the Intelligence guy ask the question, heard Bekker say, "No . . . ah, Mr Druze?" A moment later the phone rang. Worried that Bekker might arrive and yet develop cold feet, they'd worked out the diversion of the telephone, with Sloan calling from a back room. If Bekker could hear the receptionist talking, he'd be encouraged to act.

The Rose Chapel was small, with fifteen dark wooden chairs facing the coffin. The plaster walls were a pale shade of rose; the woodwork an antique cream. A closed pair of double doors was straight ahead of Bekker, apparently leading to the depths of the funeral home; they were sized to take a coffin on a gurney.

The coffin itself was to Bekker's right, on a dais within a plaster alcove. Roses were molded into the plaster, and individually hand-painted. The dais was covered with a rose-colored drape, a deeper shade than the walls. Bekker could see the side of Druze's head and his heavy shoulders under a dark suit.

Beauty was pushing through now, anxious for the celebration, moving him. He could hear the receptionist

353

talking, faintly, far away, and he moved to the front. His hand went to his pocket, found the scalpel. He pulled the tube off the end and moved next to the coffin.

Druze's head was large, he thought. Not just a pumpkin, but a big pumpkin. His face had been liberally worked with makeup, so the patchwork of skin grafts was barely visible. The nose, of course . . . not much you could do about that. He frowned. Too bad. Druze actually had been something of a friend. A man you could talk to. But he had to go; Bekker had known that from the beginning. Murder was something you didn't share, except with the dead.

Lucas pressed his eye to the hole in the double doors. He couldn't see Bekker as he came in, couldn't see his beautiful face as he went by. Bekker paused, just for a moment, in front of the coffin, looking down. Lucas could hear the receptionist muttering in the hall, and then, suddenly, Bekker was on Druze, bending over, the hand out of sight, but working over him. . . .

Bekker glanced back over his shoulder, then reached across Druze's face with his left hand and lifted his eyelid. The eye beneath was intact, but dull, dry, a piece of leather, staring sightlessly and unflinchingly at the ceiling. His heart pounding, the pressure in his veins, the murmur of the receptionist's conversation providing him with the necessary security, Bekker plunged the point of the scalpel into Druze's eyeball, and then turned the handle, like a corkscrew. He felt some of the weight leave him, a pressure gone from his shoulders.

Quickly, quickly, his mouth open, panting, he did the second eye, looking over his shoulder, twisting the knife. . . .

And he was free. He felt it, almost as if he were being

lifted from the floor. He did a little step, Beauty coming on, and looked back at Druze.

The eyelids were open, wrinkled and pulled up, like fragments of dead leaves. His heart beating hard and with joy, Beauty reached out to smooth them down, round them carefully, the scalpel still in his hand. He stepped back.

"Cut his eyes, Mike?"

The voice broke on him like a bucket of ice water, crashing down, snatching his breath away, each word hurting, a sharp stone: CUT HIS EYES, MIKE?

Bekker whirled, the scalpel still in his right hand.

Davenport was there, leaning in the double doors, wearing a dark leather jacket, a pistol in his hands, pointed not at Bekker but to one side. He looked wired, his eyes wide, his hair dirty, his face unshaven. A thug. Another man came in from the left, and then a third, Stephanie's dope-addict cousin, Del. The receptionist was behind them.

". . . 'Cause if you cut his eyes, Mike, we got you for the kids, too. We just dug them up today and the medical examiner says they were done with a knife just like that one, a scalpel. Is that a scalpel, Mike?"

Bekker stood speechless, the words bouncing through his brain, GOT YOU FOR THE KIDS, TOO, and Davenport moved in on him. One of the other cops, a thin man, said, "Be cool," but Bekker had no idea what that meant.

Lucas moved in on him, the pistol in his hand. Bekker was startlingly beautiful in the soft light coming off the rose plaster, a violent contrast to the leathery patchwork face of the man behind him.

Lucas' mind was pure ice: he could do anything when his mind was like this, he thought. Some of it was the speed. He'd been up three days now, but felt awake and in control, sharp, as sharp as he ever had. He reached Bekker, brushed past him, ignoring the scalpel, stretched past him, lifted Druze's eyelids with his left hand, just as Bekker had. Bekker turned away.

Lucas, ice, stepped away from the coffin and glanced at Sloan.

"Cut them right through. Want to take a look?"

Lucas was crowding Bekker with his hip, and Bekker tried to move back, letting the scalpel slip from his fingers as he moved. It bounced off the deep carpet, the blade pointing at him like a steel finger.

"Got them both—really did a job," Sloan said, bending over Druze's body.

"What I want to know," Lucas said to Bekker in a conversational tone, "is why you killed Cassie Lasch. Why'd you have to do that? Couldn't you just have done Druze? Just gone in there, stuck the gun in his ear and pulled the trigger? You could have stashed the photos anyway and we'd have gotten the point. . . ."

Bekker's mouth was open, but no sound came out.

"I need an answer," Lucas said.

"Cool," said Sloan, catching his coat sleeve.

"Fuck cool," said Del, moving up on the other side of Bekker. He put his face four inches from the other man and said, "I knew Stephanie longer than you did, Mike. Loved that girl. So you know what?"

Bekker, caught between Lucas and Del, shrinking back against the wall, still didn't answer.

"You know what?" Del screamed, his eyes wide.

"Hey, now," said the Intelligence cop. He had Del by the coat.

"What?" Bekker croaked, half under his breath.

"I'm going to beat the snot out of you, m'boy," Del said. His right hand came around in an arc and hit Bekker in the nose. Bekker slammed against the wall, his nose broken,

356

blood gushing down his chin. He put his arms up, crossed his face.

"Wait," Sloan yelled. He tried to step around Lucas, but Lucas pushed him; and before Sloan could recover, Del hit Bekker twice more, once with each hand, evading Bekker's feeble block. Bekker's head snapped back twice more, the back of it knocking the wall like a judge's gavel, and another cut opened on his eyebrow. The Intelligence cop was on Del's back, and Sloan wrapped him from the front and pushed him away. Bekker was moaning, one hand cupping his nose, a high, dying sound: "Eeeee . . ."

"That's enough, that's enough!" Sloan screamed. They hauled Del back, and Bekker dropped one of his covering hands.

"No, it's not," Lucas said quietly. He was less than an arm's length from Bekker. Sloan and the Intelligence cop were struggling with Del but looking toward Lucas.

The pistol came around like a whip, the front sight leading the arc.

"'Member Cassie, motherfucker?" Lucas said, the words as much a groan as a scream. Saliva sprayed into Bekker's face, and Lucas had him by the throat with his left hand. Bekker had time only to flinch before the sight sliced across his cheek and the side of his nose. A ragged furrow opened in its wake. Bekker grunted from the impact, a pain like fire ripping through his face.

Lucas, precise, quick, moving with the easy coordination of a speed-bag man, hit Bekker with the gun a dozen times, leading with the sight.

Ripped his forehead, twice, three times, opened his eyebrows, carved bloody canyons across his nose, the left cheek, then the right, sliced through his lips, his hands a blur . . .

Sloan hit Lucas in the back, wrapped up one arm. Lucas flailed with the pistol, a last wild swing ripping across Becker's chin, opening the flesh as effectively as a chainsaw.

Lucas, mind blank, focused, could barely feel Sloan's arms binding him, barely feel the Intelligence cop sweeping him off his feet, barely feel the uniforms barreling into the room, pinning him.

Even as he went down, his eyes were focused on Bekker, his hands straining. Sloan had the pistol, was twisting, his thumb under the hammer. . . .

Lucas was aware of weight on his chest, and Sloan, then of Sloan looking away, looking back up at Bekker, who was sliding a bloody path down the plaster walls. Sloan was looking at Bekker's face, and Lucas heard Sloan say, "Oh Christ, ah Christ, ah sweet Jesus . . ."

The doctor's face was a mask of blood and curling, wounded flesh. Even Druze might have turned away, had he been alive to see it.

In ten minutes, the world was moving again.

Lucas sat on a hard wooden bench in the entry, Sloan next to him.

Del was down the hall, his hands in his pockets. The Intelligence man, two uniforms and the paramedics were with Bekker. When they brought him out, on a gurney, one of the paramedics held a drip bottle above him, the line plugged into one of Bekker's arms. He was conscious. One of his eyes was puffed nearly shut, but the other was open.

He saw Lucas, recognized him, and a noise came through his ruined lips.

"What?" Lucas asked. "Hold it. . . . What'd he say?"

The paramedics stopped and looked down. Bekker, struggling, one eye open, blood running into it, tried to sit up, put the words together. . . .

"You should have . . ." He lost it for a moment, then came back, a red bubble of blood on his lips.

"What?" Lucas asked. He stooped over and the blood bubble burst.

"You should have . . ."

"What, what, motherfucker . . . ?" Lucas shouted down at him, Sloan on his arms again.

" . . . killed me . . ." Bekker tried to smile. His lips, cut nearly in half, failed him. "Fool."

32

Lucas sat outside Daniel's office, six feet from the secretary's desk. She had tried talking to him but eventually gave up. When the secretary's intercom beeped, she tipped her head toward the office door and Lucas went inside.

"Come in," Daniel said. His voice was formal, his office was not. Papers were scattered across the top of his desk and an amber cursor blinked on his computer screen, halfway down a column of numbers. A veil of cigar smoke hung in the room. Daniel pointed to the good guest chair. "What a fuckin' week. How are you?"

"Messed up," Lucas said. "I'd only known Cassie for a few days, and I don't think we would have lasted . . . but shit. She was pulling me up. I was feeling almost human."

"Are you going back over the edge?" Daniel's face was questioning, concerned.

"Christ, I hope not," Lucas said, rubbing his face with his open hands. He was exhausted. After the arrest, he'd gone home and crashed, slept the night and the day through, until he was shaken out of bed by Daniel's call. "Anything but that."

"Hmm." Daniel picked up a dead cigar, rolled it between his fingers. "You've heard about the answering machine."

"No, I've been out of it. . . ."

"One of the crime-scene guys—you know Andre?"

"Yeah . . ."

"Andre was going through Bekker's office, and a secretary said she'd seen Bekker coming out of the next office down from his. She thought he was just doing some housekeeping for his neighbor, who's off in Europe on a fellowship. Anyway, Andre gets on the phone and calls this guy in Europe, tells him what happened, gets his okay, and they check out his office. There's an answering machine in his desk and it's turned on. Andre pushes the button and the tape just stops; it's been rewound. But when he pushes it again, it starts running, and it's a message from Druze to Bekker, telling him it's done. . . . We went back to the phone company, checked it, and the call came in a half-hour after the woman was killed at Maplewood. There's another fragment of conversation under that, just a few words, but it's Bekker."

"So that ties it," Lucas said.

"Yeah. And there are a couple of other things, coming along."

"What about Loverboy?" Lucas asked.

"I pulled Shearson off the shrink. Shearson thinks he's the one, but we'll never know. Not unless he just comes out and tells us." Daniel rolled the cigar between his palms. He looked more than unhappy.

"What's wrong?" Lucas asked.

"Shit." Daniel backhanded the cigar butt at the wall, where it bounced off the black-and-white face of Robert Kennedy and fell to the floor.

"Let's have it," Lucas said.

Daniel swiveled his chair to look out the window at the street. Spring was definitely coming, the days stretching toward summer. The street was sunlit, although the temperatures hung in the forties. "Lucas . . . God damn it. You beat up Bekker. His fuckin' face . . . And remember that pimp, that kid, Whitcomb? His goddamn attorney has been back to Internal Affairs—Whitcomb's family don't believe a word of that pimp story, they think their little boy fell into the hands of a bad cop. They're talking about the courts. . . ."

"We've handled it before . . ." Lucas suggested.

"Not like this. You've been in fights. These people . . . Shit, these people didn't have much of a chance."

"Whitcomb is a fucking violence freak," Lucas said, leaning forward. "Has his attorney looked at the girl he worked over?"

"Yeah, yeah. Whitcomb's a criminal—but you're not supposed to be. And now there are rumors about you going into Druze's apartment. Too many people know about it. If you tried to deny it at a hearing, you'd be perjuring yourself. And there's more. . . ."

"Like what?"

"A guy from Channel Eight was talking about making a formal complaint that you gave special privileges to one of the reporters from TV3. That wouldn't be any big deal, normally, except that Barlow picked it up, and decided that you fed her confidential investigatory material."

"You could quash that," Lucas said.

"Yeah. That. Or any one of the others. But the whole bunch . . ."

"Cut to the action," Lucas said. "What're you telling me?"

Daniel sighed, turned back and leaned over his desk. "I can't fuckin' save you."

"Can't save me?" Lucas said it quietly, almost pensively.

"They're gonna hang your ass," Daniel said. "The shooflies and a couple of guys on the council . . . And I can't do a fuckin' thing about it. I told them that you'd maybe had some psychological problems, they were straightening out. They said bullshit: If he's nuts, get him off the street. And you've killed a few guys. You see that *Pioneer Press* editorial? *Our own serial killer . . .*"

"Jesus Christ," Lucas said. He levered himself out of the chair and took a turn around the office, looking at all the black-and-white mug shots, the smiling sharks, a lifetime of politicians. He stopped at the color, the Hmong tapestry, the Minnesota weather calendar. "I'm gone?"

"You could fight it, but it'd be pretty bad," Daniel said. "They'd be asking about the break-in, about the fight with Whitcomb and about Bekker's face. . . . I mean, Jesus, you look at a picture of the way Bekker used to be, and his face now. Jesus, he looks like Frankenstein. On top of it all, you haven't gone out of your way to win any popularity contests."

"There are some people in the press. . . ."

"They'll turn on you like rats," Daniel said. "Nothing gives an editorial writer more satisfaction than seeing somebody else booted out of his job."

"I've got friends. . . ."

"Sure. I'm one. I'd testify for you . . . but like I said—and I'm a politician, I know what I'm talking about—I can't save your ass. As a friend, I tell you this: If you resign, I can turn it all off. I can short-circuit it. You walk away clean. If you decide to fight it, I'll stand with you, but . . ."

"It wouldn't do any good."

"No."

Lucas stared bleakly at the weather calendar, then nodded and turned to face Daniel. "I knew I was getting close to the end of my string," he said. "Too much shit coming down. I just kind of wish . . ."

"What?"

"I wish I'd dumped Bekker. Damn it. . . ."

"Don't talk like that. To anybody," Daniel said, pointing a finger at Lucas. "That can only bring you grief."

"When do I go?"

Daniel tipped his head. "Soon. Like now."

"Do you have a sheet of department paper?" Lucas asked.

Lucas hunched over Daniel's desk, writing it out in long-hand, two simple sentences. *Please accept my resignation from the Minneapolis Police Department. I've enjoyed my work here, but it's time to pursue new interests.* "Twenty fuckin' years," he said, as he dotted the *i* and crossed the *t*s in *interests.*

"I'm sorry," Daniel said. He had turned his back again, and was staring out the window. "The retirement'll be there, of course, if you care. . . ."

"Fuck retirement. . . ." Lucas looked at his hand, found that he was holding a square of pink paper, a receipt from a tire store. On the back was a list, with the word "Loverboy" at the top. He crushed it into a tight little wad and tossed it toward the big plastic basket that stood in an alcove behind Daniel's desk. The paper wad rimmed out, and they both watched it bounce across the rug. "I dated the letter tomorrow—I've got some official things to clean up. And I want to slide some of my files over to Del."

"Okay. Del . . . I know he pounded on Bekker, but he doesn't have the history . . ."

"Sure. If there's a problem, if Internal Affairs gets on his case, tell them to talk to me. I'll take the heat for it."

"Won't happen. Like I said, I can contain it, if you're not around to goad them. And I can do something else, I think. I can take your resignation and put you on reserve. . . ."

"Reserve? What the fuck is that?"

Daniel gestured helplessly. "It's nothing, right now. But maybe, if you get out clean, let things cool down, we could get you back. . . . If not full-time, in some kind of consultant capacity . . ."

"Sounds like bullshit," Lucas said. He looked at Daniel for a moment, then said, "You could do more than contain it . . . but you can't, can you?"

Daniel turned, uncertain. "What?"

"You can't have me around. I'd . . ." He looked at

Daniel for another long minute, then shook his head and said, "I'm outa here."

Daniel, still confused, said in a rush, "Do something, Lucas. You're one of the smartest guys I've ever known. Go to law school. You'd make a great attorney. You got money: see the world for a while. You've never been to fuckin' Europe. . . ."

As Lucas was going out the door, he stopped, and he turned back again to look at Daniel, who was standing behind his desk, his hands in his pockets. Lucas looked for a long three seconds, opened his mouth to say something, then shook his head and walked out, pulling the door closed behind him.

From the chief's office he went down to the evidence room, signed for the box on Bekker and started through it. The physical evidence was there—plaster casts of the footprints at the Wisconsin burial site, the pieces of the bottle used to kill Stephanie Bekker, the hammer used to kill Armistead, the notes from Stephanie's lover.

Tape pickups had been used to preserve the lover's footprints from the floor of Stephanie Bekker's bedroom. They'd been sealed in plastic bags, with a label stapled to the top of the bag. They were gone.

After checking out of the evidence room, Lucas got his jacket, locked his office and walked up the stairs to the street level, out past the bizarre but strangely interesting statue of the Father of Waters, and onto the street.

Where to go? He waited for the pull of the guns, down there in the safe in the basement. They'd be glowing, wouldn't they, like a luminescent brand of gravity. . . .

"Not a lot left, fuckhead," he said aloud to himself as he wandered toward the corner.

* * *

365

"Hey, Davenport." A uniformed cop was calling from the door to City Hall. "Somebody looking for you."

"I don't work there anymore," Lucas shouted back.

"Neither does this one," said the cop, holding the door open and looking down.

Sarah, in a pink frock and white shoes, toddled through the door looking for him, her face breaking into a happy smile when she spotted him. She had a pacifier in one hand, waved it and gurgled. Jennifer was a step behind, her face flushed with what might have been embarrassment. The whole scene was so blatantly contrived that Lucas started to laugh.

"Come here, kid," he said, squatting, clapping his hands. Sarah's face turned determined and she came on full-steam, dashing toward a soft landing in Lucas' hands.

"So we start talking, if it's not too late," Jennifer said as Lucas tossed the kid in the air.

"It's not too late," Lucas said.

"The way you were the other night . . ."

"I was full of shit," Lucas said. "You know about . . . ?"

"Sloan heard rumors, and called me," Jennifer said. She poked her daughter in the stomach and Sarah clutched Lucas' neck and grinned back at her mother. "I think Sarah's got a future in the TV news business. I coached her on going through the door, and she did it like a natural. She even got her lines right."

"Smart kid . . ."

"When do we talk?"

Lucas looked down the street toward the Metrodome. "I don't want to do anything today. I just want to sit somewhere and see if I can feel good. There's a Twins game. . . ."

"Sarah's never been."

"You wanna see a game, kid? They ain't the Cubs, but what the hell." Lucas lifted Sarah to straddle the back of his neck and she grabbed his ear and him with the pacifier. What felt like a gob of saliva hit him in the part of his hair. "I'll teach you how to boo. Maybe we can get you a bag to put on your head."

When Lucas had gone, Daniel gathered his papers together, stacked them, dropped them into his in tray, shut down the computer and took a lap around the office, looking at the faces of his politicians. Hard decisions. Hard.

"Jesus Christ," the chief said quietly, but aloud. He could hear his heart beating, then a rush of adrenaline, a tincture of fear. But now it was ending, all done.

He stepped back toward his desk, saw the paper wad that Lucas had fired at the waste-basket. He picked it up, meaning to flip it at the basket, and saw the ball-point ink on the back. He smoothed the paper on his desk.

In Davenport's clear hand, under the heading "Loverboy":

—Heavyset, blond with thinning hair. Looks like Philip George.
—Cannot turn himself in, or even negotiate: Cop.
—No hair in drain or on bed: Cop.
—Called me through Dispatch on non-taped line: Cop.
—Extreme voice disguise: Knows me.
—Served with S. Bekker in police review board study.
—Knew Druze was the killer.
—Didn't call back after advertisement in newspaper and pictures on TV: Already knew Druze was dead and that he was S. Bekker's killer.
—Had Redon flower painting on calendar; same calendar at Institute of Arts has cyclops painting for November; changed it for weather calendar.
—Assigns fuck-up to chase phony Loverboy.

*　　*　　*

Then there was a space, and in a scrawl at the bottom, an additional line:

—*Has to get rid of me—that's where IA is coming from* . . .

"Jesus Christ," Daniel said to himself.

He looked up, across the office at the weather calendar, which hung on the wall amid the faces of the politicians, all staring down at him and the crumpled slip of paper. Stunned, he looked out the window again, saw Davenport tossing a kid in the air.

Davenport knew.

Daniel wanted to run down after him. He wanted to say he was sorry.

He couldn't do that. Instead he sat at his desk, head in his hands, thinking. He hadn't been able to weep since he was a child.

Loverboy wished, sometimes, that he still knew how.